Praise for the first e

"The subtlety, and fairness, with w.... MW01038813
ing frameworks [Nietzschean valor, Christian pragmatism,
inductivism] stand as the novel's crowning intellectual achievement, side
by side with the artistic one: a convincing tale of murder and ruminating
guilt." —*Janus Head, a journal of Philosophy, Literature and Psychology*

"Troncoso excels as a narrator, a storyteller, and a creator of vivid characters and images." —*Southwest Book Views*

"A suspenseful psychological thriller in the tradition of *Crime and Punishment*." —*The Believer Magazine*

"The issues of identity, the connection between Helmut's own identity and his sense of guilt concerning the professor's sympathies, and the political and philosophical issues . . . make the story itself so rich. . . . *The Nature of Truth* is an interesting and provocative read." —*Review of Contemporary Fiction*

"I hope it isn't the kiss of death to invoke the name of Dostoyevsky in praise of Sergio Troncoso's impressively lucid first thriller, published as part of Northwestern University's Latino Voices series. As Dagoberto Gilb says in a jacket quote, 'Troncoso has widened the field for all of us.'" —*The Chicago Tribune*

"*The Nature of Truth* is a thriller that explores the philosophy of truth and whether one truth is more important than another. This well-written, fast-paced, introspective novel raises many questions about truth and evil, and wonders if eventually 'murder even defeats the murderer.'" —*Multicultural Review*

"For his psychological complexity, Troncoso's Helmut Sanchez is in good company with the likes of Leslie Marmon Silko's estranged Tayo and Dostoyevsky's guilt-ridden Raskolnikov. And *The Nature of Truth* is a unique meditation on redemption and retribution that tackles racism, homophobia, and anti-Semitism with sensitivity and skill. Troncoso's legacy is in having expanded the social and geographical terrain of the Chicano narrative with enviable aplomb." —*The El Paso Times*

"Troncoso recognizes that, though truth lies within the community, a failure to acknowledge the validity of other communities is the root of lethal lies." —*The Forward*

The Nature of Truth

Sergio Troncoso

Arte Público Press
Houston, Texas

The Nature of Truth is made possible through a grant from the City of Houston through the Houston Arts Alliance.

Recovering the past, creating the future

Arte Público Press
University of Houston
4902 Gulf Fwy, Bldg 19, Rm 100
Houston, Texas 77204-2004

Photo by Sergio Troncoso
Stained glass window by G. Owen Bonawit
Sterling Memorial Library, Yale University
Cover design by Mora Des¡gn

Troncoso, Sergio, 1961-
    The nature of truth / by Sergio Troncoso.—Revised and updated [edition].
        p. cm.
    ISBN 978-1-55885-791-9 (alk. paper)
    1. Holocaust, Jewish (1939-1945)—Historiography—Fiction.
2. Mexican Americans—Fiction. 3. German Americans—Fiction.
4. Holocaust denial—Fiction. 5. Retribution—Fiction. 6. Scholars—
Fiction. 7. Psychological fiction. I. Title.
PS3570.R5876N38 2014
813'.54—dc23
                                                                2013038548
                                                                CIP

♾ The paper used in this publication meets the requirements of the American National Standard for Information Sciences—Permanence of Paper for Printed Library Materials, ANSI Z39.48-1984.

Originally published by Northwestern University Press in 2003
Revised and updated by Sergio Troncoso in 2013

14 15 16 17 18 19 20 21 22   10 9 8 7 6 5 4 3 2 1

For Laura

Acknowledgements

Thank you to Northwestern University Press for first publishing The Nature of Truth in 2003, and to Arte Público Press for publishing this revised and updated paperback edition in 2014. The story remains roughly the same, with a few important changes. I tightened the language and, I hope, removed what was not essential, all with the goal of making this novel a good experience for readers.

I also want to thank Yale University and so many individuals there who have been instrumental in nurturing my love of philosophy in literature. The university was my haven as a graduate student enthralled with ideas and literature. The late Professor Maurice Natanson guided me through the history of phenomenology as a teacher, and helped to deepen my appreciation of teaching as a craft when I was his teaching assistant for an undergraduate course in "Philosophy in Literature." The late Professor John Hollander invited me to become his teaching assistant in "Daily Themes," and showed a generosity toward this graduate student who was not even in his English department. I have never forgotten that. I also want to thank Professor Karsten Harries for teaching me about Nietzsche and Heidegger, and Professor Michael Della Rocca for reading the first edition of the novel. I wrote my first short story at Yale, about a Chicano calling his *abuelita* on the Mexican-American border to argue about Heidegger. I wanted to break stereotypes, to communicate a complex idea through a story, and to cross geographical as well as intellectual borders. Yale was this unique place that encouraged these disparate worlds to come together, and I will always be grateful for that opportunity to be a part of it.

My deepest gratitude is reserved for my wife Laura. She has been by my side for decades, since we first jogged together by the Charles River to Fresh Pond, and back. Our two sons, Aaron and Isaac, have taught me about curiosity and courage. I have tried to teach them about the tenacity and character that I learned from my parents—their *abuelitos*—Rodolfo and Bertha Troncoso. As I have said many times, "Ysleta has as much to teach Yale, as Yale has to teach Ysleta."

The Nature
of Truth

Sergio Troncoso

Chapter One

Helmut Sanchez yanked the steel ring of the creaky wooden door and stepped blindly into the dark castle that was Yale's Sterling Library. He pushed open the inner foyer door. A puff of steam hissed from a radiator in the shadows. The air inside was cold and damp. In front of him, two lines of students waited to check out books at the circulation desk under the watchful eyes of the mosaic of the Goddess of Knowledge. Another line surrounded the copy machines, which flashed and droned like baby dragons trapped in boxes. Without stopping, Helmut displayed his ID to the bored security guard and veered into the first floor stacks, toward Mr. Atwater's office. Jonathan Atwater was the assistant librarian responsible for interlibrary loan requests.

"Hello?" Helmut said, with a studied meekness, knocking twice on the oak frame next to the opaque glass, like a gumshoe's door. A genteel older gentleman, about forty-five, hunched over Gabriel García Márquez's *Cien años de soledad*, his spectacles on the bridge of his pink nose. Puffy light brown eyebrows and a head of thin gray hair distinguished Mr. Atwater's patrician face. He wore a candy-apple red bow tie and a perfectly starched blue oxford shirt. A dozen books, in German and Spanish, were fastidiously arranged on his desk in front of him like a mini-fortress. Helmut noticed a small red leather edition of Goethe's poems atop a stack of white papers and manila folders.

"Helmut. Please, come in," Mr. Atwater said, warbling just a note higher than normal. "Sit down. Here. Take a look while I

1

bring you a cup of coffee. Bought it on Saturday at an old bookstore in Meriden. Only thirty dollars for that edition!"

"But I was on my way–" Helmut protested weakly, but Mr. Atwater was already out the door and bounding down the hall. Helmut glanced at the poetry book in his hand, a leather-bound edition with gilded pages from the late nineteenth century. He reluctantly sat down on the black wooden chair emblazoned in gold with the crest of Yale. *Lux et Veritas.*

"This is what you came for, I presume," Mr. Atwater said, striding into the room, handing Helmut four volumes, and placing a Harvard-Radcliffe mug of coffee on the edge of the desk in front of Helmut.

"Thank you very much, Jonathan."

"Here's the confirmation for *Geschichte und Literatur Österreichs*, just sign at the bottom."

Mr. Atwater handed Helmut two sheets of paper, the first a barely legible pink carbon of Helmut's original request, the second an agreement to return the books by such-and-such a date to Yale, which would return them to the library or archive that owned them. "What a *quest* for those!" Mr. Atwater continued. "At least we finally found them."

"Thanks." Helmut drank half a mug of coffee and pushed the four volumes into his backpack. All morning his head cold had dizzied him at the oddest moments.

Suddenly Helmut had the eerie feeling that something was wrong, that he had seen a mistake but had not recognized it for what it was. He signed the second sheet of paper. He folded it back and glanced at the first sheet. Ach! he thought. He had originally requested *Österreich in Geschichte und Literatur*. There it was, in fading blue ink. This was the *wrong* literary review for the years 1957, 1961, 1965 and 1970. Mr. Atwater had made a rare mistake. Helmut's shoulder's slumped. He felt bloated and depressed. He handed back the sheets to Mr. Atwater.

What would be the point of telling Mr. Atwater he had wasted a month looking for the wrong review? Helmut gulped down the rest of the coffee and stood up. "Thanks again. I'll give you a call next week."

Helmut smiled politely and marched toward the circulation desk. Outside, it was gusty and warm for March. He might as well peruse these four volumes of *Geschichte und Literatur Österreichs*. He didn't have much to lose. If Mr. Atwater was right, they were obscure, if not rare, reviews. What would have been the point of deflating Atwater's enthusiasm when precious few cared as deeply about books anymore? Helmut's back ached, but the bike ride to Orange Street was quick and his backpack didn't seem too heavy.

Not until a few weeks later on April 29th did Helmut open the 1961 volume of *Geschichte und Literatur Österreichs*. The Thomas Bernhard article for his boss Professor Werner Hopfgartner had been mailed weeks ago. The semester was near its end, and finals would begin in a week. Helmut was putting the final touches on Christa Wolf. Before Hopfgartner left for his summer vacation of hiking on the Alps, the professor and his assistant would bounce the essay back and forth a few times. Helmut had indeed discovered a few articles in *Geschichte und Literatur Österreichs* he might include in the professor's Compilation.

Before his retirement, Hopfgartner envisioned the Compilation as a synthesis and expansion of his ultimate views about literature and philosophy. German culture in the nineteenth and early twentieth century, the professor wrote, had achieved a community as distinct about the good and the right as that of classical Greece. What the professor's clear and convincing prose advocated, in an almost revolutionary tone and certainly with a poetic cadence, was the creation of a set of real community values. Then, and only then, would adherence to such values be authentic to a culture. Individuals in such an authentic society would blossom into *true human beings*, the full potential of man. Anything less would be "fakery" or "decadence" or "the moral abyss of modernity" or "the bleakness of the soul." Modern society, Hopfgartner concluded, was on the bleak and lonely road of pernicious individualism and nihilistic hedonism.

Wednesday night-Thursday morning Helmut was reading an article in *Geschichte und Literatur Österreichs* on the American revival after the Kennedy election. It was 2:30 a.m. and Helmut desperately needed a distraction from the brain chatter that kept him awake. Suddenly, in the table of contents of the second quarter issue from 1961, he noticed that a W. Hopfgartner had written a lengthy, three-page letter to the editor. Helmut's heart leapt. What a fantastic coincidence! he thought. Perhaps Mr. Atwater's efforts had not been in vain.

Helmut didn't immediately read the letter, and instead checked the biographical lines at the end. The author *was* indeed a W. Hopfgartner who had also been a professor of literature. So there was a chance, however slim, that this W. Hopfgartner was the selfsame Werner Hopfgartner who now employed him.

The year 1961 was the year Professor Hopfgartner had arrived in America as the newest tenured professor at Smith College. After the Wall had gone up in Berlin, a spiritual incarceration had been plastered atop the existential malaise of the Continent. A double burden, Hopfgartner had once mused to his research assistant, which had simply been too much to bear. Helmut dropped the 1961 volume into his backpack. He would copy it tomorrow. Maybe he'd read it over the weekend. The Christa Wolf final rewrite had been delayed long enough. Helmut turned off his reading lamp and reset his alarm clock.

The sun was bright overhead by the time Ariane Sassolini, Helmut's girlfriend, drove him back to Orange Street, about a twenty-minute drive from her apartment in Hamden, Connecticut. They had spent another delicious Saturday night together. Helmut's bicycle was still locked to the backyard fence. His apartment upstairs was quiet, clean, empty. Finally, he had a little time to relax and be peacefully alone. He changed into shorts and a T-shirt, and bounded down the stairs. He bought a copy of the Sunday *New York Times* at the grocery store on Pearl Street. This was definitely a day for the back porch. He shoved open the kitchen door, which he rarely opened, and it led, through a murky and filthy hallway, to the back staircase and to another rickety door with peeling lime-green paint. Beyond this second door was the back porch of the third floor. Tender, mint-green leaves had sprouted from the old elm that hovered over the porch like a gnarled hand. Last year's leaves—dried-up, yellow-brown and crunchy—were packed into piles in each corner.

Helmut dragged out an old beach chair, a mug of coffee with milk, a milk crate to use as a small table, the newspaper and a stack of photocopied articles, including W. Hopfgartner's "Why I Am Neither Guilty Nor Ashamed." The chair was as comfortable as he remembered it had been. A perfectly cool breeze meandered in from the north. The air was finally dry after the rainstorm last night. A squirrel pranced across the porch railing, unafraid. He pushed the newspaper away and refilled his coffee mug and settled himself on the porch again.

"Why I Am Neither Guilty Nor Ashamed" was short enough, just three pages. Helmut started to read it. Immediately his stomach twisted into a knot. His left foot, dangling over the railing, at once stopped bouncing to an unknown beat. The letter was a response to a prior issue of *Geschichte und Literatur Österreichs*. That previous issue had been dedicated to expurgating Austria's complicit role in the *Anschluss* and the Nazi atrocities of the Second World War. Of course, it was true that the cultured citizens of Vienna had cheered the triumphant Adolf Hitler on Währingerstrasse with an evident proto-fanaticism. And who didn't already know that the dreaded SS had been composed of more Austrians than Germans?

In any case, the letter from this W. Hopfgartner derided all such pandering as "weakness and indecision." Vague "foreign influences" were at work. It declared, in a staccato prose, that Austria had done nothing wrong in the war. In fact, the premise of the war had been "correct" in any case. Only its "practical implementation" had been distorted by the excesses and digressions of a few idiots. What had been this correct premise? The letter mentioned only an amorphous "authentic value system" for the German people. Only with this value system would the genuine Teutonic character be realized, in itself the highest embodiment of man. The rambling letter ended with a call to all Germans and Austrians, especially the new generations coming of age and those about to be born in the next decade, the future leaders of the Third Millennium.

"Rid yourselves of this guilt and this shame!" the letter exhorted its readers. "Believe not, in such a blind fashion, these accusations of what your parents did during the war. These lies will emasculate you. The German self will thus be destroyed! The great German spirit, so corrupted by guilt and shame, will not even be capable of correcting past excesses. How will we ever soar back to our splendor, creativity and productivity? This is the only way. A future free of guilt."

Helmut Sanchez felt sick to his stomach. How could anyone have written this garbage, in 1961 or at any other point after the war? What kind of sick mind would rationalize away this massive moral black hole? Millions of Jews murdered simply because they were Jews. Millions of gypsies and Catholics and countless political prisoners and so-called subversives slaughtered by a regime gripped by a frenzy of murderous thinking. And this, exactly, was what had always troubled Helmut about the Holocaust and the war in general. That Germans, he felt, had a tendency to think too far, to an abstract and rigid self-righteousness that could all-too-easily devalue the simple aspects of daily life. Such a murderous abstractionism could be used to justify crushing something today for the sake of an escapist ideal of a far-off tomorrow.

Of course, the student Marxists at Freiburg were also like this. Religious terrorists who killed in the name of God were no different. So this fanaticism of the ideal was not limited to Germans, nor to fascists, nor even to the field of politics. It was a beast of the mind! Helmut thought. Elusive. Multifarious. Immortal.

Helmut had once dated a younger student from Karlsruhe, Stephanie Henke, a special girl. At a concert, she had been so overwhelmed by Beethoven's *allegro assai* conclusion to the Ninth Symphony that she cried and shrieked non-stop into the deathly silence at the end of the concert. An incredible orgasmic fury! What was even more shocking was that those around her, the prim and proper of Freiburg, approved of this primeval release with their admiring looks. Apparently this wild girl had really understood the heart of the music. Little did they notice the desperate gleam in her eyes, the spasmodic little twists of her head processing in a rapid-fire loop, the slash scars on her wrists.

During finals the previous semester, Stephanie had locked herself in the bathroom and screamed, "I will die a complete failure!" After a tense hour, Helmut had forced open the door and saved this beautiful creature from herself. So Helmut understood only too well that this murderous thinking was still pervasive and even part of his blood.

But what was his blood? Who was Helmut, really? That was the question that had tormented him all his life. Helmut Sanchez had always hoped his Mexican blood would save him from a freefall into his German heritage. Yet certain parts of this heritage also captivated him, especially German philosophy and poetry. So instead of saving him outright, these mixed legacies confused him. He had never really felt at home with German culture, but in many ways he had harbored the same doubts about American culture. He was neither American nor German nor Mexican. He was neither here nor there. Sometimes he still felt like a fat, lonely, little boy. In any case, now he was on his own. He could still pull himself above his own wretched ambiguity about who he was. There was no need to doubt himself when his heart was clear. He could still feel repelled by W. Hopfgartner's letter. Helmut could still understand what was right and what was wrong.

Before he tucked the letter away in an empty blue folder, Helmut read it again Sunday night. He memorized the flow of thought. The ridiculous justifications and qualifications. The conviction and exhortation of its style. Even the seeming plausibility and rationality of what it said. In Helmut's head, there was still one well-formed doubt: perhaps this W. Hopfgartner was not the Werner Hopfgartner at Yale with the endless stream of inamoratas. Hopfgartner was indeed a common German name. Also, Professor Hopfgartner had been a professor in the Federal Republic of Germany, and the journal was from Austria. But more pressing in Helmut's mind was the need to find out more about *his* Werner Hopfgartner. Could the professor be the same vile character who wrote "Why I Am Neither Guilty Nor Ashamed"?

Chapter Two

On Cross Campus, a festive air seemed to soften the edges of the pale yellow stone walls of Yale. Four male students, two of them shirtless, tore through the newly planted grass at the center of the quadrangle, grunting their way through a game of Ultimate Frisbee. One young woman, wearing white shorts and a Harvard T-shirt, lay listless on the edge of grass, her back against a blackened wall. Her eyes were closed. Her face was pockmarked with acne scars. Three blue examination books rested carelessly on her lap. Subject: Organic Chemistry. Grade: in the thick red slash of a hurried marker, ninety-three. Her hair was scraggly and unwashed. The armpits of her T-shirt had yellowed. Yet a beatific smile was on her face. And the sun seemed warmer than ever.

At the other side of the quadrangle, another young woman, in a short, black skirt and a black blouse that seemed a second skin over her slim and attractive body, danced wildly on the grass. From the third floor of Calhoun College, Madonna's "Holiday" pulsed through two speakers. Her name was Alesha Brown. A piece of paper was in her hand. *Hol-i-day! Cel-e-brate!*

"Alesh! Hey! I just *heard!*" another girl shrieked from the dorm window with the blaring speakers. "Aiyyyi! Three ninety-two kicks ass in Cambridge!" *Oh, yeah! Oh, yeah!*

Alesha Brown smiled and danced and waved the piece of paper over her head as her roommate started dancing, too, each mimicking the other and swaying to the rhythm of the music, their hands outstretched toward the heavens. *Let's celebrate!*

"Alesh! To Rudy's, honey pie! I'll call Marla and Tina! Pa-r-ty!"

"Can't! See ya at dinner, Sweet Face! Got one last thing to do! And I'm outta here!" Alesh yelled, still swinging her arms as she planted her bare feet in the espadrilles she had shed on the grass. Her shoulder-length chestnut hair shimmered in the sunlight. As she skipped toward Harkness Hall, her pointy breasts bounced against her blouse. One of the boys playing Frisbee missed a long pass because he was staring at this beauty sprinting past them, at her sleek, long legs and tight waist, and that magnificent, perfectly protruding ass so out of reach for all of them. Alesha Brown was gorgeous. She was savvy. Now she was on her way to Harvard Law School. Almost.

She pulled open the heavy wooden doors of Harkness and immediately dashed into one of the restrooms next to the German department's office. Alesha strode into an empty stall, peed quickly and brushed her hair with a long pocket comb from her purse. She splashed water on her face, rinsed her mouth and double-checked the row and schedule of birth control pills on the small pink plastic grid of pills. She glanced at her watch. It was five minutes past 4:00 p.m. She stared at a test schedule somebody had pilfered from the hallways of Harkness and posted in the restroom. TAKE BACK THE DAY! somebody had scrawled on it in heavy, blue ink. Two full weeks of finals remained for everyone else, but not for seniors. *Cel-e-brate!*

Alesha Brown knocked on Werner Hopfgartner's door. She imagined the old professor looking up slowly and frowning. He was probably reading the article on Max Frisch he had just published, the one he had bragged about in class, the kind he had regularly published with the greatest of ease years ago. Alesha remembered a conversation Hopfgartner had casually mentioned before, that "young bastard Rittman" cutting Hopfgartner with, "You must be *so* looking forward to doing nothing," and Hopfgartner stiffening angrily in his chair as if the Jonathan P. Harkness Professor of Literature and Philosophy should be ready for the trash heap!

She rapped sharply on the door again, and heard a chair slowly drag across the wooden floor. Professor Hopfgartner had also
bragged to her about other forthcoming "excellent articles" on
Thomas Bernhard, and another on Christa Wolf, and another, all
in one final, glorious year for old Werner Hopfgartner. It was as if
Hopfgartner were collecting gems and admiring them. But of
course, Alesha had never seen the prof in the stacks, only Helmut,
his little gnome, oblivious to the world, to everything and everybody, in the darkness surrounded by books.

"Yes? Alesha, *mein hübsches Mädchen*, please come in."

The professor's large basement office in Harkness Hall resem-
bled a grand, disheveled closet. An ornate wooden desk was posi-
tioned diagonally across a far corner, facing out, so the old man
could easily scan his lair. Behind the professor, near the fireproof
ceiling, a row of rectangular windows revealed, through heavy
wrought-iron bars, an occasional pair of sneakers pounding the
sidewalk of Wall Street.

Against one beige wall was a row of metal cabinets, about
chest high, on top of which were more books, piles of papers and
a Styrofoam cup. In front of these cabinets, a bare, wooden chair
was angled toward the professor's desk, for supplicants. Here Alesha sat, crossing her legs tightly in front of her. Against the other
wall was a comfortable, blue sofa with a glass-topped coffee table
in front of it, strewn with more papers and copies of articles. Surrounding the hallway door, like a multicolored arch, were teak
bookshelves. Alesha tapped her foot impatiently on the linoleum
floor and possessed a cheery look about her.

"Well, Alesha, your final, right? Excellent as always," Professor Hopfgartner said in a thick, German accent, yet still enunciating every English word clearly, tediously, as if he directed a
spelling bee. He handed her the blue books, glancing at the supple roundness of her breasts. Werner Hopfgartner's eyes, like quiv-
ery blue moons, darted to and fro. His face had the chiseled look
of salmon-colored granite. He flicked off his reading glasses and
poured himself another shot of bourbon. The liquor was never far
from his fingers.

"My God! Didn't know you'd already finished grading. I'm so psyched! This is great!" she squeaked, sliding her body forward to the edge of the chair.

"You need only apply yourself, my dear girl. I've told you that many times before. Remember last year? One of the *best* in *Contemporary German Literature*. And you did it all on your own," Professor Hopfgartner said, not looking at Alesha, flipping through a stack of term papers on his desk. Apparently he had the wrong class. "I don't know what happened at the end of this semester. I didn't see you at the seminar for—what?—the last four or five weeks?"

"I'm sorry, Professor Hopfgartner. Really and honestly. God, this last semester was a killer. Law school apps, my senior paper– I pulled two all-nighters in a row, and almost a third one, to finish it! I almost *died*," she said, not really worried, tapping her heel against the floor to some unknown rhythm. She crossed her legs again, dangling her arms indifferently by the sides of the chair. Even if it took three hours and she missed dinner, she wasn't coming out of this room until it was over. This was it. She had just won her own glorious ticket to ride. Just this, and she could finally walk away from Yale, free and clear.

"I know you're a smart girl. *Lebendig*. I saw it in your eyes immediately as soon as you walked into my class last year. A smart girl with a great future. Beauty, a good mind and something special. Something *extra*. A thing many others don't have and can't learn. Guts. Fight. *Hunger*," he said, still pretending to look for something she knew he didn't have. "But this semester, well. Maybe it was just too much to do. Too short a time."

"I almost did everything. Except for this class. I thought I could catch up later," Alesha said in a pleading voice, high-pitched like a plaintive, feline growl. "I loved your class last year! You're the best professor I've had at Yale! I just had to take your class this semester. Absolutely had to! And now I've ruined everything! Don't know what I would have done if you hadn't *saved* me at midterm! Don't know what I'm going to do now." Tears were dripping over her rosy cheeks. She stared directly at Hopfgartner. Her foot was still rapping the floor.

"Now, Alesha. Everything will be fine. You are an excellent student. There's no need for this. Your final paper isn't here, right?"

"Oh, my God! I tried so hard! I was trying to do everything! I just simply couldn't! I don't know what to do, Professor Hopfgartner. Please help me! This is the only thing I have left," she said, wiping her eyes on her sleeve. "What am I going to tell my parents if I can't graduate?"

"*Nein, nein.* That's not going to happen, my sweet Alesha. We have an understanding, *richtig*? No need for panic. But you do know, that paper was worth a third of your grade. It was an important paper. Some of your classmates spent months working on it. I don't know how I can dismiss it completely."

"Maybe this is asking too much. I'll say it. I don't know what you'll think of me. I enjoyed being with you in March. It was the best thing that happened to me all year. I mean it. It was absolutely thrilling! I dreamed about it over and over again. There! I've said it! I just don't know what to do," Alesha said seductively, in a husky voice this time, at the edge of her chair. She brushed back her chestnut hair again, thought about winking at the old geezer, but knew she had to play her part in this pleading, painstaking chase. A crude move could easily ruin it. As soon as he stood up, she stood up, too, seemingly quivering, her back straight like a rod, waiting with her eyes as wide open as his.

Professor Hopfgartner strode slowly toward her until his bluish, burgundy jacket brushed against her chest. Although he was taller than she—just under six feet, while Alesha was five-feet-eight inches tall—she was statuesque, muscular, angular, even lithe, but he only stocky, creakily slow, stiff, like an upright turtle just in sight of a delectable treat. Werner Hopfgartner raised a chubby, blotchy hand to her cheek of silk and light and caressed it, almost as a grandfather would.

"Are you sure about this, *mein Liebling*? Do only what is right. For *you*."

"Yes," Alesha whispered, edging closer to him, "This is what I want."

She reached up and kissed him slowly on the mouth. His whiskers were rough, and he smelled of bourbon and stale cigar smoke. Her lips fluttered over his mouth, and just before she pulled away she flicked her tongue ever so delicately over the dry edge of his upper lip.

"I enjoy being with you," she repeated as she stepped back, clasped his hand between hers, kissed it and lifted it gently to her left breast. Werner Hopfgartner's eyes were owl-like. He took another step back, almost coming to attention as he gazed at a full view of his prize. He marched to the door and locked it.

The professor turned off the fluorescent light above them and flicked on the reading lamp on his desk. As he pulled the window curtains shut, she glanced at the wall clock and noticed it was just past 4:30 p.m. Almost perfect, she thought. Already the halls were quiet without classes, and the finals that had started at 2:00 p.m. were about to end. The last secretary would also be gone exactly at 5:00 p.m. She would give the old man a splendid farewell to his penultimate year. He turned around, and Alesha was already waiting for him on the couch. He took off his jacket and folded it on the seat of his desk chair.

"My dear, come here," he murmured to her hoarsely, and she slid closer to him and began kissing him ever so slowly on his neck, over his cheeks, on his lips. At mid-term, Alesha had been too quick, too aggressive. Oh, how the old man had chastised her! He exhorted her to take a certain pace, stepping back and threatening to stop, then and there, if she insisted on her haphazard idiocy. But Alesha Brown was a smart girl. She learned quickly. She had been almost delicate by the end of that first tryst, pleasing him to the very pit of his stomach. Much, much better than a Sarah Goodman, Hopfgartner had once mumbled, who would always be cursed with a certain clumsiness.

Alesha breathed heavily, and fluttered tiny kisses over the professor's face, waiting for his next move. If it took a century, she didn't care. This was easy, it was relatively quick, and last time—although she hated to admit it to herself—she had almost finished. The old guy could really do it if he was given half a chance. Soon she would be off to Europe for two months with her roommates.

She felt one of the professor's hands, a gnarly, impatient claw, grab one of her breasts, and she moaned softly. The hand jumped from breast to breast, intermittently squeezing hard and fingering her nipples lightly. Alesha closed her eyes, rested her head against the back of the couch and pushed her chin up as Werner Hopfgartner greedily licked her neck and panted, "*Ja, meine Schöne, ja.*" Suddenly, another hand swooped in between her legs and grabbed her crotch roughly. She was reminded of a wrestler hoisting an opponent by the trunks for an explosive body slam. Alesha spread her legs willingly. She thrust her hips into that clamp of fingers, yet he pulled quickly away. Only a test, a taunt, a declaration to invade a boundary at will. The swoon and whim of power. "*Ja, mein Alles.*"

"Please," he said quietly, tugging at her blouse. Alesha pulled her black blouse over her head one hand at a time. This time she didn't immediately remove her brassiere, but waited for him to do it. Professor Hopfgartner pinched it open from the front, with nearly a casual ease. Alesha's big, brown eyes feigned surprise. He kissed her lower neck, his face like sandpaper, and plunged into the soft whiteness of her breasts, sucking them in spasms, as if gagging on the plethora of skin and fat, and—Alesha swore later—biting her nipples until they were raw. Oh, and how delicious these pinches were! Her skin almost breaking. A precipice. Then a sweet reprieve. Was she already somewhere high above Place de la Révolution or Montparnasse, a light breeze dancing across a darkened terrace of red and yellow roses? Or was she actually still at Yale?

She sensed another hand rub the inside of her thighs rhythmically, the gray and shiny head still attached to her chest like a lamprey. Alesha stared at the gray cabinets in front of them and imagined a cloudy afternoon, a lonely fountain with cherubic angels. Professor Hopfgartner suddenly grunted in a protracted, phlegmatic cough, and just as abruptly a claw yanked aside the crotch of her panties and thrust two sharp fingernails into her vagina. She yelped, and then exhaled rapidly, rewarding him with another languorous moan. "*Ja, meine Schöne.*" His fingers flickered inside her like tiny ballerina legs. Alesha began to relax and open up and steady her breathing with soft little whimpers. Her skin was radiating warmth, and she was wet. She was a very smart little girl.

"Let me kiss you down there, Professor Hopfgartner. I want so much to please you," she pleaded, almost out of breath, her body arched on the sofa seat and nearly sliding off. So she was fucking a dirty old man who was so insecure, so weird, that she hadn't even seen him naked the first time. That wasn't going to happen today. Hey, doggie-style was sweet for her too. But this time Alesha Brown wanted a good hard look at it.

Werner Hopfgartner stared at her with huge, blue orbs. Astonished? Daydreaming? Simply calculating his fortune? He unbuckled his belt and unzipped his khakis and pulled his pants and boxer shorts to his knees. The professor looked as if he were sitting on a newfangled sofa-toilet. Before Alesha kneeled in front of him, she unhooked her skirt and dropped it on the floor behind her with an effortless twirl of her body.

Even in this near darkness, she could see that his skin was a glimmering white, like the scales on a lizard's belly. His paunch hung above his little soldier and created what seemed like a rocky, white cave. Rocky because enormous ridges of wrinkles, more like wavy folds and creases, crisscrossed his abdomen and dangled from his thighs. And white because his hair was frosty, brittle, only softer and darker atop his testicles. A faint acidic scent wafted up from his loins, as well as the much more overwhelming odor of the elderly. The smell of fine dust and decay. She kissed his little soldier, but she was taken aback. It was *tiny*. A wrinkled, deflated pinky! Could this have been what had really nailed her before?

"*Ja, mein Liebling, ja. Nur langsamer, bitte. Verstanden?*"

"*Natürlich, mein Herr.*"

It seemed hours before he started to come around. She knew it would take time. In March it had taken at least this long, if not longer, with her hand blindly groping at the bulge in his trousers until her wrist was sore. Now she was clearly focused. The thing-in-itself in front of her without a barrier between them. What would Heidegger have said about possessing such a delicate morsel of an object? Salty and almost creamy. Like the underside of kugel. Alesha nearly laughed, but quickly stifled herself. The professor would not have understood. Ah, was that a tingle? A precious quiver from the near-dead? Finally this old soldier heard the clarion call to another good fight.

Like a water balloon slowly being filled, the professor's penis became erect at a ceremonious pace. And she encouraged it heartily. Alesha licked and caressed it, teased it and withdrew. She barely seemed to notice his studied silence. She herself was almost hyperventilating, trying to maintain that flow of interest as a torrent. To aggrandize it. To convert play-acting into being. Anything less, and she would have dissolved into tearful laughter. Allow a sliver of doubt into drama, and the impossible would metamorphose into the ridiculous.

"Professor, please, my God! I can't wait any longer!" she screamed and tore off her panties. In the next instant, she was prostrate on the sofa, still panting furiously like a quarter horse, and he was inside of her. His talons clenched her perfect, half-moon hips. His face flushed with blood, gasping.

Perhaps Werner Hopfgartner would have been no match for these muscular thighs and perfectly tapered back and rock-like biceps and triceps had Alesha released herself completely to him. She gave him only what she imagined he could take, and then just a bit more for herself, enough to keep her happy and on the way toward ultimate freedom. Back and forth. Slowly and then a little faster. To one side and then gently to the other. Like the only perfect song they could have between them. She moaned, this time for real. She was definitely on her way out of the nether world of New Haven.

And then something awfully strange happened. Stranger than even a 74-year-old man having sex with a young vixen of twenty-one. Just as she had almost willed herself to the precipice, despite flashes in her mind that she was fucking a bowel of oatmeal, a sharp slap stung her behind like a splash of acid. Slap! Slap! Slap! Alesha tried to wiggle away, but *he* had her now. The pain was bright against her skin. She thought she saw red spots in the darkness. She pushed against him more forcefully. Slap! Slap! Slap! She liked it. Oh, such exquisite pain! Slap! Slap! Slap! She pushed harder and screamed. Who was fucking whom now? Slap! Slap! Slap! His fingers were like bait hooks on her thighs. Slap! Slap!

Slap! What utter, impossible sweetness! What tremendous power! Slap! Slap! Slap! She exploded like a super nova. For years thereafter, she would fondly remember that moment of heaven and think of how he had done her such an unexpected favor. When Alesha Brown finally came down from her black universe, she heard the professor's own sonorous explications of joy. "*Mein Gott! Mein Gott!*"

After a few minutes of silence, she finally wiggled free. He immediately turned off the reading lamp, and they dressed in complete darkness.

"Ready, Alesha, my dear?"

"Yes. Here I am."

The fluorescent lamp above their heads flickered and snapped into an almost painful brightness around them. Alesha sat on the sofa, combing her hair, not one stitch out of place. The professor stood at the doorway, still without his jacket but otherwise unruffled, the crease on his khakis razor-sharp. Only his hair betrayed any evidence of the previous tussle, spiky at the temples, matted down with sweat on his forehead. Alesha stared at the professor and almost giggled, but said nothing. A wet spot, the size of a quarter, punctuated the round bulge on his crotch. Suddenly it seemed to her an endearing symbol to remember him by.

"That was quite wonderful," he said, still motionless by the door, ready for this final exit.

"For me too," she said, picking up her purse and slinging it over her shoulder. "I'm going to miss you so much."

"You have been a wonderful student. An *excellent* one. And I am confident about your future. If you ever need my recommendation, I will give you only the best one. You deserve nothing less."

"Thank you, Professor Hopfgartner. Maybe I'll stop by before graduation. Please take care of yourself."

"I'll certainly be here. Good luck, again," he said, the door open. She reached up and kissed him on the lips again, and this time he seemed shocked, his eyes bulging out of their sockets in a fiery azure. But the hallways were deserted. There was no one around. Only a few hallway lights were still on.

As Alesha Brown walked away and pushed through the hallway doors—she turned around for one last look—she saw Werner Hopfgartner felt quite satisfied with the perfection of all of this, as if he had just sipped the last drop of a fine and exquisite whiskey. That was the look on his face. Soon the old man would begin his long walk home, and that wonderful burning sensation around his loins would make his face glow pleasantly, too. She imagined before the professor readied himself to leave that he would listen carefully, because if Hopfgartner was anything he was careful to the point of paranoia, trying to detect any inadvertent squeak of a chair moving, or a sneeze, or even the *click click click* of a computer keyboard. But if there was nothing, if Harkness Hall seemed empty of life, then Professor Hopfgartner would lock his office door, walk home and relive every second with her in his mind.

Chapter Three

Helmut Sanchez, even at twenty-six, appeared far too serious for his own good. Everyone had said he looked like his mother. He looked like his mother, yet he acted like his father. His thick black hair had a tendency to grow too fast, so that if he waited four weeks between haircuts his hair became helmet-like. His face possessed high cheekbones, an angular chin, a Roman nose. The skin pale, not ruddy, more the color of a contemporary Greek or Italian man, for whom he was repeatedly mistaken. And yet, Helmut was in fact half German and half Mexican, or at least *New* Mexican.

Only its practical implementation had been a distortion? The excessive digression of a few idiots? I must be going out of my mind! Of course, it can't be the same person. I should just forget about the whole thing. It's none of my business anyway.

There was a knock at his office, a converted small storage cubicle in the basement of Harkness Hall. Helmut glanced at the battered—yet still accurate—wall clock above his metal bookshelves. It was almost 1:00 p.m. Before he said a word, the door opened.

"Hi," said Ariane, her brunette hair shimmering against her olive skin.

"Let me just save this," Helmut said, punching his keyboard. He should stay and finish Hopfgartner's essay. The old man would surely be looking for him today.

"Missed you." She swooped down to kiss his cheek. "Forgot to shave this morning?" She rubbed his neck as he exited the word-processing program.

"No time to take a shower."

"So that's what that smell is."

"Thanks."

"You know I *love* it. Every last bit of it," she whispered into his ear and took a nip. A sudden spasm electrified his neck and shoulders; at once his back was rigid. Helmut stood up, pulled her gently against him, his hands on her hips, and imagined, in a lingering kiss, he was about to shatter like a statue of mica.

"Did I tell you the Eggman gave me a raise on Friday?" Ariane said as they walked on Chapel Street.

"That's great! I'm proud of you. I mean it." Helmut squeezed her hand. As they crossed the corner of High Street, at Yale's British Art Museum, a little boy approached them. His trousers were shredded at the ankles. He wore the few remaining threads of filthy high-top sneakers. On one cheek, the black skin suddenly switched to bright white, as if the boy had been burned and the skin grafts had not matched. This black-and-white boy was about eleven or twelve years old. But what struck Helmut was how this chubby boy smiled shyly at them. A fat little boy alone.

Helmut and Ariane stepped inside Atticus Book Café. The little boy held out his hand and looked at the ground, as if Helmut's stare had been too forbidding. But many memories had simply been flooding Helmut's mind. Before the glass door slammed shut, Helmut stopped it with his heavy shoe, waved Ariane forward and bent down to find the little boy's eyes. As the little boy grinned, Helmut took out a five-dollar bill and planted it in the small palm. Yet instead of feeling better, Helmut at once felt cheap and stupid. It was now much worse leaving the little boy in the street. It was much worse when the glass door shut between them.

Helmut and Ariane sat down at a table next to the section on European History and Philosophy, the air thick with the steamy aroma of cappuccino, blueberry muffins, ham-and-cheese croissants and chamomile tea. The tables in the café section were half-full. The coffee bar was empty except for a young woman reading Thomas Mallory's *The Tales of King Arthur*.

"You know, that's how I looked when I was in grade school," Helmut said, glancing at the glass door. The little boy stood like a sentinel at the doorway, his back toward them, occasionally fingering something in his pocket. Suddenly he popped a handful of raisins or chocolates into his mouth.

"Like that?"

"Yeah, I was fat. Nobody liked me and I don't think I liked anybody either. Nobody likes you when you're fat. They tease you," Helmut said. "I can only imagine what it's like for him, with that face."

"Children can be cruel. I was teased because I looked like a horse, or so they said. All arms and legs. Big nose. I was clumsy."

"In Germany, kids called me 'fat little brown turd.' Once, I was 'invited' to a birthday party, but when I arrived—my mother had dropped me off—they handed me a brush and a rag and said I was only there to clean bathrooms," Helmut said quietly. "They pinched my nipples and my butt. They chased me into the bathroom. I cried and cried—for hours, it seemed. Finally after the party was over, I heard a sharp knock at the door. It was Frau Schnell. She yelled at me for being an 'ugly little boy,' and told me to go home to 'your people.' Everybody can be cruel. Especially when you're not like them."

"That's awful. But you're not fat now."

"I know. But you never forget. Even when I'm old, I'll probably still think of myself as a fat little boy."

"Hey! Look," Ariane said, handing him a book off the shelf next to them. It was Werner Hopfgartner's treatise on Nietzsche and Heidegger. "Read it already?"

"Not really. You know, I'm not a bleeding heart." He flipped through the first few pages with little interest. "I don't think caring means giving money away. But nobody's going to take the time to help that boy. Where the hell are his parents? I won't help him either, I'm guilty too. I can hardly take care of myself."

"I'll take care of you, my sweet." She reached out to hold his hand, then took a bite of her muffin and drank her coffee.

"I loved being with you Saturday night," he said quietly, still feeling guilty and ashamed about all sorts of things. "You know, you're the best thing that's happened to me since I came here." He was a coward, he thought. Why couldn't he simply say to her, *I love you.* Was it too much? Was it saying something new, an irreversible step into an abyss?

"*You* were quite thrilling this weekend. Over two hours." Ariane's whisper was low and husky, and her big brown eyes opened wide and stared at him in mock astonishment. Her hair flickered between blue black and dark brown. The silky smooth skin of Ariane's oval face glowed warmly. Only her aquiline nose seemed out of place. Helmut and Ariane, in fact, looked like distant cousins from the same cluster of villages on the Mediterranean.

Helmut at once seemed lost in Ariane. The Florentine with a green card who made love like a jaguar. He really did love her. Without her, he'd be alone and unhappy. And it wasn't just the pleasure of their lovemaking. It was the whirlwind she created around her. This kindness mixed with steely determination. Ariane had assumed her place next to him, sure of what she wanted. She expected the rest of the world to play along with her or move aside. She was the way she was. Nothing hidden, yet still a surprise. She smiled at you and took you in but never seemed to lose her own self. He, however, was here and there and nowhere, in exile.

If Ariane was also a young immigrant trying to gain a foothold in the land and promise of America, why was Helmut Sanchez the one in exile? Over the many years, he had heard different, more complex versions of his fateful beginning, and filled in the rest with his imagination. His mother, *née* Eva Sanchez, had insisted to her husband that their baby be an American citizen, especially after the German authorities had refused to give the couple a straight answer about whether their child was entitled to German citizenship. "Morons!" Mrs. Hirsch screamed, "Let those *cabrones* keep this stinking country to themselves! My son's an *American*, and damn proud of it too!" Johannes Hirsch didn't say much, embarrassed about this misunderstanding. He knew his wife's German was not more than a mishmash of German words, English phrases, and exasperated, virulent denunciations in Spanish, particularly when someone offended her pride. Quietly, without letting her know it until the very end, the dutiful Sergeant Hirsch had used his few military connections to speed up approval of little Helmut's German citizenship papers. So, by the time Helmut entered the *Gymnasium*, the fact that their son was a citizen of both Germany and the United States was almost forgotten. But instead of granting him an embarrassment of riches, this dubious beginning had bestowed upon Helmut the child, and now Helmut the young man, a sense of being adrift, away from home, in between two worlds.

After finishing his *Bakkalaureus der philosophischen Fakultät* in Freiburg, Helmut took a stab at determining his ambiguous homeland, once and for all. Perhaps it was another rash act in a series of such acts. But then again he knew he had to decide his future, and only that might bring him the chance of peace. So at his university graduation, Helmut renounced his German citizenship, changed his name to his mother's maiden name and set off for America. After *her*. By this time, his father was already dead, inadvertently crushed by a Bradley Fighting Vehicle during routine NATO military exercises near Marburg. His mother had returned to New Mexico, begging Helmut to follow her when he was finished with school. What choice did he have? Helmut had to follow his mother. Eva Sanchez was the only real family he had left. His father's family was completely alien to him. But by chance, Helmut had landed in New Haven and discovered it wasn't so bad, after all, to be on your own. And so his mother was still waiting for him in the scenic Sacramento Mountains, increasingly frustrated by the son who was merely as impetuous as she had been.

"Helmut, *m'ijo*," she would plead to him, "You don't need a job on the *East Coast*. Come over here. You don't need to work at all. I've got plenty for both of us. It's so beautiful here. I've got *five acres*! Bear and deer are everywhere. Pine trees!

"Everyone here is beginning to think I lied about you. You know that? Pedrito told me the other day—he thought it was *funny*—that maybe I just paid some guy for his graduation pictures, for his pictures as a little boy! They don't think you exist, *m'ijo*! I'm beginning to have doubts too," she said over the phone, more resigned than ever to the stubborn independence of her son. Indeed, he had put himself in exile.

After lunch, at the southern entrance to Harkness Hall, Ariane wheeled around and kissed Helmut, leaning against him and almost toppling him over.

"I'm going in too," he said, his arms around her waist. Many thoughts invaded his mind. When could he say it simply, without *thinking* about it? He wanted to be with her, and he also wanted to be alone.

"Thought you were done for the day." She yanked open the oak slab of a door. Her biceps curled under her billowy blouse and then relaxed to a flat, taut surface of olive skin. They walked inside.

"I'm finishing some work for Hopfgartner. I'm dead if it's not done today."

"He's taking advantage of you, Helmut. You know that, don't you?"

"I promised to have it done today. I just want him off my back. Hardly have anything to do this summer while he's gone."

"Well, you deserve a break. Twenty hours a week! As far as I can tell, you're here mornings *and* afternoons."

"I'm not always doing his shit, you know. Sometimes I'm just reading."

"Just don't work too hard."

"Call you tonight," he said as he walked down the stairs into the dimly lit hallway that looked like a cave.

Helmut clicked on his computer, and while the virus scan skipped through the files, he started a pot of coffee. The basement offices felt empty. A pair of fluorescent tubes, in the middle of the basement hallway, pushed aside the darkness with a pulsating gray light. The only noise Helmut could hear was the faraway echo of an occasional slamming door one floor above. He imagined he was deep within the bowels of an almost deserted freighter that coursed and creaked across the sea. Who else was on this ship? Did they know he was here too? He left his door open. It was hot enough in this cramped space.

After two hours, Helmut was almost done touching up the Christa Wolf bibliography. There was one reference he'd have to check tomorrow at Sterling. Maybe Mr. Atwater could give him a hand. But the writing was finished, and Helmut could give it confidently to the old man for his final comments, and that would be that. In just under two weeks, Professor Hopfgartner would be in Europe, and Helmut would be more or less free for the first half of the summer. Free, except for *that*. Those pages in a blue folder. An odd and obscure little thing Helmut had almost forgotten about while he had been with Ariane. A couple of pages of German prose that had gripped his heart like a bloody, rotted hand from the grave. A *curse*, really.

A door banged shut at one end of the basement hallway. Only one final exam was in progress in the Harkness basement, and it had started two hours ago. Helmut heard quick, short footsteps on the linoleum floor. *She* walked by again, without so much as a glance into his open office. In her short black skirt and black blouse, she almost melted into the hallway darkness, except for her beautiful, young legs. Helmut heard her rap against the door next to his.

Was Werner Hopfgartner still here? Helmut had forgotten to check for a sliver of light underneath the professor's door when he returned from lunch. That had been careless of him. Helmut heard the professor's door open, and she walked in. She wasn't of course the *only* she, yet she was certainly the most exquisite: terribly young and tender, absolutely bold, not the least bit careful or doubtful or guilty. In a way, she reminded him of Ariane, and in a way she did not. Ariane Sassolini was loving and passionate, and not just voracious.

Helmut closed his door and locked it. He stepped beside the computer keyboard, saved his work and turned the machine off. Murmurs now seemed to emanate from the wall he shared with the Jonathan P. Harkness Professor of Literature and Philosophy. He could occasionally hear a sentence or two through a ventilation grate on the wall a foot from the floor. He slid into his reading chair with a book on his lap. The blue folder was next to him. Wild thoughts consumed Helmut's mind like a fire. The professor and one of his conquests. The very best one.

"*Ja, meine Schöne, ja.*"

It comes to all of us from nowhere, this cursed evil. Why me? I am not even a part of that generation. I should simply stop reading these pages. Ignore them. None of my business at all. Let evil fuck up the world for all I care! Why should I give a damn? Please, dear God, what should I do? I'm sick of this feeble mind.

"*Ach! Nein! Hier. Besser. Ja, viel besser, mein Liebling.*"

First I should find out the facts. I don't even know anybody's exact involvement. It could be a horrible mistake on my part. Should I tell Ariane about my suspicions? Maybe I should find out the truth first. Piece by piece. A methodical investigation. Certainly I'm good at that.

"*Mein Gott! Mein Gott!*"

What terrible rubbish! What abyss of words! It will never end even with my grandchildren. It was simply a nightmare. My blood. I can't escape that. But then, again, why escape? Why not confront and act now? I should at least find out who it really is. Exactly who. These words. The thought and prose of that nightmare. My God!

"*Ja, ja, ja! Mein Gott! Ja! Mein Gott! Oh, mein lieber Gott!*"

Helmut Sanchez carefully balanced the blue folder on his knee. The room was finally quiet. Slowly he read the German words. These carefully chosen words. The style rhythmic and assured. The logic clear, almost convincing, finally ghoulish. He heard a door slam shut, and the same hurried little footsteps stomped down the empty hallway again. After a few seconds, he heard a faraway door close like a muffled explosion. An echo.

When he had read "Why I Am Neither Guilty Nor Ashamed" for the first time this weekend, he had been expecting nothing out of the ordinary. But as one word led to another, and an idiotic thought connected to a dangerous one, Helmut couldn't believe his eyes. These *words*. He wanted to stop reading. He wanted to *will* himself back in time before he had ever set eyes on these words. He read the pages to the bitter end again, and put them in a blue folder. Maybe the utter shock of reading them was greater because Helmut had been expecting nothing when he had picked up the pages this past weekend. If you open a closet where your winter coats are stored for the season and find, instead, the red, wormy head of Mrs. Johnson from across the street, on a spike, then you, too, might be especially shocked out of your mind.

Helmut heard Hopfgartner's door close with a soft click. The knob was jiggled once and then twice to check the lock. And then more footsteps, plodding softly, nearly gliding, made their way down the hallway too. Did they almost pause in front of his door? Of course not. It was Helmut's imagination again. After a few minutes, he heard the faraway door close again.

These words more than thirty-five-years old. From an obscure literary journal. "Why I Am Neither Guilty Nor Ashamed." The language still evoking the bitter, copper stink of blood in the air. A fog of blood.

Chapter Four

It took all of Helmut's focus to finish the final rewrite of the Christa Wolf paper before Professor Hopfgartner departed for Europe. Helmut put "Why I Am Neither Guilty Nor Ashamed" out of his mind. It was the only way to get any work done. Or to get any sleep.

Finally Hopfgartner left for Zürich on May 16. The next day Helmut mailed the Christa Wolf piece and stopped working on the professor's Compilation. In the gloom of a seventh-floor carrel, he poured over the professor's articles and books. But now his work was not for the official version of events, but for the truth about Werner Hopfgartner.

Anything before 1961, the year the professor departed from Europe. That was Helmut's goal. Was this W. Hopfgartner *his* Werner Hopfgartner? The secret would be somewhere buried in the past, before the professor's escape to America.

Helmut retrieved the professor's books and opened the one on Goethe. This was a classic treatise on the relationship between philosophy and literature in Germany, and its antecedents in ancient Greece. Another book was on Heidegger and Nietzsche.

Immediately Helmut noticed the complete difference in writing style between the various books. The mind of a schizoid? The first two books were perfect academic interpretations of their subjects. Not one comma was out of place. But the earliest book, on Heidegger and Nietzsche, the first finished after 1961, was notable for its attack on poor Nietzsche. It was an emotional, unrestrained polemic that condemned the philosopher's intellectual wander-

ings. This obscure book might contain a link to writings the professor published in Europe prior to his arrival at Smith College in
Amherst.

What did the professor find so distasteful about Nietzsche?
The philosopher tended to be "all-too-German in temperament,"
whatever that meant, while also being anti-German in his criticism of the country's obsessive behavior about itself and its great-
ness. Nietzsche, it seemed, would take no prisoners. He'd douse
his own culture with a torrent of condemnation. He'd rail against
the metastable relationship between the mind and the body, this
ever-confusing being of vicissitudes. He'd even attack his own
ideas, exposing his mistakes with a keen glory. Nietzsche pierced
the belly of every sacred cow in sight! *That's* what unnerved Hopfgartner. This philosopher, with such a great and inherent capabil-
ity for thinking, repeatedly overlooked the power of taking a
stand, of declaring that such-and-such was right, here and now, of
establishing *this* as the truth. Nietzsche tore at himself needlessly,
or so wrote the professor.

But Werner Hopfgartner was dead wrong about Nietzsche, Helmut thought. This character of self-criticism and openness was the
very reason that Helmut felt he could trust Nietzsche. This kind of
philosopher would fight against his own dogmatism. He'd question
himself and become even more rigorous in his thinking. Why did
the old man pamphleteer against this "intellectual wildness"?
What was there to be afraid of? What Nietzsche did took guts.

Helmut flipped through the bibliography of the Nietzsche
book. It was closing time, and his stomach was grumbling. The
bibliography was a mishmash of bulletins, books, articles and
speeches. Journals with volume and issue numbers but no date.
Some of the journals Helmut had not even heard of. He checked
the other books. These strange or incomplete references appeared
only in the Nietzsche book. How odd.

The next morning Helmut walked into the newspaper room of
Sterling Library. He had already marched to Jonathan Atwater's
office, where a small yellow note on the glass door said the librarian could be found in the newspaper room.

"*There* you are," Helmut said cheerily, trying to lift this cloud over his head. In his hand was a list of the most peculiar references from Hopfgartner's Nietzsche book.

"Indeed. Saw my note, did you?" the librarian said circumspectly. He wore a pink oxford shirt and a bolo tie, with a hexagonal turquoise center beaded in silver at the edges.

"Yes, I did. Could you take a look at these? Really need your help this time."

"Let me see."

Jonathan Atwater studied the sheet of paper carefully. He pushed his glasses against the bridge of his nose and scribbled a few unintelligible words in the margins. "These can probably be found, Helmut. But it might take time because I've got to look for them in certain collections that are not ordinary, although not quite extraordinary either. It's just that these journals are unusual, maybe out-of-print."

Helmut noticed Jonathan Atwater's face. It wasn't particularly friendly. Of course! Helmut thought. He had not even said hello. My God! Why did he zero in on his work like a madman, at the expense of even his best friends? Hopfgartner had always treated Helmut like that, and he hated it.

"Whatever you can do, Jonathan," Helmut finally blurted out, awash in guilt. "I'm sorry I've been piling up these requests, but—"

"Oh, my dear, *please!* I'll have none of that now!" Mr. Atwater exclaimed, a grin finally spreading over his face. "A proposition."

"What?"

"An *invitation*, Helmut. To my favorite Chinese restaurant, for dim sum. On Broadway, near the Co-op."

"Today?"

"Why not?"

"I'll stop by at 12:30," Helmut said, and waved goodbye. He knew the price to be paid for Mr. Atwater's help was feeding his fantasy that they might have a relationship one day. At least Jonathan Atwater was never boring.

～ ～ ～

The Imperial Room was bedecked in gaudy red velour. Red velour on the walls. Red velour on the faux-French chairs with round, beaded backs and stubby gargoyle claws for legs. Even red velour on the waiter's notepad. The color of blood. Mr. Atwater and Helmut sat in front of the windows on Broadway. Young Chinese waiters brought them water, steamed towels, menus, a bowl of crispy fried noodles and a tiny tray of hot mustard and sweet sauce.

"Taking a summer vacation?" Mr. Atwater asked, as he pointed to the steamed pork buns and the rice noodles with shrimp on the metal cart. The Chinese waitress, stoic and small, splashed the soy sauce over the noodles and dropped both trays on their table. She sped off to another corner of the restaurant as if she were on fire.

"Don't think so. Got too much work. I don't have the money anyway." A rice noodle slipped down Helmut's throat, sparking a riot among his taste buds. With a delicate precision, Mr. Atwater ordered sticky rice, crispy-skin duck and fried pork dumplings.

Another Chinese waitress with a cart, who seemed even more agitated than the first, pushed the trays onto their table and left in a panic. Helmut stared at the man in a suit behind the cash register, who smiled nervously in their direction. The waitresses huddled together and whispered to each other as they glanced at their table, too.

Didn't Jonathan notice their attitude? Helmut wondered.

"Too bad. I'm going to Andalusia," Mr. Atwater said. "Two blessed weeks. Oh, I can't wait! It's been years since I've been to *España*. A little flamenco, a good bowl of gazpacho and who knows! I may never return to *Los Estados Estúpidos*."

"My boss is over there."

"Hopfgartner? In Spain?" The librarian's face turned white. He gulped half a glass of water and calmed himself. "I don't believe it."

"No, Switzerland and Austria. In the Alps, I think."

"Oh, I see. Not even in the same country, Helmut. *Shame on you*. You're becoming such a damn Yankee. Now that I think of it, you don't even have a German accent. A strange mix. Not even Spanish, really."

"My mother. Blame her, if you want. She said she didn't want me to speak English like she spoke German."

"A wise woman."

"She was-is. You know Werner Hopfgartner?" Helmut asked suddenly. Should he mention the awful letter to Mr. Atwater?

"A while ago, probably before you started to work for him, I helped him research a few topics. Nothing special. Tell me about your mother, Helmut."

"She's from New Mexico. She lives there now."

"How did she meet your father?"

"He was a German soldier training for NATO. At Fort Bliss in El Paso."

"Fort *Bliss*? What a name! A soldier. How romantic. He swept her off her feet and took her to Germany. What a saga!" Mr. Atwater stared dreamily past Helmut, almost with tears in his eyes.

The librarian listened intently as Helmut recounted the story of his parents' courtship, how his mother had trouble adjusting to German culture, his mother's return to New Mexico as a widow. Mr. Atwater seemed thoroughly enthralled. Their conversation was spirited and even humorous. Yet as Helmut looked into Mr. Atwater's eyes, he kept thinking he found it disgusting to imagine himself penetrating another man's anus, let alone a woman's or even the wonderful roundness of Ariane Sassolini's sculpted behind. And so the meal left him at once satisfied and perturbed.

The results of Mr. Atwater's search arrived in bunches throughout the summer. The first interoffice letters to Helmut announced disappointments. A review could not be found or a particular volume was missing.

The first successful search yielded two little-known journals from the 1950s. One was nothing but Hopfgartner's bland review of three "recent" German books on related themes. But the other journal was an astounding confirmation of Helmut's worst fears. A Hopfgartner article expanded on the defense of Austria's innocence during the war. The "story" of the Holocaust, it argued, was simply an extortionate guilt trap. Vienna did not owe the newly created state of Israel one Austrian shilling. If the Federal Republic wanted to "waste" its money on foreign aid to a country that would never forgive it for "supposed crimes against humanity," then it should do so, but alone.

Werner Hopfgartner, *his* Werner Hopfgartner, wrote that Austria was bound, as was any "great nation," to its own principles of honor and statehood. Without these, Austria would be incapable of defining itself. It'd be mired in the political guilt manipulation these *Ausländer* were attempting to impose on them by fiat. How could they be the judges and embody the standards by which Austrians should be judged? The professor wrote: "This 'outside judgment' is sheer nonsense! Don't let it seep into your consciousness like a poisonous stream. We Austrians should determine the moral good of our own community. See these efforts for what they are: a crass imposition of guilt, an international dictatorship of morality. Nothing less! Austria will find its own *authentic way*. By our own blood we are bound, and by nothing else! Know in your heart that they will *never* understand us. Know that the cowards among us, these nonauthentic citizens of our land, have simply emasculated themselves. They've ceded the possibility of possessing our *natural* vision of the truth."

My God! Helmut thought. It *was* Hopfgartner! Without a doubt.

In late July, Atwater found more journals. One again hit Helmut like a sucker punch. This essay, written in 1952, argued that the war had indeed been "a profound Germanic failure." But the "Movement" had been a success. The "Movement" in question was an informal group of intellectuals and political commentators with a "communitarian" ideology. They had long advocated raising German consciousness about the emptiness of modern living and the danger of unrestricted freedoms without accompanying responsibilities. This group called for a "New Day" when the human essence of freedom could be joined with "authentic" political action and community.

"To win this New Day," the professor wrote, "a new bond must be created between Western individual freedoms and society. Our freedoms must be *embodied* in our community, not suppressed by it. Yet this 'community' will not just guarantee anonymous individual living. We cannot be a community of lonely strangers! That is the abysmal path of the United States. *Our* community will be truly grand. Its true leaders will define our community culture. They will embody the values of each citizen without shunning the self, and its uniqueness. Our hearts, our *blood*, will lead the way! Relativism and chaos will be the demons of other countries, not ours! Raw clashes between citizens, a morality of the victorious, of the most powerful—*not* of the right and the true—these diseases will not infect us! *We* will know what is right. *We* will live in truth."

Helmut's head spun. What abstract nonsense! Did Hopfgartner not read his own words? The holes in his arguments were gargantuan. How would a community choose these "true leaders"? What criteria would be used for such a choice, and by whom? Was "authenticity" to spring out of nowhere, from a charismatic charlatan's naked assertions? Could the community or groups within it have the right of dissent in the face of a leader's declarations? Oh, how easy it was to leave the most important questions unanswered!

But these flaws weren't the worst part for Helmut. He already assumed that many Germans, especially of the old school, had a penchant for authority and for following orders like good little soldiers. The opposite of the East Coast. Here in America, bizarre excesses were celebrated simply to shock and disgust. It was voyeurism at its apex.

If Germany was the land of authority, America was the incubator of materialistic and hedonistic anarchy. Maybe Helmut was simply condemned to his own special purgatory, an outsider in Freiburg, a traditionalist in New Haven. But the cultural mêlée of New York still seemed nearly out of control to him. So the professor was in some sense right about the reasons for the problems in America.

What *did* surprise Helmut were the professor's comments on National Socialism. The 'intellectual movement' of the Nazis a "success"? Its practical and political implementation, its massacre of innocents, a mere "unfortunate digression" of what was genuinely good theory and idealism? What blood-splattered blindness! Helmut thought. These quasi-religious abstractions yearning for a "pure German freedom." These were ideas that were simply embraced by brutes and manipulators to purify Germany of whomever they deemed bad blood. *That* was the truth. The vagueness of what exactly this German freedom would practically be was an empty placeholder waiting to be filled by the next smooth-talking demagogue. Not to see this plainly was to inhabit an alien world with a different moral sense. A world of absolutes. A world without discourse. The opposite of the practical world. Why would you even call this absolutist world 'moral'?

Finally, it was simply astonishing for Helmut to realize he had been helping, and even admiring, the man behind such radical views.

Chapter Five

The path from the cottage led only to the village square nestled within a small valley of the Swiss Alps. There was nowhere else to go except into the forest. The smaller paths led nowhere. In the forest underbrush were meandering routes, one to a stream, another to a clearing, a third to a meadow populated by small white butterflies. These paths, in fact, had originally been worn into the grass by animals. It was best, if you did not yet know your way, to stay on the main path to Berg. Many a visitor had been lost in the dark forest for hours, especially after these seemingly innocuous paths split and split again, into smaller, more wayward routes.

Wasn't it only two years ago when Heinrich Maienfeld, who had been visiting for a week, became suddenly disoriented by what he called the "sameness" of the forest? Sameness, indeed! Hopfgartner thought. Maienfeld had been lucky he didn't freeze to death or become the evening meal of some hungry beast. Every tree was different. Every rock. Every path. Maienfeld had spent too much time in Munich, Hopfgartner concluded. He knew this forest as his best friend.

Holding a cane with an ornate silver wolf's head handle, the old man marched into the outskirts of the village of Berg.

Himmelfarb's was open, so he went there first. In front, two ruddy-cheeked workers in identical gray overalls, German to the core, laid stone after stone into this patch that had become a dip in Hauptstrasse. Hopfgartner had noticed the problem a year ago, and mentioned it to Himmelfarb, who simmered into a rage. Himmelfarb had asked the authorities almost four months before to fix the "hideous hole" in front of his shop. They had finally gotten around to it. No wonder Himmelfarb seemed happier this summer.

"*Gruss Gott, Herr Himmelfarb*," Hopfgartner said, strolling in front of the anise-flavored cookies, gingerbread men, *Walnussschnitten*, poppy seed and fruit tarts, and other *Kleingebäck*.

"Oh, Herr Professor, what a thrill it is to see you! Did you see the men outside?" Himmelfarb asked in a deep growl. He was a huge man, with fat cheeks, a voluminous belly covered by a white apron, and thick, plodding legs. His head was bald except for wisps of gray hair behind his ears. Himmelfarb's face was as expressive as his size, downright jolly. "Finally!"

"Of course, you are happy with their work?"

"Well, between you and me," Himmelfarb said in a hushed tone, already with the box in his hand for Hopfgartner's *Honigkuchen*, "they are *Dummköpfe*. But they do what they are told. I've had to watch them every hour to make sure their work is *flawless*. I've waited long enough! I'm not about to accept second-rate work."

His stubby fingers struggled over the tiny knot of the red string wrapped tightly around the cake box. Himmelfarb cleared the phlegm in his throat, which bulged like another small bald head under his pink chin.

"You are right, of course."

"Everything up at your cottage in good order? We had a terrible early frost last winter. I wondered about your water lines, if Karl had gotten there in time. Ours froze up and cracked open. *Eine Katastrophe!*"

"Everything's in perfect condition, thank you. Here you go."

"*Gott sei Dank!* Have a beautiful walk back. There's nothing like the summer," Himmelfarb said.

A block north from Himmelfarb's—in an alley which contained a butcher shop, a small real estate office and a two-story square building that had once been the *Rathaus* when his parents were still alive—Hopfgartner found the post office. One of the tight-lipped *Frauen* behind the counter's ornate, wrought-iron window brought him a stack of letters, two flat parcels, half a dozen magazines and journals. He nodded and made arrangements for his mail to be delivered to the cottage once a week, a task he had neglected since his arrival in Berg.

On his way back to the cottage, he walked by the Hoffmann house at the edge of the village. He didn't know which family lived there anymore, probably a son or daughter of Ilse, maybe even a grandchild of hers. *In Frieden leben, meine Liebling,* he thought. Finally, he reached the forest and the path homeward.

Inside the cottage, flames crackled in the old stone fireplace. Enough heat emanated from the blaze to warm the rustic living room. An old French rug covered the dark wooden floor in front of his father's reading chair. On the walls, which were built of dark wood too, hung old landscape paintings from his mother's family. There was a bookshelf that long ago Werner Hopfgartner had dragged downstairs from one of the bedrooms. The bookshelf was full of leather-bound volumes of poetry, philosophy and history. These were his father's books, a few from his mother or her family, his own additions, some books without a clear origin, books from previous centuries. The bookshelf was next to a window in the middle of the living room, within arm's reach of his father's chair. His father would never have approved. Hopfgartner sat in the chair and read his mail. The evening was unusually cold even for this mountainside.

He opened a letter.

Mein Gott, the professor thought, what in the world is this? In English, he read:

Werner Hopfgartner, you will never escape your perversions. You horrible bastard! I know about them. I know about everything. You will be found out if it's the last thing I do. There will be no sailing into the sunset. There will be no beautiful life ahead. No future! You've ruined enough lives already. You've ruined my life. Yes, I was one of yours. But I'm not going to just walk away. Everything will be known soon. You will pay for everything you did to me. To all of us. Fuck you!

The note was typed on a white sheet of copy paper. The postmark was from New York. It had been mailed eight days ago, in a light-blue envelope with diagonal red and blue stripes along the edges, the kind of envelope you could buy in any drugstore. The postage was common American stamps, the exact amount for a letter to Switzerland. The address was typed, his exact Berg address. Even the mail codes were correct. Who knew his summer vacation address? Probably dozens of individuals. Professors, other colleagues, students, friends, secretaries. He'd been coming here for at least twenty years. The letter had been mailed from New York, and with the correct address. So it was most likely someone at Yale, someone there now or someone who had once been there. It could be anyone.

Hopfgartner crushed the letter into a tight ball with his thick gnarly fingers. He was about to fling it into the fire, but stopped and reread it and shoved it into a stack of personal papers. He was surrounded by cowards, he thought. Hopfgartner tore open a Parisian journal of history that contained a small piece he had finished last winter. His friend Maienfeld was in here too. Now *that* was a pleasant surprise! He reread his own article first.

Chapter Six

Helmut received another interoffice mail notice from Mr. Atwater late Friday afternoon. A few hours prior to the Labor Day weekend, Helmut was near the end of Hopfgartner's Compilation. The old man had phoned Helmut in early August and said he'd be back in New Haven by the second week in September. Helmut didn't panic: the Compilation would be finished. And in a strange way, it was Helmut's best work: clear, thorough, and purposeful. Yet his obsession to finish it was anything but noble. His mind roiled in disgust. The only way to free himself from Hopfgartner and his sick ideas was to finish this work quickly. Then Helmut would have time to think about what to do. Should he give these two articles to anyone, to another professor perhaps, and let them decide what to do? Did these forty-year-old words matter anymore? Mr. Atwater had found the last batch of articles by Hopfgartner. Helmut packed up his things and left Harkness Hall.

On his bicycle, he sped through the night, the late August air a bevy of cool spirits around him. His clothes were in his backpack, along with a compass for the mountains of North Adams, his toothbrush, Ariane's favorite Lindt chocolate bar with pistachios, and a moth-eaten collection of obscure pamphlets. Tonight they'd flee New Haven for the serenity of the forest.

≈ ≈ ≈

"So that's why we had to push it to the gas station last week! The radiator!" Helmut said, watching the flash of lights alongside I-91. They were careening down an on-ramp at sixty miles per hour.

"Well, the hose, a coolant hose was leaking," Ariane said distractedly, pumping the gas to beat the semi that wasn't about to let them into freeway traffic without a race. The Corolla's motor buzzed like a swarm of hornets. She pulled left on the steering wheel, thudding across the giant triangular reflector grid, and punched into the first lane, a few feet in front of the truck. Helmut's heart leapt, and then relaxed. Ariane sped into the travel lane. The truck fell behind, two shiny eyes in the distance. "Jerry replaced the hose, flushed the radiator. It was full of muck. Changed the oil. He said the Blue Demon's in good shape now."

"Love the Blue Demon. Reminds me of a spaceship at night."

"We should be there before midnight," she said, more relaxed after setting the cruise control. The speedometer read seventy-five miles per hour. They'd take I-91 North to Hartford, past Springfield, all the way to Greenfield, Mass., and then Route 2 West to North Adams. This was the easiest way to Savoy Mountain, with the worst traffic probably before Hartford. And best of all, it was a perfect late summer night, cool, clear and dry.

They fell into a good rhythm. The dirt was moist and full of pine needles. It was better that Ariane led, since they couldn't walk abreast in this increasingly thick maze of pine trees, fallen branches and spiky bushes. Up the mountain, she was quicker and stronger than he. She always found the right way to go even when they could see nothing ahead. He had only to follow her. His heart thumped hard inside his chest. What was happening to his lungs up here? Helmut thought, between gasps. They'd shrunk in this thin air!

He had shoved the Hopfgartner pamphlets into the second drawer of the pine bureau in their room. He wasn't hiding them, really. Why leave them out and have to explain them? He had trouble explaining it to himself why he had brought them. Was it because Hopfgartner would be back in two weeks? Was that a deadline? Or was Helmut thinking of ignoring what he had found? Maybe he *did* want to reveal everything to Ariane.

"Get your butt over here! Take a look at this!" Helmut heard from somewhere beyond a hill of short pines that seemed to drop off into the sky.

"Where are you?" Still marching upward, he scanned the short horizon for Ariane's red flannel shirt. He saw only a thick mesh of dangling branches.

"Up here! Nowhere else to go!"

He found her in a cove of junipers, at the peak of this hill. Beyond was a lush green valley. Ariane had already dropped her backpack and begun to spread a blanket on the bed of pine needles, dried leaves and fine grass.

"What do you think?" she asked, standing up for a second look. Helmut focused on their surroundings. His breathing slowed. His backpack dropped to the ground. There was no sound except for their voices. The view for miles was spectacular.

"Great," he said, tugging at the back of his shirt to ventilate it. The air was surprisingly cool.

✑ ✑ ✑

Ariane was on her back, her head resting on the lump of her backpack. She nibbled at the last bit of her sandwich.

"Why don't you ever go home?" she asked.

"What do you mean?"

"I mean, Are you ever going to visit your mother in New Mexico?"

"Why do you call it 'home?' I've never *been* there."

"Your mother's there."

"So?"

"Don't you miss her?"

"Well, I guess," Helmut said. "But it's not my home."

"Why not? Isn't home wherever your family is? Even if you've never been there?"

"I don't know what 'home' is. I don't miss the mountains of New Mexico. My mother's there, sure. But it's not like I want to go back to being a kid."

"That's not what I mean. Don't you want to talk to your mom, to have dinner with her, to help her out?"

"I do that already. I talk to her. Maybe I don't help her out much, but I call her."

"It's different face-to-face. Don't you think it's better to kiss her in person than just call her on the phone?"

"Sure. Why don't you go home?" he said, opening up another can of Diet Coke.

"I don't know. Sometimes I want to. I want to see my sisters. I'd like to spend some afternoons with my mother. Cooking dinner. Laughing at stupid jokes. Seeing their faces. Trying to avoid their questions about my love life. I miss the little things the most."

"So you think you'll go home one day?" Helmut said, at once realizing what this would mean for them.

"Not for a while. Maybe never."

"I don't understand. You just said you *missed* them."

"Well, I do," she said, still lying flat on the blanket, her eyes closed. Ariane heard the crunch of the Corn Nuts and held out her hand. Helmut shook a pile of them into her palm. "But I don't think I belong there anymore. Not in the same way as before. I know what you mean: you can't go back. But maybe I could go back, as a different person, in a different role. I just don't know if they would let me be somebody else. It's so easy to slip into old habits."

"Maybe they'll change."

"Maybe *we'll* change."

"Can I ask you a question?" he said.

"What?"

"Why are you talking about 'going home'? Are you tired of me?"

"What? Of course not!" Ariane said, looking surprised. She propped herself on her elbows and stared at him. "You know how much I love to be with you."

Helmut was quiet for a moment. Ariane sat up and took his hand. He squeezed it. "Ariane, I love you with all my heart."

"You mean that?"

"Of course I do. It took me long enough to say it. But I love you. Yes, I do."

"Tell me what you mean," Ariane said softly.

"What is this, hermeneutics? Took me long enough to say it, now you want me to explain it too?" he said too sharply.

"Please. It's important to me. Just tell me what you mean. In words."

"I mean I want to be with you for a long time. I don't know if that's forever, but it's as far as I can see into the future. I mean if you go back to Italy I want to go with you. I don't care about my job. I don't care about my mother. I don't care where I live. I just want to be with you." A few tears slid down his cheeks. Helmut was having trouble breathing again. "What you said about your family, I know it's true for me, too. I love everything about you. The muscles on your back, your beautiful legs, the way you walk. Your gorgeous nose. I love that you do your pushups and sit-ups every morning; that your favorite cereal is Grape Nuts. That sometimes you're bossy and sometimes you're sexy. Sometimes in the same minute! I love you with all my heart, Ariane. Don't know what else to say."

"I love you too." She kissed his hand.

"Why do you think it took me so long to say it?" Helmut asked. He wiped his cheeks.

"It's hard to say if you mean it. It'll be a year in a couple of weeks. A year since we started going out."

"Think that was too long?"

"For what?" she asked, rubbing his back and neck.

"For saying 'I love you.'"

"Feels just right to me."

Ariane pulled him down on top of her and kissed him. They were both lying on the blanket, dots of sunlight surrounding them like tiny suns. She kissed his cheek, kissed his eyes and pushed against him. His lips caressed the pores of her neck, which swirled with the scent of her sweet perspiration. He felt intoxicated and overwhelmed. Ariane exhaled appreciatively. There was nothing more she wanted to do than to love him. Helmut unbuttoned her shirt, unsnapped her bra and kissed her breasts. Gently she held his head in her hands.

～ ～ ～

"Ariane, a question," Helmut said as they marched downhill. They had tried descending hand in hand, but outside of the small clearing at the top, the footing was treacherous.

"What?" She wiped her brow, found her footing and held out her hand as he skidded to a stop just above her. She walked up and hugged him. "You okay?"

"I want to ask you a question."

"Shoot." Ariane started down the mountain again, more slowly this time. He was right behind her.

"Have a scenario for you. Need your advice," he said, catching his breath.

"Scenario?"

"Say you're digging into your family's history. Doing a genealogy. And you find something horrible. Something that's really disgusting. What do you do?"

"What do you mean 'what do you do'? It'd be exciting. Love to know the dirt on an old Sassolini. You know I have an ancestor who fought with Napoleon?"

"That's not what I mean. What if you were doing this history and discovered something awful about somebody *alive*. Say, your grandfather."

"My grandfather! Ugh! Depends. What's this about?"

"Well, I'm helping one of my mother's friends. Looking things up at Yale." Helmut lied, and ducked his head to avoid branches smacking his face.

"You found something about his grandfather? What?"

"I don't really know."

"Why is he asking you what to do?"

"Not really *asking* me. When I talk to him, I get the sense he doesn't want to know. I could just pretend it's a dead-end."

"What about what he knows?" she asked, picking up speed down an incline. The pine needles and the moist dirt crumbled under her feet. "Seems cowardly he wants you to make this decision for him."

"Cowardly? He has to live with it."

"Maybe you're right. I'm just the peanut gallery. But I think he's the one who has to decide what to do. He just can't forget what he knows."

"That's pretty much what I told him."

≈   ≈   ≈

It was Sunday night. They'd return to New Haven the next day. Ariane was asleep next to him. The mesh of her hair, like a sea anemone brown and fibrous, glistened on the white pillow behind her head. Her face had no wrinkles when she slept. Her olive skin seemed to glow in the darkness. Helmut pulled the quilt over her shoulders.

It was cold at night on Savoy Mountain, and it seemed particularly cold in this room on the second floor of the inn. He stepped on the wooden floor, and it creaked, but she did not wake up. Helmut opened the pine drawer and removed the old papers. He tiptoed to the red plaid window seat and turned on the small reading lamp above his head. The pamphlets felt exceedingly fragile, as if the coffee-colored pages might crumble when he turned them. But they didn't. It was a few minutes before 1:00 a.m.

It was insomnia, Helmut thought. Why should it matter anyway? Why should these old words make a difference now? How could any words really matter, now or forty years ago? It was what you did that counted. Not what you thought, not what you said, but what you *did*.

The professor's article in this *Monthly Bulletin from Vienna* was a reprint of a magazine op-ed piece originally written in 1949. Was it still a surprise to Helmut that this "historical analysis" was replete with distortions? Maybe it shouldn't have been, and maybe Helmut should've expected these insanities against common sense. But even Helmut Sanchez wasn't so easily hardened. Werner Hopfgartner exposed, in the most inflammatory language, the atrocities committed by Russian soldiers in Vienna. He did this to justify the brutality of the German army in the Soviet Union. In other words, the Third Reich had been correct all along to assume these brutish foreign hordes needed to be conquered by the superior forces of Germany. Only the "physical failure" of German soldiers had left them vulnerable to these "Slavic-Asian animals," not their moral failure or the failure of German reason.

Red Army soldiers in Vienna? Helmut suddenly remembered a story from his mother. It was about a New Mexican woman, a distant friend of his mother. This woman was an expatriate Austrian who now lived in Alamogordo, New Mexico, the mother of three boys. She had married a Mexicano from Juárez and eventually ended up in an art class with Helmut's mother.

Maria Theresa, with her little brother, had been walking to the grocery store a few weeks after Russian soldiers first marched into the Danube valley. She was fourteen years old. Six Russian soldiers in a truck stopped them, and briefly interrogated them. Those new and ominous invaders usually ignored children. Two of them grabbed her from behind and dragged her into the truck. Another simply punched her brother and pushed him to the ground when he tried to help her. The truck sped off, to an isolated farm on the outskirts of the city. These Russians, one a lieutenant, raped her repeatedly until she fainted from the pain and lost blood. When Maria Theresa finally regained consciousness, her only thought was to beg the Almighty to kill her.

But the Russians didn't let her go. The lieutenant kept her and used her for a while. Later he sold her to a man who owned a farm near Lvov in the Ukraine. Maria Theresa became a servant and, really, a slave to this wealthy "landowner," a regional Party boss. A schoolteacher saw her and inquired about her education, and the teacher was told to mind her own business, or else. The teacher returned secretly to hear the story of how a young, blond Austrian girl had come to live in the Ukraine without even a good grasp of colloquial Russian. After months of secret planning, the teacher helped Maria Theresa escape the farm one night. She hid inside a grain truck heading west. Then, with the help of other families the schoolteacher knew, Maria Theresa traveled day and night for four days and nights until she'd simply collapse into another stranger's arms for another journey. After reaching Vienna, she discovered most of her immediate family missing or dead. Maria Theresa feared the Russians would be looking for her. So she immediately took a boat to America. She wanted the Atlantic Ocean between her and the nightmarish demons that tormented her sleep.

So Helmut was sure atrocities had occurred on every side during the Second World War. But that wasn't the point. The point was that the Germans *began* the war when they invaded Poland. The point was that the Germans were again the aggressors on the eastern front in their war with the Soviet Union. The point was that the Germans created and implemented genocidal policies to obliterate those deemed not pure enough. And most of all, the point was that if a nation did start a war simply to conquer others for its own benefit, then the reactions of those who eventually defeated the warmongers had to be understood in the *context* of the idiocies that started the war in the first place.

The slippery morality of the professor's article. The convenient forgetfulness of causes and their role in the hideous endgame of the war. The sheer denial of proper context and real blame. What a corrupt liar! Helmut thought, in the darkness next to Ariane. How could anyone ever forsake the obvious, the *human*, in understanding the terrible wrongness of Germany's role in the war? In a sense, then, Helmut was still surprised.

But compare a grisly movie scene with the sight of your own mother stabbed, dying in your arms. You would then know the thunder of *real* shock, the swoon of what mattered, when it twisted disgustingly toward you. This was what Helmut read in one short paragraph, a paragraph he nearly skimmed over:

> *Without a doubt, my friends, just as we have lost the war, we Germans and patriots are also in danger of losing the ideological battle to understand the war. Already ad hominem attacks against all Germans and Austrians have become commonplace. The explanation for what happened, in this insipid reductionism so typical of modernity, is centered on who we are, that Germans, by the simple fact of being German, are evil and corrupt to the core. I myself have faced this challenge personally, by having to refute ridiculous accusations that I participated in the goings-on at Mühldorf and even the infamous Dachau. That's what the future holds, unfortunately, personal attacks to define*

*morality, vilification of individuals until a bloody circle of
internecine warfare becomes the norm and we live under the
bleak sun of relativism and tribalism.*

My God, thought Helmut, what was this? Mühldorf? Accusations? Who made them? What exactly were these allegations?
What sordid hidden history had Helmut stumbled upon?

The night seemed to close around his reading light and suffo-
cate him. Only until a certain moment could he gather himself
enough to think about sleeping again, to plan for tomorrow. That
moment came when one thing became clear in his mind. Helmut
decided, irrevocably and adamantly, that he had to get to the bottom of this puzzle. As soon as he had the chance, before Werner
Hopfgartner returned from Europe, Helmut would break into the
professor's office and dig out the truth about this nefarious past.

Chapter Seven

Helmut had to wait until Friday to carry out his plan. The professor would be back in a week. The classrooms were deserted Friday night, the end of the first week of the fall semester. Helmut had already found the keys in the German department's offices.

He had so much work to do that his staying late wouldn't seem out of the ordinary. He had told Ariane he'd see her Saturday. Maybe they'd bike down Rim Road, near East Rock Park. Helmut walked slowly through the darkened hallways of Harkness. There was an Italian professor with his light on, but his door closed. A coquettish older secretary from the French Department was working too. Helmut went to the restroom, returned to his basement office, sat down and distractedly edited the first draft of the Compilation. After a while, he'd take another walk. If he was alone, he'd go to the main office and enter Werner Hopfgartner's private study.

It was almost 9:00 p.m. before the last person left. The last hour had been a temporal agony for Helmut. What if the security guard discovered him in the professor's office? A guard would soon make the rounds of the Cross Campus buildings, turning off the lights and locking doors. Perhaps he could tell the guard he was working on a project for Professor Hopfgartner and needed to retrieve papers from his office. It was the truth! Helmut thought.

Helmut tucked a manila folder under his arm as a prop. It contained a printout of the first twenty-six pages of the Compilation. He walked to the professor's door. A fluorescent bulb pulsed in the basement hallway. He fumbled with the keys and the lock. Finally he pushed the door open, flicked on the lights and locked the door behind him.

Helmut dropped the manila folder by the door, a reminder not to forget it on his way out. Over a stack of books on the floor, he groped for the string to draw the thick white curtains closed. Someone might see the light and decide to stop by and welcome the professor back to New Haven. Helmut calculated he had at most two hours, and certainly no more than three.

The office was a pigsty. Piles of books and papers were strewn on top of the desk, over the coffee table and sofa. Even the two chairs that faced the professor's desk were littered with books. Against the wall was the bureaucratic gray row of eight shoulder-high filing cabinets.

The files. Helmut had decided only these could contain the secret to the accusations against the professor. It was also possible that the professor might not have kept anything so controversial. Or he might have hidden the evidence from his past at home. It was quite possible that Helmut would find nothing shocking or extraordinary in the office. But he was willing to take this risk. Maybe in his office, the professor had tucked away one tidbit that pointed to his participation in the war. If Helmut discovered that evidence, he'd be on his way toward the truth.

In the first few filing cabinets, Helmut found Hopfgartner's handwritten drafts and finished articles. Then other essays, reprints, reviews of postwar German authors, chapters of books, old galleys with their corrections in bright red ink, a drawer devoted to book contracts, payments from academic reviews and miscellaneous financial records. Helmut rummaged through papers for an hour and a half. His heart stopped thumping wildly. Maybe nothing was there after all, Helmut concluded. What was the point of chasing these ghostlike words?

The last two filing cabinets were locked. Helmut yanked open the main desk drawer and hunted for the keys. He found keys on three interlocking rings. One small key opened the locked cabinets, and immediately Helmut's heart pounded faster. This material predated the professor's 1961 arrival in America. The articles and manuscripts were from the early 1950s.

Three files had no date whatsoever. At once Helmut flipped immediately to these yellowing pages in the back. One was a French newspaper clipping from 1946. Helmut read the story of a Lithuanian businessman. His family had been kidnapped by the Nazis in 1943 and presumably killed after the plunder of Vilnius on the battle road to Moscow. The article was uncertain about the fate of his family. The businessman had been the only one to escape the German war machine, and had even evaded the black cloud of the Red Army.

After the war, this survivor settled in Paris and organized a non-profit center to locate and reunify Jewish war refugees and their families. He became the center's director. But he never found his own family: a beautiful daughter with an operatic voice; a devoted wife he loved to such an excess, even after the near-certainty of her death, that his colleagues at the refugee center said he wasted away waiting for her return; an infant son full of promise. The businessman had vowed never to remarry, had dedicated poem after poem to his beloved. He had recited the stanzas quietly on the Seine every Saturday at dusk. Finally these murky waters seemed to wash away the pain forever. The day before this newspaper article appeared, Vladek Litvak had committed suicide.

Helmut flipped through more pages in the unmarked manila folders. He found a document approving an application for Austrian residency dated December 21, 1944. He also found a letter instructing an official to forward the professor's government pension to an account with Deutsche Bank A.G. in Munich. And there was another short letter in response to a query by an investigative German commission established after the war. In this last correspondence, Werner Hopfgartner simply stated that he had been a low-level political attaché in the *Wehrmacht*, specifically in the southern command section based in Munich. Hopfgartner said he had held this position for less than two years before the end of the war. Previously, he had been a member of the *Reichsstudentenführung*, the Reich Student Leadership, when he had been a philosophy student at Heidelberg. Helmut scanned more of the pages and discovered the commission's response. It thanked Werner Hopfgartner for his cooperation and indicated the facts he presented matched what they had learned from numerous government files and indices. His name, the commission wrote, had been cleared of any wartime criminal behavior.

To Helmut, the professor's brush with the war seemed typical of many septuagenarians in Germany. They had been young men who joined the Nazi war machine just in time to be blamed for its colossal failures. By then, the assault from the Allies had gained unstoppable momentum. The real planners and malevolent geniuses behind the belligerent philosophy of *Lebensraum* and racial genocide had either died in battle, fled to Argentina, committed suicide or were planning secret lives as innocuous farmers in the Bavarian countryside. This young generation of the war was left holding the bag, so to speak. They had never easily accepted the brunt of the guilt for what they had not started. They were novice implementers, nothing more. Cowardly and slavish, but probably not evil.

At the University of Freiburg, Helmut had known professors of this ambivalent generation. Some accepted full responsibility for the entire country, for every death. They'd hope to wash away their sins with extreme self-flagellation. Others, however, denied they had played any significant role as twentysomething soldiers. For Helmut, it was now clear that Werner Hopfgartner had been in Munich during the war. It was also clear that he might have been an enthusiastic participant in Nazi propaganda as a student. Just those facts would, no doubt, be embarrassing if they were ever revealed at Yale. But at this point in the professor's career, on the brink of retirement, such an embarrassment might be unimportant and even inconsequential. Certainly there was nothing here about Mühldorf and Dachau. The letters seemed perfunctory clearances, probably issued to millions of good German soldiers.

Was Hopfgartner nothing more than an ugly moral wart in the rancid corpse of Nazi Germany? Would Helmut have been so pure? What would he have done if he had been a young man in Germany in 1944? Would he have mouthed preposterous theories to fit into the intellectual milieu? Would Helmut have served in the army dutifully? Would he have jockeyed for a non-combat role in Munich? Or would he have possessed the presence of mind to know the danger of such murderous thinking? Who among us had the courage to oppose even the greatest blasphemy when it meant your immediate torture and execution?

It was late, only twenty minutes before the Cross Campus guard began his midnight rounds. Helmut calmly walked into the hallway, unlocked the door to his own office and copied the sheets in the three unmarked files. He hadn't even skimmed half of the pages. Maybe he had missed something. Maybe he'd take the incriminating information and deliver it somewhere, to someone. Maybe Helmut might just go home and feel idiotic about hounding an old, vain man and dump every sheet and article into the trash. What was he thinking anyway? Why should he be responsible for ferreting out the war activities of Werner Hopfgartner? Had Helmut not stumbled upon the information and persisted in his mania to find the truth, Hopfgartner's "official face" would have remained his true one. More importantly, it wasn't as if Helmut had discovered a gem beyond astonishment. True, he had unearthed what would be a scandal at Yale. But did he merely want to disgrace an academic who had once promulgated morally repugnant ideas?

It was no use trying to go back, to consider whether he had been right to do this, Helmut thought. The more he pursued it, the more he could not escape this quest. Yes, he could ignore it, or leave it to others. But then he'd exempt himself from knowing firsthand what was right and true. He wasn't a coward. Ariane was right. This was his problem because he had first been perplexed by it. It would be his solution because he would pursue it to its logical end.

"What are you doing here?"

"What?" Helmut wheeled around, startled. He had almost fainted when he heard the familiar voice behind him. The copy machine in his office droned and wheezed to a stop. It was Ariane.

"What are you doing here? I *knew* you'd be here. Hopfgartner's office is wide open."

"Oh, yes, I know that," he stammered, quickly collecting the copies from the machine. He slipped them into the blue folder with the other essays. His hands were shaking nervously, yet he was also strangely elated.

"I asked you a question, Helmut," she said angrily, "and I expect an answer. What the *fuck* are you doing here?"

"Had work to do. The Compilation," he said, dropping the blue folder into his backpack. He zipped it shut and turned off the copy machine. "He's back next week. But I'm finished."

"I called you at home and I knew you'd be here. Are you out of your *mind*? It's almost midnight! I had to see it for myself. I know you'd lie to me. Just had to come here and see it for myself."

"What? What are you talking about?" Helmut picked up the keys on his desk and began to collect and arrange the files he had taken from Hopfgartner's office. Ariane was standing at the entrance to his office, seething. Her brown eyes bored into his whenever he dared to glance at her.

"Do you blank out like an epileptic? Is that what it is? Do you suddenly lose your common sense for days at a time and start doing the *stupidest* things?"

"I don't know what you're talking about."

"Why are you working here at *midnight*?" she asked, almost shouting at him. For a moment, Helmut thought she was about to slap him. He had never seen her like this before. "He pays you to work half-time and you're working sixty hours a week! Does he have something on you? Is that what it is?"

"Course not. I let this Compilation go for too long. I had to rush things. But I'm done. Please, let's go. We biking tomorrow morning?"

"I think you're crazy," she said. Helmut strode quickly into Hopfgartner's office, dropped the files into the cabinet and locked it again. Ariane was in the hallway, her eyes watching his every move. "He lets you inside his office when he's not here?"

"Well, not really. This was an emergency. Had to finish this before he came back. Please don't tell anyone."

"You were stealing stuff from his office. Is that it?" Ariane said, almost smiling at him as they walked down the hallway. "Hah! *Now* I understand."

"Yeah, right. What are you talking about?" Helmut was light-headed and suddenly flustered. Red spots erupted in front of his face. "I wasn't stealing anything."

"Don't worry. I won't tell anyone."

"Thank you."

"It would've been better if you were stealing. A thief is better than a workaholic slave." They locked the main office and exited Harkness Hall. "Wanna ride?"

"Can't. We need the bike tomorrow, don't we?"

"Right. You gonna be okay?" she asked. Helmut walked her to her car and kissed her.

"No one's on the road. I can't believe you came here looking for me. And you say *I'm* crazy. See you tomorrow, okay?"

"Going home?"

"*Yes*, I'm going home."

Ariane drove off in her Corolla, and Helmut felt exhausted. He rode his bike up Hillhouse Street, and turned on Trumbull toward Orange Street. As he sped through the night, Helmut couldn't stop thinking of Vladek Litvak. Why had this man decided to end his own life even after overcoming so much pain? Wouldn't living always be worthwhile even if you had suffered the torture of your family's murder? Wouldn't life give you, at least, the possibility of redemption, of starting anew, of creating another love? Helmut couldn't imagine not wanting even the simple pleasure of riding his old ten-speed at night, free in the darkness. And maybe that was the problem. Maybe if certain events happened in your life—events you did not cause, like accidents, assaults or the murder of your family by hateful tyrants—then the rest of your life could never cut itself away from this wound. History would eat up the future until you had none, or at least until you lost the desire for one. Helmut still believed that somebody with incredible fortitude, and maybe faith, would put history in its place. Couldn't you make the future into something better than what the past had destroyed?

Helmut wasn't sleepy when he reached home. His head ached. He took off his shoes and clothes and slipped on a pair of blue shorts and a white T-shirt. He threw the copies of the unmarked files on the bed, and began to study them more carefully. His four-inch foam mattress, on a sheet of plywood atop cinder blocks, seemed Spartan but sufficient. Ariane had always hated that bed.

Helmut read the copy of the residency form again. Why had Werner Hopfgartner left Germany so late in the war, in December

1944, just before the American army liberated the concentration camps the following April? How could Hopfgartner have been so prescient? Or had it been blind luck to escape just in time? How did he secure Austrian residency in the midst of such chaos, when surely many other Germans were also fleeing the defeat and imminent occupation of their country? He scanned each document again, this time meticulously. To his own amazement, Helmut found other references to Vladek Litvak. A letter sent to Paris in 1946, several months after the newspaper article on the Lithuanian's suicide. A letter that had apparently included a cashier's check for three thousand German marks to the Jewish refugee center.

Why would Hopfgartner have sent an anonymous contribution in the name of this Vladek Litvak to Paris? Helmut asked himself. Had the professor been so taken by this story that he had whimsically given such a generous sum of money? Of course, the immediate aftermath of the war had been a nightmare for everyone. But why give money to a charity whose purpose was to alleviate the agony you helped create? And didn't the professor himself later write that Austria should pay nothing to Israel in war reparations? Werner Hopfgartner, the selfless giver? That seemed almost metaphysically impossible.

It was three in the morning. Many other things didn't make sense in these files. For example, an old American military pass was issued to W. Hopfgartner to travel in the occupied area of southern Germany in September of 1946, and renewed in January of 1947. Hadn't the professor been eager to abandon the Third Reich in December of 1944? Why would he have returned twice, a mere twenty-four months after his escape? Surely Germany would have been a devastated landscape. What shock for any proud German returning to his homeland! Helmut imagined. And why would Hopfgartner have returned and risked being captured by Allied troops? He would have been perfectly safe in Vienna. Werner Hopfgartner must have had a powerful reason for returning home.

The other important discovery that perplexed Helmut was a cryptic note in English and German. He found it scribbled on a sheet of paper stuck between two other files he had copied. It read, in the professor's letter-perfect script:

American Files
Melk– Die Fragmente der Vorsokratiker
Key– Sankt Peter (natürlich!)

For Posterity? Defiance? Sieg Heil!

Sieg Heil? Helmut blanched. But the most obvious question was: What did "American Files" have to do with "Fragments of the pre-Socratics"? From his philosophical training at Freiburg, Helmut immediately understood this to mean the ancient written fragments mentioning Heraclitus, Thales, Anaximander, Pythagoras, Democritus, Zeno, Parmenides, Anaxagoras and Empedocles. Obviously, these fragments, studied for millennia by ancient Greek scholars, were not even in the same time frame as anything American. Was this a random list of books the professor kept for some strange reason? Moreover, Helmut vaguely remembered that the title *Die Fragmente der Vorsokratiker* referred to a famous book compiled by two German authors, the standard edition for references to pre-Socratic thinking. But he thought the authors were Kriels and Manz, or something like that, certainly not "Melk." On Monday, he'd find out the exact names at Sterling Library.

The note's reference to Saint Peter was the most obscure. How was this related to the pre-Socratics or to American files or to the word "Key"? Was "Key" the wrong last name of an author, as he suspected "Melk" was? Or did this refer to an actual key to open a door, for example? It probably wasn't an author's name only because the professor, in his fastidiousness, would have also underlined "Saint Peter" if this had indeed been a reference to a book. So Helmut was left with the possibility that "Melk" was a name of something besides the author of a book. He also possessed the near-certainty that "Saint Peter" referred to the apostle or to a place named after the apostle.

Yet the fundamental reason Helmut became obsessed with this note was the repugnant Nazi salute "Sieg Heil!" scrawled in heavy black letters. What a vulgar taunt! Helmut thought. Certainly the professor had written this note many years ago, probably in the late 1940s. Helmut was staring at events even beyond his father's time. Yet that "Sieg Heil!" still reached out and grabbed Helmut by the throat. It was Hitler's jig on paper!

This unrepentant declaration rang in Helmut's ears long after he put away the note and tried to sleep. These horrible words danced around him as he searched for an elusive comfort. When he did sleep, he dreamed of Nazi storm troopers marching row by row and chanting "Sieg Heil!" They marched up a hillside and crashed open the wobbly doors of hovels in the bright orange dawn of the New Mexican desert. The adobe shacks seemed laughingly defenseless. Soldiers ransacked bedrooms and living rooms, and pounced on *los de abajo* without mercy. A girl was shot scurrying under a bed. A piercing scream. A young father was slashed across the face. He was pinned to the ground. One soldier jumped up and rammed his bayonet into the man's stomach. Laughter, as the father's face drained away from this world. The room filled with silence and shadows. Outside, as Helmut slept, the New Haven dawn unfurled onto streets empty and bleak.

Chapter Eight

Frazzled, Sarah Goodman walked down Temple Street. She had taken three hours to grade baby German's first oral test of the fall semester. She hadn't even started *thinking* about the reading list for her Comprehensive Exam in December. She didn't have a senior faculty adviser yet. What was she writing her dissertation about? The prospectus was due next spring! Sarah thought, panicking. She started to hyperventilate, but calmed herself by the time she reached the back entrance to Clark's.

In Des Moines, Sarah Goodman had always been the Smart One. Yes, she was a bit nervous, and even pushy once in a while, at least by Iowa standards. But Yale had changed her. After two years in New Haven, her own mother barely recognized her. An occasional lack of focus had transformed into wildly spasmodic green eyes. Her left temple and upper cheek also twitched whenever she wrote a paper. Her hair, a gorgeous, strawberry blond, was often unkempt, uncut, straw-like. Her complexion astonished her mother at Christmas. "You look like a ghost!" she exclaimed to her daughter. "Are you okay at Yale?"

Sarah was not okay. She was hurtling toward a cataclysm, but her family would never hear a peep from the Smart One. She was barely making it as a graduate student at Yale, and "barely making it" meant "failure." It meant that you were worthless, that people were being "kind" to you, that maybe you wouldn't be able to land a job, even at the University of Iowa. Why hadn't she gone to law school when she'd had the chance? Sarah had asked herself dozens of times.

Only her figure, it seemed, had survived Yale. Her rumpled, brown-plaid shirt and dirty jeans camouflaged a very nice body. She was one of those women who made it almost illegal to wear blue jeans and a T-shirt, with her perfectly round and tight behind, her perky breasts and these exquisitely taut thighs. Sarah often consoled herself with the certainty that   although she was not a Yale genius—she was still bright and definitely good-looking.

Werner Hopfgartner had certainly noticed. Why had Sarah let it happen? Was she out of her mind? At least he had been friendly. In fact, Professor Hopfgartner was her best "friend" in the entire department. The graduate students were interested only in mind games that undermined her already weak confidence. The rest of the faculty was neurotic, elusive or even more hateful than the students. For two years, Sarah had been desperate for friends. When Werner Hopfgartner reached out to her, she grabbed his hand and plunged into a startling escapade. She had been embarrassed, and deeply regretted it, yet at least she had a connection with someone at Yale. Someone who would give her the benefit of the doubt. Professor Hopfgartner always left the door open for her, and that was better than being desperately alone.

Sarah opened her mailbox in Helen Hadley Hall and gasped. It was the printout of last semester's grades. She hurried to her single room on the third floor. A serene, cheery Indian graduate student grinned at her, Bharat Patel from Mathematics, or maybe Physics, but she smiled sheepishly, and waved, and ran up the dusky stairs. She slammed the thick, wooden door, tore open the letter and flung herself on the creaky bed.

Oh, my God! she thought, staring at the printout. Three High Passes and only one Honors!

Her head drowned in a cascade of thoughts. Sarah was sure she had written four superb papers. She had nearly suffered a nervous breakdown in May! *Three* HPs! How could this have happened to her? Last semester, only Professor Hopfgartner had given her a touch of academic glory. Only one Honors, and from Werner Hopfgartner!

Sarah sobbed until her mind felt numb, and she fell asleep. She awoke when it was dark outside. She thought somebody had knocked on her door. Maybe they wanted to eat dinner with her. She didn't bother to get up. They didn't knock twice, and that was that. She'd eat dinner alone again. Her window was open to the little pine cove between Helen Hadley and Yale Health Services. For hours Sarah had often stared at that little patch of green heaven, having read another Max Frisch or Thomas Mann novel. For a second Sarah imagined jumping. But then she spotted the languid blinking of her answering machine's tiny red light.

"Sarah, this is Professor Neumann," a woman's voice said in a measured tone. "I need to discuss something important with you. I need your *help*. Could you come by my office tomorrow morning, say, around ten? I hope you are well and had a good, productive summer."

What the blazes was this about? Sarah wondered. She needed her help? Why? That shrimpy bitch had already canned her work with a High Pass! In fact, of all four courses, Sarah had had the least hope for Neumann's seminar. The woman was relentless, aloof and forever surly. And yet, Sarah had obsessively focused on Neumann's paper. It was the *best* paper she had written in two years! And only a High Pass! She was a stupid dreamer! Now Neumann needed her "help." For what? To finish pounding her into oblivion?

She was exactly on time arriving at Professor Neumann's office in the Harkness basement. The room was brightly lit and sparsely furnished. Regina Neumann showed Sarah inside. Professor Neumann was a particularly difficult character to understand. Sarah had heard that Neumann inhabited many dissimilar worlds, and yet she was not insane. The professor was a stern taskmaster, a brilliant poet, a perceptive essayist and even a loyal mentor, if you could crack the shell of severity that encased her. Sarah had never heard anybody question the quality of Neumann's mind, even the older gentlemen, most of them European-born, who had anointed the professor to a tenured position over a decade ago. Neumann produced not only exemplary literary criticism, but more astonishingly, was an original and greatly admired writer in her own right. She had the heart of poet, the mind of a logician. That was Regina Neumann.

Although Sarah had never discussed it with anybody, she secretly believed even Regina Neumann had flaws. Her white, almost phosphorescent skin, next to her short jet-black hair, betrayed a certain fragility. Most students interpreted this luminosity for mental brilliance, and in a way it played a role in her success in the predatory environs of the academy. She was unapproachable. But Sarah imagined a true wolf could have easily cut through this façade and smelled the fear, the weakness, that perhaps lurked in the professor's eyes. Or was Sarah projecting? At Yale most knew Regina Neumann had never married, that she dated only occasionally. Her parents were German, yet she had lived her adult life in Canada. Finally, everybody knew she loved her work and never to disturb her when she didn't want to be disturbed. The old lions in the department had seen the professor as almost the perfect match: an excellent scholar of German poetry, a non-political recluse and a woman to boot! Their little den would be left intact and, for a while anyway, spared the political pressures of the "diversity" crowd.

"Sarah, hello. Take a seat." Neumann wore a long black skirt with a pale purple silk blouse; her small body seemed lost in the waves of fabric. Only her black eyes—floating in the luminosity of her skin—propelled this professor-queen into the dead space in front of her in a startling manner. "I called you to discuss something terribly important. A private matter, first. But also something that concerns this department."

"Okay," Sarah said, almost in a whisper.

"Before we get into this, I want you to know I'm your friend here. You haven't done anything wrong. I'm just trying to help you. This is about Werner Hopfgartner."

"Okay," she said. "I understand." Yet Sarah Goodman did not understand. In her head, she was panicking. She didn't want any trouble. She was afraid of this woman. She was afraid her Yale dream was metamorphosing into her worst nightmare. Who was Regina Neumann? Sarah certainly didn't know.

"For several years now," Neumann began, "I have heard rumors that Professor Hopfgartner has been having affairs with undergraduates and even graduate students. I've decided to do something about it. If these rumors are true, then, as you know, they violate the most basic academic and ethical standards. I've talked to several students this summer. You're not alone. I'm on your side."

"Thanks. But . . . I don't know what to say, Professor Neumann."

"Just tell me the *truth*. You don't need to go into details."

"What'll happen to him? I mean, he's about to retire, isn't he? Whatever he might have done, he's actually helped me a lot."

"No one is trying to hurt anyone here," Neumann said firmly. "What needs to be avoided is the abuse of students. I am only trying to find out the truth. If it happens that Werner Hopfgartner did violate Yale's policy, then he might receive a reprimand or a more severe penalty. But the question now is whether he'll ever be held accountable for his actions."

"That sounds like vengeance," Sarah retorted without thinking.

"Vengeance?" Regina Neumann's black coal eyes pierced Sarah Goodman like arrows. "Sarah, we're talking about *justice*, about doing the right thing. You may have a good relationship with Professor Hopfgartner. But if he did have a sexual relationship with you, he was abusing his position. He was using you. I think we should stop this kind of manipulation and exploitation, don't you?"

"Well, yes. But 'manipulation' and 'exploitation,' that's not what happened. I'm not sure what *did* happen. I don't want to characterize it wrongly."

"I just want the truth, Sarah. You're a good student. But I don't want you to make the mistake of thinking there's some ambiguity about Yale's policy. To put it bluntly: the question is whether or not Hopfgartner slept with you. Even if you weren't in his class at the time, you were still in this department. That constitutes an abuse of power if it happened. Did it?"

"It's not as easy as you think." She was not going to cry, Sarah told herself. "I only want to do the best I can at Yale. I don't need this," she said in a muffled squeak. A tear rolled down her cheek, and she wiped it away savagely.

"I'm sorry, Sarah. Please, here." Professor Neumann handed her a white tissue. "How about some coffee?"

"Thanks."

"Be right back."

When Professor Neumann returned with two white Styrofoam cups of coffee, a reassuring smile was on her phosphorescent face, yet her eyes were still sharp.

"Professor Neumann, I'm okay, really." The hot coffee incited Sarah's empty stomach into a growl. "I've thought about it and I don't really want to get involved. Nothing terrible has happened to me because of Professor Hopfgartner. I may have made a mistake, but I'm really okay."

"Well, Sarah, I'm afraid it's not that simple. This problem goes beyond you. If these allegations are true—and you haven't yet given me an answer—then they affect many past and present students. Don't you want to stop this kind of thing from happening to other students?"

"Course I do."

"Well, if we don't do something about it now, we're only helping to support the atmosphere in which this happens. I'll be on your side, from start to finish."

"I appreciate that, professor. But I don't want to be involved like this. Nothing terrible happened to me," Sarah said in an exasperated tone. She wanted simply to stand up and leave.

"Let me be perfectly clear. I've talked to other students, Sarah. They said basically the same thing. All of them undergraduates or former graduate students. You're the only graduate student still here. We don't have a choice. We must work together on this. What do you say?"

"All right," Sarah said slowly, terrified at not only being alone in the department, but also being the target of a senior professor's wrath. There was no way out, she thought. "I slept with Professor Hopfgartner last year. In January."

"Good. Very good. There's just one more step that's necessary for this to become an official matter. You need to repeat these words to the chairman. Professor Otto. Don't worry, I'll be with you. I'll set up a meeting for tomorrow and call you."

"Okay," Sarah whispered. She was about to burst into tears. She said goodbye and nearly sprinted out of that suffocating room.

"*Grüss dich*, Victor. I've just finished my recommendations for the new faculty appointments, if that's why you're calling. I think we should offer Maienfeld the visiting professorship next year. He's first rate."

"No, *listen*. This is more important than any of that. Remember, this is a personal call, from one friend to another."

"What are you talking about?"

"Neumann has just arranged a meeting for tomorrow to charge you with sexual harassment. She's got a student of yours, Goodman, who's coming in with her."

"What?"

"That's all I'm going to say. If this Goodman woman charges you, I will be forced to ask Yale to start disciplinary hearings against you. After that, you're *guilty*, in everyone's eyes, regardless of the outcome."

"*Danke schön*, Victor. From the bottom of my heart. You are a good friend."

When Sarah picked up her phone a few hours later and heard Werner Hopfgartner's heavy German accent, she almost peed in her jeans. But then a great sense of relief washed over her, inexplicably, and she felt calmer than she'd ever felt at Yale. His voice was warm and friendly. She knew exactly who Werner Hopfgartner was. Maybe he was not a perfect friend, but then who was? At least he listened to her and treated her with some intellectual respect. She remembered their long discussions on Plato and Aristotle. That's how she had imagined her life at Yale back in Iowa. Hopfgartner invited her to lunch, and strangely, she felt relieved when she said yes.

Except for the normal pleasantries, they didn't say a word until they were seated in a private booth at a place in Hamden. The dark restaurant was empty except for another couple. Sarah's heart thrashed with a mixture of excitement and fear.

"Sarah, please tell me what this is about. Are we not *good friends?*"

"Oh, God! Professor Hopfgartner. I don't know what to say. She pushed me into it! That's the truth!" Sarah said in a breathless tumble of words. She lowered her voice, looked around, but no one was nearby. "I don't want to have anything to do with it."

"I'm glad to hear you say that. I have the greatest respect for you, Sarah. Together we can find a solution."

"I feel trapped. All I want is to finish my Comps, and get my dissertation going, and get out of New Haven." Sarah felt a sudden wave of heat hitting her face. Maybe it was the beer she was sipping on an empty stomach. She had nothing left to lose.

"Let's see what we can do, *meine Schöne.*"

These affectionate words, so out of the blue, gripped her heart.

"But what we did was a mistake, Professor Hopfgartner. My mistake and your mistake."

"And you are absolutely right, Sarah. I made a terrible mistake and I'm sorry. But I still feel a genuine affection for you. You must believe that."

"I do," she said, tears in her eyes. Her mind was spinning. She thought she might faint, but took a deep breath and gathered herself into a shaky equilibrium.

"Sarah." Hopfgartner held her hand tightly. "We'll get through this together. Friends help each other."

"How?" Sarah gave herself up to him. At Yale so much had gone wrong for her. She wanted to be picked up and held.

"First, you must go in there tomorrow with Neumann and tell the chairman nothing happened between us. That we just have a good working relationship."

"But she'll destroy me! She practically threatened me already!"

"Listen, Sarah," Hopfgartner said reassuringly. "Listen to me very carefully. Regina Neumann can't touch you as long as I'm around. And I'll be around, in one way or another, for years to come. I also have many good friends at Yale and beyond. Professor Neumann will be angry for a while, but you simply have to avoid her. Go into that room tomorrow and tell them nothing happened, and get out of there without saying another word. I know Otto won't press you for details or explanations, really. After that, I'll protect you from anything else."

"Professor Hopfgartner, I already told her what happened. I'd be lying to her face. My God!"

"Sarah, *please*." He squeezed her hand gently. "You can do this. A few minutes and everything will be fine. After you come out of Otto's office, you can become my student, if you want. I will be your advisor for your dissertation next spring."

"What? You mean that? Would you really do that for me?" Sarah had never dreamed of asking Werner Hopfgartner to be her thesis advisor. She had thought their tryst had forever poisoned that well.

"I not only mean that, *mein Liebling*, I will do it happily and enthusiastically. If you come out of that office cleanly tomorrow, I will be your mentor. Not only will I be your advisor, Sarah, I will help you. With your Comprehensive Exam. And after we finish your dissertation, I'll do everything in my power to find a good job for you. Sarah, I will help you. That's what I promise."

"I don't know what to say. Professor Hopfgartner! I just don't know what to say. My life has been in ruins for so long. I thought I was a complete failure. Maybe there is a way out! I'll do it!"

"I knew you would, my dearest Sarah."

"I'll do it," she said more quietly. "Whatever it takes." She fell silent for a few minutes. Sarah imagined returning to the University of Iowa, a triumph. She could be a professor of German on the tenure track, with some excellent publications already in hand. Her mother would be so proud! Her mother who had never left Des Moines, and who was probably twice as smart as she was. "I'll do it," she repeated.

A sly smile came to her lips. It was her turn to shock the professor. A ferocity filled her eyes, the ferocity of an animal. "Professor–" she continued.

"Yes, dear Sarah?"

"I want to sleep with you again."

"*Entschuldigung*? Are you *serious*?" Werner Hopfgartner exclaimed, truly flabbergasted. His fork dropped from his hand and clanged onto the plate.

"I want you to fuck me. That's what I want."

"Sarah, are you sure about this? I mean now, before tomorrow?"

"It will only make things easier for me. Yes, please."

"Let's go then."

"So ex-Stasi tried to kill him?" Victor Otto huffed in his customary gravelly voice. He seemed genuinely intrigued by the tale. Professor Otto, chairman of the German department, was a pear-shaped man, about two hundred pounds, five feet seven inches tall, small shoulders and reedy legs. A bulldog's sneer usually settled over his thick lips. Yet when he was happy, a fire would light up his gray eyes, almost like a child's eyes, and the snarl would disappear. Now he had a look of intense curiosity as he listened to Regina Neumann.

"No, but they are looking for him. That's what he believes," she said, a picture of utter serenity all afternoon. It was ten minutes past 1:00 p.m. Sarah Goodman was a bit late for the meeting Neumann had been anticipating for a long time. But there was no reason to worry. She had spoken to Sarah this morning, after having tried to reach her late yesterday afternoon and evening. Sarah sounded happy over the telephone, and certainly Neumann herself felt a deep satisfaction with her own life. Finally, she was about to defeat one of the last nagging devils in her own conscience.

"It's incredible to think you could be killed for writing essays on police corruption. What a twisted world! The old Stasi couldn't even prevent television broadcasts from West Berlin, but now they want to attack a poor writer? That's simply preposterous," he said, passing a chubby hand over his huge bald head. Otto the Eggman.

There was a soft knock at the door. A stone-faced Sarah Goodman walked in and sat across Professor Otto at a small conference table to one side of the expansive office. Professor Neumann sat a few chairs away, at one end of the table. "Please sit down, Ms.

Goodman. Make yourself comfortable. Would you like a cup of coffee?"

"Okay," Sarah said meekly, glancing at Regina Neumann, who offered her the slightest of smiles and a comforting wink.

"Ariane," Otto said quickly into the telephone, "could you please bring Sarah a cup of coffee? And please call Rooney in the president's office and tell her I'll be at the budget meeting after all." He hung up the phone. "Now, Sarah, I want you to be at ease here. Whatever you say, of course, is strictly confidential. I know you've talked to Professor Neumann already and I want you to know I'm glad that you did. If, for some reason, our graduate students are in trouble or are being subjected to unethical behavior by members of the faculty, we want to know. We want to help you and I will personally do everything I can to help you. And so will Yale. Okay?"

"Okay." The secretary brought a cup of coffee and left it in front of Sarah.

"Now, Sarah. Is that okay if I call you 'Sarah'?"

"Sure," she said, smiling.

"I don't really know you, but I do remember your application. From Iowa, right?"

"That's right."

"Okay, I want you to tell me, in your own words, what happened between you and Werner Hopfgartner. Just tell me what you can say comfortably. That's all."

"Nothing's happened. I have a good working relationship with Professor Hopfgartner," Sarah said clearly, brushing back her blond hair easily. She took a gulp from her coffee.

"Sarah!" Regina Neumann gasped.

"Sarah. Let's take this slowly. And calmly." Professor Otto glanced at Professor Neumann. "You have nothing to fear. I want you to tell me the truth. Has Professor Hopfgartner ever sexually harassed you in any way?"

"No, not at all. He's been the best professor I've had at Yale. A perfect gentleman," she said, her eyes riveted on Otto's head.

"What are you *saying?*" Neumann exclaimed. "Sarah! This is incredible!" She pushed her seat away from the table. Her face was bright red; her small shoulders were shaking.

"Sarah, listen to me carefully. I want you to tell me the truth," Otto repeated, holding up his hand at Neumann to stop her in her tracks. His eyes were affixed on this stoic, oddly carefree young woman. "Did you or did you not tell Professor Neumann yesterday that you had an affair with Werner Hopfgartner?"

"No, I did not." A vein in Sarah's neck throbbed.

"You've never had a sexual relationship with Professor Hopfgartner?" Otto shot back, as if slapping her.

"No. Of course not."

"You lying, stinking bitch!" Regina Neumann exploded, suddenly standing up, in an utter rage.

"Regina! My goodness!" Otto exclaimed, suddenly wheeling around to face his colleague. "Sit down and calm yourself, before you make another grave mistake."

Neumann's face was contorted. Her black coal eyes wanted so much to kill. But Otto's serious, forceful words finally reached her, and she sat down, still transfixed on Sarah Goodman.

"I want to apologize," Professor Otto said, "on behalf of my colleague for that outburst. There is no excuse for that."

"That's all right," Sarah said, her blue eyes still riveted on Victor Otto.

"Are you absolutely sure you don't want to tell us anything?" Otto asked slowly.

"I've told you the truth."

"Thank you. You can leave now, Ms. Goodman."

As soon as Sarah closed the office door, an unrelenting clamor of obscenities and near-words and screams shook in the air. The secretary, Ariane Sassolini, seemed stunned at her desk, and Sarah walked out quickly into the bright fall afternoon. She was already late for the first meeting of the German Table at Trumbull College.

Chapter Nine

Wednesday, September 16 was Mexican Independence Day. Helmut knocked on Werner Hopfgartner's door. Sarah Goodman, a graduate student and one of the old man's girlfriends, pranced out happily, not even glancing at Helmut on the way out. This was Helmut's first meeting since the professor's return from Switzerland. The Compilation was in his hand. All one hundred fifty-six pages, plus footnotes, bibliography, an explanatory appendix and even a first crack at an index. If nothing else, Helmut had been thorough.

Hopfgartner welcomed him into his office, then spent a few minutes reviewing Helmut's work.

"This is quite good, Helmut. I will have to read it more carefully, of course. But I have to say, quite candidly, this appears first-rate." Hopfgartner's fleshy red face smiled. He seemed giddy and drunk.

"Here, you see, we might need a chapter division. *Meiner Meinung nach*, you could leave it as you have it, but it might be better to break it up," the professor said quietly, perusing the manuscript at a more measured pace now. Hopfgartner poured himself another full tumbler of bourbon and reclined in his chair, engrossed, quietly pleased, still basking in this and other victories at hand. "This note on East German writers is exactly right. Helmut. *Helmut.*"

"Sorry, Professor. I'm just tired."

"As well you should be. It is obvious you had a productive summer."

"Did my best."

"Well, this is *sehr gut*. Just leave it with me and I'll return it to you in a week or so. As a reward, I am not giving you more work until then," Hopfgartner said and sipped the last drop of bourbon in his glass.

"Thank you." Fuck you! Helmut thought.

Helmut trudged back to his office and closed the door. The blue folder, which contained every article and file from Hopfgartner's past, was inside a large manila folder stashed at the back of the filing cabinet in his desk. He had determined that "Melk" had nothing to do with the book *Die Fragmente der Vorsokratiker*. The authors were Hermann Diels and Walther Kranz. Meanwhile, his cross-referencing of the word "Melk" with the authors Diels and Kranz, the "pre-Socratics," and ancient Greek philosophy had turned up nothing of significance. He had also tried to find a link between "Melk" and "Werner Hopfgartner," and "pre-Socratics" and "Werner Hopfgartner." Nothing. His head throbbed. It was almost 5:00 p.m. He heard Hopfgartner leave his office next door. A few minutes later, as he quietly sat at his desk, Helmut stared at the doorknob as it turned slowly.

"Hey, wanna ride home?" Ariane asked.

"Sure," he said, his face still drained of blood.

They sat on Helmut's back porch, drinking Coronas. It was a beautiful autumn afternoon, warm but dry. A splash of dusky, orange sunshine filtered through the maple leaves.

"I don't believe it," Helmut said.

"She was screaming for an entire hour," Ariane said. "Believe it. Little Regina looked like a radish by the time she came out. The Eggman soaked his head the rest of the afternoon and missed his meetings. What a train wreck!"

"Hopfgartner's lucky."

"Smart, not lucky. Smart and evil. He got to her. I know it," she said, licking off the last drop in her bottle. Ariane jumped up and brought back two more beers from the kitchen.

"I saw her come out of his office at four," Helmut said.

"Goodman?"

"Yeah."

"Knew it! He got to her. He just won't stop. He just won't give up. That's how he is. He wanted to humiliate Regina. He had to show he was in control."

"Maybe he just didn't want to be busted. She didn't have any proof anyway."

"You know he sleeps with them. Everyone knows that."

"Sure I do," he said, ignoring that second bottle for the moment. "But first, if you're going after him, you better have proof. Second, you won't get any because they don't care."

"You think women want to hook up with that nasty old man? You out of your mind?"

"I didn't say that. I said they don't care. He picks them out carefully. Picks the ones who don't care, who wouldn't mind. Weak ones, greedy ones. He's not stupid, you know."

"Maybe he's your hero."

"Oh, come on! That's not fair. You know he turns my stomach. I don't think what he does is right. But getting pissed off at him isn't enough to get him. Look at Regina Neumann. She only gave him more power. Bastard probably thinks he can never lose. Maybe I shouldn't tell you the proof I have."

"Spill your beans, sweetie, or I'll smash this bottle on your head," Ariane said, glaring at Helmut. She had already gulped down two beers.

"Okay. But you really can't say anything. To *anyone*."

"Fine."

"Well, I found some articles Hopfgartner wrote in the forties. He was in the German army. A Nazi sympathizer."

"Articles? From *1940*? Oh, yeah, *that's* relevant. Ancient history."

"You don't know what he said. He defended what the Nazis did, wrote against feeling guilty for the Holocaust. He supported their ideas," Helmut said, revealing more in one moment than what he imagined he would ever tell her. Her casual dismissal goaded him.

"So? Who wasn't a Nazi back then? I've got a great uncle who was in Mussolini's army. He's dying of emphysema. Might even be dead already. My family's been fighting over this since I was a little girl. That's the past. Forty, fifty years ago! What does that have to do with anything now? Hopfgartner's fucking students and getting away with it! Maybe that's not important to you."

"Course it matters to me. All I'm saying is it shows his character. These are his words. It's what he believed."

"The forty-year-old past versus what's happening now. Your 'proof' versus what we all know to be true. Maybe Hopfgartner was a Nazi. But I care about what happens today. Regina Neumann isn't my best friend, but she doesn't deserve getting her face kicked in."

"I agree with you," Helmut said. "All that matters is what happens now. But what if what you don't know from the past changes what happens now. I mean, what if you treat someone better than they deserve because you don't know what they did years ago?"

"That's not the case here. We know he's having affairs with students."

"Okay, we know about the affairs. But we also know, and please don't get angry, that some of these students wanted to sleep with him. Hopfgartner didn't tie them up in his office."

"That's disgusting. If there was your kind of proof, Hopfgartner would be in big trouble at Yale," she said. "Maybe."

"That's my point. We need proof to have justice, not just mob rule. Something concrete."

"Like kicking him in the balls. Tell you what I think and don't you get angry. The abuse of women is important to me because I'm a woman. That's all the proof I need against that idiot. Nazi stuff's important to you. Maybe because you're German. But you're still looking for proof against him. 'Finding proof' is just a matter of who's looking for it and what they want to find in the first place. Don't you think?"

≈ ≈ ≈

The next day Helmut sat in front of a library computer terminal at Sterling. He was running another search on "Melk." He turned around and found Jonathan Atwater staring at the computer screen's list of twenty-seven references to "Melk."

"You know," Mr. Atwater said, "the Melk monastery on the Danube is such a great place to visit. Made a point to see it after I read *In the Name of the Rose*."

"There's a monastery there?"

"Of course. A grand place. I'm positive you've heard of it. Search your memory banks."

"Jonathan, interested in lunch today? My treat," Helmut said, standing up and grinning.

"My goodness," Mr. Atwater said. "Certainly I am."

"On one condition. Tell me everything about Melk. You really overestimate me, Jonathan."

"What on earth do you mean?"

"I haven't even heard of this Melk monastery in Austria. Can you believe that? Umberto Eco? I'm just an ignoramus."

"Nonsense. Stop this Dostoyevskian self-pity. Why Melk, anyway?"

"I ran across a reference to it in a book. Just didn't understand it."

The monastery, Mr. Atwater explained over lunch, was a masterpiece of Baroque architecture, standing on a cliff above the Danube. The ancient walls were pale yellow. Thick red-clay tiles covered the roof. After his visit to the chapel, Mr. Atwater had spent a few more moments on the balcony overlooking the river. And then he had gone on to Linz. As Helmut listened, he hoped in his heart he had found an important piece of the Hopfgartner puzzle.

Helmut returned home with a computer printout of the references to the monastery and several travel books on Austria and European monasteries. What could a monastery on the Danube have to do with Werner Hopfgartner's war activities? With the note on "American Files"? Hopfgartner had indeed escaped to Austria immediately after the war. And the Melk monastery was in Austria. But how cunning could Helmut's mind be? He was now making absurd connections between the Holocaust and an ancient monastery, between an old man at Yale delighting in his last year as a professor and Umberto Eco's dreamscape of medieval secrets and plots! Ariane was right, he thought: He was lost in a futile library search for yesteryear's demons. Maybe it was time to step back and reconsider his quest. Then, incredibly, from out of the book he was reading, a demon leaped out and bit Helmut's hand. The Melk monastery was a Benedictine monastery whose patron saints were Paul and *Peter*. Could this be true? Sankt Peter? Sankt Peter! Helmut nearly overturned his metal bookshelf yanking out the files on Werner Hopfgartner. He frantically flipped through the pages. Helmut found it. The note. Printed in the professor's own hand, this note from the late 1940s. Sankt Peter!

But what did it mean? What possible connection could there be between Melk, the book on the pre-Socratics, the word "Key," and Saint Peter? Turning to descriptions of the Benedictine monastery at Melk, Helmut found what he took to be the right answer to this question. His heart was pounding. The Melk library! Helmut concluded ecstatically. What other possible relation could there be between the pre-Socratic book and the Melk monastery? This had to be the answer. The library at Melk was acclaimed for its unique collection of seventy-five thousand rare books and manuscripts. This treasure trove of ancient and medieval and eighteenth- and nineteenth-century wisdom surely contained the *magnum opus* of Diels and Kranz.

Helmut thought for a moment and then concluded, in a manner that was still tentative yet increasingly more self-assured, that the professor's note had to refer to the book on the pre-Socratics in the Melk library in Austria.

Maybe, Helmut reasoned, a secret key led to files about the professor. The key might be hidden in the book. He would have to find it. Or the book itself might have been encoded with a linguistic key to finding such files. Or perhaps the book simply contained the files themselves.

If his conclusion was indeed correct, at least up to this point, then only one thing was left to do: He had to travel to Melk, find the book and step into whatever truth might be concealed there.

Chapter Ten

Getting to Europe was a blur. Packing the week before Thanksgiving. The trek to the New York's Kennedy airport. The takeoff, which Helmut dreaded, grasping Ariane's thigh until they had cleared the clouds. The dull and interminable transatlantic plane ride. The scramble to find Hotel Döbling on the crazy map of the trolley system in Vienna. Finally, the sweet repose of a hot shower together.

Helmut was happy to be free of the New Haven bleakness. They would stay two nights in the jewel of the Hapsburgs. The first night they would be alone. The second night they would have dinner with Helmut's friends on Sporkenbühelgasse. They'd rent a car and drive to Linz. Then to Salzburg.

That night, they left the hotel to attend a concert of Gregorian chants at Votivkirche. They took the No. Thirty-eight, which passed in front of their hotel on Gymnasiumstrasse, and exited at Schottenring, near Währingerstrasse. But his mind was obsessed with only one thing: *Die Fragmente der Vorsokratiker* at Melk. His questions would finally have answers. He had no doubt about this at all.

They walked hand in hand into the massive church. The ancient columns and ornate stained glass reminded him that Europe often felt like a living museum. That odd sense cascaded from every dark crevice and weird figurine, from the stale smell of incense and rotting wood. A great silence trembled around him. The silence of the holy. It shocked him. He was in another world now, not the grimy non-world of New Haven, Connecticut. The choir sang its first note. The stone walls seemed a fortress around him. He glanced nervously around. Was he about to faint? He fixed on Ariane's sweet face, her big brown eyes, her silky smooth skin. He was amazed to find himself here again. Surrounded by strange faces. Some old. Others pretty and young. None black or brown. Faces whispering in German. Faces foreign and yet familiar, like primeval memories. This air crushed him. The very light of the sun seemed different, muted. Helmut glanced at Ariane again, the serenity in her eyes. He touched her straight black hair and imagined losing himself in this thicket.

After the concert, they boarded a trolley toward Grinzing, although Helmut complained this was what tourists would do. Ariane wanted to sample the famous beer and wine and compare it with what they would soon find in Italy. She promised she had discovered a *Biergarten* frequented by the locals, not a kitschy tourist joint. The Eggman had indeed given her detailed directions to a place south of Josefsdorf, through the vineyards, miles from the popular Grinzing stop.

A few pedestrians roamed the narrow sidewalks. Others patiently waited in the open-air stations for their trolleys. It was eerie that Vienna was so dead at night, bereft of the bustle and irreverence of New York and even without the sense of lurking danger on a desolate New Haven street. There was simply nothing in Vienna after six o'clock, just block-long bureaucratic offices and a smattering of empty cafés with stiff waiters ready at the door. The few souls on these streets were probably students from the nearby University of Vienna, or tourists desperately looking for a good time. The legalized prostitutes, in their neon-colored Roman wrestling shorts and glittery high heels, wouldn't be out before 10 p.m.

It occurred to him that Vienna felt like a ghost town even during the day. Sure, the streets would be full of Viennese, but you still couldn't tell who they were or what was on their minds. The exact opposite of a place like Manhattan. There, everything was in the open. New Yorkers pushed you if you were in the way. They gossiped with their friends on the subway so that you overheard who was cheating on whom, whose mother couldn't stay out of her children's lives, what bar had the best Happy Hour on Amsterdam. On

Graben, however, you rarely overheard small talk. You heard enigmatic references if you heard anything at all. The citizens of Vienna ignored obvious strangers to their country. They seemed serious and self-possessed. Words revealed who you were. Words exposed you. In silence, mystery was still a possibility. In silence, a one-way bridge could still be imagined between your dreary quotidian reality and the grandiose self-worth in your mind.

At the *Biergarten*, in a barnlike hall behind a stone house, wooden picnic tables were packed with families, students and an occasional tourist. Helmut and Ariane grabbed an empty table near the back wall. The *Mädchen* with liters of beer and pitchers of wine on wooden trays, seemed as surly as the diner waitresses off I-95 on the Connecticut coast.

Two young couples sat down at their table. When the young woman next to him overheard Helmut's English, she offered a hello and asked where they were from. In rapid-fire German, with the slightest American accent, Helmut explained he was originally German and Ariane was Italian, but that both of them lived in America. He turned to Ariane and began to translate what they said, but three of the four knew passable English. So instead, the Austrians insisted on translating to the lone non-English speaker. Two were in medical school at the University of Vienna. One was beginning his career as an architect. The non-English-speaking woman was a kindergarten teacher. They marveled at how Ariane and Helmut had ended up in America. The med students in particular had always dreamed of visiting the United States.

"The best medical work, yes, arrives from America here. *Also* it is important English to learn," the woman sitting next to Helmut said coolly as she picked at her *Kartoffelsalat*. Her name was Anna. She reminded him of a carefree and irreverent gypsy, with a red bandanna dangling from her slim, muscular neck. She wore tight black jeans that matched her feathery short black hair, and ankle-high zipper boots.

Across from Helmut, Ariane and the architect discussed their favorite European churches. Walter, the other med student, a wiry fellow with spectacles, sat across from the gypsy. He asked Helmut about New Haven. The schoolteacher stared vacuously into the garden. Another round of beers arrived.

"It's just a few hours from New York. A really small town. But there's so much crime around Yale. In fact, I think New York is safer than New Haven. Last year a graduate student was shot to death near the campus," Helmut said casually, trying hard to glance around the gypsy's unblinking eyes. Suddenly he felt someone rub his leg underneath the table. Thunderstruck, Helmut glared at the gypsy med student next to him, who offered him such a friendly smile. In a stupid reflex he immediately regretted, he glanced at her breasts through the open collar of her white shirt.

"Isn't it *richtig*," Walter pronounced, "that everyone in America on drugs is? So much of a drug problem you Americans have. Isn't that why *diese schwarze Leute*, the niggers, commit so much crime in New Haven?"

Helmut stared into Walter's eyes, which seemed innocent enough. "Walter," Helmut said, without any anger, "you really shouldn't use that word. The word 'nigger' is considered derogatory and offensive."

The gypsy med student beamed at him, and propped her face on her bespangled hands.

"No, no, no. I have heard this word in—*wie sagt man?*—television music rap. *They* use this 'nigger' themselves to describe."

"I know, but it's still not right. Most Americans don't use it. It's really a bad word. Anyway, not everyone uses drugs. Drugs aren't the only reason for street crime in New Haven," Helmut said, and gulped his beer. He couldn't drink more than what he had in his mug.

"*Aber nein!*" Walter interjected loudly, glancing at the gypsy for support. "But this is what I have heard. America full of cocaine is. We have no drug problem. No race riots. No problems. You can walk safely in *Wien* any time of the night."

The gypsy's leg curled around Helmut's calf and then slipped out tantalizingly. Helmut ignored the overture again and focused on the face of this bearded jackal.

"Every country has problems. Some publicize them more than others. What about the Israeli embassy in Vienna? Tell me about *that*?" Helmut shot back. "Why does it have guards with Uzis at the entrance? Wasn't it recently bombed? Didn't fanatics threaten the Israelis when your great hero Waldheim was accused of being a Nazi?" Maybe this last goad was excessive, but Helmut didn't care. "*Ach!* President *Waldheim!* He was attacked because what happened years ago. Foreigners brought down Waldheim. No one cares here about that!"

"Why is there so much racism in this country? Don't put your head in the sand!" Helmut retorted, smiling right into the jackal's maw.

"*Eine Luge!*" Walter exclaimed, almost shouting, practically in a seizure. Ariane and the architect stared at the other end of the table, and resumed their conversation.

Walter was still seething. "Not at all truth. Americans, you think always you know everything for everyone. Cultural imperialists!"

"What? We don't tell anyone what to do. We face up to our mistakes," Helmut said sharply. "We don't run away from them. That's the very reason why you hear so much about us in Austria."

"Not truth at all. Vietnam, that failure? Tell me about it," Walter sputtered. He wiped his mouth and gulped down the rest of the liter in front of him. His Adam's apple twitched, and Helmut had the urge to rip it out. "America in decline is. Decaying like a corpse. Look at your streets. Look at your people. Germany and Japan have passed you. The Muslims want to destroy you."

"At least we don't burn down refugee centers! The Turks and the Muslims have it just as bad here."

"He is right, Walter," Anna said suddenly, turning to face Walter. "*Was?* You too?" Walter looked betrayed by the gypsy. "This is ridiculous!"

"It is time you listened. Austria has many racists. Is it the only country *so*? No, *natürlich*," Anna said, still facing Walter and speaking slowly. Walter seemed crushed. "I don't know about America, I know it has its proper problems."

"*Ach! Perfektes Amerika!*"

"Listen to me, Walter. America is *nicht perfekt. Österreich auch.* To be perfect. To be right. *That* is our problem here. Maybe in America, Helmut will tell us, everything is perfect, so nothing is right. I don't know. But we have a different problem here. In Austria, one thing is right. One idea, one people, one way. Always it is like that in Europe. The idea changes, but the mania for One Idea does not. Why do we follow ideas like hungry animals following food?" Anna said, now turning to face Helmut again.

"Well, I don't know," Helmut said, also deflated.

Anna was dead serious about getting an answer to her question.

"Maybe we should use them differently," Helmut continued. "Ideas, I mean. Maybe we should use them as tools to improve our lives, but not as monsters to torment us. But that seems stupid, too. Stupidly unclear. The power of ideas is that they affect our actions. They're not just fantasies. Ideas should bother us. They should cause us to act. But they shouldn't destroy us."

"*I'm* the stupid one!" Walter suddenly exclaimed. "Please my rudeness forgive! Anna, of course you are right. I needed only a minute clearly to think. It's the beer! But we are still friends, no?"

Ariane and Helmut soon said goodbye. He waved politely to Anna the gypsy, who had slipped her address and phone number into his hand under the table. As they started down the gravel road in front of the *Biergarten*, Ariane punched his arm.

"Why are you always getting into a fight?"

"*Me*? I started it?" Helmut protested meekly. As soon as she turned her head to the road, he threw the crumpled ball of paper into the empty field.

They walked through farm roads for hours, cold and numb. The full moon was so bright it looked like an interminable dawn.

"Do you mind if we stop at the Melk monastery when we drive to Linz?" he asked, holding her hand.

"Sure, why not? It'll be a nice way to break up the drive. What's in Linz anyhow? Why don't we drive straight to Salzburg? We'll get there late, but it might be worth it."

"I wouldn't mind that," he said.

"Okay. I'll call the Gasthaus Zur Goldenen Ente and see if they can take us a day early. More time in the Wachau sampling wines. And the monastery. Maybe an old castle along the way. I can't wait!"

The next morning they awoke late, showered quickly, and soon strolled through Heldenplatz, on their way to the Kunsthistorisches Museum. Near the Stadtpark, they discovered an obscure bistro with homemade sausages off Himmelpfortgasse and stopped at a second-floor *Kaffeehaus*. Helmut called his friends at Sporkenbühelgasse. Helga was a young divorceé who taught German at the Goethe Institut and her partner, Anton, was a bookseller and perennial graduate student in history whom Helmut had met in Freiburg. They told him to come over with Ariane around seven.

Ariane and Helmut meandered through the narrow streets. Every other building seemed encased in scaffolding. They stopped at a small lonely plaza with what, from across the street, appeared to be a man kneeling on the ground. The man's back was oddly flat and rigid. It was a statue of a rabbi in supplication. In front of the rabbi was a wall of names and dates. It was a new Holocaust memorial. Helmut studied the names, and no Sanchezes were on this list. Only the names of the dead. A sickening number of names. He turned to look at the stone rabbi again. Its human features were barely sketched on the boxlike block atop the cobblestones. He noticed a line of faint graffiti scrawled across the flat back of the rabbi. *Judenrein*, the graffiti read in nearly scratched-off black paint. *Judenrein*, in a most truthful and hideous glory. Austria was indeed free of the Jews.

At Sporkenbühelgasse, it didn't take long before Helmut asked Anton and Helga about the statue of the rabbi.

"I didn't see any graffiti," Ariane said from the small kitchen. Anton and Helga Schmidtz kept an eclectic, homey nest resembling an attic jam-packed with objects from another time. At the end of the living room was a large bay window.

"On the rabbi's back. Maybe they tried to clean it off, but it was there," Helmut said, a beer already in hand.

"Please, Helmut. Tell Ariane to sit down. There is nothing more to do here. I'm just bringing out a few snacks," Helga said, poking her head out of the kitchen. She was a Dane with a facility for languages who had lived in Vienna for fifteen years. She had austere blue eyes, snowy skin with the sheen of peach fuzz and a sudden, explosive smile. "I'll tell you, they've had so much trouble with that memorial."

"Hah! That's putting it mildly!" Anton roared as he sauntered in from the bedroom. He sank onto the couch next to Helmut and passed him his latest monograph. In contrast to his angular and graceful common-law wife, Anton Schmidtz was stocky, taller than she was, like an unstoppable tank. With every lurch, his black hair brushed against his pale forehead in thick strands.

"The memorial," Helga continued, carefully setting a tray of vegetables on the coffee table, "was commissioned years ago. The veterans of the war didn't want it. Some students protested *for* it. Merchants were more worried about the impact on tourism, the 'reputation' of the city. I think I read a story about the rabbi being vandalized, but it wasn't graffiti. Neo-nazi morons had taken a hammer to it."

"Even that's completely too generous for our beloved Vienna," Anton said, with a dismissive wave of his chubby arm. "The politicians, as always, started this descent into disgrace. They're to blame. The eunuch we have for a mayor and his 'girls' in the city council, they lobbied against placing the memorial in the plaza in the first place."

"Why?" Ariane asked. She sat next to Helmut on the couch and squeezed his hand affectionately.

"Anton, are you paying attention to these lovebirds? They might teach you a thing or two."

"Me? Ho!" Anton blared, and leaped up from his slump and kissed his wife on the cheek with a great grin. "But let me finish this story. Our philosopher-kings were at the peak of their powers. 'Oh! The construction work will create traffic jams! Oh! It will be so unsightly! Oh! Every regulation must be enforced, to the letter. Vienna is not a barbarous city!' An absolutely disgraceful display."

"I'm surprised they allowed it in the first place," Ariane said. Helmut took a swig of his beer. She reached for a carrot strip and dipped it in the mustard-colored dip next to the crudités. "Wow, what is this?"

"My creation. I'll give you the recipe only if you keep it on your side of the Atlantic," Helga said with a wink.

Anton stroked his beard carefully, his eyes boring into the empty space in front of him with his black, prosecutorial eyes. "I wouldn't be surprised," he said, "to find these political cowards behind this campaign to deface the memorial. They invited these small acts of terrorism, didn't they?"

"Maybe this sounds stupid. But when I saw those awful words . . . on that poor rabbi. It was a *shock* to realize it still exists," Helmut said quietly. "Like a dagger into my own heart. I don't want to bring everybody down. But it affected me strangely. Just wanted to know more about its history, why it was there."

"Ah, still the Helmut of my younger years! My dreamer, my philosopher, my muse!" Anton thundered into the silence, bringing an awkward moment to a quick end. "Your heart on your sleeve, that shine in your eyes! I still remember fondly how you brought our classmates to shame with your passion. What you say is right. Absolutely right! When they attack that statue, they attack *us*. We are all Jews now. Every last one of us. We should never forget that."

"Oh, listen to you. You and your metaphysics!" Helga said with a slight smile on her face. "Yes, we are all Jews now, when no more real Jews are in Vienna. When the only Jew we have on our streets is made of stone."

"As usual, my dearest, you are my better half. Abstractions aren't nearly enough. Abstractions *dehumanized* us once before. Tomorrow I'll gather a group from the bookstore and clean up that blasphemy at the memorial! I'll do it alone if I have to!" Anton proclaimed defiantly.

"My goodness, what a panther! You see what you have done, Helmut. You've brought him back to me. The old cranky loveable beast from Freiburg is back," Helga said, squeezing her husband's thick knee. Ariane beamed at Helmut.

Helmut, again, discovered the deep satisfaction of being with his old friends from Freiburg. The way in which Helga passed each tray and glass. Anton's baritone guffaw. The gleam in Ariane's eyes. Then the liquor hit Helmut like a two-by-four. He heard his friends, slouched on the sofa, arguing about the old Soviet Union and *glasnost*. The discussion floated above him. A sudden sharp peel of laughter pierced the air. His head was awash in fifty-proof neurons. He thought about the rabbi, alone and vulnerable in the plaza.

As if a bolt of lightning ripped through him, Helmut felt his mind soar and plunge. A wave of sympathy flooded over him. He felt like a Mexican *compadre* commiserating with his buddies about the pain of their lives, the loves and the tragedy of it all. A bit unsteady, he stood up. He blurted out a jibe about the dreamy, sedate jazz on the stereo. Carefully he made his way to the shelf of music at the other end of the living room.

He couldn't believe his luck. This could not be more perfect. His blood was boiling. He turned off the jazz and flipped on an old album of folk dances. The noisy chatter behind him swayed back and forth in a wavelike roar. He cranked up the volume and wheeled around and dragged the coffee table to one side. He stood up straight, his arms upright and defiant like a matador.

"What is a night in Vienna without dancing?" Helmut shouted. "Are we not friends for life? Get up and dance, you fools!"

Ariane shot up immediately, laughing and grabbed Helmut's waist and kissed him. Anton and Helga stared at each other, still in shock at this apex to the evening. Then they burst out laughing too, like the teenage lovers they had once been. The rash music, the alcohol and their laughter conjured such lost and singular magic that by the time "Hava Nagila" roared to its crescendo they twirled around in a circle, arm-in-arm, the reverie stupendous and limitless and almost holy.

A few hours later Helmut and Ariane were walking home through the empty streets, quietly elated, her body warm against his. Lying awake in their hotel room on their final night in Vienna, Helmut remembered the bliss and his friends and the songs as they floated away from him. He closed his eyes and tried to sear this memory into his soul forever, before a dull and ceaseless throbbing engulfed his entire body.

Chapter Eleven

They sped along the Danube's muddy waters in their Volkswagen Passat. Melk was less than an hour away. Helmut had thought about his plan and reviewed the papers while Ariane had showered that morning. Maybe, Helmut thought, he could just find what he was looking for, take it and be done with it. He had carefully tucked Professor Hopfgartner's note into his pocket.

Trying to anticipate Ariane's possible hurry to reach Salzburg, he told her he wanted to look for a rare book Jonathan Atwater had mentioned. The Melk library possessed a copy. He would try to speak to the authorities about borrowing it, or at least about later sending correspondence from Yale to start the borrowing process. She could tour the monastery grounds in the meantime.

"Is that okay with you?" he asked, his eyes fixed on the road.

"Hey, if you wanna spend your vacation in the library, that's your problem."

"Thanks."

"Who's this book for anyway? For you?"

"Yeah."

"Greek philosophy? Thought you were writing a piece on modern German literature."

"It's not for work. Just something I'm interested in."

"Didn't know you were still interested in philosophy. Who's 'interested' in philosophy? Sorry, but I don't get it."

"Weirdos, I admit."

"I mean, what's the point of thinking about life? Why not just try it out?"

"Maybe philosophers think they can somehow preserve it, in words, or maybe they think they can make sense of it. Some people just like philosophy. Like me."

"Rather read a good novel."

"But philosophy has the chance of being more than a novel. Of being true. Don't you think?"

"Well, maybe not. I'd rather get out there, I'd rather do it."

They parked the Passat in the Melk monastery's gravel lot, and walked up the hill. In a small foyer beyond two statues at the entrance, Helmut bought tickets and noticed a sign that warned the monastery would close next week for the winter. They were lucky.

Ariane found a map to guide her to the imperial bedrooms and galleries. Helmut told her he would meet her at the monastery's chapel after he finished his business in the library. They kissed quickly. The female guard scowled at them from behind a glass booth. He ran off through a vast courtyard, past a fountain. The monastery's grade school was to the left, the church up ahead. The library was through a hallway next to the church and across a balcony overlooking the Danube. He fumbled through his pant pockets, panicked for a second and found Professor Hopfgartner's cryptic note.

Why was he so excited? Maybe, Helmut imagined, he had made a mistake. If he had, he would drop everything. He would enjoy his vacation with Ariane and stop pursuing this quixotic truth. Already this was not normal. Who would care about the truth anyway? He might anonymously drop the professor's files in somebody's mailbox, maybe a university official of high rank. Why should he be strapping reason and justification and guilt onto his wonderful time with Ariane?

He pushed open the massive bulk of the library door. Inside, a dank stench of decaying books drifted over his face. It was empty. Not even a guard. A display of books was under a few bright rays of the sun at the center of a vast marble floor. Heavy round wooden tables and a few chairs lined the perimeter.

On a far wall was a map of the library's contents. Medieval and ancient philosophy was on the opposite wall. The shelves and their books were locked in cages! What had he been thinking?

That he would just walk up and steal a book? Diels and Kranz was inches from his fingertips. Was anything behind it? Should he ask a guard to take him to the librarian? But for what? To help him steal a book? Helmut dug his fingers into the thick metal net and rattled the cage like a savage animal. He wheeled around; he was still alone. He reached into his pocket and burned his eyes onto Hopfgartner's note:

American Files
Melk– Die Fragmente der Vorsokratiker
Key– Sankt Peter (natürlich!)

For Posterity? Defiance? **Sieg Heil!**

Why had he followed these accursed words to Melk? Helmut asked himself. Why had he wasted so much time? Suddenly he remembered. Saint Peter. Key. There had to be at least one statue of Saint Peter at Melk. Could it be that simple? The key to the bookshelf. Helmut ran back through the halls to the monastery's chapel.

Three worshippers were kneeling in the near-empty pews of the airy church, a couple in the back and an old woman near the center. Helmut marched slowly down the middle aisle, feeling the heat from God's eyes upon him. He knelt quickly at the threshold of the altar, and sat down in the front pew. The couple was leaving. In front of him were the statues of Saint Peter and Saint Paul. His eyes traced the outline of Saint Peter's face, with the hollow eyes, the robe of marble, the feet in humble sandals. Where could a key be hidden on this statue? What was he going to do, strip search Saint Peter? There had to be a cavity somewhere. He turned around. The old woman was still on her knees, praying. Helmut stood up quietly and knelt down at Saint Peter's feet. The key had to be where it could be easily reached. Behind the left heel was a discoloration of sorts. Head down like a beseeching peasant, Helmut reached up toward the discoloration. He rubbed the silvery spot. It gave way! It felt like clay, and came out as one plug.

Behind it was a key, which Helmut squeezed in his hand until his palm hurt. He stood up. The old woman was gone.

He ran back to the library, to the spot on the wall where *Die Fragmente der Vorsokratiker* stood dusty and imprisoned. The small key unlocked the metal gate in front of the shelf. The gate door creaked slowly open. He grabbed the book, stuffed it in his coat and pushed the gate shut. Thinking for a second, he jerked the gate open again and removed a handful of books. He reached into the space behind Plato's early Socratic dialogues. He felt nothing but cobwebs and a thick, sooty dust. Then his fingers touched something smooth. A raised part of the wall. Something standing flush against the shelf wall. It was smooth, with a loose flap. He wrenched it free. It was a leather-like pouch about the size of an accordion file. It read, in functional block letters, "U.S. Army." He slid the pouch next to the book inside his overcoat, pushed the other books back into place and slammed the metal gate shut with a clang.

He found Ariane waiting outside the church door and nervously told her he was ready to leave. She said she had waited to see the church with him, but he walked quickly away from her as if he had not heard her words. Helmut focused beyond the rows of pews, toward the front of the altar. The old woman was standing with a guard who peered at the ground at Saint Peter's feet. The guard bent down on one knee and picked up what looked like a rock from the floor.

"I'm gonna puke, I'll wait in the car."

"What's wrong?"

"You look at whatever you want."

"Wait for me!"

He ran through the gravel courtyard, slowed to a march in front of the guard reading *Die Neue Kronenzeitung*, and ran downhill to the parking lot. Before Ariane reached the car, Helmut shoved the book and pouch underneath his seat, scraping his knuckles on a sharp wire. Then he vomited a spurt of yellowish liquid, a mixture of cheese chunks and cracker bits and apple juice and acid, which spilled out in a redemptive and absolving stream at the foot of the car door.

Chapter Twelve

It was the right thing to do, Sarah thought. Her mother would do it, even with the pain. The professor couldn't be angry after two months. She wouldn't be out of control. Sarah *had* to do it. Everything else was going so well. She would ace her Comps. Hopfgartner was really putting her through the ringer. He could be relentless when he had to be. With a split personality, he could be tough and oh-so-sweet too, when you got to know him. It was just such a difference when he decided to help you, when you were on *his* side. But it was also scary. Sarah was in now, and maybe for a while, but his moods went on and off like a light switch. She thought she was in until she left Yale. She should make the most of it. God, she hadn't worked this hard in two years, but she was ready for those Comps. She just had to finish these books, prepare those answers, check for any loose ends or off-the-wall questions. Sarah had to get ready to be grilled by the old man one more time, after Thanksgiving. Everything was set, except for one thing. Sarah just had to talk to Neumann. She wouldn't be out of control. Who knew what she would do if she began to hate Sarah forever.

"I'll just sit there and take her best shot," Sarah said to herself. "I'll let her punish me. I screwed her completely and she'll want revenge. I'll let her have it. I'll let her have the power. Then she won't be able to hate me forever and I won't have to look over my shoulder for the rest of my life."

Sarah Goodman dried her naked body with the thick blue towel her mother had bought at the new Wal-Mart just outside of Des Moines. The shower stalls were empty. Most of the other graduate students in Helen Hadley Hall had left for the weeklong Thanksgiving break. It was her last big chunk of time before her Comps in December. It was Friday, the last "official" day before the break. Regina Neumann had her normal office hours for her students from 9:00 to 11:00 a.m.

Sarah unlocked her room. As she turned the knob, a man with a clear Indian accent asked, "Sarah, you are still here?"

Sarah turned. It was Bharat Patel. "Oh, my God. You scared me, Bharat," she said, out of breath. She propped open the door with her right calf.

"I am sorry. I just wanted to say 'hello.' Not too many of us are here for the break," he said, that signature smile on his face. Bharat Patel never seemed to suffer any of the internal turmoil of most graduate students. He didn't sit around and gossip with the other Indian students in the communal kitchen. He was always polite; he smiled this wide, toothy and handsome smile whenever he saw you. Everyone liked him, but if he had close friends they certainly weren't in Helen Hadley. Sarah had heard from others that he worked extremely hard, and once in a while he did look exhausted. Yet he still smiled. She took notice because Bharat seemed especially friendly toward her. They had cooked dinner together a few times. The last time she had also noticed his thick forearm muscles, the way he moved so lightly, like a graceful middleweight. His skin was smooth and richly dark. When he smiled, it seemed as if shiny light bulbs glowed inside his cheeks. Even so, she really didn't know who he was.

"Sorry I'm a little jumpy. Sort of spooky when everyone's gone."

"Spooky?"

"You know, like a haunted house. Like Halloween and spirits and ghosts."

"Oh, spirits. Don't worry, Sarah. I am not a spirit. You are so funny," he said, smiling again.

Suddenly she realized she was naked under her robe. But he didn't seem to be checking her out. She folded her arms over her chest anyway. "So you're here for the break too?"

"Yes. I must finish my prospectus this semester."

"This semester? Wait a minute, isn't this your second year?"

"Oh, yes it is."

"And you're finishing your prospectus already?"

"Yes."

"That's unbelievable! How?"

"Well, Sarah, I will tell you. I don't have a choice. I don't have money after the second year. No more scholarships in India. I have to apply for dissertation scholarships this year or I can't come back. My family has no money to give me. But my adviser says I will have no trouble finding a scholarship. He told me, you know what he told me, that he will give me the money himself if he has to."

"Wow. What a great guy."

"Oh, he is very great. A great man. A Nobel winner. But I will not take his money. I must finish this semester and start my dissertation on Riemann's Hypothesis in January. I know I will do it."

"When you want a break, let's cook dinner together again. Just slip a note under my door," Sarah said, and returned his smile. Who was this Bharat Patel? Now, for some unknown reason, she really wanted to know. A strange peace seemed to emanate from his shiny brown eyes.

"I would enjoy that very much. I will write you a note," he said, and waved goodbye as he glided down the hall to the other end of the third floor. He disappeared into the darkness.

Sarah pulled on her old jeans. Sarah hadn't heard a word from Professor Neumann since the incident at Otto's office. If the other students knew the gossip, she hadn't heard about it. They still treated her with a smug disdain. Maybe Neumann had already put the situation behind her, had kept it to herself and had just decided Sarah had been manipulated by someone more powerful than her.

After two months, Sarah was more certain than ever about her lie. It had been exactly the right thing to do. Now she was getting real help from Hopfgartner. She was more confident than ever about her work. Her glorious dream was now a concrete plan. In three years, when she returned home, there would be no messy compromises of living unfulfilled. She'd have the best of both worlds. Only one last potential obstacle remained.

Sarah knocked on Regina Neumann's door. She was sure the professor would be expecting no interruptions during her office hours. Everyone was leaving for the Thanksgiving holiday. The professor was probably deep in thought and focused on writing more poetry, like Rilke, one of her favorites. The knock at the door would interrupt her chain of thought, and perhaps upset her. Still, during the holidays, who wouldn't be in a pleasant mood? As Sarah waited, pondering whether to return to her room, she heard clearly, "Please come in."

"May I please talk to you for a few minutes?" Sarah asked from the open doorway, with a soft, hoarse voice that surprised her.

"All right," Neumann said coldly. The professor's jaw barely moved when she uttered those words. Her entire body was deadly still, as if a self faraway had said the words without her consent. Her black coal eyes glowed with a strange fire. Her face turned dead white, like the face of a porcelain doll.

"I know you're very angry with me, Professor Neumann. I just wanted to say I'm sorry for what I did. I truly am. But I had no choice."

"You had no *choice*?" Professor Neumann hissed.

"I am just terribly sorry. That's what I wanted to say most of all. You didn't deserve what I did to you. I hope you accept my apology. I just didn't want to get involved. I'm not as strong a person as you are." The wooden door had closed like the lid to a crypt behind Sarah.

"Sarah, you listen to me very carefully," Neumann replied in a pitiless monotone. The professor seemed possessed by her demons. There, and yet not there. Sarah imagined screams in this silence. She imagined violence, yet the room was still. She imagined an animal mouth after her flesh, yet only logic and reason and the flaming arrow of truth seemed pointed at her heart. What kind of damage could the truth cause? What harm would words ever do to her? "You have done nothing to me. Nothing at all. I know you lied. Otto knows you lied. You're simply Hopfgartner's liar. If that's what you want to be, that's your business. What concerns me is what effect it will have on you and your work."

"What do you mean?"

"Well, I noticed this first in your Goethe paper last year and this only confirms it. That paper, if I am not mistaken, was basically 'using' the viewpoint Humboldt developed long ago to analyze German Romantic poetry. In fact, 'using' is probably too kind a word. You basically borrowed his analysis."

"But Professor Neumann! What are you saying? I cited him several times in my footnotes and certainly in my bibliography. I almost worked myself to death on that paper!"

"Please, you tell me yourself if my reading of your term paper is incorrect. Did you or did you not cite Humboldt simply in the periphery of your main analysis, as if he were merely tangential to your paper?"

"Well, I don't know. I guess I did."

"But wasn't that how you structured your entire approach to Goethe?"

"Yes, ma'am," Sarah said, her voice a whisper.

"Well, that's my point exactly. Intellectual dishonesty will eventually catch up with you, Sarah. You are being trained to be a scholar with the highest standards. Those who read your work may not tell you directly, and maybe they should, but your intellectual dishonesty is plain to them and certainly plain to me."

"I did my *best*," Sarah stammered, tears in her eyes.

"You are an adult now, Sarah. Search your own heart. See if the work you have been turning in, the work that has gotten you this far, see if it is not derivative, naïve and often superficial. That is not what we do at Yale. There is no substitute for originality, for the hard work of the mind. It's better that you learn that lesson now."

"Yes, ma'am." Sarah's whole body was shaking. Tears streamed down her cheeks. She wanted to vomit.

"The problem, I believe, the reason you may never become a true scholar, is that your dishonesty, unfortunately, has become part of your character. Now, of course, you may find a job in some small university of low repute, but whatever you produce will most likely be worthless, unless of course you change your ways. Now the question is whether you can change the heart of a liar. I have often seen that you cannot. Why? Well, in the academy, those who are dishonest are often those who do not have the mental ability for originality. To compensate for a lack of innate ability, they lie. The ruse works for a while, but then they are uncovered for what they are. The university may preach opportunity and diversity and having an open mind. But what it practices is the search for truth, and this search is relentless and brutal. While the 'outcomes' may not be clear, it is clear who can pursue them honestly, and who cannot. It may be better for you to do something worthwhile, Sarah. That's my advice to you. Don't waste your life chasing unachievable dreams."

Sarah stood without moving. After a few seconds of dead silence, she said, "Thank you, Professor Neumann." She opened the door and stumbled into the hallway, stunned.

The streets seemed a watery blur. As she walked through Yale to her room in Helen Hadley, Sarah repeatedly tripped on the sidewalk cracks on Temple Street. She sobbed uncontrollably. A priest from St. Mary's Church, who was fixing a broken latch on the back door of the chapel, saw her and stopped his work and asked if he could help her. She shook his hand for no reason at all, blurted out that she was from Iowa and thanked him for being so kind. But she couldn't look him in the eye. A drumbeat inside her head shocked her with a bleak fury. Miraculously she made her way home, and when she arrived collapsed onto her bed, blinded by her tears.

Sarah woke up early in the evening. She had slept most of the day. Her head pulsed like a hot chunk of magma. She could see the orange streaks of the setting sun on one corner of the white window frame.

Professor Neumann's accusations swirled in her head. The bitch, Sarah thought, had extracted her revenge. None of it was true. Neumann just wanted to tear her apart. Was Sarah really "intellectually dishonest"? She hated herself. In her heart, Sarah felt worthless and wretched. Why had she ever bothered to come to Yale? Why had she done this to herself? Why hadn't she stayed in Iowa?

What was she going to tell her family? She had lied to everyone! Sarah thought. She had lied to her mother and her grandmother. Straight A's in German literature? An essay winner? The recipient of the University of Iowa's summer scholarship to study in Germany? All of it lies! Ingenuous, derivative crap! That hateful bitch was right, Sarah concluded. She would never be like her. She would never produce anything of lasting value.

The drumbeats were louder in Sarah's head. Her mind swelled, and then released her into an abyss. She couldn't go forward and she couldn't go back. She was a failure. A liar. She imagined what her mother would say, and her devastating disappointment.

"Mama, please," she muttered to herself, "I just wanted you to be proud of me. But I lied to make up the truth. I lied to pull myself up from the muck I know. I lied and lied and hoped, somehow, it would metamorphose into the truth. I know who I am now. I know what I am. I know at least that much!"

Sarah was at the window's ledge. The cold November wind lifted up a few strands of her blond hair. The air seemed to call her forward. The evergreens swayed so peacefully, too. Suddenly she realized what she was about to do, and a terror gripped her. She gasped and crumbled to the floor in tears. A sharp knock was at her door. Slowly the heavy wooden door opened by itself.

"Sarah? I found your keys in the lock, and you know New Haven, so I . . . Sarah! What is wrong?" Bharat rushed forward. "Did someone attack you? Sarah! What happened? Please talk to me." He hugged her shoulders and cleared away the wet strands of hair from her face. He pulled the window closed, and she collapsed into his arms.

"Oh, Bharat! I hate myself!"

"But no, Sarah! You are a *good* person!"

"Please don't leave me alone. I don't know what to do."

"Of course not! I will stay with you. What is this sadness I see? What happened to my Sarah?"

"I'm a liar, Bharat. I'm a complete liar. I don't deserve to be at Yale."

"Oh, that's nonsense, Sarah. I am sorry to tell you this, but you are wrong about yourself. You are just digging a pit for your soul." His loud reproach startled her. She dried her eyes. Bharat was angry; at once he looked like a different person.

Sarah told him what Regina Neumann had done and ascribed it to a bitter "professional rivalry" between Neumann and her own adviser. How could she tell Bharat the truth? He would think she was a liar and a slut.

"But she's right about me, Bharat," Sarah whispered, barely able to talk. He was brewing black tea for her. She sat on her bed, her back against the wall. The skin around her eyes was puffy and raw. He nimbly went about gathering utensils, cups and napkins. He left briefly to get food for both of them from his room. When he returned, he immediately stroked her hair and rubbed her cheek affectionately, a gentle reassurance of his presence.

"No, Sarah. I am sorry if I am contrary today, but this professor is *not* right about you. You must understand that in your own heart. I will tell you something you may not want to hear. But I think you are much too vulnerable for your own good. You seek validation from the outside only. In mathematics, you *know* when you are right, if you have made a mistake. At least most of the time. 'Most of the time' is ninety-nine percent of the time. You might overlook an assumption that needs a proof. Or your own proof might have a fallacy. But if you work carefully, step by step, you will know you are right. My adviser is but to confirm my conclusions, and often I must explain exactly what I did. Other mathematicians will also check my work, undoubtedly. I know that in the social sciences, in German literature, it is not as clear-cut. But the principle should still hold true. If you can work carefully and confirm rigorously what you have done, using your own tests, then the outside world will come to you. Not the other way around."

"But I've been dissatisfied with my own work. I know I've lied to myself about the quality of my work here. I don't deserve to be here. She's right. I just want to get by and go back home. I'm stupid and lazy."

"Sarah, just listen to yourself. This woman has destroyed your confidence. Didn't you tell me that you were finally making real progress with your own adviser? That's how it's done. Very slowly. Didn't you tell me that before?"

"Yes."

"Maybe that is what you need. Someone on your side, not someone kicking you and making you feel like nothing. Stay away from this Neumann. She has obviously forgotten what it is to be a teacher," Bharat said, refilling her cup with tea. "That is the first thing. The next thing is to know there is nothing wrong with your desire to return home. 'Academic achievement,' at a place like this, is often the achievement of power without spirit. It is winning by annihilating your opponent. I went to a philosophy seminar once. And the talk was so imprecise, which I had expected. But what was surprising was this fight to the death, this who 'won' and who 'lost.' It's as if some in the humanities have taken the precise rendering of results in the real sciences to fields that are by nature imprecise. So you are left with imprecise debates declaring their certitude with nothing but loudness and guile. 'Being right' is just the current whim of a herd of eloquent idiots. Don't mistake me. I believe truth in the humanities exists. But it is the practical understanding of the human spirit. They will know more about that in Iowa than in a transient community like this one. You will only gain if you return home."

"Maybe I should."

"After you finish your work here," he said quickly, a grin on his face.

"After I finish my work here," she repeated and finally smiled in return. He had laid out two dishes heaped with basmati rice and curry chicken with spinach. "Bharat, can I ask you a personal question?"

"Ask me anything."

"Well, did you like me before?"

"I like you now."

"I mean, Were you interested in dating me?"

"Frankly, yes," he said, embarrassed.

"And now?"

"I still like you," he said. Sarah leaned over and slowly kissed his lips.

"Bharat, if you want to, you can stay here tonight."

"Thank you, Sarah. Thank you very much. I will tell you, quite frankly again, that is more than I ever dreamed of. And I will also tell you that you have completely succeeded in confusing a good mathematician. You are the expert here. But let us do one thing for both of us. Let us wait. You will pass your Comps, and I will see if my head stops spinning, even just a revolution or two. I want to be with you very much, Sarah. But let us wait a bit, and then that night will be a perfect one."

"Okay, it's a deal."

Chapter Thirteen

In Salzburg, Helmut first glanced at the contents of the pouch. It was packed with yellowed sheets of paper, and included transcripts of several conversations. He closed it after a few minutes. He didn't need to read it just now. He had what he wanted, and it was time to enjoy himself with Ariane.

The Sassolini villa in Florence astonished Helmut. Two huge wrought-iron balconies overlooked the heart of the city. A labyrinth of rooms, whitewashed and neat, extended from an enclosed courtyard bursting with hanging vines, trees and flowers. The family had owned the building for generations. Ariane's father was a lawyer for the government; her mother managed other family properties in Florence. One sister was a fledgling model; another was a high schooler. Her twin brothers were mischievous brats who upended every room they invaded. An older brother was studying to be a lawyer like his father.

Everyone was curious about Helmut. That he had expected. What *was* surprising to him was the fearful deference they paid to Ariane. She seemed to grow in stature as soon as she walked through the front door. Glowing with pride, Mama Sassolini hugged her daughter at every turn. The twins taunted Sofia, the youngest sister, but not Ariane, whom they approached warily.

When the beautiful sister, Adriana, came home, Helmut put the puzzle together. Mama Sassolini and Ariane were cooking their welcome-home dinner. Adriana said hello to Helmut, who was relaxing in the parlor. She asked him about renting an apartment in New York, and what difficulties she would face if she were a model. She asked him if he had ever traveled to Los Angeles. Her English was a mishmash of Italian and English words and phrases, and Helmut did have trouble understanding her. But the real reason was that Adriana was stunning. A perfect face, with the most seductive almond eyes he had ever seen. A body so proportioned that Helmut could not help but imagine discovering endless bliss over every curve. Adriana wore a tight black skirt with a blood-red silk blouse, and no bra. Yet, as their awkward attempt at conversation dragged on, her allure faded like a weakening scent. Helmut realized she just wasn't that smart. Not dumb, but naïve. Maybe immature.

Helmut asked Adriana about her older sister, how Ariane had been as a child. Adriana rolled her lovely eyes and recounted the story of a young rebel. A girl who had been thrown out of Sunday school for arguing that the virginity of the Virgin Mary was preposterous. A young woman who had screamed at and fought with her father about what she wanted to do with her life, where she wanted to go. A sister who left for America without her parents' blessing. Adriana Sassolini said that without Ariane, the trailblazer, the younger siblings, particularly the girls, would not have enjoyed the freedoms they took for granted every day. By dinnertime, when Ariane's father returned home and greeted him with a warm, but formal hello, Helmut felt the tension swell in the house. The father and daughter found each other in the living room. Without hesitation, Ariane jumped into her father's arms. Tears streamed down Don Sassolini's fat cheeks and big nose. The man and the child sobbed in each other's arms. Ariane was finally home.

A few nights later, Helmut began to flip through the old army pouch he had found at Melk. Several hundred pages of material were bound together with clips. These formed small piles of documents, transcripts and carbon copies. He examined the transcript of a conversation between Captain Johnson and Mr. Drabek. Mr. Drabek had originally been from Estonia. German soldiers had captured him two and a half years ago. Helmut looked for a date. At the top of the first page in tiny block figures, he found the numerical cipher: 160646 14:30. Next to it was "U.S. Third Army: Military Trial Records: Dachau, Germany."

The conversation was really an interrogation. Captain Johnson asked questions about Mr. Drabek's trek to various concentration camps and finally to Dachau. Mr. Drabek would answer dutifully. The transcript contained brackets where the translator would add commentary on the exact meaning of a phrase or what he thought Mr. Drabek had really meant to say.

The story Mr. Drabek told was grim. Captain Johnson pressed him for details about Nazi atrocities. Mr. Drabek described the repeated beatings and torture of prisoners weakened by malnutrition, starvation and grueling marches toward southern Germany. The prisoners had been made to stand abreast in excrement-filled boxcars. There had been countless suicides. Summary executions were carried out behind farmhouses, and in the middle of desolate roads. Fathers were executed in front of their families. People were forced to dig graves and then fill them with the bodies of friends and family. A German soldier laughed after committing murder. Jews. They wanted Jews, Mr. Drabek said. They were obsessed with killing Jews. Mr. Drabek had survived, he explained, because he wasn't a Jew and because he was a good mechanic.

Captain Johnson devoted the last third of the interrogation to the grisly details of several incidents that occurred near the Dachau camp. Mr. Drabek claimed to know the names of some Germans who had perpetrated heinous acts against prisoners. He was asked to confine himself to eyewitness accounts of outright murders or fatal tortures of prisoners. Mr. Drabek indicated he had seen the guard Johann Lübeck smash his rifle butt against the face of a woman, a Mrs. Paslavsky, after she pleaded for the release of her daughter. The daughter had been dragged to the medical barracks, although she had not been ill. There were rumors, Mr. Drabek said, that German doctors were conducting experiments inside, with huge vats bubbling with a smoky liquid. Mrs. Paslavsky, her face bloody, latched onto Lübeck's leg and swung wildly at his groin. He shot her in the stomach, in front of the other prisoners. Two other guards rushed out, screamed at Lübeck and dumped the moaning woman into a cart. Lübeck pushed the cart to the far edge of a fenced field, and dumped the body into a ravine. Then he picked up a bucket with yellow powder. With a practiced motion, the guard pitched arcs of color into the ravine as if he were spreading seeds in a field.

Mr. Drabek continued. An alcoholic sergeant with a psychotic temper routinely conducted surprise inspections in the middle of the night, and dragged men into a storage shed. Those who returned were badly beaten, bones broken, even sexually abused. Three men never returned. One inmate discovered a severed hand dangling on the camp's barbed wire. He recognized a ring on the hand as belonging to one of those three men. The name of the sergeant? Sergeant Rudolf Spranger, Mr. Drabek answered. He had the ring, if Captain Johnson wanted to see it. He had traded some quinine for it. The ring saved his life. But Captain Johnson didn't want to hear about the ring.

There was one other thing. Mr. Drabek said it was the worst because he saw it happen. He didn't know the name of the man involved. The incident happened before any of the other things he had already told Captain Johnson about. Not long after he arrived at the Mühldorf camp, in the autumn of 1944, Mr. Drabek was working in a remote field, digging holes for a line of fence posts. It had been a sunny day. The work crew was near a thicket of trees and bushes, just beyond where the fence would be. It looked like a beautiful island of green to him. He was digging when he thought he heard a yelp. A puppy's yelp. The sound came from the thicket. Mr. Drabek saw something move. He couldn't be sure, but he thought he saw the soft whiteness of a hand or a leg. Then he saw a young German soldier on the far side of the trees. He wasn't one of the regular guards. The soldier was walking toward the thicket. Mr. Drabek saw something move again. Someone was there. The soldier reached the trees, glanced back. He didn't pay any attention to the prisoners. They were far in front of him. The soldier slipped inside the thicket and took something from his breast pocket. Mr. Drabek saw a flash of metal. The soldier, just dark shadows and sunspots in the trees, unzipped his pants. Mr. Drabek thought he was going to pee. But then he fell to his knees, on top of a bush, what Mr. Drabek thought was a bush. Legs flailed in the branches. He heard a high-pitched moan, a woman's moan. Then nothing. The bushes stopped trembling, the legs stopped flailing. He saw a figure hunch over a bush and fiddle with something for a few minutes. Then the soldier stood up and fixed himself. As the soldier walked back to the barracks, away from the prisoners, he cleaned several pairs of handcuffs on his trousers. Mr. Drabek turned to the thicket again. Nothing moved anymore. There was no sound.

Mr. Drabek didn't know who the soldier was. He saw him once more, the next day. But the soldier had not been at Dachau when the Americans arrived. Mr. Drabek remembered the soldier's face, though. With deep blue eyes and ghostlike skin. A young man in a trance, this solider. He walked right past Mr. Drabek, who noticed the index finger on the soldier's right hand was in a splint. That's all Mr. Drabek remembered.

Helmut shook his head clear and left the papers beside his bed and tried to fall asleep. The next day, he and Ariane said a tearful goodbye to her family. He looked at the files again on the transatlantic fight home. Ariane dozed next to him.

Helmut flipped through another packet of testimony. It was a conversation between a Captain J. Miller and a Vytis Petruskas. Helmut read:

031146 11:30. You Americans are good. Let me tell you. But I have seen things that were not so good. Your soldiers, some of them, were not good. They did terrible things. It's true. Who doesn't hate the Germans? I certainly do. But you Americans must be careful you do not become like them. Not like them. Please. That would be such a waste. That would give me nothing to believe in anymore. I love America. America saved us from dying. America came to us. The soldiers who opened up Dachau were our friends. They helped us out. They gave us so much food my friends got sick from eating those first days when we won our freedom again. I love America, really. But I have to say this. At the end of March 1945. Right before the liberation. The exact date? I don't know the exact date. Half of my mind is gone. You should be happy I'm still alive telling you this. Okay,

I'll go on. May I have a drink of water? Thank you. I think it was in March, maybe the last week. Okay? There was chaos everywhere. You didn't know who was German and who was a prisoner. The Nazis were running away, the war was lost. I know two of the guards tried to steal the prison clothes from me and my friends. They wanted to hide from the Americans, from the Soviets. Prisoners roamed around in bands; groups of Nazis were everywhere too, scared and trying to hide. We just wanted to hide to keep from being shot by anyone who might want to shoot us. Mistakes could be made.

A group of ten prisoners from Dachau, I was with them, we hid in the forest to wait for the Americans. The Germans had already left everything behind. We had food but no weapons. For days we could hear bombs exploding around us. We just wanted to survive long enough for the Americans to control the territory. We didn't want to die. At that point, our prison uniforms were the only things to keep us from being shot on the spot by the Americans. That was all we had. Who would the Americans believe? Real prisoners or guards dressed as prisoners? Those devils might even say we were the Germans. This was our nightmare. One day in the forest, three of us went searching for food. We were on a hill coming down when we heard voices yelling. We didn't understand the language completely. It certainly wasn't German or Russian. We thought it was English. A group of about fifteen soldiers had just captured seven German soldiers. A woman was with the Germans. Maybe an officer's wife. The Americans were angry with the Germans. They were shouting at them. One of them was screaming out of control, raving. Screaming and pointing at the Germans. Another American soldier ran behind a clump of bushes and dragged out several bodies. Others helped him. Bodies of dead American soldiers. That was the first time I saw a black man and he was a body without life. Their hands were tied behind their backs. They had been shot in the head. Four Americans. It was horrible to see this. Blood was everywhere. Now more American soldiers were yelling too. At each other. The Germans waited patiently, their arms raised. One American who was guarding the Germans was nervous, a blond

*fellow. He kept looking at the two who were screaming at each
other. The other guard wasn't nervous. He seemed bored. This is
the one who fired the first shot. He shot one of the German prisoners in the chest, then the head. Then another one. The nervous
one started shooting too. One soldier rushed to stop the shooting,
but was grabbed by another soldier. More soldiers shot their
weapons. The Germans were motionless, like cardboard. They
fell back with bullets ripping up their uniforms. The only one
they didn't shoot was the German woman. The cold American
soldier, the one who started this, raised his rifle to shoot her too.
But he didn't. He grabbed her and started ripping off her clothes,
touching her. A good American soldier pushed the attacker off.
When the other one got up to fight him, the rescuer hit him and
screamed at him. Then he turned around and shot the woman in
the head before she looked up to thank him. That's what I saw.
No, I don't know who they were. I don't know anything about
those American soldiers. We ran back up the hill before anyone
could see us.*

*May I have another drink of water? I have one more thing
to say. One more thing before I go. You have been asking about
what the Germans did to us when we were in the camp, right? I
have just one thing to say. I made a promise to someone I met in
Vilnius, when the Nazis invaded us and dragged us from our
homes. I promised my friend I would take care of her daughter.
Yishka died soon after the city was invaded and we were captured. The horrible thing was that she died slowly, of an infection, my beautiful Yishka. I felt terrible I could not get anything
for her wounded leg and the German soldiers ignored me when
I told them I needed something for her. What does this have to
do with the camps? Well, if you wait a minute you will see. You
Americans are so impatient! I waited long enough to be rescued.
You can wait a few minutes for me to finish. Okay. Before Yishka died she asked me to watch out for her daughter. This happened when we were already heading south, in boxcars full of
prisoners. The Germans just threw poor Yishka off the train
when she died, like a sack of rotten potatoes. Yishka's daughter
stayed with me. I was like her father now. The girl was not just*

*beautiful but strong. An epidemic of malaria broke out among
the prisoners and she got sick. But she did not die. We made it
together to Mühldorf after many days of struggle. There, I
thought, if we could stay together we would be rescued after the
war. There were rumors that the Americans were advancing,
that the Russians were also attacking from the east. The last few
months we knew something was about to happen. The guards
would gossip anxiously. We hoped and then we would lose hope.*

*But at Mühldorf I did not keep my promise to my friend
Yishka. The Germans slaughtered her daughter. When did this
happen? The October before we were liberated. She had such a
beautiful voice, this young angel. I had heard her sing once when
we were being taken south to Mühldorf. But maybe she was too
beautiful. One military officer, not much older than her, grabbed
her one day, yanked her out of the women's barracks. My friends
told me she fought like a tiger and even hurt the German bastard. She grabbed a finger and almost twisted it off. But this only
made it worse for her, I think. He punched her and tied her
hands with shackles. Not only did he drag her out while the
guards kept everyone else away, but he never brought her back.
She was gone. That was the last time anyone saw her. No one
knew exactly what happened to her. The German officer soon
disappeared too. But I have no doubt she's dead. I have no doubt
about this at all. That's all I have to say. What was her name?
Anja Litvak. A child of God.*

Helmut remembered the name Litvak from the papers in
Hopfgartner's office. Could Anja have been the daughter of Vladek
Litvak? Could this nightmare be true? The director of the refugee
center who had committed suicide in the Seine in Paris? After the
suicide, the center had been the recipient of Hopfgartner's anonymous donation. After the suicide, Hopfgartner had obsessively
kept the old newspaper article for decades in his office cabinet.
Anja Litvak, the daughter with the divine voice, from Vilnius,
Lithuania. Anja, in the trees, Helmut thought. Anja Litvak, one
young German soldier's perverse delight when no one was looking. One worth three thousand marks of guilt. The reason why the

professor had recklessly stole documents from the authorities and hid them in the Melk library after the war! Werner Hopfgartner's own guilt had betrayed him! Next to the sleeping Ariane, Helmut pushed his seat back and stared into the dawn of orange clouds in the horizon above the Atlantic Ocean. Thirty-five thousand feet above the earth, the sea of this reddish orange seemed to go on forever.

An icy snow covered the ground in New Haven. A northeaster had blown sheets of snow and rain across the coastline. The streets were deserted.

After Helmut dropped off Ariane, he drove home. His mind reeled. He imagined Anja Litvak shackled and tortured. He imagined her brave attempt to fight back, and that coward looking over his shoulder. Helmut imagined the carnal rape. It had been a clean and merciless destruction of innocent life. What an appalling lack of consequences! he thought. Only for a moment did Helmut think about turning in Werner Hopfgartner. Would the authorities believe Helmut had found these documents in Melk? Would they believe the documents referred to Hopfgartner? Would they believe the evidence–Hopfgartner's handwritten note about the files in Melk, the old French newspaper article and the letter with the cashier's check for the refugee center? Would they believe Helmut had found this evidence in Hopfgartner's cabinet before the old man destroyed the originals? Would they believe anything at all? And in that moment, even after Helmut imagined that everyone would believe what he believed, this wasn't enough. Turning Hopfgartner in was not nearly enough. Having Hopfgartner discredited and kicked out of the university, and even having him incarcerated forever—none of these punishments seemed enough.

'Enough' wasn't even the right word for it. This wasn't a matter of compensation or comparison. It wasn't a matter of revenge. Helmut felt a personal connection to this act, its history, these years of deception, its resolution. He was a part of this truth. It was *his* truth now, to carry forward, to complete. It would have been the height of absurdity for him to try to communicate what he felt and what he reasoned. It would have been like trying to explain why you were truly in love with a particular person and how you *knew* what real love was. The experience of universal love linked you to every human being who had ever been in love. But it also particularized this love, with your own feelings and circumstances and capacities, so that no one else would know it as you did.

Anja Litvak was his angel, Helmut thought. Anja Litvak was his child. Anja Litvak was his blood. Helmut could not keep her out of his mind. He imagined he could have saved her even at the price of his own flesh. He imagined he could have freed her from that thicket of bushes and trees, and protected her. Helmut imagined a peace and a perfection that just wouldn't allow for a death whose purpose was to fulfill simple greed or lust. He wanted to will into being a world without a murder all-too-easily born of the hope that no one was watching.

When, from these depths, Helmut Sanchez decided he would destroy Werner Hopfgartner for the murder of Anja Litvak, Helmut did so with the knowledge that this world wasn't perfect. His dreams were just dreams, and this world was a nightmare to be possessed. It was his turn to stake his claim.

Chapter Fourteen

What was morality anyway? Helmut asked himself. Wasn't it simply being caught and punished for what you did? That was 'wrong.' Or escaping responsibility for your crime? That was 'right.' Wasn't that the rotten scheme? Helmut knew no one else would understand his reasons. He didn't need to wait for anyone's approval. The rational calculation of his murderous plan unfolded in the weeks after his return to New Haven. It started as a detailed dream, then became a blueprint and finally seized him as an inevitability that awaited only the crepuscule of this day.

Helmut didn't want to slip on the ice outside and inadvertently plunge the nine-inch stainless steel Cutco knife into his chest. He dropped the knife into his backpack, collected the notes from the research he had done the night before at Sterling Library and added a short sequel to the Compilation that the professor expected this week. He was late for work.

Helmut worried that the long blade of the Cutco knife would rip his backpack, so he tore off a piece of cardboard from an abandoned box on Bradley Street and wedged it around the tip of the blade. The streets were empty. Everyone, except a few graduate students, had left for Christmas vacation. Yale had shut down to avoid paying exorbitant utility bills. The blanket of winter cold was oppressive. The German department was holding its last faculty meeting of the year that night to discuss the schedule for reviewing incoming graduate applications and to vote on several faculty appointments for next year. Werner Hopfgartner would be at this meeting. Afterward, he would probably have a drink with a few colleagues in the faculty room. The department maintained a stock of expensive liquor for its senior members. Then the professor would walk home, as he always did. Werner Hopfgartner would toddle down Hillhouse to Sachem, then to Whitney Avenue, just across the Hamden town line, and past Edgehill Park. Whitney was more like a highway at that point, flanked by a narrow sidewalk. On one side of the walk, thick evergreens sat atop a hill; on the other, a snow bank was often piled high. It would be like walking in a ravine. At that spot, the professor would be momentarily hidden from the street view. The streets would be dark and abandoned. There, Helmut would wait for him. His hands trembled inside his sleeves.

When he reached Harkness Hall, his face was numb from the cold. Helmut patted his cheeks, stomped his shoes on the thick webbed mat at the entrance and pushed open the foyer doors. Inside, the air was pleasantly warm. His footsteps echoed down the cavernous hallway, and in the empty classrooms. Downstairs, in the maze of offices and seminar rooms, it felt even more deserted. The lights were off. A faraway door slammed shut. Helmut found his office door and turned on the bright fluorescent light and closed the door behind him.

His first shot of caffeine woke him up. Helmut turned on his computer. Everything had to be normal. He had to work as if nothing would happen that night. No little mistake could bring the suspicion of murder back to him. He had purchased the Cutco knife long ago, at a garage sale on Bishop Street. He would get rid of it as soon as the deed was done.

The location he had selected was perfect. He had imagined the scenario, and its possible variations, a thousand times. A week ago he had visited the site. It had been empty. Cars seldom passed through that part of Whitney Avenue at that hour. It was the professor's regular walk home from Yale. Street crime in New Haven was rampant. Just this semester, two drug dealers had shot each other, and an undergraduate had been caught in the crossfire. Who would assume the professor's death was anything but another random tragedy in this godforsaken town?

And afterward, Helmut would stay out of sight. School was officially over. Only three working days were left before Christmas vacation began for Yale employees. He would have minimal contact with people during that time. The chairman and several other people were leaving in the morning for a conference in Europe. It was possible that Helmut and a couple of the secretaries would be the only people around to mourn the gruesome death of Werner Hopfgartner. Helmut might even shed a tear. But the tear would be for Anja Litvak. The tear would be for the truth.

It had taken more than two weeks after he returned from Italy before Helmut overcame his wild hatred for Werner Hopfgartner. For a few days, Helmut simply wanted to strangle, then and there, the distracted old man who so casually strolled the halls of Yale, absorbed in his bourgeois, academic life, far removed from the blood of his past. But each day, Helmut forced himself to *think* about his hatred, not to act on it. A drastic act would only hinder the progress of true justice, Helmut reasoned. The truth would have its final incarnation in his careful plan, and his escape. What was certainly not needed were official accusations, and a careful consideration of the 'facts,' and the considered resolution that something had to be done, and the conclusion, from informed and expert opinion, that there did indeed exist possible transgressions, but not quite enough, of course, for any serious punishment. Only swift justice was necessary. Justice after decades of escaping blame and reveling in a life of lies. Yes, justice! Helmut declared to himself. *Real* action! *Real* morality! A morality of blood and consequences and impact! Enough with debated half-truths and lies and obfuscations! Enough with this emasculation of the living truth! What was not wanted was another philosophical seminar of nothing, from nothing, for the purpose of nothing. So Helmut did not immediately smash the professor's bulbous face into the stone walls of Harkness. He would take his time. He would use his well of hate to plan what should be done, to detail the act that would fulfill his moral reason. Imagining what he would do to Hopfgartner gave Helmut a strange, fluttery pleasure.

Helmut took a swig of coffee. He locked the door and turned off the overhead fluorescent light. He unzipped his backpack, took out the knife. It was nine inches long, shiny, with a weighty feel to it. Helmut discovered the most comfortable position was to hold it with his palm underneath the handle, his arm ready to plunge into his target. The blood, he thought, might disgust him. But the deed would not. Certainly the wrinkly pink face of Hopfgartner, shocked at his own bitter end, would be enough to carry Helmut through any difficulties.

It would only be a sweet and total victory if Helmut escaped detection. He had imagined every contingency. He knew how the investigating authorities would view the crime. Nobody would implicate him. The deed would soon be done and he could begin again. With a washcloth, Helmut meticulously wiped every inch of the blade and the handle to rid the knife of his fingerprints. He dropped it into his backpack and zipped the flap shut.

His nerves could not be a problem. Helmut had nothing to worry about. Not only had he planned everything in his head, but he was right. His *act* was right. He tried to push away the possibility that at the crucial moment his mind would be filled with doubt. It was simple. He would take the knife and kill him. He would make it appear like a robbery or an assault. He would leave quickly, discard the knife and reach his apartment safely. The next day he would be shocked upon hearing the news. He would be shocked and go about his business in mourning for the old bastard. In time, the brouhaha would end, Helmut would take his vacation, and by the time he returned to Yale the incident would begin its gentle fall into the oblivion of the past. Simple, he repeated to himself. Everything would be straightforward and simple. He would not lose his nerve.

The act was carefully planned. If he failed, it would be a failure to carry out an almost mechanical process. It would be a failure to perform. He had to be clear about his purpose and the simple steps to achieve that purpose. There could be no ambiguity here, no room for conflicting emotions. Maybe his head would reel a bit, but he would control it. His will would control any tendency to lose his mind at the moment of truth.

Helmut paced inside his small office and poured himself another cup of coffee. He pulled open the desk drawers, then forgot what he was looking for. On the computer screen, the rows and rows of amber words seemed to call him; the incessant hum of the machine seemed impatient, too. He had done no work at all. Who would care about Hopfgartner's work by tomorrow? He just needed to relax. He still had hours to go. He had to be patient.

Trying to get rid of his headache, Helmut massaged the top of his head, his temples and his neck. He walked hurriedly to the restroom and washed his hands. He walked back to his office, locked his door again and sat quietly in the half-light of the small, barred window behind him. He tried to work, but his head throbbed. He heard footsteps in the hallway, and his heart froze. The steps stopped in front of his door. The doorknob rattled.

"Helmut, are you in there?" Ariane asked.

He stayed quiet.

Oh, Ariane! My most precious love! You are but the bride of a monster! How can I tell you what's in my heart? How? Maybe you would laugh at me. Maybe you would recoil in horror. Your eyes, yes, the mere sight of your eyes! That would be enough to dissolve this hatred into specks of dirt. I don't know, Ariane. Suddenly I don't know anything anymore. Why, dear God, did you come for me? Why just at the moment when I need to cut away from all flesh, when I am about to leap into this murderous act? You would call it 'despicable.' You would turn away from me if you only knew! That would be worse than killing myself. That would be a million suicides. Ariane, what should I do? Am I a raving lunatic? What's wrong with me? Murder? Am I completely out of mind? Will I really kill Werner Hopfgartner? With a knife? What demons have possessed me! That almost seems laughable. Will I shed human blood with a knife? Absurd! Maybe I won't do it. Maybe this is just a nightmare in my waking hours. Maybe . . . I don't know anymore.

But Anja. I hear Anja's voice. Maybe I am insane. I hear her crying. I see her alone in the trees. I remember being alone and humiliated. I remember, too, the fat little boy hiding in the bathroom. And I see this man, Ariane. I see this evil man, Ariane. He laughs everyday still. He has had years of laughter. He has triumphed over the screams of others, he has triumphed with blood on his hands. And he laughs still. God has cursed us! He has either cursed us or He was never here

to begin with. We've pretended God was here for our own sanity!
That's the truth! We've pretended evil is punished and good is reward-
ed. A perfect scheme! With certain qualifications and explications for
any exceptions or irregularities! Of course, God is with us! To protect
us, to make our world safe and good! Hah! The ultimate lie in a world
of lies! Just open your eyes! Look for yourself! You will see exactly
what I see!

Oh, Ariane, forgive me. What I am about to do is not a 'crime.'
You will not agree, I dare not tell you! This act will save my soul. How
can I live in this world if I don't act? I would lose my right to be a
human being. And yes, you will say, Why should human beings care
about the truth? It's excessive, this caring. It's bizarre to want to live
in the truth, is it not? Real truth-seekers, those who would die or kill
for the truth, they seem out of place somehow. Better to have that
bureaucratic instinct and call for committee hearings to resolve the
matter! But I will not do that. I can't do that. Maybe what I will do
has nothing to do with the truth. Maybe that is just another fantasy
from the same place that created God. In that case, I will kill him sim-
ply because I want to. For no reason at all. I will kill him because of
our humiliation and destruction and because of their laughter. I will
kill him to see it can be done. I will kill him because I am alive and
because he will be dead. I will kill him because I don't know anymore.
I will kill him simply to know I can. Darkness, give me the strength!

After a while, Helmut heard Ariane walk away.

The faculty meeting was scheduled to start at 6:00 p.m. It was
now 5:00 p.m. Helmut's stomach churned. He had forgotten to eat
lunch, and now he felt weak and nervous. Harkness Hall was
deathly silent. Everyone had fled the upstairs offices for home.
Where should he wait for the meeting to end? How would he find
out if Hopfgartner and the other professors were having a drink
afterwards or simply going home? The faculty conference room
was on the third floor. The faculty lounge was next to it.

At 6:45 p.m. Helmut closed his office door, the backpack
slung over his shoulder. He trudged up the stone steps in thumps
that seemed preposterously loud to him. On the third floor, the
hallways were empty. He heard faint voices at the end of the hallway, from inside the conference room. Through a narrow door

window, Helmut glimpsed the faculty of the German department around a huge table. A professor Helmut didn't recognize was speaking.

My God! Helmut realized. Werner Hopfgartner wasn't there! Helmut craned his neck to scan the room. Maybe the professor was behind the wall to the left. Helmut needed to be sure. It was quite possible the old man had skipped the meeting entirely. That would be a disaster. Should he wait like a fool? Helmut found a secluded spot in the stairwell at the far end of the hallway. He could hide behind the double doors, but still keep watch through the narrow door windows. No one would use those stairs to leave the building. From there, he could see the door of the conference room and entrance to the faculty lounge. Yet he would be hidden.

Why had he been waiting in his office? Hopfgartner might have already escaped. Helmut would never be able to summon the nerve—the will—to do this again. Even now, as he waited, the absurdity of his plan shook his bones. What was he thinking? Was he really planning to slit a man's throat with a knife? Was he was completely out of his mind? But Hopfgartner had sacrificed an innocent girl to satisfy his selfish pleasures, Helmut reminded himself. Hopfgartner embodied every self-righteous social climber without a conscience. The old man deserved to die.

A door creaked open down the hall. Helmut heard a loud conversation. The meeting was breaking up. Two professors went quickly down the main stairwell. Several others entered the faculty lounge. Still others lingered in the conference doorway, arguing, laughing.

And there was Hopfgartner! He chatted with a young colleague, Zachary Kohl, who had joined the department last year. They strolled into the lounge. For some unknown reason, Helmut nearly burst into the hallway and screamed.

Helmut's plan was on track. Thus far everything was perfect. He had to wait for the professor to leave the faculty lounge. He checked his watch. It was already 8:20 p.m. The longer the old man stayed in the lounge, the better. The later it got, the fewer people would be on the streets of New Haven. Helmut could enjoy the cover of darkness. His plan could finally reach its perfect moment. Everything had to be right. Everything had to be absolutely perfect or he would not risk this folly. If events unfolded perfectly, then the plan and the deed would also come to be, without question. This seemed clear to Helmut Sanchez. This incredible perspicacity overwhelmed him with a giddiness that threatened to erupt out of control.

He heard a door slam shut below him. Then footsteps. On the stairs, rising toward him. In a few moments he would be caught! He could only escape into the hallway, but faculty members still lingered at the conference room door. The footsteps were a floor below him. Helmut stuck out his head into the hallway. The last straggler walked into the lounge. He pushed through the stairwell doors, hurried across the hallway and slipped into an empty seminar room. The stairwell doors fell softly shut. The footsteps rose to the top of the stairs. And stopped.

Helmut glanced nervously around the seminar room. He had forgotten his backpack in the stairwell!

The stairwell doors opened. A security guard walked out. He was holding Helmut's backpack! In a moment the guard would open it and find the knife. Then he would discover Helmut's name on his papers and books. Helmut was panicking.

The guard trudged down the hall, the backpack slung over his shoulder. At the doorway of the lounge, he smiled sheepishly at the congregation of German professors drinking on the ruby leather couches.

Helmut dashed out the seminar room and through the stairwell door, and raced down the narrow steps to the first floor. He had to cut off the guard and retrieve his backpack. A rage exploded inside of him like a flash of lightning.

He caught up to the guard outside Harkness Hall, under the smoky amber lights of Cross Campus.

"Hey! Excuse me!" The guard turned around slowly, with the chubby face of a grown child. Immediately Helmut's spirits soared.

"Hi," the security guard said, with a heavy horse-like breath in the December chill.

"That's my backpack. I was talking to one of the professors on the third floor, right before the faculty meeting—I work here—

and I left it by mistake," Helmut said, out of breath, faking a sub-servient mixture of modesty and embarrassment. His mind was racing. He fought the urge to just yank the pack out of the guard's hands and run. He reminded himself to stay calm, but his face was perspiring. "That's my backpack all right."

"This is yours?" the fat guard asked warily, holding up the heavy pack at eye-level.

"Yes, sir."

"Well, it's a good thing I came by, mister," the guard said, genially. "'Cause, you know, all sorts of things get stolen at Yale. They blame the bums. And maybe those guys do snip a few things now and then. But I tell you, I've seen students with sticky fingers too."

The guard still held the pack at his side. He wasn't exactly frowning at Helmut, yet his smile was gone.

"I believe it. Sign of the times, I guess," Helmut blurted out. The sweat dripped down the side of his face. He looked around. Cross Campus was deserted. Their bodies were practically hidden by the evergreen bushes at the entrance to Harkness Hall. Helmut shivered at the thought that had slipped into his mind.

"I was going to return it to 'Lost and Found,' but I guess I could give it to you right now."

"Thanks."

"If I was going by the book, and I usually do, I should turn it in. Don't you think?"

"Well, yes. But it's mine."

"Oh, I don't doubt it at all. You look like you're telling the truth. I'm sure you're an honest guy," the guard said with a sly grin, shifting his heavy torso on his thick, stumpy legs. "You say you were talking to a professor in the hallway before the meet-ing?"

"That's right. I really have to go. I'm in a bit of a hurry."

"Well, that's the weird part. Not that you're in a hurry. Every-one at Yale's in a hurry. Zip, zip, zip. That's how I see them. Zip-ping off to the library. Zipping off to class. Zipping off to play Fris-bee. No, that's not the problem. You say you work here?"

"Yes, in the German department."

"Ah, *German*! Got my worse grade in Mrs. Peterson's German class in high school. Never got the hang of it. The verbs at the end, in the middle, split up. What a mess!"

"Excuse me," Helmut interrupted, now incensed. The idiot was toying with him. He would hand over the backpack now or Helmut would snatch it away! No, that would be stupid, Helmut reasoned. He should calm down, and just play the game. "I'm sorry to sound rude, but I have a lot of work to do and I have to get going."

"Well, the problem is I found this backpack in the third-floor stairwell, not the hallway. That's why I think I should go by the book. Nothing against you, of course."

"Look. I don't know how it got in the stairwell. But if you turn it in to 'Lost and Found,' I'm doomed. I lose a night's work and maybe more. I don't know if I can come back to get it before the Christmas vacation. I don't *want* to," Helmut said, his eyes feverish, quick and fierce. "Please look in the bag."

"What?"

"Open the bag and look inside. My name's Helmut Sanchez. Just check any paper or book inside. It'll have my name on it."

"Well, I don't know. We don't really have the right to inspect anyone's personal belongings."

"Please, just look in the bag. It's perfectly fine with me," Helmut said, fighting to mask the desperation in his voice. The deep wrinkles on the guard's gray uniform seemed strangely to incite him, shifting languorously with every movement of the guard's massive body. Suddenly Helmut was cold again, and his hands were shaking. He seemed on the brink of an explosion.

"Okay, let's see," the guard said almost cheerfully. He tugged at the thick, black zipper that sealed half the pack. He opened it only a hand's width, felt around, frowned slightly and began to pull something out. It was a paperback English dictionary. He opened it. "Okay. Here it is, 'Helmut Sanchez.' Just like you said. Sorry for all the trouble."

"Thank you very much," Helmut said, the backpack in his hands. He exhaled in relief. "Thanks again."

The guard waddled away with a wave of his hand. Helmut opened the backpack in the foyer. The knife was where he had left it. He hurried up the alternate stairwell to the third floor of Harkness Hall.

He peeked inside the faculty lounge. Professor Hopfgartner was sipping one last shot of bourbon before dinner, his legs crossed like a young woman's legs, modest, casual, seductive. Hopfgartner smiled, uttered a brief sentence, and stood up. Helmut barely got out of sight before Hopfgartner exited the lounge door.

Helmut hurried down three flights of stairs and waited in the basement shadows for the professor. Finally, Werner Hopfgartner appeared, walking slowly. He unlocked his office door. A few minutes later, the professor emerged with a long black coat, a vermilion silk scarf tightly wound around his neck, a cone-like wool cap on his head, his Austrian, wolf's head walking stick in one hand, a small leather briefcase in the other. He locked his office door and exited the building on College Street. Helmut ran to the Wall Street exit. The backpack thumped against his back.

Shifting shadows danced in the empty streets. Not one car was parked next to Scroll and Key or Sprague Hall. Helmut hid next to the thick evergreens of Woodbridge Hall and waited for the professor to cross Wall Street on College. There he was!

Helmut shook his legs over the cold ground. He made his way slowly toward College, and crossed the street and turned left toward Hillhouse, keeping the professor in sight. On Hillhouse, just in front of St. Mary's Church, Helmut saw the professor walking briskly ahead, faster than his own pace. Helmut wanted Hopfgartner to be one or two blocks in front, to make sure the old man took his normal route home. Once the professor started up Whitney Avenue—the only street that could take him to Blake Road—then Helmut could run on a parallel street, like Prospect, overtake the professor and cross back onto Whitney near Edgehill Park. There he would wait for him at the thicket of trees across the Mill River dam.

The professor hiked up Hillhouse, nimbly stepping over chunks of ice and ridges of snow piled on the curbs and driveways. With each crisp step, Hopfgartner touched the metal tip of the walking stick on the ground and swung it forward, like a pendulum. He disappeared inside long stretches of darkness. Helmut caught only glimpses of the old man in the amber light that filtered through the branches.

It was all unfolding so fast. It seemed as if Werner Hopfgartner himself might have been hurrying to meet his destiny on Whitney Avenue. Helmut's heart beat savagely inside his chest. Sweat drenched his face. He followed a few hundred feet behind the professor. The moon was nowhere. An overcast sky of lead gray clouds hovered above them like a claustrophobic ceiling. Helmut felt like he was falling into a bottomless pit. He inhaled deeply and tried to control his breathing.

The professor turned right on Sachem, toward Whitney Avenue. Helmut stopped at the corner and watched the professor turn at the Peabody Museum on Whitney.

Helmut started to run. The footing on the slate sidewalk of Prospect was treacherous. No one had shoveled away the snow. The sidewalk was intermittently covered with mounds and ridges of packed ice. His knees buckled and almost gave way. The professor would take about forty minutes to walk up Whitney Avenue, to the Mill River dam.

Helmut could have easily beaten him by three or four blocks if he had trotted leisurely up the hill on Prospect. But he rushed into the night like a madman. He sprinted over snow banks, sliding and slipping. His face glistened with perspiration. His cotton shirt was soaked under his black leather jacket, which gleamed like shiny plastic. A cat jumped out of a bush and streaked across the street. As he turned back to face the sidewalk, he skipped over a patch of ice, lost his balance and crashed face first onto the sidewalk, his backpack bouncing off his back and into the gutter.

Helmut jumped up, picked up his bag and started running again. His right shoulder ached, and the right side of his chest felt as if his lung had trouble expanding. Glancing at the base of his left thumb, he picked out a chunk of gravel lodged into the skin. Blood oozed from punctures in his palm.

He almost slipped and fell again at Canner Street. The pain in his chest seemed to expand with the warmth of his body. His shoulder throbbed. He stopped, checked his right knee and discovered a rip in his trousers. A nasty scrape. More blood. The injury stung sharply. Blood was trickling down his leg.

His thick black hair matted against his scalp, Helmut finally turned and sprinted down East Rock Road. At the corner of Whitney, his knee buckled for a second. He thought he saw Hopfgartner striding up the avenue, about five blocks away. Helmut couldn't be sure, but he knew he was far ahead of the professor. He ran past the entrance to Edgehill Park. The closed Amoco gas station was across the street and next to it was the barn-like museum for Eli Whitney. A few cars raced around the perilous bend adjacent to the Mill River, heading toward Whitneyville. At the Mill River dam, past the wooden bridge next to the museum, Helmut finally slowed to a walk. He could hear his heart beating inside his chest.

The paved sidewalk ended and became a narrow path stomped out of the weeds along Whitney Avenue. Snow had been pushed against the curb in uneven mounds by the snowplow. At the bend toward Whitneyville, the silent river snaked closer to the road on the opposite side. At this point, the walking path was nestled between Whitney on one side and a steep hill on the other. Pine trees and brush covered this hill. Along this secluded stretch, several hundred feet from Blake Road, the path veered into the hill and away from the road. A space of several strides was hidden not only from the houses high on the hill but also from the cars on Whitney. It was a byway through the trees. Helmut found the perfect spot behind a row of bushes and the trunk of a pine tree. He crouched, a knee on the ground, catching his breath.

It was inky black in that small bend in the pathway. Through the bramble of leaves and branches, Helmut could hardly see the road and the river beyond. Behind him the leafy underbrush rose precipitously. He had a clear view of the entrance to and exit from this bend. A streetlight by the Mill River dam, a single bulb of amber light, barely illuminated the shadowy murk. He yanked open his backpack and almost plunged his hand straight in. Was he out of his mind? He patted the inside pockets of his leather jacket and found his gloves. Why wasn't he wearing gloves when he fell on Prospect? He thrust his hands into the furry lining. He knew his blood would smear the gloves' inside, but what choice did he have? Then he gripped the knife, which felt heavier than before, like a sword, and set it down beside him. He closed his backpack and pushed it out of the way. The knife was in his left hand. Through the gloves, a sharp coldness surrounded his fingertips.

Helmut heard only the wind through the pine trees. The street was quiet. He waited for what seemed like hours, and still nothing. Crouching on his toes, he shifted his weight around; his left hand ached. Where was Werner Hopfgartner? Had he taken a different way home? Helmut's head was dizzy. Would he truly murder Werner Hopfgartner? Minor hotspots of pain erupted over his body. Helmut imagined Anja Litvak in pain, and all alone. He imagined Anja in the trees above him, waiting too, and wanting what he wanted. But why should he be the one? Why should he soil his hands too? He was not like Werner Hopfgartner! He wasn't! What on earth had his evil mind done to him? Helmut thought, exhaling for what appeared to be the first time that night. Helmut was about to get up and run down Whitney Avenue, but then he heard the distinctive click of the cane on the ice and distant footsteps.

The footsteps were getting closer, just coming around the bend. A wave of fear suddenly hit Helmut's face. What was he doing? Why was he here? Bits of snow cracked underfoot, not more than a few feet away. A certain elation mixed with dread overtook Helmut like a red cloud. Werner Hopfgartner took the slight turn of the pathway into the trees. The knife dropped from Helmut's hand and clanged against a rock.

"Who's there? I know someone's there!"

Helmut hesitated for a moment. His vision was blurred. Tears streamed down his cheeks. "You bastard! You horrible bastard! I know about Mühldorf! I know about Anja!"

"Helmut? What? Is that you?"

"You monster!" Helmut screamed at Professor Hopfgartner, standing a few feet away in the half-light. "You disgusting animal! You don't deserve to live!" Amid the shadows, Helmut could see and not see the professor's blue eyes. Hopfgartner held up his walking stick with the lance-like metal edge pointed at him. "I know!"

"So you do. I see," said the professor in a steady, deep voice Helmut had never heard before. It reminded him of a bear's growl. Hopfgartner planted his legs apart and grabbed his walking stick with both hands. "I found out everything! I have the documents! You liar! You murderer!" The blood pumped wildly through Helmut's head in a red frenzy, and he felt dizzy. He wanted to vomit. "You have been even a better researcher than I imagined. But this truth will stay between us. It will never escape these shadows, you young idiot."

"I will tell everyone, you monster!"

"What a stupid, stupid boy you are!"

Suddenly Hopfgartner's figure disappeared into the shadows. A heavy blow from the walking stick's sharp metal wolf's head smacked Helmut square on the left temple. Stars erupted in front of Helmut's eyes, and he crumpled to the ground. Another blow struck him on the neck, and another cracked against his ribs. Hopfgartner was on top of him, the stick gripped in his hands. The stick against Helmut's throat. The professor was choking Helmut.

For a second, Helmut seemed to lose consciousness. The moment was almost lost. Then he feebly grabbed at the old man's throat, flailing with his other arm. In the darkness, Hopfgartner's sweat or spit dripped into Helmut's eyes. The walking stick was pressed further into Helmut's larynx with what seemed extraordinary power. The young man gagged, and his legs kicked weakly at the old man's back. In one final gasp, Helmut struggled to free himself and reached for the ground behind his head. Helmut's hand touched the knife's handle amid the pine needles. Coughing and almost unconscious, he clutched it tightly, lurched forward with all his might and jabbed the knife into Hopfgartner's chest. The professor moaned loudly, dropped the walking stick across Helmut's chest, and fell back.

Helmut Sanchez struggled to his feet, stood back, astonished. The blood rushed back to his head. The knife was lying next to Hopfgartner. The professor was gripping his chest, quivering and coughing. In the shadows, everything seemed in slow motion. Helmut grabbed the knife. He jammed his boot onto the professor's throat. With both arms upraised, Helmut thrust the knife home, deep into Werner Hopfgartner's abdomen. Blood sprayed over his gloves and jacket. The professor screamed hoarsely and shivered to a stop. The blade had hit ice on the other side. A pair of headlights suddenly flashed across the road and disappeared. Helmut looked frantically around him. He was alone. He had to think. He knelt over the professor and tore open the top buttons of the coat. A pool of blood spread over the cold ground. The professor's coat and shirt were soaked with blood. Helmut grabbed the professor's wallet and picked up the knife. He had blood smeared on his jacket. His pants were streaked with it too. He wiped the knife clean on the pine needles on the ground, grabbed a handful of leaves and wiped himself clean. He was panicking. Helmut grabbed his backpack and dashed down Whitney Avenue, the very picture of a macabre madman, blood-smeared, a nine-inch knife in one hand, his eyes dilated in wild abandon.

What was he thinking? Immediately he ran off the road, stepping into the bushes adjacent to the Mill River. He ran up to the river and flung the knife a good twenty meters beyond the water's edge, the knife spinning like a Ferris wheel of death, blade over handle. It splashed dully into the water. Another car drove by. Helmut waited, and then jumped out of the bushes and sprinted down Whitney to East Rock Road. He turned west, toward Orange Street. The sidewalks were dark and empty. At East Rock Park, he pulled the wallet open, pinched out whatever money and credit cards he could find, and jammed the wallet deep into a trash barrel. He was out of breath and suddenly cold. What had he done? My God, what had he done?

At the bridge on East Rock Road, Helmut wadded up the money and flung it into the river. He found a secluded spot off the road and buried the credit cards after scraping a shallow hole in the cold dirt. He covered the spot with leaves and twigs. Now his knees were muddy. Blood was caked on his leather jacket. His gloves were grimy and black. He stood for a moment, collecting his wits, listening to the river. He was almost home. One more thing had to be done, he thought. His clothes. He turned on Orange Street and shunned the streetlights, zigzagging through the neighborhood like an animate shadow. In the darkness, from a distance, no one would notice the blood on his clothes. Only the appearance of his gloves was grotesque: sooty black and smeared with blood.

At the door to his apartment, Helmut peered up and down Orange Street. Then he went inside. He stripped off his clothes, including his shoes, and dumped everything into a plastic garbage bag. Only his leather jacket he spared, and his belt, which seemed untouched.

He was naked. His wounds suddenly throbbed again. His throat was a bright pink, and one side of his head was tender to the touch. He tightly tied the bag, shoved it underneath the kitchen sink and began to clean his jacket. By the time he was satisfied he had removed every trace of dirt and blood, the leather was dripping wet. Helmut hung the jacket in his bedroom. Then he turned on the shower. The steamy water at first scalded his skin. But then it soothed him. One side of his head pulsed as if an embedded worm ached to escape. The water sluiced over the wounds on his knee, cleansing him. Helmut found flaps of torn skin and pulled them off, wincing. His back ached, and he wanted to stay under the water's onrush forever, but he had too much to do.

He dressed in jeans, a T-shirt and a brown sweater with frayed edges. He had to destroy the clothes in the bag. He couldn't just throw everything away. It was almost midnight. Frau Hopfgartner had probably called the police already. They might be searching for the professor at that very moment. Helmut had no time to lose.

Helmut peered out his third-floor window. Nothing moved. He grabbed the plastic bag under the sink, threw in the stack of newspapers next to the door and ferreted out a matchbook from a vase full of matchbooks in his bedroom. On Pearl Street, he looked like a criminal Santa Claus who had been reclaiming his gifts.

He crossed State Street and found a near-empty trash barrel underneath the I-91 overpass. He wadded up several sheets of newspaper, lit one and dropped it into the barrel. The lip of the barrel glowed softly with the fire inside. He fed more newspapers into it, let them burn hot and then dropped in his shirt, which burned cleanly, his underwear and socks, and finally his pants, which almost suffocated the flames. Finally, he dropped his shoes into the blaze.

As Helmut stood watching the fire, a lone figure walked toward him from the overpass shadows. A black man, an old vagrant who offered him a swig from his whiskey bottle. Helmut declined politely. The two men stared into the barrel's firelight, their faces concentrated on it as if it were an oracle's vision of the future. Helmut thought about leaving, but he wasn't sleepy, and he felt safe there somehow. The old man told him, in a gravelly voice, that he was from New Orleans. He said it hadn't been a bad winter yet, that the cold was just good enough to keep a man on his toes, but not freeze him. He had tried living in society—the old man recounted, talking to himself and talking to Helmut—but society had thrown him out. There really wasn't any society at all, he continued. It was just nasty people, some with the mind to push you out, and others who didn't give a shit what you did.

After half an hour, Helmut started to leave, but stopped, found his wallet, and grabbed the bills inside. He gave them all to the old man. As soon as Helmut Sanchez disappeared into the shadows, he turned around and saw his companion with a branch fishing out the shoes from the bottom of the barrel. Who would care about those half-melted shoes anyway? The soles were still good and perhaps a bit toasty in the cold night air.

Chapter Fifteen

Regina Neumann had always loved the serenity of her red-brick house, which sat on St. Ronan, a quiet, tree-lined street of affluent homes that belonged to lawyers and businessmen, and a few lucky senior professors. Hers was the smallest house on the block, surrounded by high, thick evergreens trimmed into perfect rectangles by an old gardener who spoke only Spanish. She didn't know her neighbors, and only the gardener interacted with them, and he had been instructed to say only a Yale professor lived in the house. But that was all. She was content to be a recluse. She didn't bother anyone, and she didn't want anyone to bother her, and her yard and garden were just about the best on the block.

Inside the house every morning, the sun streamed into the bedroom on the second floor. It struck the varnished wooden floors and reflected on the glass doors of the bookshelf next to the bed. Inside her bookshelf were rare first editions in English, German, French and Spanish, mostly poetry, but also a few novels, and even two rare manuscripts purchased at an auction in London. A small Japanese alarm clock was next to her bed, but no radio or television was nearby. In fact, her house did not have a TV set. The four walls of the spacious living room were lined with books, journals, literary reviews and several bound collections of rare newspapers and magazines. The house itself was always warm despite the bitter cold outside. Invisible infra-red beams criss-crossed the first floor. Any interruption of the beams would trigger an ear-splitting alarm immediately notifying a private security service and the police. The alarm system could only be turned off from the second floor, if she was waking up, or from inside the garage, if she was coming home. On every first floor window, and perfectly parallel to it, was a small blue sticker from the First Federal Security Company. The on-light of the second-floor alarm panel pulsed without interruption like a tiny red star.

Under the blue down comforter, Regina Neumann lay warm and naked. In the morning light, her face seemed more ephemeral than ever, like glistening mist. Although her eyelids were shut, you could almost see the outline of her black coal eyes through her gauzy skin. The phone rang, and those eyes popped open, immediately looking fierce.

"Hello."

"Professor Neumann, hello. This is Ariane, from the department office."

"Ariane. Give me just one second," Neumann said and put the cordless phone down and rubbed her face. She stood up and put on a thick, red robe and picked up the phone again and walked to the alarm panel in the hallway. She punched in the code. She glanced at the grandfather clock in the hallway. It was a few minutes past 9:00 a.m.

"Okay. Please go ahead," she said.

"I'm sorry to bother you at home, Professor Neumann, but I have some, well, terrible news. Professor Hopfgartner was murdered last night, on Whitney Avenue."

"*What?*"

"Mrs. Hopfgartner called me this morning. I'm calling the senior faculty first, whoever is still in New Haven. I've left messages for Professor Otto at the conference in Berlin."

"Werner Hopfgartner is *dead?*" Neumann gasped. Her heart fluttered inside her chest. She sat down on her bed.

"Yes. It's horrible. It happened on Whitney Avenue. A robbery. The police have already been asking questions."

"I, I don't, I'm *stunned*, Ariane. That's unbelievable! Thank you very much for calling me. You say it happened *last night?* You mean, after the faculty meeting?"

"Yes, I think so. He was walking home."

"That's simply astonishing! Please call me if you need anything. I'll be at home most of the day. My goodness, that is terrible news."

"Okay. Goodbye."

As soon as the phone's red light turned off, Regina Neumann shrieked like a bobcat. She dashed downstairs and into the kitchen, grabbed a steak knife and rushed into the living room. She found Werner Hopfgartner's book on Goethe. She opened it, took the knife in one tremulous hand and began to slice out page after page until the floor was littered with paper. When she stabbed the near-empty binding, the knife wrenched free and cut her robe, just missing her ribs. She dropped the knife, and her tears gushed out. The fucked-up piece of shit—she mourned to the heavens—had gotten away with everything!

In the world revolving around the Yale campus, the news had spread like a new atmosphere. In Harkness Hall, Ariane Sassolini was barely in control of her emotions. She had reached the senior faculty who were still in New Haven. Victor Otto had called back from Berlin and said he would notify everyone there. The president's office had instructed her to refer all inquiries from reporters to them. Under no circumstances was she to give any details to the media.

A few minutes before 11:00 a.m., Helmut walked into the office. Ariane jumped into his arms and told him in gasps what had happened to Professor Hopfgartner. Tears streamed down her face. She was terrified, and he hugged her so she would not collapse on the floor. Finally, he staggered to an empty chair and slumped into it as if he had been shot. Helmut felt crushed by this pain around him. For a moment he felt sick to his stomach about what he had done. One thought overwhelmed him. Not that he had caused random or abstract pain, but her pain and her anguish. Ariane's grief seemed unbearable, and that was what made his eyes well up with tears.

Ariane told him Frau Hopfgartner had, at first, seemed remarkably composed, even cold, when she had informed the office early that morning. But later, one of Werner Hopfgartner's neighbors was at the house, a professor from the School of Architecture. He called the German department, too. Ariane asked him about Mrs. Hopfgartner, and he said she was resting. The professor had already phoned the three Hopfgartner children, none of whom lived on the East Coast. They were on their way to New York. The family doctor was there too, apparently sedating the poor woman. The police had stopped by to ask a few questions and said they'd return after Mrs. Hopfgartner had rested for a while.

Ariane and the other secretaries had been able to piece together this much: The professor had been murdered last night on Whitney Avenue; a jogger had discovered his body in the pre-dawn hours. Helmut felt cold. He sat down in a chair and buried his face in his arms. For a moment he thought he would black out. Ariane came over and rubbed his shoulders to comfort him. He heard her crying behind him. What on earth had he done?

After a few minutes, Helmut staggered back to his office. Not in front of Ariane's desperate eyes, he felt calmer, more rational. Why had he not stopped himself before he was trapped inside the shadows of Whitney Avenue? Why hadn't he walked away? Yet, after the fact, he felt little remorse for what he had done. He knew in his heart he had done the right thing. It did unnerve him to think of Werner Hopfgartner as suddenly a husband and a father and even a *victim* of murder. Helmut had never expected to feel anything for the old man. Last night, he had at first felt only a rage inside him, and then a fear of what he was about to do. At the last moment, he had been overcome by weakness, by these incessant waves about who he was and who he was not. The night had unfolded as a series of unexpected catastrophes. As Hopfgartner choked him, a wild and desperate anger had consumed Helmut, an anger not to pass out, an anger not to give up, a rage not to allow a repeat of Anja Litvak's murder. But now after the deed was done, the morality of his act seemed murkier, even questionable. What had he done?

How could he ever reveal his secret to Ariane? Helmut asked himself. He loved her with all his heart. How could he shatter her, and his own self, by telling her about his murderous act? He sensed a dreadful pall over his life. What, dear God, had he done? He clicked on his computer, retrieved the files of the Compilation and the sequel to the Compilation. What was the point of working on these lies now? Did he even have a job anymore? He had killed his own boss!

Helmut replayed the events of the night before. Had he overlooked any detail that could lead back to him? The police might even question him about his relationship with Werner Hopfgartner. They would no doubt question the professors who had been at the faculty meeting. No one from the department had seen him.

What would he say if the police interrogated him? Would his face betray his guilt? More than anything else, he had to act like someone in shock, fearful. How could he pretend not to know when his head exploded with every detail from last night, with every reason behind it?

That morning he wanted only one thing: to keep existing. Nothing else mattered. He wanted to let the world carry him along for a while. He wanted time to pass. He wanted to be far away from what he had done.

The phone rang. It was Jonathan Atwater. He had just heard the news. Incredibly enough, Mr. Atwater was even more distraught than Ariane. Helmut offered to have lunch with him, and then asked if Ariane could join them.

"Of course," Mr. Atwater gushed. "My God, of course! We need each other now." Helmut called Ariane, who thought lunch with Mr. Atwater was a good idea. She had received more calls from the president's office. A memorial service for Professor Hopfgartner would be scheduled after the Christmas holidays.

Helmut introduced Ariane to Mr. Atwater and then clasped her hand as they walked briskly down College Street to Claire's Cornucopia. Mr. Atwater and Ariane were chatting about Professor Hopfgartner and the details of the morning's disastrous news. Helmut stared at them, amazed at their easy rapport. Why was he the one who searched obsessively for a reality behind every face and every surface?

The restaurant was nearly empty. The bone-chilling cold had probably kept most Yalies inside.

They sat down next to the windows facing the Taft Hotel. Mr. Atwater's mood was gloomy and disturbed. Ariane told him what she knew about the murder. The librarian's face turned white. For a second, Helmut thought Jonathan Atwater might faint. He seemed stricken to the core. Helmut asked him, gently, how well he had known the professor. What Mr. Atwater revealed, first in bits and pieces, then in an emotional outpouring, was remarkable.

"Oh, dear Lord, where should I begin? I met Werner Hopfgartner at a Heidegger symposium about five years ago," Mr. Atwater said. "But that's not really the beginning, my dear Helmut. I had seen him in the library before. Werner came to the reading room on Fridays. A handsome man, mysterious. Don't remember exactly what caught my eye. . . . You know what it was? Oh, this sounds so superficial. Promise you'll forgive me?"

Helmut said they would.

"His birthmark, right over his lip. Just like my mother's birthmark," he said. "But Werner never talked to anybody in the library. That's so infuriating to me! These eggheads are like ghosts! He'd sit in his corner and read European newspapers. After a while, he'd eat a granola bar. Like a squirrel. Once I almost told him he wasn't supposed to eat in the library, but I stopped myself. Why should I be the library policeman? He wasn't bothering anyone and he was most certainly neat. I'm a compulsive Felix myself.

"Our paths truly crossed at the Heidegger symposium. These lectures are so exciting. You hear people from all around the world. I asked a question—I've read some Heidegger—but I don't know that much. This claptrap about being-in-the-world makes me dizzy. But I thought the speaker was being too hard on poor Heidegger. The fellow struck me as an arrogant dolt. He was French. Need I say more? I asked him why he was connecting Heidegger's flirtation with Nazism to his political philosophy. I'd just been to "Amadeus"—wasn't that F. Murray Abraham *fantastic?*—and in my mind, the point of it was that despicable people often create wonderful things. Why should we attack the great music or literature or theory of a worm because he was a worm? I didn't put it quite like that. But the French professor answered with a flourish I didn't understand. Werner Hopfgartner asked the next question and, like a bulldog, wouldn't let the French bastard waltz free! Werner was terrific! Much more sophisticated and precise than I ever could be. It was a wonder to watch him press Mr. Europa with points about 'the nature of philosophical truth' and its flying free of its originator to stand on its own. It was truly exciting. They went at it for a while, quoting arguments and philosophers as if they were flinging arrows at each other.

"Anyway, after the lecture, I was picking at my chicken salad in front of the buffet table at the Whitney Humanities Center. Werner came over and introduced himself. Oh, I tell you, I was *shocked!* Absolutely shocked he would even notice me. He told me I had asked an 'excellent' question, which had not really been answered. We sat together on the stone staircase, munching on our food. I was trying not to say anything too stupid. Why ruin his good impression of me?

"I saw Werner again at Sterling, in front of the copy machines. He was marching down the hallway. And he remembered me! I tell you, I was thrilled! *Now* he would say hello. We first had lunch together. Very first time *I* asked him out, when I spotted him on Wall Street. You know what the best part was?"

Ariane shook her head, almost in a trance. Helmut rubbed his forehead and glanced around nervously. "Werner *never* treated me like a child. It's true. I'm not a graduate student, a professor, nor even an undergraduate. I work in the libraries, for God's sake! I read because I *love* to read, not because I'm trying to parrot some mentor.

"Werner would tell me about the latest works on German Romanticism and the critique of Deconstruction. He *hated* Deconstruction. It was literary anarchy to him. I loved his stories. He'd tell me about the real personalities behind these critics. He knew most of them. It was simply grand for me! My personal lecture over lunch. He never became annoyed with me, even when I asked the stupidest questions. He'd bring me books of exciting new German writers and poets whenever he went overseas for a lecture. Soon I started stopping by his office. One thing led to another. Oh, it happened so fast! You know how it is, my dear. Soon we were deeply in love."

Helmut turned to Ariane and gulped. She reached across the table and clasped Jonathan Atwater's hand.

"We got along so well," he said. "We'd spend hours talking about books, art, politics, opinions. Nonstop. Suddenly we'd realize it was late, time to go home. Oh, it seems like a dream now. Maybe I make everything into a dream, with time. We couldn't be without each other for more than a few days. Like teenagers! It was ridiculous. We attended foreign film festivals in Manhattan, hiked up Sleeping Giant State Park. On different weekends, we drove to Bar Harbor, Northhampton and Gloucester, to explore old bookshops and antique stores.

"But you know, my dear, it wasn't a dream at all. There were awful things too," Jonathan continued, his gaze transfixed on the New Haven green. "I, I don't know if I should talk about this now. But it's true! He always said, 'Never run away from the *truth!*' Werner had a bad temper. He wasn't an easy man to be with. God, I don't know how I let it happen! Maybe I was just blind, I don't know. You lose perspective. You forget what's right and wrong. You become confused. Werner would explode with rage," he whispered, tears in his eyes. "He'd hit me, he wouldn't mean to do it, I know that in my heart. But sometimes he'd hurt me. God, was I an idiot? I don't know what I was thinking. But I *loved* him! I know that. I loved his intellect, his wit. I loved him because when he was happy and inquisitive he filled my soul with absolute joy. That's also the truth! I don't want you to have the wrong impression of him. At one point, he hadn't had an outburst for months. We started talking about being together permanently. He was nearing retirement. I told him we could move to Boston, to Pembroke Street. I have many friends in that neighborhood. Werner said he couldn't leave his wife. Of course, he didn't love her, but he still couldn't abandon her in New Haven. He felt guilty for dragging her here, from her precious Vienna. But later Werner seemed to be changing his mind. Maybe he finally got sick of these dreary streets. We would argue about it constantly. I finally challenged him. Why was he caving in to the expectations of society,

his children, his colleagues at Yale? Was that the *truth*? Who cared
about what he did after retirement? He'd still receive his Yale
checks in the mail. Thank goodness it's not yet illegal to be gay in
the Ivy League!"

Jonathan Atwater wiped his eyes, took a deep breath and finished his story.

"We were so close to escaping. We almost made it out. Then,
disaster! I don't know what happened. He said he didn't want to
see me anymore, didn't even want to talk to me. I imagined it was
someone else. Oh, it seemed so final! I deserved an explanation.
The best two and a half years of my life were ending in a nightmare. And from him, nothing. Suddenly I was a leper! Finally I
went to his office. I wanted an explanation. He told me to calm
down. He told me to stop screaming at him, that he would explain
everything. He could hardly look me in the eyes! He was hurting
too! I told him I would leave him alone as soon as he gave me an
explanation. I just wanted the truth. Sure, we had had fights. But
we always worked them out. We were on the verge of leaving for
Boston! Then he told me. That miserable bitch! His wife had
found out. She had always known his many 'conferences' and 'lectures' were nothing more than escapes with his latest mistress.
Werner had been cheating on her for years! This mean creature.
Werner hadn't touched her for aeons. She hated him for bringing
her to New Haven. She blamed him for destroying her life in Vienna. She had accepted his 'disgusting animalism' or overlooked it
or resigned herself to it, I don't know. She had overlooked his
affairs as long as they were unimportant. How can love be unimportant? She'd compare Werner to their German shepherd in heat.
She'd say he was like the dog humping the cast iron stable boy
next to the front door. What a witch!

"But Frau Hopfgartner became suspicious. About *me*! She had
absolutely no idea. She must've noticed something different this
time around. Werner was spending too much time with his latest
'mistress' and she knew it. Werner was falling in love. Oh God,
how cursed love is! One weekend, she followed us to Northhampton. She finally saw my face. She found a hotel room, spied

on our 'wanton immorality,' she was aghast to see her husband happy and affectionate with a homosexual.

"'My Lord! What kind of degradation is this!' she screamed at Werner when he returned to Hamden. She demanded he cut off all ties with me immediately. She threatened to obliterate his life. How was she going to ruin him? Werner never told me. But I understood it was something so utterly important, beyond simply cheating on her or being bisexual. It scared Werner to pieces. I'd never seen him like that. It was an impenetrable wall. Werner would not give me one clue. He just told me it was over. He told me to leave him alone, to please leave him alone or I would cause him incalculable pain. It frightened me! What could I do? I loved him, so I left.

"This happened about two years ago," Jonathan said, his chest heaving, still in tears. "Ever since that day, I have never been whole."

Ariane scooted her chair next to Mr. Atwater and hugged him. Helmut covered his face with his hands and closed his eyes. The world was spinning out of control.

Chapter Sixteen

At 4:00 p.m., a detective from the New Haven Police Department walked into the German department to ask a few questions. Mainly he was interested in reconstructing the professor's last day. Ariane told him about the scheduled faculty meeting and gave him a list of the professors who had attended the meeting, plus their phone numbers. She told him that many had immediately left for a conference in Berlin, and gave him the hotel's phone number, too.

Ariane asked the detective if he knew what had happened. He said the investigation was just beginning. The coroner, he told her, was working on the body to discover important details about the fatal injuries. In the detective's opinion, a mugger had murdered Werner Hopfgartner, knifing him during the struggle. During their search of the area, the police had found Hopfgartner's wallet in a trash can, minus any money or credit cards. It looked like a case of being in the wrong place at the wrong time.

Before leaving, the detective asked the secretaries why Werner Hopfgartner was walking the dangerous streets of New Haven in the middle of the night. Wasn't that odd? The professor, Ariane explained, had this long-standing habit of walking home, even in the worst weather. Hiking the paths of the *Wienerwald*, they called it around the office. Many other professors also walked home, but they lived only about a mile away. The detective thanked her, and said he might be back for more information.

In his apartment, Helmut paced nervously after coming home from work that night. He opened the cabinets underneath the sink to reassure himself that no traces remained from the night before. His reality had to be reality itself. He had to remember what he had actually done, not what he wished he had done. As soon as his eyes did not gaze upon what he affirmed in his head, doubt would seep into his mind. Was blood smeared in some remote corner of his apartment? Had the credit cards not been buried deep enough? Perhaps his clothing hadn't burned completely and could be traced back to him. What thousands of possibilities! Helmut imagined. He tried to calm himself. He sat down and drank a cup of Red Zinger.

How could he absolutely be certain he had done everything right? He had to retrace his steps. It would be preposterous—suicidal—to return to the scene of the crime. It was too late to correct anything there. But what if he had missed some detail afterwards? Should he assume the mental picture of what he had done that night was correct? He had to check reality with real-time sight. His mind would certainly fool him. It had uncannily possessed him before, when he had found himself in the shadows of Whitney about to do what he could not do. And yet, the deed had still been done.

Helmut picked up the leather jacket. He examined it inch by inch under the light of his desk lamp, holding a wet paper napkin in case he discovered a speck of blood. But the leather was absolutely clean. Helmut stared at the napkin. The bloodied napkins from the night before were still at the bottom of the wastebasket! How many more of these mistakes were strewn behind him like arrows pointed at his back? He lifted the plastic garbage bag out, removed every bit of junk mail with his name on it, and tied up the bag tightly. Helmut dumped his own garbage in a trash can in the alley, and disposed of the garbage bag with the bloodied napkins about two blocks away, in a Dumpster behind the Belnord Apartments.

He walked down Pearl Street and bought a submarine sandwich. He wasn't going to sit in his room and worry. Outside, he could replay the places and events of the previous night. He might uncover more mistakes. The whole episode had been a ghastly mistake! he thought. But if he discovered a small, important blunder and couldn't fix it, at least he might anticipate how to respond to it if somebody else discovered it too. When he got home he would also clean his apartment from top to bottom. Then he'd bike to Ariane's for their twelve days of Christmas vacation together. His apartment would be immaculate; every corner and crevice would be scrubbed clean. Yes, he was probably okay. He was probably safe.

He had one last errand to do. Had anyone noticed the rings around his eyes? No one had said anything. He thought about poor Jonathan Atwater. Helmut had never intended to cause him so much pain. How could Jonathan not have seen the evil in the old man? Certainly Frau Hopfgartner had known about it. This must've been how she had kept her husband shackled to her side.

Up ahead, Helmut saw the cavernous darkness underneath the I-91 overpass on Humphrey Street. On the slope rising from the road up to the overpass, he focused on a cardboard box with 'Whirlpool' printed on its side. The box walls jiggled; something had moved inside it. Not a soul was on Humphrey or State Street. Traffic on I-91 droned overhead.

Helmut walked up the slope to the cardboard box. He realized he didn't know the old Cajun's name. "Hey, New Orleans!" Helmut yelled. The old man stuck his head out of the refrigerator box. He said hello politely enough, but he still sounded wary. Helmut said he had been there to warm himself by the barrel fire the night before.

"I brought you something to eat. If you want it."

"Shit, yeah," the old man grumbled.

Helmut held out the submarine sandwich in a paper bag. In the darkness, a hand took the bag from his grasp. The fingers felt rough and gnarled, like an old claw. Helmut heard paper rustle. He asked how he had been. No answer. Helmut was about to leave when he heard a grunt and the paper bag being folded and fussed with.

"You a Yalie?"

Helmut said he wasn't. He just worked for Yale.

"Good. 'Cause Yalies turn my stomach. Been over here trying to tell me what to do. Think they own you just 'cause they feed you."

Helmut said he didn't care what New Orleans did. He wasn't a politician.

"Liberals and conservatives," the old man snorted. "They're all a bunch of bastards. Wished the Man would just end it all and burn every living sucker in Hades."

Helmut asked him what the Yalies had done to him.

"Shit, don't get me started down that road. Won't get a good night's sleep, I'll be so agitated. They come up here every so often, pushing a needle in my face. What the hell! Don't do drugs. Just whiskey goddamnit. Want to be left alone. One of 'em gave me a condom. Wish I had a use for it. Ain't had me a woman in years. Damn Yale bastards. Don't know the first thing about you. Don't know the first thing about shit. Ain't the worst of it. I'll tell you a story, young man.

"Used to be living by Whalley Avenue. Near the Holiday Inn. Had my own place in an alley. Shared it with a friend of mine. We were good buddies even though he was a Yankee from Boston. Didn't mind him at all. We shared food and whiskey and beer and didn't bother each other at all. If he found something good, he told me. Did the same. But the damn best part was nobody messed with us. Warehouse chief knew we were sleeping in the alley, but he didn't care. Said hello and even gave us new boxes every couple months, with flaps and steel wiring on the outside, long as we didn't cause any trouble. And we never did. Even told him when two kids had been scoping out the place. No trouble at all. It was nice."

Helmut said it sounded like a good place.

"Didn't stay that way," the old vagrant said. "No sir. Was them Yale bastards that ruined it for Hoagie and me.

"Hoag and me used to go to the soup kitchen at the church on Broadway. Their meat once gave me the runs, so I didn't eat it. Didn't much like anything but the bread and the fish soup and the apples. Good ol' Hoag used to eat everything on his plate. He had a steel bucket for a stomach. He liked going there. Went with him only when I was too hungry to sleep. Had other ways of getting food. Yale's just a food machine if you know where to look. Hoag and me went to the church. It'd been getting warm for a while and I hadn't been for a couple of weeks. Hoag kept yammering about a kid at the soup kitchen. Kid wanted to *study* ol' Hoag and he acted like the kid had asked him to move in with him. Hoagie was a sure-fire sap and as soon as anyone was kind to him he'd get all stupid."

Helmut asked what kind of study the student wanted to do on his friend.

"Damned if I know. All Yale ever does is study us, or feel big for feeling sorry for us. Don't need that shit. Kept being told the North's more enlightened than goddamn Dixie. Poor black folks supposedly had it better up here. Shit if they do. Been here over ten years now, up to Boston and down to New York City. Know what I've seen? Mama-suck. They treat you like Mama-suck. Like you know nothing about nothing. Like a man can't or won't do for himself. They expect you to be a little nothing shit so they can be big. Sorry feelings never did it for me. Just a different way of putting you down 'cause you're a nigger. That's all it is. Damn Hoagie fell for it and look where it got him."

Helmut asked New Orleans what happened to Hoag.

"Done arrested him and beat the crap out of him. Hoag and me went to one of them castles at Yale. Kid wanted to do an *interview* with ol' Hoag and he asked me to come with him 'cause he didn't really know Yale. Like an idiot, I went. Went up to where the kid told us to meet him. Went and waited in a corner where no one would see us, inside the gates and next to bicycles rusted up and mangled. We'd see other Yalies, eating and laughing and carrying on. But no kid. Waited and waited 'til it was dark and I got tired and told Hoag I wasn't about to wait anymore. Hoagie said he'd take a look around.

"I waited for Hoag. Took a leak and thought I could still get myself some scraps from the Dumpster behind the big white castle next to the cemetery. Fucking Hoag. I was getting real pissed at him. Then I saw the police. Saw students running and yelling. Somebody crying. Couldn't see much 'cause it was dark. But I heard 'em drag out Hoagie. Heard him screaming that he was looking for somebody, that he hadn't touched her. 'Interview! Ain't been interviewed, you Christ-fuck!' Damned if I didn't hear them

kids laughing at Hoagie. I got the hell out of there. The next day
Ralphie The Snake asked me what party Hoag and I had been to.
Told him I didn't know what he was yammering about. Told me he
had found old Hoag by the railroad tracks next to the coliseum.
Moaning and in pretty bad shape. I went looking for him. Never
found him. Never came back to the warehouse, either. And after
some bastards broke into it, manager said I had to get out of the
alley. Said he was taking too much heat about it. Said he was sorry.
I didn't mind his I'm-sorry. I knew he was."

Helmut tried to make out the old man in the shadows. He told
New Orleans about his father's death in Germany, about how
much he missed him although he had never really known him.
Helmut told him about his mother in New Mexico, and about how
he didn't like New Haven and wanted to leave it soon. New
Orleans said he didn't blame him. What was Helmut waiting for?

"No need to wait to be happy if your family wants you," New
Orleans said. His family had run him out of Louisiana. His broth-
er-in-law and his uncle, the preacher, wanted to kill him for phi-
landering and propagating his seed and slapping his woman.

"Leave before your heart's dead as wood," the old man continued. "This town's a deathtrap."

"I will. But certain things are keeping me here."

"What kind of things? A woman?"

"Yes, my girlfriend."

"Is it love?" New Orleans asked. "'Cause if it's love, might be
worth staying until you can take her with you."

"I don't know what love is."

New Orleans chortled and coughed so loudly Helmut thought
the old man would choke. Then he gurgled and made a sound like
a muffled backfire, and a big ball of phlegm splashed onto the hard
ground.

After New Orleans settled down, he told Helmut he was most
likely in love.

"Love's the kind of thing you know you don't have when you
don't have it. But when you have it, well, you won't *admit* it. It's
that kind of powerful thing, love is. When you have it, it has you.
That's the best, but most terrifyin' part," New Orleans said. Before

he met his wife, he had also been in love. He still remembered this woman's face, the softness of her skin, the way she would twirl herself around him like a whirlwind. New Orleans said he couldn't tell him what love was, but only that he once had it, and he had lost it, and lost her, because he had been afraid of it, afraid it would somehow emasculate him. And he had been dead wrong. Since this time, he had been trying to find again "a kind of living on earth in complete glory." But he never found it with his wife. Nor with any other woman. Not in Louisiana. Certainly not in New Haven. And probably not ever again. So if he had found love, the best thing was to grab hold of her and ignore the witless part of his manhood. Helmut might not ever get a second chance.

The old man thanked him for the sandwich and the company, and Helmut said goodbye to his Father Confessor. Helmut walked home, thinking about New Orleans asleep in his Whirlpool box. How do you sleep in a Whirlpool box? How do you sleep when you're hungry? How do you sleep when you're haunted by what you have done?

Chapter Seventeen

Jack Rosselli slammed the phone down and roared to no one in particular, "Doesn't anyone speak English anymore? Goddammit!" Another detective, flipping through a file across the room, glanced up and grinned at the burly, middle-aged man. Rosselli's thick, brown hair was graying at the temples. He studied the file on the murder of a Salvadoran couple by a gang of blacks shouting "Kill the crackers! They're stealing our jobs! No justice, no peace!" One victim had been a dishwasher at a Mexican restaurant on State Street for six years, seven days a week, fifteen hours a day.

Juan Samaniego had been granted political asylum in the United States although he had lied about having been pursued by 'death squads' in San Salvador. In fact, Samaniego's house in Quetzaltepeque had once been mistakenly peppered with bullets by a roving band of yahoos who thought it their birthright to torment their rivals. Juan and his wife, Clarita, fled El Salvador and its culture of random violence. But unfortunately, in the United States, they crossed paths with another gang and another violent society.

The months before, Detective Rosselli had heard about a clandestine group from Hartford, Connecticut. They took bats to workers at construction sites and other businesses that lacked the "proper" proportion of African Americans. The rapid, smash raids had left two people dead, several with broken arms or legs, and one man had suffered a spinal injury. The authorities got a break when one gang member defected and agreed to be a mole. "Martin" was a Southern Baptist who had been appalled by the violence

147

and the increasingly random attacks against those having nothing to do with racial discrimination.

The mole had recently revealed the organization's plan to attack other minorities believed to be responsible for keeping blacks in oppressive conditions. Mexican Americans, Koreans, Vietnamese, Puerto Ricans, Guatemalans. So maybe the murder of the Salvadoran couple was linked to the Hartford group. But there was just one problem. No one could—or would— identify the members of the gang. The closest eye-witnesses were a young mother and a grandmother who lived across the street from the Samaniego residence. They told police they had heard gunshots, then seen three, maybe four, black men bolt out the apartment's front door.

The police canvassed the area for other witnesses, but discovered no reliable information. No one had heard or seen anything at all. The apartment had been ransacked; the television kicked in. Clothes were strewn everywhere, as if the hooligans had been searching for something in particular. Money and jewelry were missing, but it didn't appear the Samaniegos had had that much to begin with.

Rosselli had tried to call a Salvadoran refugee center in New Haven. The woman who answered the phone said, "*Ahorita viene el jefe de comer.*" A big waste of time.

He still had to check out Juan Samaniego's place of work. Maybe someone there could give him a piece of useful information. Didn't anyone give a damn anymore? Maybe he could get Frankie Rodriguez to take over this idiotic case. At least Frankie could call the damn refugee center and use his broken Spanglish. Jack Rosselli only knew '*mañana*' and '*chingada.*' Anyway, Frankie owed him big for the Cowboys-Giants game.

A secretary dropped a manila folder in his in-box. He frowned at her and then winked. It was the dead professor's preliminary autopsy report. Rosselli wondered whether and why the old guy had fought back.

Show one ounce of disrespect to a mugger and you're dead, Rosselli thought. Give him a bad look. Bingo. The professor probably understood only the never-never land of Yale. Maybe the old guy didn't know the language of the streets. The right and wrong looks. The movements. The absolutely wrong thing to do. Never fight back. They hated it when you fought back. They hated when a victim told them, in words or looks, that he was better than they were, that a gun in the face made him angry, not pliant. Fuck morality, should and shouldn't. The only thing that mattered was who was on the wrong side of the gun or knife, and who wasn't. The power of hate. The power behind hate. The power to hate. The punks on the street thought: If I can kill you, I can own you. They never taught that at Yale, Rosselli imagined. The muck of raw life. It was worse than the wild kingdom, because on the streets they didn't always kill you to eat you. Sometimes they just wanted you dead. Period. Why? Who knew? It was society. It was people who found out they could win at certain murderous games. Rosselli was just there to do his job. His game was to find them and stop them.

He read a certain section of the report over and over. It was a description of the angle of the two wounds, their approximate size and nature, and the damage caused by them. One wound had pierced the heart and part of the left lung. The angle of this wound was about forty-five degrees, if the professor had been standing straight at the point of attack. The wound was jagged and by itself would have eventually been fatal. This was probably the first wound; it caused a shock reaction as soon as the knife went in. An instinctual lurch that only helped the blade cut enough of the tissue and arteries near the heart to cause massive internal bleeding. The second wound was almost exactly perpendicular to the line of the body. Cleaner and deeper than Wound A. The coroner suspected, and Rosselli agreed, that Wound B occurred after Wound A. The professor was probably not moving much at the time of this second attack. Because of the clean entry and exit of this wound, right into the abdomen, deflecting off the spinal cord, and slipping out through the back, this wound suggested the body was braced against a hard surface. No convulsive lurch forward or backward had "dirtied" this trajectory. The professor was probably on the ground at that point, right where he was found in the morning. That second thrust had been the *coup de grace*, for insur-

ance and out of pure malice. The coroner had discovered metallic
fragments embedded in the spinal cord, which might give them a
better idea of the make or composition of the blade.

Rosselli had already found something interesting about the
murder weapon. The width of the knife was estimated to be
between one and a half and two inches. The length about nine to
ten inches. Jesus. This part of the coroner's report only confirmed
what Jack Rosselli had suspected when the New Haven police conducted its initial investigation of the crime scene. On Whitney
Avenue, Rosselli had examined the wounds and immediately
noticed their size. For knife wounds—and he had seen hundreds
of varying shapes and sizes during his twelve years as a regular
cop and ten years as a homicide detective—the professor's wounds
were on the large side.

At the scene, Rosselli had thought that maybe after the professor had been stabbed a struggle had enlarged the entry points
and distorted the external perspective. He had hoped the coroner
would give him more definitive conclusions. His first suspicions
had been absolutely correct. One-and-a-half to two inches wide.
Nine to ten inches long. This matched the rough average ratio of
length to width of the knives he had read about, and what he had
experienced in the field. His quick and dirty numbers had been
right on the money, almost too perfect. His own calculations at the
scene, although he had at first hesitated to believe them, had the
length of the knife to be no less than eight inches and probably
not more than ten inches. Now he had no doubt at all. Hopfgartner's killer had used a huge knife. A butcher knife. And that cast
doubt on another of Rosselli's original suspicions: that the killer
was a local thief who robbed Yalies reckless enough to walk home
almost three miles in the dark.

The report gave him another piece of information: Werner
Hopfgartner had died sometime between ten and midnight.

So the old guy had been stabbed twice with a damn butcher
knife, or something the size and heft of a butcher knife. Yet it was
rare for knife attacks to involve such a large weapon, unless they
were family disputes where someone might grab a weapon out of
a kitchen drawer. Professional thugs and other young assholes

almost never carried butcher knives. They usually preferred all manner of switchblades, sufficient to do the job and easy to hide on their bodies. A butcher knife would be for the deranged, the familial, the amateurish. So the probable size of the knife undermined the theory that this crime had been a routine mugging gone fatally awry.

Which left the question: Who'd want to stab the old guy?

Rosselli kept coming back to the second wound. If it had been robbery, the bad guy would have taken off as soon as he nailed the old man with the first blow, and removed his wallet. According to the coroner, the professor was in no shape to put up much of a fight after it. So there must've been a *reason* for that second, horrifying stab. Either the attacker had really lost his temper with the professor, or he simply wanted him dead, and that was the point. Of course, the second blow might have been to avoid being fingered by the old man, in case he survived. But Rosselli didn't think so. Over the last decade of urban crime in New Haven, he had learned that most street criminals weren't careful or farsighted enough to eliminate their victims just to avoid being caught. If they killed somebody they were robbing, it was because of a flash of psychotic anger, or because they despised the class or race of the victim, or because this wasn't a mugging in the first place, but a killing, with a convenient opportunity to use a human ATM.

Scratch marks had also been found on the professor's neck. The wounds from an attack from behind? A lunge for the wallet as the professor resisted? DNA tests were being conducted on the neck, the torso and the clothes of the victim, for any traces from the killer. But unless Rosselli was damn lucky and the killer not only had been arrested before but also had his DNA stored in a databank, this information would lead nowhere. The Good Samaritan jogger had also performed CPR on the old man, so the jogger's DNA was also in the mix.

Then there was the issue of the wallet. It had been found in a trash can at East Rock Park. To Rosselli, this indicated several things. The perpetrator of the crime had walked (run? driven?) from Whitney Avenue near Blake Road, where the professor was found, to East Rock Park. Probably down Whitney Avenue, crossing left on East Rock Road. So either the bad guy lived in the area near East Rock Park or he simply crossed near Wilbur Cross High School to someplace beyond. Could it have been a high school kid? Rosselli made a note to check reports of recent knifings at the school, to see if anything matched his murder weapon. But what kind of idiot would bring a butcher knife to school? Rosselli asked himself. Also, no prints other than those belonging to the professor had been found on the wallet. The money and credit cards were gone. Only one distinguishable footprint had been found near the body. A footprint in blood. But nothing else pointed to a particular suspect. Maybe the punk would eventually use the credit cards at Home Depot or Wal-Mart and so be identified. But the detective didn't think that was likely.

Within thirty-six hours of the killing, Rosselli had interviewed, via the international operator, almost everyone who had seen the professor at the faculty meeting. These professors had said much the same thing: It had been a routine meeting to discuss departmental business, and nothing unusual had happened. The professor had left the meeting at about 9:15 p.m. or 9:30 p.m. after a quick drink with his friends in the faculty lounge. The professor had departed alone. Rosselli had also already interviewed Mrs. Hopfgartner. She had said, in a plain and unemotional voice, that yes, her husband had mentioned he was coming home late that night because of a faculty meeting. These meetings, she said, usually meant her husband would miss dinner, arriving home as early as 9:00 p.m. and sometimes as late as midnight.

Rosselli asked only routine questions of Mrs. Hopfgartner, and indeed he received straightforward answers. Mrs. Hopfgartner was obviously upset by her husband's death, even distraught. But she also seemed cold in a way. Rosselli took that to mean the murder ended a relationship that had probably endured for years without affection. He had seen it before. He had also witnessed the chasm of a lover's grief.

So with all of this information, what was he left with? Already it was Friday, and next week would be Christmas, finally. Getting in touch with the professors hadn't been easy. The detective had a stack of other cases also demanding his attention. He was falling behind. Yet he also knew that unless he came up with something soon, the professor's case would quickly slip into the oblivion of unsolved crimes. The first two days of any case were crucial. Rosselli already didn't have a good feeling about this one.

The detective was left with these vague possibilities. An opportunistic thief—probably an amateur—had spotted the professor strolling on Whitney Avenue. He waited until the old guy was out of sight of traffic, and then nailed him. The professor did something to provoke his assailant, and ended up dead. The bad guy wanted the money and the credit cards, but not the briefcase, which was left next to the body. The perp had planned to nail someone that night, which was why he grabbed a butcher knife from home when he had begun his safari. No other crimes, not even a burglary, had been reported that night in the neighborhood.

Another scenario was possible, in Rosselli's mind. It was less probable than the first one. The crime had been not primarily a mugging but a killing. That led to the question of who wanted to kill Werner Hopfgartner. No doubt, it would have been someone the professor knew. Almost anything could incite that kind of rage. An office rivalry. The end of an affair. Rosselli knew the power politics at Yale were vicious. But he couldn't imagine another Yale professor committing this brutal crime.

He made appointments with two professors who had not attended the Berlin conference and who had also been at the faculty meeting: Michael Rittman and Regina Neumann.

Rosselli hung up the phone after talking to them. He was tired of making phone calls. There was no personal interaction, no reading between the lines, no little hint from a certain glance or inappropriate laugh about where to dig for relevant details. In most cases, almost everybody loved to talk about the victim. There was this strange fascination with being a part of an unresolved story. His job was to filter through the nonsense. But to do that, he needed to look people in the eye.

But Rosselli already had doubts about the second scenario. The professor was about to retire this year; the secretaries had told him that. Why would a professional rival kill him now? No, if this had been a killing, then it would've been a crime of *passion*. It could have been a graduate student angry about his or her ruined career. A jilted lover. Perhaps a secretary or one of the professor's minions. Maybe a jealous worshipper from the undergraduate ranks. To Detective Rosselli, those possibilities seemed far-fetched. They did, however, fit better with his idea that the criminal had been an amateur or a demented individual stalking the professor. Hadn't a physics graduate student walked into the departmental office at Yale two years ago and unloaded a 9mm Glock? A secretary and the student's dissertation adviser had been killed; an associate professor had been left a vegetable. So even the wildest scenes could unfold behind these walls of ivy.

There was one big problem with pursuing this second, less plausible line of inquiry: politics. Rosselli had no proof. If he was wrong and started to ask questions about the professor's enemies at Yale, he'd be responsible for encouraging the rumor that someone at Yale University had murdered Hopfgartner. The university possessed real power in New Haven. It was the city's biggest employer and landowner. Without Yale, New Haven would be another Bridgeport. Half the politicians in Connecticut had a Yale connection. The pressure from the chief of police and even the mayor would be incredible. They would ask him why was he hounding the good and prosperous citizens of Yale. What proof did he have? He definitely needed to be careful.

Rosselli decided to wait for the rest of the coroner's report. Other leads might trickle in. He'd recommend that the university offer a reward. Beyond that, he wasn't excited about pressing for a long shot. Rosselli wasn't stupid. If he were younger and ready to save the world, if his waistline were six inches smaller, if he didn't know how wild guesses usually turned out . . . he might go for it. But not now. He'd keep his appointments with these two professors. Maybe he'd go back to the secretaries and chat with them about office politics, quietly, without alarming anyone, just to satisfy his own conscience.

Chapter Eighteen

Rosselli went Friday morning to Professor Michael Rittman's office on the third floor of Harkness Hall. Hopfgartner had been murdered Wednesday night. Yale felt like a wintry medieval ghost town. The German department was still buzzing with activity, but the secretaries and assistants in the other departments had left for Christmas vacation. A few teaching assistants graded papers, or frantically wrote their own, in the closet-size, dust-filled cubicles beneath the eaves of Harkness Hall.

Rittman was a bearded man in his early forties, with wire glasses that looked tiny against his thick, protruding forehead and shock of black hair. He greeted Detective Rosselli with a meek smile.

"It was simply the last faculty meeting of the fall," Rittman said. "Very straightforward. We argued about who'd start the first review of the incoming graduate students. We voted on the visiting appointments for next year. Three of them. Maienfeld, one of the visiting professors, is one of Professor Hopfgartner's best friends. I still can't believe Werner's dead. What an absolute shock! He was like a father figure around here. Loved and hated."

Rosselli perked up. "Hated? People actually *hated* him?"

"Well . . . not universally. He had a few great allies too. That's just the way it is. You get together with your friends, mold the department in a certain way. You defeat your enemies and try to prevent them from gaining the upper hand. Over the past two or three years, Hopfgartner seemed less directly involved in these squabbles. Maybe he was just waiting to retire. He'd been at it for more than three decades. What a lousy way to go out."

"You don't seem too shook up about it."

"Well, I don't really know *how* to react. Maybe it'll hit me later. I thought he was a *great* professor. When I came into the department, I came because of him. He helped me find my way. I certainly would never have gotten tenure this early without his support. But he could be heartless if you turned against him. I also thought he was marking time. Maybe if he had retired a few years earlier, none of this would've happened."

"At the meeting, what did Professor Hopfgartner say?"

"He supported Maienfeld, that I remember. But not much else. He stayed around for a drink afterward. But that's about it."

"What kind of a mood was he in?" Rosselli asked.

"Mood? I don't think he was in any particular mood."

"He wasn't angry or depressed?"

"No."

"He didn't seem preoccupied with any problems?"

"Not really. It was rather a dull meeting. I had work the next day and I didn't notice anything out of the ordinary."

"What time did Hopfgartner leave the meeting? You remember that?"

"Well, I left at 9:40 p.m. I'd promised my wife I'd be home no later than ten. And I think Professor Hopfgartner left about half an hour earlier."

"No one left with him?"

"No."

"You said before some people hated him," Rosselli said, leaning forward. "Had anything important happened the last couple of days or weeks? Any political fights? Any disappointments or successes?"

"May I ask you a question first?" Rittman asked, suddenly intrigued. He stroked his beard carefully.

"Sure," Rosselli said, with a practiced smile on his face.

"Are you seriously considering the possibility that someone at Yale killed Hopfgartner?"

"Not really. But it might help to know everything about the professor."

"I mean, I thought he was killed by a mugger on Whitney. Isn't that what happened?"

"That's what probably happened. That's what our investigation has focused on as the most likely possibility. But I still need to look at every angle. I wouldn't be doing my job if I didn't. The more I know about the victim, the more I'll know if other possibilities are realistic too. Any information, even about personal matters, will be helpful. I can assure you, Professor Rittman, if it's not pertinent to the case, this conversation will remain strictly between you and me."

Rittman carefully thought about what he might say. He seemed to want to say it, whatever it was, and Rosselli would let him.

"Well, detective, where do I begin? Hopfgartner was known to be very 'popular' with certain undergraduates and graduate students."

"What do you mean?"

"He slept with them. Not many, but every once in a while. Don't misunderstand me, he was an excellent professor and a great scholar. That's probably what gave him the power to do it for so many years. That, and his political connections."

"Didn't anyone ever complain or try to stop him?"

"Werner was careful about it," Rittman said. "His relationships were consensual, or at least that's what I heard. He was clever. Never forced himself on anybody. I just know no student ever filed a complaint against him. I certainly didn't *like* the situation. But it was hard to do anything about it."

"You know the names of these students?"

"Only one. Sarah Goodman."

"What are you *not* telling me, professor?"

"Well, Sarah Goodman actually denies everything. But that's not important. She's just a graduate student trying to make her way through Yale. I don't know her very well. I've heard she works hard and is quiet in class. Several months ago, at the beginning of the semester, there was a 'confrontation.' I think that's probably the right word. Another professor, Professor Neumann, tried to get Sarah to accuse Hopfgartner of sexual harassment. At the last moment, Sarah denied everything. It saved us from an external

scandal, but it also created the most difficult months in this department in a long time. It was almost forgotten when this happened."
    "So Neumann was after Werner Hopfgartner?"
    "That's right. I think she just wanted the truth to come out
before Hopfgartner retired. I can't blame her, really."
    "Why do you call it a 'confrontation'?"
    "Listen," Rittman said, with a glimmer in his eyes.
    "What?"
    "Just listen. What do you hear?"
    "It's quiet. Like a library."
    "And that's what it's like most of the time," Rittman said.
"Once in a while, of course, there's a lively discussion in one of the
seminar rooms. Voices are raised. But they die down after a while.
And you certainly never hear blood-curdling screams of profanity
in these halls, at least not very often. But that's how Regina Neumann exploded after her meeting with Sarah Goodman and Victor
Otto, our chairman. The secretaries didn't have to gossip about it.
Everyone heard. It was simply astonishing. And from Professor
Neumann? I don't think she's recovered from it yet. I still hear
those disgusting words ringing in my ears."
    "I see. Is that it?"
    "Yes, that's it. But it's just an aside to his last months. I hon-
estly believe it's not important, at least not anymore."
    "Thank you very much, professor. I'll call you if I need any-
thing else."

    Rosselli decided it was better not to start poking around about
Regina Neumann yet. He had a meeting with her in less than two
hours, just before lunch. It was simultaneously wonderful and terrible luck. It could be everything, or nothing. He had to gather
more information before this appointment. If she did have something to do with Werner Hopfgartner's murder, it was better to
catch her by surprise, to know already what she did not expect
him to know. But a female assassin with a knife? And a Yale prof
to boot? That was highly unlikely, although not impossible.
Rosselli turned into the main office.

"Ariane, hi again," he said. "Where is everybody?" He slumped into a chair in front of the secretary's desk. He had about ninety minutes before the Neumann interview.

"One secretary left early for vacation. To Aruba. Don't know where the other one is this morning. It's been that kind of week."

"I'll bet. I need to check Professor Hopfgartner's office. Just routine."

She handed him a ring of keys. "The long one is the deadbolt. The other one opens the door handle." Ariane looked like she hadn't slept in weeks. Her eyes were bloodshot.

"I'll bring these back in a jiffy," Rosselli said.

"No problem."

"Oh, one quick question. Who knew Professor Hopfgartner really well? Who were his buddies?"

"I think Professor Otto was one of his good friends. But I don't think they were buddies. It's not like that around here. They got along. Hopfgartner wasn't very social. He never just hung around. After my boss, I'd say it was Helmut."

"You mentioned him before."

"Helmut Sanchez," Ariane said. "Professor Hopfgartner's research assistant. A friend of mine. Helmut saw him every day. Can't say he *liked* him—Werner Hopfgartner always gave him too much work—but I think Helmut knew him pretty well."

"Is he around today?"

"Sure, here's his number."

"I'll be right back with the keys."

Rosselli unlocked the door to Hopfgartner's office, flicked on the lights and went directly to the desk in the corner of the study. He opened the thick curtains of the basement windows. Where would the professor have hidden a pressing worry, a threat? the detective asked himself. If a crushing financial burden had plagued Hopfgartner, would he have left the details at home for his wife to find? How about a letter from a mistress?

Rosselli opened a drawer. Bingo, he thought. A box of condoms. Trojans. Finely Ribbed for Her Absolute Pleasure. And a bottle of Viagra. So Rittman had been telling the truth. Rosselli wondered if Rittman had dropped the Neumann tidbit because he wanted to mess her up. At least she tried to do the right thing, turning in a sexual predator. Rittman might just be ratting her out. What did they do at Yale all day? Play their little games?

The detective searched through the drawers. He found a set of small keys, probably to the cabinets. Rosselli also found term papers and a document called "A Compilation and Synthesis of Recent Criticism." He couldn't even understand what the first paragraph meant. Yale was light years away from the life of a working stiff, Rosselli thought. But wasn't he the one who was supposed to solve their little problems now?

He bent to look into the lower drawers. A twinge of pain shot up his back. He pulled the whole drawer out and set it on the desk. He found papers and more papers. Bills. Two files, on "Drafts" and "Proofs." One on "Investments." Another on "Tax Deductions." Rosselli glanced through them. Hopfgartner was certainly in good shape financially. Maybe he should have quit and moved to Florida.

Rosselli went through other drawers. More files. Old student papers. Recent articles and reviews. A file labeled "Current Reading." The guy had been a pack rat, he thought. Who filed his newspapers?

The detective discovered another file labeled "Correspondence." He opened it. On top was a letter from the previous month, to a man named Maienfeld. Four single-space pages. It was more indecipherable, abstract garbage. This was a *letter*? Rosselli asked himself. No wonder no one had any buddies at Yale. It was like one book talking to another book. Rosselli found similar letters written in German and French. He wondered why Hopfgartner had written Maienfeld in English.

At the back of the file, the detective discovered the responses to the letters. Hopfgartner even stapled the envelopes to the back of the letters. The old guy had been unbelievably anal.

Behind the "Correspondence" file, Rosselli came across a small, wrinkled note.

Werner Hopfgartner, you will never escape your perver-
sions. You horrible bastard! I know about them. I know about

everything. You will be found out if it's the last thing I do. There
will be no sailing into the sunset. There will be no beautiful life
ahead. No future! You've ruined enough lives already. You've
ruined my life. Yes, I was one of yours. But I'm not going to just
walk away. Everything will be known soon. You will pay for
everything you did to me. To all of us. Fuck you!

Bingo. Rosselli understood *that*. The note had been sent that
summer to Switzerland, from New York. Unsigned, of course. Had
it been Neumann's first attempt to scare the old man? She sent the
letter, worked herself into a lather and then had the rug pulled
from under her by the department's shenanigans, Rosselli imagined. So she stabbed Hopfgartner. It seemed so perfect.

But Rosselli caught himself. He needed to pull back for a second look. He already knew Professor Neumann had a way with
words, especially when Hopfgartner was the subject. But he still
needed to connect her to the letter. And then he had to connect her
to Wednesday night. Maybe the detective had something here, and
maybe he didn't. But *somebody* had sure hated this son-of-a-bitch.

Rosselli knocked on the thick door, and the door opened
slowly. Regina Neumann shook his hand, and the detective was
dumbfounded. She was a fragile little thing! Her tiny hand felt like
a feather in his beefy palm. How could she have had the strength
to plunge a butcher knife into Hopfgartner's spine?

He took off his coat and sat down across from her desk.

"Thanks for meeting with me, Professor Neumann. I really
appreciate it. I know it's been tough for everyone around here."

"Professor Hopfgartner's death certainly was the last thing
anyone expected. Have you found anything yet? Do you know
who did it?" she asked, her black eyes shining in the wintry half-
light that filtered through her windows. Strangely enough, all the
lights in this office were off. She wore a bright, white turtleneck
sweater, which gave her pallid complexion an angelic aura.
Rosselli shifted his weight, his back still aching.

"That's just why I'm here. I need to find out as much as I can about Professor Hopfgartner and what happened after the meeting. Problem is, everyone tells me the same thing. 'The meeting was no big deal. Hopfgartner left around nine-fifteen or nine-thirty p.m. He left alone.' That just doesn't leave me with much to go on. I'm pursuing some possibilities, but nothing concrete yet."

"How can I help?"

"You were at the faculty meeting?"

"Correct."

"When did you leave?"

"At eight-thirty."

"Before the end?"

"Yes. I had to be somewhere else by nine."

"Did you notice anything peculiar about Hopfgartner during the meeting? Did he seem preoccupied with a problem, anguished in any way?"

Regina Neumann burst out laughing. It was a self-absorbed, sinister laugh. Jack Rosselli frowned.

"I am sorry, detective. I just would never use 'anguished' to describe Werner Hopfgartner. He was not that kind of man. He seemed his old self."

"What kind of a man was he, then?"

"He was just a man."

"Was he a great man, beloved by his students? Respected and esteemed by his colleagues?"

"Certainly many enjoyed the fact that he was here. He had been a professor at Yale for a long time, long before I arrived. Some of his early work was quite good."

"You don't seem to be terribly enthusiastic about him, if you don't mind me saying so," Rosselli said. He thought about the letter in his portfolio.

"I don't mind at all, particularly because you're right. Anyone will tell you, if you simply ask, that I was not the best of friends with Professor Hopfgartner. We had our disagreements." Neumann spoke, looking right through the detective, to a place beyond both of them.

"You mean about having sex with his students?" Rosselli said bluntly, surprising even himself. Her casual boredom incited him to push her. A real criminal would not have changed her expression now, but Regina Neumann did. She glared at him as if she had just noticed a puny mosquito engorging itself on her blood.

"You are absolutely right, Detective Rosselli," she said coldly. "I *hated* him with all my life."

He watched her, and waited.

"I wish to God I had killed Werner Hopfgartner," she continued. "I hated that despicable old man."

"What did you do after you left the meeting?"

"I, along with Professor Steiner, went to the Round Table at President Nathan's house."

"The Round Table?"

"It's a dinner for faculty members with the president of Yale. He invites three or four departments at a time. A politicking session. Generally a waste of time. But somebody has to beg for money."

"When did the dinner end?"

"A few minutes after midnight."

"And you were there the whole time?"

"Yes, indeed I was. There are seven other faculty members, and President Nathan of course, who will give you any details you wish to know about our dinner. It was rather boring," Neumann said, the slightest smile on her lips.

"Did you have anything to do with Hopfgartner's murder?"

"I imagined it many times. But I did not touch him."

"You didn't answer the question, Professor Neumann," Rosselli said irritably. In his gut, he knew she wasn't the killer. She couldn't have been the killer. That knife, Rosselli remembered, had hit ice as it was plunged straight through the professor's body.

"No-I-did-not-have-anything-to-do-with-the-murder-of-Werner-Hopfgartner," she said in a condescending, staccato tone. "I simply hated him completely," she added in a normal voice, as if that would be enough to mollify Rosselli.

"So you played it *safe*," Rosselli said snidely into her face. This time she looked angry. Immediately her deathlike pallor disappeared. "You wanted to kill him, yet you did *nothing*."

"I hated him. I don't care if the whole world knows it. Search my office if you want. I'll give you the keys to my house. I have nothing to hide."

"Oh, but you *do* have something to hide," Rosselli said, reaching for his briefcase. Neumann looked vaguely amused.

"Nothing to hide. Your *life* is nothing but hiding! 'You will pay for everything you did to me. To all of us. Fuck you!' Did you write this garbage?"

Regina Neumann didn't move. Her white skin seemed to transform itself into the whitest ceramic. "Yes," she said in a hoarse whisper. "I wrote it."

"You didn't have the guts to confront him? You mailed him an anonymous hate letter? Was that going to cleanse your soul and redeem you? 'Nothing to hide.' Hah! I bet. Now you want to tell the world that you wanted to kill him? Why are you wasting my time?"

"You're out of line, detective!"

"You simply wanted to kill him. How nice."

"He was a cock-sucking shit! I would have cut his penis off! I would have buried my fingers into his wretched blue eyes and ripped them out! I hated him! I, I . . . " Professor Neumann stared into her nether world, looking and not looking at Rosselli. She seemed to shake without moving.

"'Would have' means nothing," the detective said coolly, getting up from his own chair and shoving the letter back into his portfolio. "That's all you people do. 'Would have'."

"I . . . I . . . I killed him! I grabbed his neck and choked him! I took his life! I am the one! Where are you going, detective?" Neumann shrieked as he turned toward the door. "He was mine! That bastard was mine, I tell you! Detective!"

"I don't know who or what you are," Rosselli said glaring at her at the door's threshold. His ears were ringing, and his head was bursting with a fresh headache. "But you better get some help."

"I killed him! Detective! That is who I am! Truth! Blessed truth! Detective!" Neumann screamed even as the door closed tightly shut. As he walked away, Rosselli imagined that in a few seconds the professor would suddenly realize she was alone again. In a moment, yes, a self deep within her mind would emerge, and finally glance about the room, and understand that a shuddering silence was better now. Soon Neumann would be back in the world of cool politeness and exceptional brilliance. The world at Yale. She needed just a moment or two, and she could free herself again from the dark dreams of her primordial truths.

Detective Rosselli found a telephone and called Helmut Sanchez. They made an appointment to meet at Sanchez's office in about an hour. It was lunchtime. The detective's headache dissipated as soon as he walked toward Chapel Street. Frightful bitch, he thought. What the hell was her problem? She had treated him like some dope, though. New Haven and Yale didn't get along? Surprise surprise. One was in the gutter, the other was in the clouds.

The important thing was that Rosselli was sure she wasn't the killer. She could have had someone do it for her, but he didn't think so. She would've been tap dancing if she had been behind it. No, somewhere out there was somebody who had hated Hopfgartner as much as—maybe even more than—she did. Or maybe, it had been a street punk after all.

Chapter Nineteen

Helmut's heart raced after he hung up the phone with the detective. He fought against his panic, and forced himself to calm down. He had to think.

A detective wouldn't make an appointment if the police thought he was the killer, Helmut thought. The police would have exploded through the doorway and dragged Helmut out. In a way, his brown-bag lunch had saved him. He had been about to eat when the detective called. Helmut would never have had the presence of mind to delay the meeting if he had simply answered the phone. "How about in an hour?" Helmut had said, staring dumfounded at his lunch. Helmut had sounded so cool, so calm, hadn't he?

Helmut needed to catch his wits. He had to prepare himself. His face was streaked with sweat. The detective was coming to ask routine questions, Helmut told himself. Nothing more. There was time to relax. Time to think everything was normal. Time to calm down.

Nothing pointed to him. Or nothing that he knew of. How could Helmut answer the detective's questions without displaying the dread that engulfed his head? The detective's visit was just an interruption, a nuisance. Wasn't that the way to see this meeting? The wretched detective needed information. Helmut could provide it casually and carefully, couldn't he?

Yesterday, Ariane had told Helmut the police wanted the phone numbers of all the professors at the faculty meeting. They were piecing together Hopfgartner's final day. That's what Rosselli wanted. Nothing more. The cops simply wanted a picture of Hopfgartner's routine.

But why? Helmut thought, panicked. *Why don't they believe the old bastard was mugged? What's led the police away from that line of investigation? What idiotic clue have I left to point the police back toward Yale, to me? I have to save himself. It's in my hands now. I have no other choice. Oh my God, I have just a few minutes.*

Helmut sat at his desk and tried to work. He tried to think himself into being calm.

It's just another day of work. I was shocked to hear about the murder. I didn't know the professor that well, although I had worked for him for three years. What else will this detective ask?

It's a matter of will. A matter of drama. I have to think of himself as an actor. What is real and what is drama anyway? It is simply a matter of convincing myself and everyone else to believe. What's this blather about the real truth?

Helmut had to create a new truth. He had no choice. He would create a calm, relaxed truth. Yes, he worked for the professor, Helmut imagined he would say. No, he had nothing to do with the professor's murder. It was a terrible tragedy. New Haven was a dangerous town. Crime was destroying this community. He was working, and had just eaten lunch. He was waiting for Christmas vacation. Yes, that was his mood, Helmut thought. That was the truth.

Suddenly Helmut thought of sweet Ariane. He thought of their time together. Thought of her beauty. And it calmed him. It gave him something to live for. Yes, he would think of her.

There was a knock at his door.

"Please come in." Helmut gulped for air.

"Hello. I'm Detective Rosselli."

"Helmut Sanchez. Please sit down." They shook hands, and Helmut sat down. Beneath his desk, his right leg nervously pumped with a piston-like rhythm. The detective leaned heavily on one elbow, which sank into the soft arm of the black, vinyl chair in front of Helmut's desk. His thick neck was flushed.

"What can I do for you, detective?"

"I'm here about Werner Hopfgartner," Rosselli said, fishing out his notepad and a pen from his portfolio.

"I figured as much."

"You worked for him, didn't you?"

"Yes, sir. I'm his Research Assistant. I work half-time. I can't believe he's dead. You know what happened?"

"Not yet. I need your help on some details about Professor Hopfgartner." The detective twisted in his seat uncomfortably.

"Sure. Anything I can do." Helmut began to relax. It was just an interview. He was good at interviews. He thought about Ariane, and how much he loved her.

"Tell me about Hopfgartner. Did you see him the day he was killed?"

"Yes I did. Wednesday morning he gave me instructions on a rewrite he wanted me to finish before leaving for the holidays. I usually saw him once a day. Either to give him what I was working on or to get another assignment from him."

"Was he a good boss?" Rosselli asked. "I'm trying to find out what he was like. What he did every day. What he *really* liked to do. Did he have any *peculiar* characteristics?"

"Well, he was usually aloof. The professor kept to himself. He wasn't the type to chat about anything. You know, businesslike. Sometimes I felt a little intimidated by him. I mean, he was a fair man, in terms of my work. He never really got angry. And I did the best I could," Helmut said somberly. Why these odd questions? What did this detective already know?

"I'm sure you did." The detective twisted awkwardly again, as if his back, the softness of the vinyl chair, or the bulkiness of his body bothered him. "But that's not exactly what I'm looking for, son. Let me be perfectly clear. I talked to other professors. They've already given me a picture of a man who, let us say, was a bit of a Romeo around campus."

"You *know* about that?"

"Of course. It's my job to find out."

"You think someone he knew killed him?"

"Probably not. But I need to check everything out. That's why I'm here."

"But the secretaries told me Professor Hopfgartner was mugged!" Helmut said insistently. What else would this detective find out?

Rosselli frowned slightly and then quickly smiled. "Well, yes, of course, they're probably right. Just trying to be thorough. Did you know any of the professor's lovers?"

"I can't believe someone here killed him. That's impossible! It just can't be true," Helmut exclaimed. He fought a wave of dizziness. He searched the detective's face for some clue to his thoughts. Werner Hopfgartner—Helmut thought—deserved to die. That was the truth. "I'm not sure."

"What do you mean, Mr. Sanchez?"

"Well, I know what the professor did. These 'meetings.' I think everyone who works on this floor knows. In a way, we're all guilty of being bystanders, of letting it happen. Professor Hopfgartner didn't exactly try to hide it."

"You know any of their names? That's what I need to know," Rosselli said irritably. He seemed impatient to finish and return to his office. As the detective twisted once more in the chair, his stomach rumbled too loudly.

"I saw two of them come in and out regularly. But I don't know who they are. Just don't know their names."

"What did they look like?"

"Can I ask you something?"

"Sure. Go ahead."

"You really think one of these girls killed him? Is, is that really possible?" Helmut muttered, out of breath. He sensed a trap.

"I don't know that. Anything is possible. At this point, you could say everybody is a suspect. It's just a matter of gathering information to the point where someone is singled out, where we can pursue a lead to its logical conclusion."

"Please pardon my questions, Detective Rosselli. How does 'information' become a 'lead'? Why should a 'lead' reach a 'logical conclusion'? It's just that I struggle with a similar set of questions in my own work."

"Of course, son. Seems like I've been answering as many questions as I ask. It's not a problem. When I don't have something obvious from the beginning, I start to look for more information about the victim. I look at the victim's relationships. Nine times out of ten, the answer's right there. Love relationships. Hateful rivalries. Family squabbles. Problems at work. Of course, that depends on whether the crime was committed by someone the victim knew. But most murders are," Rosselli said, gently adjusting his position in the chair again.

"So you don't have anything 'obvious' yet?"

"No, we don't." Rosselli frowned.

"Well, I mean, what's going to be 'obvious' to you? Of all the information you get, how do you decide *this* is a 'lead'?"

"That's tough to answer. It depends. Depends on the case, the person murdered, what was found at the scene. Depends on peculiar things. I'd have to say it simply sticks out in my mind. It's *there*."

"Would you say its 'experience'? Something like that?"

"That probably right, son. Guess I've done enough investigations to know what to look for."

"What happens when it's an odd murder? Say something beyond your experience? What do you do then?"

"Well, I'd have to say every murder is different in some ways, and the same in others. The motivations for murder never change: jealousy, greed, hate, anger and sometimes, simply for the hell of it. Because it's fun for some sickos. Guess you could say it's all about power. So in a particular case, I first look for a motivation to murder the victim. Sometimes it's easy to spot. Other times it's a twisted tale. The other important part of the puzzle—the way the victim was killed—is probably the hardest part. It could be anything and could point you in any direction. I've probably seen at least a hundred ways to snuff out a life."

"You know how I would do it?" Helmut asked, startling even himself with the question. He swayed in his seat. He felt as if he were observing his own interview from above. There and not there.

"How?" Rosselli said, annoyed. He gave Helmut a quizzical look.

"You see, I think the problem is always the murder weapon. What do you do with it? The club, the gun, the ax, the knife. And can they trace it back to you? I would use something random, something I owned or could get my hands on, but something that didn't belong to me in particular. Say a knife I had found. Then the problem would be how to dispose of it once I killed him."

"Killed who?"

"Werner Hopfgartner, of course. Isn't that who we're talking about?" Helmut smiled crookedly, his pupils dilated. His heart thumped wildly inside his chest with a great elation. His mind floated beyond him.

"Well, I guess we are," Rosselli said. The detective glanced quickly around, as if he were unsure of his surroundings.

"I would've flung the knife into the river, buried it under a pine tree. *That's* what I would've done. No one would ever find it even if they knew it was there."

"That wouldn't be a bad plan at all, but usually a murderer, even an experienced one, makes mistakes," Rosselli said good-naturedly. "The heart sometimes trembles when the mind wants to act. The more exceptional the act—and murder is, if anything, one of the most exceptional things we do—the more incalculable the tide of emotion necessary to finish this act. Sometimes it's there. More often it abandons you at the crucial moment. Now let's just get back to where–"

"Just one moment, detective," Helmut interrupted softly, glaring at the wall next to Jack Rosselli. "Please, indulge me just a bit more. Our little talk has been so helpful to me. I may never get another chance to ask a professional everything I want to know about how you search for the truth."

"Okay. For posterity, so to speak," Rosselli said quickly, forcing a thick smile.

"What if there was no doubt in my mind? No reason to be nervous, no source for my muscles to shake uncontrollably and betray me?"

"But there is *always* doubt. Before or after a murder. Sooner or later it bubbles up and that's when mistakes can be made, when the truth comes out. Murder is not a natural thing to do."

"Why not?"

"Well, maybe for a professional killer or a sadist. Some deranged psychopath. But they're hardly 'natural' by our standards."

"But don't you think you or I could murder someone, if we had the right reasons? Don't you think someone 'normal' could kill and believe it was the right thing to do?"

"Maybe in self-defense."

"But not a murder *for the sake of* murder?"

"No, I don't think so. Guess I could see how you could do it. It happens everyday! But murder is never 'right.' Even in self-defense. It's just something you have to do. Some doubt would eventually creep in. I don't think you could do it without having doubt. I just don't think human beings are made like that. Murder is the ultimate way you separate yourself from the victim and from everyone else. Murder defeats even the murderer, eventually."

"I have to say I disagree," Helmut said, feeling suddenly light-headed. "I'm terribly sorry. I'm wasting your time. What was it you wanted to know about Professor Hopfgartner? My mind's gone blank!"

"Descriptions of his two lovers. Are you all right, son? You're really very pale," Rosselli said, leaning forward in his chair. He almost stood up this time. The detective dropped his notepad and pen back into his portfolio.

"Oh, I'm fine. Something's not right with me. My stomach, I think. Maybe something I ate. Maybe the flu. One was a brunette, athletic, about five-foot-eight. I think she was an undergraduate. The other was smaller, about five-foot-four or so. A blond. Also good-looking. See her all the time. Sarah Goodman's her name."

"Thought you said you didn't know them."

"Made a mistake. I'm sorry, Mr. Rosselli."

"Look, if you remember the other one's name, give me a call." The detective handed Helmut his card. Rosselli grinned as he pushed himself up heavily from the chair. "Call me anytime."

"Before you leave, please, can I ask you another question?" Helmut said, standing behind his desk. His legs felt suddenly weak.

"Okay. A quickie," Rosselli said impatiently.

"The murder."

"Yes?"

"Read about it in the *Register*. The secretaries talked about it. I imagined the blood. I, uh, the professor was probably carrying what I gave him that morning. I dreamed I was there. I, I don't know anymore," Helmut said fervently. What had he just said? His head was spinning.

"Maybe you should talk to someone. A counselor. I'm sure Yale can help you. It's quite a typical reaction when someone familiar is murdered. A certain leap of the imagination, son. Try to focus on something else. You are fine. Don't worry. We'll find out who killed him. It's a matter of time. You are safe."

"I still feel angry. I feel empty. In the trees. I remember nothing but a certainty. Now, uh, I just don't know."

"In the trees?"

"In, yes, the trees. What was I just saying?" Helmut babbled, his eyes feverish. His body swayed forward. He gasped for air, and his mind went blank. Suddenly he dropped to one knee and vomited.

"You okay?" Rosselli exclaimed, already by Helmut's side, one hand on his shoulder. "Here you go. Clean yourself up, son. Maybe you should see a doctor. A stomach virus is going around the station. For all I know I might have it too."

"Thank you. Ach, what a mess I've made! Please forgive me." Helmut wiped his face and chin with the clump of tissues in his hand. White spots erupted in front of him, and he felt his head was and was not on his shoulders.

"Don't worry about it. You okay now?"

"I'll be fine. Sorry about this."

"Sorry? Just take it easy, son. Got some on your shirt too. Right here. There you go."

"Thank you. You've been very kind. Thank you for everything."

"Look, just give me a call if you remember anything else. Take care of yourself."

The detective left and Helmut sank into his chair. He had vomited! Would the detective think Helmut was guilty? But the detective had asked only perfunctory questions. Did Rosselli secretly suspect him? It didn't seem likely. Yet this detective did not seem stupid. Would he ruminate about this spectacle Helmut had created in his office? Perhaps Helmut had delivered a seed of doubt for the detective to ponder. What kind of an idiot was he, he had wanted to confess to the detective! Was he out of his mind? Was it only a matter of time before Rosselli began to put two and two together? What in God's name had Helmut done?

Chapter Twenty

Rosselli's phone rang. On Thursday, a patrolman who had been canvassing the area of the Hopfgartner murder stopped at a European bakery about a mile from Whitney Avenue. The cop ordered a cup of coffee and danish, and listened as the owner complained about a pyromaniac near his shop. Friday, the patrolman decided to check it out, and discovered only a vagrant living under the I-91 bridge on State Street. The cop told the vagrant where he could find a shelter against the December chill, and warned him not to set fires in the neighborhood. Next time, the cop said, he'd be arrested.

Officer Murray noticed the blistered leather on this old man's shoes, which were too big for his feet. The shoes were splattered with specks of rust-colored mud. Rust-colored mud? The officer had the vagrant in front of him and was calling the station from his car radio. Hadn't a bloody footprint been found at the scene of the Yale professor's murder? Rosselli said he'd drive to State Street immediately.

Adrenaline was pumping through Rosselli's veins. Maybe it was the break he had been waiting for. The shoes! Who in the world would've noticed the shoes? Murray was in line for a pat on the back from the brass if he was right.

But once the detective got a look at the old man under the bridge, his heart sank. The geezer could hardly walk. He was frail, almost blind. And no way were those his shoes. Rosselli searched the cardboard box. No knife, no credit cards. All they had were the bloody shoes, which did match the size of the footprint near Professor Hopfgartner's body. A lab analysis would determine if the professor's blood was smeared on the leather. They would hold the old man for setting fires under the bridge. It might not amount to anything, but the old guy would be warm and fed in jail for a couple of nights. But Rosselli was almost positive the vagrant had not murdered Werner Hopfgartner.

During questioning, the old guy said calmly that he had *found* the shoes. His eyes betrayed no deceit. No panic. The old man had no idea how crucial this information was. Rosselli asked where the vagrant had found the shoes.

The old man pointed at the garbage barrel.

"Right in there," he said. "A goddamn Yalie tried to burn 'em."

Rosselli returned to the office and told a desk sergeant about the special circumstances of Officer Murray's arson arrest. But the detective's heart had stopped palpitating. Could he believe this old guy? His description of the "goddamn Yalie" had been worthless. But why a Yalie and not somebody from UConn, Albertus Magnus or anywhere else for that matter? Rosselli didn't think this bum could be making this up.

The idea of a Yalie also fit into Rosselli's improbable scenario that someone Hopfgartner knew had murdered him in a fit of passion. Rittman and Neumann had told him the professor had been fucking pretty, young students. But the description of the "goddamn Yalie" didn't sound like a pretty, young student. Maybe it could have been a jealous boyfriend. Maybe the old guy was just confused.

As Jack Rosselli saw it, he had more digging to do.

He called home. A little girl answered the phone with a haughty "Yes?" He laughed. It was Stephanie, his only grandchild. She was the best thing to come from his daughter Karen's marriage to the lawyer from New York City. Nothing pleased Rosselli more than to watch Stephanie's green eyes and dark cheeks while she figured out colorful logic puzzles.

Stephanie made it easier for him to accept that his daughter Karen had married someone who was different, from a different background. Karen's husband argued against his political views and possessed such an enormous chip on his shoulder that whatever Jack Rosselli uttered was taken as a personal attack. Stephanie's blessed arrival improved their relationship. But every once in a while, Rosselli's mind burned with his daughter's early accusations that he was a "soft racist." She said he simply couldn't accept her marriage to an African American.

Jack Rosselli's arguments with his daughter and son-in-law usually stemmed from a single source. They believed street crime was a direct result of the awful social conditions, the racism of whites and the systematic oppression of many members of the underclass. He needed more sympathy for their plight—they preached to him—not simply scorn or blame.

Rosselli agreed that, yes, he knew that racism was a problem and that it did contribute to the desperation in many who became criminals. But he believed it certainly wasn't the only explanation for criminal behavior.

A man wasn't only what society told him he was, nor what society forced down his throat, he retorted. He personally knew dozens of families in the black community in New Haven for whom racism wasn't the main issue. Some, facing the same problems as their neighbors, wouldn't succumb to the allure of drug money or the haze of crack cocaine. These families were disciplined and taught their kids to respect hard work and religion. Others, however, merely used racism as an excuse for their behavior. They were weak-minded individuals, he pointed out, who didn't really give a shit about anything or anybody. They took a grain of truth and used it as an excuse for every attack against a grandmother, for the neglect of a child and for the bitter failure to stay sober. The weak-minded were hungry for quick money and quick respect. They glorified Lotto culture, the ten-second logic of TV and irresponsible sex. The real questions were why some relished this soulless materialism, and why others saw it as the wasteland it was.

His daughter and son-in-law argued he didn't understand the pervasive racism of society. Even in New York, white people stared at them simply because they were an interracial couple. At a deli, they had once been ignored because they had smooched in front of the knishes and black olives. Rosselli asked them whether these looks of disdain only came from whites. Some blacks too, they admitted, ostracized them. And that was exactly his point, Rosselli said. Standards of good behavior had to be applied to *everyone*. The point, he continued, was that as soon as one group had, or was given, the ultimate excuse, that some external factor was so transcendent as to determine all manner of behavior, then that group would lose its sense of individual responsibility. That group would end up treating its own with much less respect. Members of such a group would become racists themselves, since that would be the distorted, reductionist way they viewed every corner of the world. Different groups, instead of joining together, would be ripped apart by their view of the "truth." The success of "racial truths" meant conflict, and chaos, and finally the tacit agreement that there existed no truth at all, just whatever you could get away with. He knew racism existed. He just didn't think it was the only problem or even the most important one now.

Then Rosselli had revealed something deep in his heart. Something he could have easily kept a secret forever. He admitted that, yes, he had first been taken aback because Karen had married an African American. He had judged Lewis by the color of his skin. He had been guilty of racism. But he told them, too, that he had changed his mind and his heart. He had gotten to know Lewis as a scrappy debater who wouldn't quit unless his wife nudged him to stop. He had spent time with his son-in-law and seen him as another New York Giants fan. He knew Lewis respected his wife. He also had witnessed how much his son-in-law loved his daughter, about as much as Jack Rosselli had once loved his own little girl. More than anything else, he said, Stephanie had opened up his heart. She possessed his blood, his eyes and, of course, his tenacity and intelligence. And for once, the three of them laughed easily together.

Yet, Jack Rosselli hadn't told them one thing, and he was thinking of it now. He hadn't told them he had finally realized how difficult a life that smart little girl would face because of racism. At the circus, he remembered the judgmental looks of white New Yorkers who had stared at them, a large burly white guy with a black little girl. The frowns of disapproval from blacks too! Some shook their heads in disbelief. Others gawked at this startling duo, this grandfather and grandchild, as they sat down in their seats to wait for the start of the show. Was it such an oddity that he could love a child who was of their race, feed her popcorn and buy her a stuffed elephant? Weren't they doing exactly what whites did to them?

After Madison Square Garden, he knew one thing with the greatest of certainty: Stephanie Slater was his grandchild, his *blood*. And he would defend her with his life.

He told little Stephanie to tell her grandmother he'd be home at 8:00 p.m.

"Eight!" the little girl trumpeted loudly and dropped the phone and yelled the message again to Rosie in the background. "Grama wants a dozen eggs and syrup! Please!" Stephanie shouted into the phone. He said goodbye and hung up the phone and laughed.

Rosselli knew he had to talk to Mrs. Hopfgartner tomorrow, on Saturday, the day before the funeral. The whole episode was beginning to irritate him. Here he was worried about investigating a murder at Yale while his family was on one of their rare holiday visits. Rosie was enjoying herself with little Stephanie, but he had hardly seen her. And what about the intrusive questions he had to ask Mrs. Hopfgartner? He had no suspects. The old vagrant could hardly identify anyone as the owner of those shoes. Maybe the detective was wasting his time.

Rosselli didn't think a prima donna grad student would have had the guts to kill the professor. Sure, if you were pissed off, you might publicize sexual harassment charges to get back at an old bastard who had betrayed you. But murder him? That felt too extreme in Rosselli's mind. Men committed most murders anyway. The scenario of a lover killing the professor didn't fit any set of realistic possibilities. Maybe it could have been a pissed-off boyfriend of the Hopfgartner's conquests. Moreover, if Rosselli asked the widow about the professor's secret sexual life, she might explode in a fury. The funeral was the next day, for God's sake! Then again, she might coolly tell him, as he suspected she would, that she had known all along about her husband's secret life.

Chapter Twenty-One

On the way to Hamden Saturday morning, Rosselli thought about what to say to Mrs. Hopfgartner. Not once during their first meeting had Jack Rosselli felt the desire to give her comfort. With Mrs. Hopfgartner, he knew immediately to be formal, concise and intelligent. She would not have tolerated an emotional display. When he phoned her Friday night to set up the second interview, she responded in the same businesslike manner, as if she had been expecting his call to conclude matters once and for all. It would be best to be straightforward again. She might even be curious about the possibility that her husband had been murdered by an acquaintance. Rosselli couldn't see any other way to the truth of the matter.

A young woman answered the door. It was Susan Hopfgartner, the professor's daughter. She had just arrived from the West Coast for the funeral. She asked the detective if the police had found anything more about her father's murder. He filled her in on what little they had. She was steely-eyed like her mother, but her pain was all too obvious. She looked like she had been crying for days. Susan thanked him for keeping the family informed and offered him a cup of coffee.

"Let me go get her," she said. "Why don't you wait in the study."

"Thank you."

"It's been such a madhouse. Michael—my brother—is arriving in an hour. I still can't believe it. My father. How could this happen? It's been a living nightmare. I always knew New Haven was

dangerous. Why didn't he listen to me? I begged him not to walk
home at night. I *begged* him! Mr. Rosselli, do you know how much
we fought over this? He never listened to me. Told me I was being
a child. Do you know anything about my father, Mr. Rosselli?"

"No, not really."

"He lived in another world. This isn't the countryside or the
forest. You know that. New Haven? I hated living here. Sorry I'm
dumping this on you."

"Don't worry. It's okay."

"I just have this huge headache this morning. Sure you don't
want a cup of coffee?"

"Okay, you win."

"Be right back. I'll tell my mother you're waiting for her."

The gloomy study was lined with books on floor-to-ceiling
oak shelves. Little statuettes were hidden inside nooks on the
shelves, as well as small ornate metal and glass boxes apparently
medieval in origin. A brass lamp, opaque and twisted, dangled
over a green leather chair. In front of a first-floor window, the desk
had neat stacks of paper and a few German magazines, a black
fountain pen, an electric typewriter to one side, a small pendulum
clock encased in glass, the clock's key and a black rotary telephone
in a corner. Rosselli glanced at the book jackets, but the titles were
in German and French. He heard the creak of the door opening.

Mrs. Hopfgartner wore a pleated blue skirt and a cream-
colored cardigan. Her wet gray hair was wrapped tightly in a bun.
She reminded Rosselli of a stern schoolmarm. But she was cordial
and even pleased to see him again.

"How are you feeling, Mrs. Hopfgartner?"

"I'm feeling better now," she said, almost surprised he would
start with such a question.

She took a seat, crossing her thin, white legs. Rosselli thought
of a bird perched expertly on a tree branch. He told her what he
had told her daughter. Nothing new had been found. It had probably been a dreadful mugging. The police still had no suspects.
Again, it occurred to Jack Rosselli that Mrs. Hopfgartner possessed
only an incidental interest in her husband's fate. She seemed impatient, ready for that snap of a handshake goodbye.

Rosselli explained that the murder rate in New Haven had been skyrocketing for several years, that sometimes, unfortunately, the police did not find the perpetrators. He also said they had found no fingerprints, and only a possible footprint, to help them search for the truth. The police were also testing all traces of foreign DNA on her husband's body. He assured her he was devoting a great deal of time to the case. But the fact remained they might never find anything definitive.

Mrs. Hopfgartner nodded studiously.

"I know you are doing whatever is necessary, *Herr Inspektor*. I have complete trust in the police. I admire and appreciate you for the hard work you do in this *Schwarzwald*," she said with her slight Viennese accent. She crossed her legs the other way and smiled and waited for him to continue.

Schwarzwald? Rosselli thought.

He didn't know what it meant precisely, but he was pretty sure it wasn't a compliment. Why would she assume they stood together against a common enemy? He had certainly never believed that racist bullshit. In a way, then, her comment made it easier to be frank with her.

"Mrs. Hopfgartner, I still need your help on some matters. The investigation is at such a point that any details would be helpful, especially about your husband's habits, his personal history, anything else that could help us find who killed him. I know this is difficult. But we have to look into even *improbable* possibilities."

Mrs. Hopfgartner frowned and looked away. Her white cheek twitched. "How much do you know?" she asked quietly, enunciating every word with care.

"I know some of what your husband did, and that in itself isn't important. I'm just following every possibility now. I think I have a good idea of what probably happened. But I have to pursue every angle, just in case. I think your husband was killed during a mugging. But there's a slight possibility it could've been something else."

Jack Rosselli held his breath for a moment. He felt as if he had stumbled into a chess game with a shrewd grandmaster.

"You think he might have been killed by an acquaintance? Is that what you believe?"

"It's just a theory I'm pursuing. I don't want to start any rumors. That's why I came to you first."

"You're just doing your job, *Herr Inspektor*. No apology is necessary for me. I will tell you that I knew about his mistresses. I know you know about them already. I can see it in your eyes. None was important. Except one. This one, the only one, I believe my husband loved or came to love in his perverted mind. You know, I myself loved not my husband, but he was still my man. We were still one in many other ways. But this one, yes, this one turned my husband into an animal. I forced him to end the relationship two years ago. If a hard man can become colder, he achieved it after that. At least in my eyes. I lost him completely then. I lost him to his perverted dreams of that horror!"

A strand of her gray hair shivered loose. Mrs. Hopfgartner tucked it back in place before she continued.

"Only *that one* could have anything to do with my husband's murder. That beast. They had a corrupt passion between them, that I know in my heart."

"Do you know the name of this woman?" Rosselli asked.

The widow smiled slightly. "It is not a woman, but another man." She lowered her gaze and stared at the floor.

Jack Rosselli inhaled deeply and almost grimaced.

"Jonathan Atwater is his name," she said.

Driving home, Rosselli replayed the visit in his mind. Who was this Jonathan Atwater? The detective tried to contain himself. He had to think it through and not just react to what seemed a real answer to a vexing series of questions. Hadn't this been a murder by an amateur and possibly by someone who worked at Yale? Mrs. Hopfgartner had said Atwater worked in the Yale libraries. Wasn't it possible that the murder was a crime of passion, not just a mugging? She had told him about Werner Hopfgartner's love for this man. How she had forced her husband to end the relationship or she would ruin Hopfgartner's career. Maybe Jonathan Atwater had blamed his lover for going back to his wife, for not standing up to her. Maybe Atwater simply decided that if he couldn't have Werner Hopfgartner, then nobody would.

Rosselli didn't know any gays, at least not anyone who had come out of the closet. For all he knew, the police force might have had a few gay officers. He certainly didn't have anything against them. He just couldn't understand them. What was this rough love, this soft violence and random sex? What was this aggression and dominance wrapped around *caring*? Maybe Rosselli had a distorted picture of homosexual love. Maybe all kinds of love possessed these elements. But one thing was certain: It was the kind of love that could be a motive for murder. More importantly, the last piece of the puzzle also seemed to fit. A lover would have known his habits, his walking route. A lover would have known when Hopfgartner attended his meetings. Maybe a mugger had killed the professor. But now there were more reasons to doubt that scenario. Now, maybe a long shot could unravel this mystery.

Before Rosselli returned to Westport, he stopped at his office in police headquarters. He needed to get an address for Atwater, who was at the moment just another wrinkle in the life and unresolved death of Werner Hopfgartner. But Atwater could certainly be much more than that.

The detective searched the computer files and found nothing. Jonathan Atwater had no criminal record in Connecticut. Rosselli called the Yale Police Department, and a friend confirmed that a Jonathan Atwater worked in Sterling Memorial Library as an assistant librarian. This friend also gave him a New Haven address, on Chatham Street, on the west side of I-91, and a phone number.

After Rosselli hung up, it struck him square in the face like a rock. He double-checked the address against the New Haven street map. Jonathan Atwater's home was on a straight line from where the professor had been murdered on Whitney, to the trash can at East Rock Park where the wallet was found. The murder, the wallet, then Chatham Street. Even the overpass where the old drunk lived was only a short detour from that straight line. Atwater could've easily walked or driven there. It would've taken just a few precious minutes. It would've been a perfectly logical path to follow without being obvious about the final destination. A multitude of roads, including the freeway itself, could take you anywhere in the city. But maybe the killer, Rosselli thought, had simply gone straight home.

Chapter Twenty-Two

Helmut held the sleeping Ariane and kissed her forehead. He tried to imagine New Mexico. He sniffed his fingers and his forearms. He still reeked of ammonia and Pine Sol and scouring powder. Before coming to her place, he had cleaned his apartment. He vacuumed the dust balls underneath his bed, and scrubbed off the rusty slime in the crevices of the toilet bowl. He threw away the bottles and rags and extra toothbrushes and scores of paper bags underneath the bathroom and the kitchen sinks. He cleaned the gray and grainy rugs, the stove, the compartment underneath the gas burners, where he uncovered a mummified piece of broccoli and three fusilli. Nothing in his apartment had been left untouched, unwiped. By the end of the day, his fingers were pink and raw. He should've worn gloves. Ariane had told him that immediately. But now his apartment was spotless, and he could be with her in peace. Maybe he could finally start believing what he had done three nights before would be forever behind him. But it wasn't.

Helmut slipped out of bed. His head pounded with a merciless pain. He kept thinking about Werner Hopfgartner. Helmut remembered the professor quivering like a piece of meat after he stabbed him a second time. He remembered the moans of agony. These sounds had resonated in his ears ever since. At the oddest moments, Helmut thought he overheard these moans again, behind bushes, next to his front door, in the backyard.

He had tried to forget that night of horror. He tried to forget how he had stumbled into the professor's nightmarish destiny and why he had pursued this truth to its bitter end. But Helmut couldn't. How could he forget that he had murdered a human being? Yes, he had hated the professor. But at the moment of truth, he had been shocked by the work of his hands. A demonic spirit had poured into his heart. And Helmut had apparently outwitted the detective. He would go free. How could he learn to live with what he had done?

Helmut walked to Ariane's living room to the kitchen. He poured water into the squat, red teakettle and turned on the stove burner. How could he get any sleep? After talking to Ariane, he started to believe that no one would find out the truth. Detective Rosselli had conceded to her that the police had no clue as to the identity of the murderer. Regina Neumann had also mentioned her "productive exchange" with the detective. But what did that mean? What leads were they pursuing? Perhaps the police would soon drop the case all together.

Other things also convinced Helmut that the police were nowhere close to him. Only he and the professors at the faculty meeting had been interviewed. He knew the police only possessed educated guesses about what happened. Ariane had also told him that Werner Hopfgartner would be buried Sunday morning. A bitter coldness would finally seep into that coffin. The earth would seal it forever. Dead and buried. What more perfect ending could Helmut have wished for? He had done what he had wanted. He had carried out his plans despite his wild emotions on that awful day.

He remembered his interview with the detective. Somehow he had stumbled through it. The vomit! Helmut remembered. What on earth had possessed him? Helmut still didn't feel very well. But at least he had finished the job. He had taken the entire godforsaken journey to its logical conclusion. So why was his mind infected with this torment?

The night before, he had reread every sheet of paper from Melk. He gasped, again, at the utter moral depravity of Werner Hopfgartner. He reassured himself that the professor had been the brutal rapist and murderer of Anja Litvak. Yes, he had been right. Absolutely right. Right to the point where he told himself he would do it all again if he had to. Yes, the world would have allowed Hopfgartner to go free, Helmut imagined. The powerful

always got their way, and the powerful always abused the power-
less. He had been right and just.

Helmut would keep those fragile documents to reassure himself in the future, to calm his nerves whenever he forgot the reasons behind his horrible act. They reminded him of who he had
been, of why he had taken matters into his own hands. His mind,
he knew, would condemn him. His mind would forget the reasons
behind the need to act, the imperative behind his flash decision.
After many years, his act could easily be reduced only to a knife
plunging downward, to blood spurting up geyser-like, to the
naked cry of a human being in pain. His murderous act had had
reason and history and goodness behind it. His murderous act had
been more than just bleak savagery.

At one point, Helmut had flirted with the idea of throwing
these documents away. It would rid him of every physical trace of
his murderous act. But then he would be left with nothing but his
memories. And that was why he could never throw them away. His
mind was his enemy. His mind might take it upon itself to question
the certainty of evil in the old man. His mind might remember only
the knife, in his own hands, the knife as part of an act without
sense and circumstance. In the future, his mind could not be trust-
ed to give him back his own self. His mind was *not* who he was.

The scalding tea stung his tongue. He would let it cool. Helmut
sat down on the love seat and imagined how his stomach was eating itself. He wanted to vomit again. His cheeks felt suddenly cold,
his chest damp. He closed his eyes and tried to imagine a pleasant
scene. But an intense, pulsating throb dizzied him. He collapsed
onto the sofa and curled up, like a fetus. He rushed to the bathroom and fell on the floor in front of the toilet bowl. A wave of light
flashed against his face. He wanted it to end. *Now . . . please . . . God
. . . stop*, he pleaded in his mind.

A yellowish liquid gushed from his mouth. He thought his
brains were pouring out. Another jet of vomit gushed out of him.
It slowed to a thread of clear slime. He waited. Helmut's stomach
felt a little better. His body was cold. His leg felt like a dead husk
underneath him. He weakly lifted one hand and flushed the toilet.
The swirl of clean water brought him to life again. He rubbed his

hand over his forehead and massaged his leg. Helmut stood up gingerly, his hands gripping the bathroom sink. He brushed his teeth and walked to the kitchen. By then, the tea was just right.

≈ ≈ ≈

When Ariane awoke, Helmut wasn't in bed with her. She thought she smelled coffee. But she found him curled up on the sofa, asleep. She stooped over him, and indeed he was breathing. She walked into the bathroom, and cranked the shower extra hot. Her feet were numb and cold. The steamy onrush brought them back to life.

Finally, she had a moment to breathe easier and not worry about the crisis surrounding Professor Hopfgartner's murder. The flowers for the funeral today, the conference in Berlin, the questions from the police—it had all fallen on her shoulders. Now, in the shower she cried softly. This relentless pressure overwhelmed her. Why should she have to work in a city where people she knew got stabbed to death? And what about Otto and the rest of these self-obsessed idiots? she thought. They had escaped to Berlin and dumped the whole thing in her lap. Not one of them had returned for the funeral.

She discovered the splash of vomit behind the toilet seat. Maybe it was better to let him sleep. She needed to buy groceries for her Christmas turkey. When she returned, Helmut would be up, and maybe he'd even keep his promise to go to church with her. Certainly he didn't have to go, and in fact he had never accompanied her to Sunday mass. But yesterday she invited him again just as she had so many times before, and instead of politely declining or arguing about it, he simply said yes. She had been surprised but pleased.

The Stop & Shop was busy, and that was a relief. The day was cold and gray, but inside, the store gleamed with light. Row after row of food, and mothers and children in the aisles lifted her spirits. She chose the bread crumbs on special, a large bag of prunes, a quart of eggnog, Idaho potatoes, the turkey for only eighty-nine cents per pound, peas and carrots, a pumpkin pie and a can of candied cranberries.

Suddenly she heard her name and felt a tap on her shoulder. It was Gregory Winters, a friend of hers who worked at Yale-New Haven Hospital. He was an intern whom she had met at a party years ago, during his very first week at Yale, a year before she had fallen in love with Helmut Sanchez. Ariane and Gregory had had a brief affair, lots of sex and not much bickering. The sex had been vigorous and even athletic, but Ariane had never believed it had been wonderful or fulfilling. And that's why she had eventually stopped sleeping with Gregory. Ever since, they had still enjoyed an easygoing friendship. Then she had met Helmut. Gregory had always been the perfect gentleman, after beseeching her with his oh-so-sorrowful eyes, and pleading for "just one more night." This scene unfolded every time they ran into each other since their breakup.

Sneaking a glimpse at her chest, Gregory said he was finished this year. He told her he was moving to Boston for a fellowship in radiology. He looked even more athletic than before, his shoulders wider and more muscular. He asked her if she had plans for Christmas.

"I'd love to have dinner with you," he said.

"I have a boyfriend," she said, smiling. "You never give up, do you?"

"You know I won't. I still dream about you. I want the real thing."

"Maybe we can have just dinner sometime."

"Okay. Hey, I have to try!" He laughed. "You know what you do to me, Ariane. You're one in a million."

"Thanks. See ya." Ariane felt sexy but certainly not interested, and remembered why she had decided to stop seeing Gregory Winters in the first place. He was a selfish man who wanted something like a concubine for a girlfriend. He was focused only on his own satisfaction. Any woman, as long as she kept him sexually satisfied and tended to his needs, would fit into the mate slot envisioned by Gregory the doctor. At the checkout line, she caught Gregory looking at her. She pumped him a generous smile and headed home.

✍ ✍ ✍

St. Mary's Church on Hillhouse Street was a gray, stone edifice with a cone-like bell tower that pierced the New Haven skyline. The church was indeed an orderly sanctuary. The steps had been carefully swept clear of snow, Ariane and Helmut noticed. The three massive front doors appeared freshly varnished. Every basin had just the right amount of holy water. Yet, the five o'clock Sunday mass was not very well attended. The students were gone; the professors had fled to the suburbs. Many had said their prayers at the early masses, for this was the last weekend of shopping before Christmas. So the smattering of worshippers lent an air of solemn proportion to the immutable walls. Ariane and Helmut sat down in the front pews. An old, white-haired priest genially scanned the worshippers and whispered a few instructions to an altar boy.

"How do you feel?" Ariane whispered to him, her hand gently on his knee. Helmut was pale and shaky. He had eaten only an apple and a yogurt the entire day.

"I'll be fine." He fixed his eyes on the cool white marble altar. A large Bible lay open on it.

"If you don't feel well, just go. It's okay. Don't worry. Here, take the keys."

"I'm not going anywhere," he whispered harshly. Her entreaties only deepened his dizzying nausea. Her caring was like a lack of oxygen around his face: it pressed against him and suffocated him. "I'm staying here with you," he said softly. She winked at him.

Helmut felt much better not having to talk to anyone. Why couldn't he wait somewhere, wait for as long as he needed, until the pain in his mind dissipated and set him free? The priest's words echoed in the vast chamber, nonsensical utterances to him, a weird and disparate ebb and flow that droned and clanged like a faraway machine. A child cried behind them. It pierced Helmut's strange bliss, and caused his throat to quiver.

Again, the space around him was quiet. He imagined the knife in his hands again. The blood pouring over his fingers. Another thrust of the blade. The open-mouthed agony of the professor. Helmut was home free, wasn't he? Why was he tormenting himself?

The congregation stood, and he followed it obediently. They did a reading from the Bible. Ariane stared ahead while Helmut glanced at her in a feverish state. His face was cold with sweat. He squeezed the keys to the Blue Demon in his hand. The church walls seemed to press against him. He imagined putrid vapors emanating from the walls and the ground. He felt lightheaded again, and tipped forward. For an instant, he thought he was going to black out. The priest jabbered on about Jesus Christ's message of brotherhood for man. The words in the Bible were repeated slowly, deliberately. Incense wafted through the dark air. The congregants expectantly awaited each phrase of this reading, each pause for meaning, for deliverance, for comfort.

An intense shudder reverberated through Helmut's body. He had to will himself to be still. He slumped into his seat. Ariane finally glanced at him with concern. He managed a crooked grin, and she almost smiled in return, pointing to the keys with her eyes. He shook his head no, and she left him alone. His body was quiet again.

Helmut imagined blood on the altar. Blood flowing from a fount in the Bible and cascading over the marble in a shiny red sheet. Thick blood flickering in the half-light. Underneath this crimson waterfall appeared a small opening to a cave. No, an open wound. Strands of uneven flesh quivered at the edges. The middle of this opening was another universe, and from this chasm erupted a cold wind. A crucified Jesus leapt out of the cold darkness and grabbed his throat and pulled him in! Meaty hands choked him, and Helmut couldn't breathe! He flailed against the force. One pallid open palm slapped his face and smeared it with rose-colored stigmata. Jesus dropped his body in a field of golden grass. A mountainside was in the distance. The God stood before him, laughing. It was incredibly cold there. Jesus took a knife from his robe, offered it to him. As Helmut reached for it, the blade slashed across his palm. Jesus smiled. A white dove flew into Helmut's face and tried to plunge its beak into his mouth. He grabbed one wing, blood smeared over the white feathers, and ripped the appendage from its body. The bird quivered on the golden grass, grotesquely flapping itself in a semi-circle. Helmut stomped it with his boot. Finally, he was alone in the field.

The congregation was on its knees now. Helmut shook his head clear. Ariane was on her knees next to him, her eyes closed. His left hand trembled. He felt the knife in his hands again. He imagined something, someone stalking him. Suddenly he was engulfed in darkness. A door closed somewhere faraway. His limbs were frozen. Helmut wanted to will himself to move, to run, but it was impossible. He was awake, but frozen.

Helmut imagined movement near the altar. His eyes stared wildly at the knife in his impotent hands, at the fingers that did not move to grasp it. He couldn't even defend himself! A light breeze brushed against his frozen face. The most fantastic fear seized Helmut's heart. A blow was but a few seconds away. His skull would be split in half! An ax! He couldn't move his head! He saw the madman's eyes for one moment, disembodied, like two lone stars in an empty universe. The ax slashed through the darkness. Helmut closed his eyes, waiting for the death blow. But it fell next to him, on Ariane! Half of her face was sheared off! Blood splattered him. His mind shattered, with the blackest grief. As his heart exploded with loss, the ax sliced through the air and decapitated him. There was nothing now, only a blackness. Not even the pain.

A hand squeezed his knee, and Helmut snapped out of his trance. People were taking Holy Communion. Ariane had gone without him and was on her knees again, chewing on her wafer. He managed to squeeze her hand weakly.

A new fear gripped him. Helmut imagined the Virgin Mary stepping out of her blue universe, toward him. He stood and faced her, trembling in the coldness reverberating from her pale skin. Her face was sad.

"Why did you kill him?" the Virgin asked Helmut.

He was in Her hands now. She waited patiently for his answer. Helmut could not find any words.

"Did you know they killed my Son and I did not want to kill them?" Mary continued, a radiance palpitating around her.

"I do not believe you," he whispered hoarsely. "But that doesn't matter anyway. I killed him because it was right. Why do you think turning the other cheek is right?"

The Virgin smiled at him and opened her arms as if to hold Helmut, but she was too far away.

"I will tell you why," she said. "It is right because it is perfect. It is a perfect idea. Free of the body, free of time. My Son was perfect too. I could honor Him in no other way. This was why He was free of the cross even as they hoisted Him toward a bleak sunset."

The blue universe glimmered brightly. In his imagination, Helmut could not quite see Her face.

"I believe your Son believed He was right. He believed Himself most of all. That is all. If He had killed another, He would not have been perfect in your eyes. So He killed himself to attain your perfection. He allowed Himself to be killed. But that is not any more perfect than killing another. It is simply easier to defend."

Suddenly the blue universe shattered like glass and the Virgin disappeared. Helmut opened his eyes. The congregants had begun to file out.

"You didn't have to be a hero," Ariane said as they drove home to her apartment again. The streets were nearly empty. He was sweaty and shivering. "I know you're sick."

"I wasn't trying to be anything. I just wanted to be with you," he said softly. "I'll be fine."

"Hopfgartner's being buried today."

"What?"

"Hopfgartner's funeral is today."

"Oh, right."

"So who do you think killed him? A mugger? I don't think so."

"So who did it?" Helmut blurted out, astonished.

"*God* killed him."

"What are you talking about? Jesus Christ?"

"Well, maybe not God directly," she said. "But what happened was in some way sanctioned by Him, don't you think?"

"I don't know. Why would God want to kill someone? Doesn't that sound strange? I would think He'd have better things to do."

"Maybe God was after Hopfgartner specifically. He wasn't exactly an angel. But that's not what I mean. I mean Professor Hopfgartner's murder was a warning to all of us. If things don't get better, then this could happen to you."

"What things?"

"The poverty. The hatred. The violence."

"What if it had nothing to do with poverty?"

"Well, then it's still about hatred, isn't it? At some level, whoever murdered Hopfgartner hated him."

"Assume you're right," Helmut said. "But why is hatred necessarily a bad thing? It could be used to fight for yourself, for what you believe in. Is it really better to love everyone around you even if they don't deserve it? Isn't that the Christian message?"

"Not exactly. I don't think the Bible tells you to be a dupe. Certainly the Old Testament doesn't. Sure, you're supposed to love your family and respect your neighbors. But you should be able to defend yourself. You should at least try to avoid your own hateful feelings and those of others."

"You see, but that's the problem. This 'avoiding.' I think if you see something wrong, you should act on it. Even if it means fighting hate with hate. What you said about the Old Testament. That's exactly right. I don't think it's about love or hate being good or bad. I think it's about abstraction versus practicality. Idealism versus realism. Jesus Christ turned love into an abstraction so powerful you didn't have to do anything to possess it or to give it to someone else. What's Christian love for a Christian anyway? Something you're born into. It's easy!" Helmut said.

"Maybe easy for you. But not me. You still need to work at it. If you don't, then your Judgment Day will come."

"That's just a threat. A faraway threat. It doesn't have any practical effect anymore. Look at all those savages murdering people for two or three dollars. Look at these terrorists who blow up a plane or a bus. They don't really care about a distant God who'll punish them. What if nothing happens when you die other than you cease to exist? Or what if you go to whatever warped version of heaven you created? What if God told them to do it?"

"Then we're in for an all-out war. God against God. Then it's simply a race to get whatever you can in this life. What a nightmare! You think that's our future?"

"I don't know," Helmut said quietly as they approached Ariane's apartment. "But I don't think it's either abstract love or terrible chaos. That's simply how the game's set up now. Why can't we have gods of justice who tell us to murder once in a while, to punish somebody because they deserve it? And to love, yes!"

"I love you." She turned off the ignition of the Blue Demon.

"Love you too," he said, and reached over and kissed her.

"You don't believe in God, do you?"

"Don't know what I believe. Maybe I'm just looking for Him in my own way."

"Maybe He's looking for you."

Chapter Twenty-Three

A northeaster buried southern New England, and the nights and days melded into a cold twilight. Ariane was in her bathrobe, reading on the bed. Helmut was under the covers, sleeping. They had made love an hour ago. A multicolored down comforter kept them deliciously warm. They had three days of blissful nothingness. Nothing but the warmth inside and the bleakness outside. Three days at home.

Helmut opened his eyes and touched Ariane's silky skin. Her huge, brown eyes were transfixed on her book.

"Ariane, can I talk to you?"

"You okay? Still sick?" She placed the book on her lap.

"Yes, I'm fine."

"What?"

"How do I tell you these things?"

"Please, Helmut. What are you talking about?" She sat up, troubled by the mask of pain on his face.

"I love you so much. I need your help. I've been having these dreams. Awful nightmares about Werner Hopfgartner's murder. I'm sick in the head, I tell you!"

"What kind of dreams?"

"I mean, I think about the professor all the time, how he died. I think about living in New Haven, about what could happen if we stay here," he said. "Ariane, I think I'm losing my mind! Violent images! I don't want them in my head! Help me." He couldn't look into her eyes.

"Please, just tell me about the dreams. Let's start there."

"They're dreams about random violence. Dreams of blood. I'm the victim. Or you're being attacked. Wild violence. Animals. Nightmares filled with fear. Indescribable fear. I think I'm drowning when I have them. I don't think I'll ever wake up. I think I'm about to kill! I, I don't know anything anymore. Maybe I shouldn't tell you this. Ariane, I love you. Please, I need you."

"My God, Helmut. I don't understand what's going on. Animals? Who's attacking us? What are these dreams about? How long have you been having them?"

"A week. After Werner Hopfgartner's murder. I love you with all my heart! I'd give you my life! I'd give you everything I have! If I could only tell you, in words, what's in my mind. Am I going crazy? Please tell me! It scares me to think like this. To think about Professor Hopfgartner dead alone on a sidewalk. Why? Why do we kill each other? Why imagine the killing? Ariane, I'm there. Why do I put myself in his place? Look, my hands. They're trembling, I can't stop! *Ach!* Too much thinking! I feel like *I* was stabbed to death! I hate this! Just don't know anything anymore. I imagine the details. They won't go away! I, I hate this! I wish nothing had happened. I wish, somehow, I had been killed instead. Am I just afraid something will happen to us? I can't be without you, Ariane. I'll sacrifice everything for you!" His eyes stared ahead at nothing, lost in another world.

"Helmut, I love you. Let's take it one step at a time. You're tormenting yourself. Something terrible happened. I feel scared too. It's okay to be scared. I'm not going anywhere. We'll work this out together. Helmut. Please. Stop crying. I love you so much. You're torturing yourself."

"I deserve it! I deserve the worst!"

"Helmut, my God. I wish Professor Hopfgartner had never been murdered too. It was absolutely horrible, I agree. I could see how it would upset you. You knew him very well. Your boss. *Everyone* was in shock. I cried too. But you shouldn't let it build up like this. Talk to me. Or it'll turn into something worse. Into dreams about mutilating animals."

"I *hate* myself, Ariane! I'm a wretched human being! I deserve this terror in my head! I *wanted* him to die! I'm completely guilty!

I know what was in my head before it happened. I can't deny that.
I'm guilty, Ariane! I'm just a despicable man! You'll leave me once
you know the truth about me. I deserve it! I love you more than
I've ever loved anyone in my life. My God! Now I've ruined everything!"

"Helmut, I love you too. I'll always love you. I'm never going
to leave you. No matter what. You understand that? I know the
goodness in your heart. I know how hard you try to do the right
thing. I know how you treat me. You are a *good person*, Helmut.
But you're tearing yourself apart over this. I admit it too. I didn't
like Werner Hopfgartner. In fact, I probably hated him too. So I'm
guilty of the same thing, Helmut. I'm guilty too. But you take it
further. You *punish* yourself for these thoughts. You agonize over
them. Why? Leave these things behind you. No one can have perfect thoughts. We try to put a good face to the world, to pretend
we don't have disgusting or bizarre thoughts. We clean these
things up as we go along. We have a dirty thought, we enjoy it for
what it is, we leave it behind. No one knows what was in our
mind. But you leave yourself open. You condemn yourself, and
agonize over your guilt. You admit you're guilty and you tell the
whole world you are. I know this sounds stupid, Helmut, but you
need to be dishonest to function in this world. You need to lie to
yourself, you need to lie to others. You need to *forget* what you
really think sometimes. It's a defense mechanism. It saves you
from too much honesty. It makes life easier. I know it's not perfection, but it works."

Ariane held his head as he sobbed and shivered on the bed. He
seemed incapable of speech. In a strange way, the more fear she
felt for him, in this deep agony, the more she wanted to love him.
Should she tell him what she wanted most to tell him? Many
things made sense to her for the first time. This critical, yet
destructive self-honesty. At once, it empowered him and enervat-
ed him. He had carried her to impossible heights. They shared a
life together. Now it was her turn to pick him off the ground.

"Ariane, oh sweet Ariane! Don't leave me! Please!"

"Don't worry, I won't."

"How can I ask you that? I'm a monster, Ariane! If you only knew . . . everything! You deserve to be *loved!* I wouldn't want you to suffer because you got entangled with a devil! I have to tell you what I am. If you think I'm insane, just leave me! I'll understand! I'll always love you. But if you don't want this, if you don't want *me* . . . I know what I deserve!"

"Helmut, I love you. I'm here because I *want* to be here. I'm staying here with you. Nothing would drag me away from you. Please, Helmut. Stop this. I've never seen you like this. I know you would give your life for me. We'll work on this together. Stop crying now."

"I thought I could control everything, Ariane. That's what I believed." He wiped his bloodshot eyes. "I know I'm a stupid man, Ariane. Thought I could control what was in my head. Thought I knew what was right, that if I knew what was right, then the rest of me would follow. I just want these nightmares to stop. I don't want to see more blood."

"Helmut, listen to me. Tell me whatever you want. When you're ready."

Helmut fell asleep on the bed, and his breathing was peaceful and profound, like the rhythm of the tide. She slipped into her flannel nightgown and bathrobe. Was Helmut having those awful nightmares again? She knew he wasn't crazy. She knew that in her heart. Maybe she was being foolish, but she did love him. The Lord would help him. Helmut was fundamentally good. It was her secret for the moment, but she wanted to stay with him for the rest of her life.

I have only been late a few weeks, Ariane thought in the darkness next to Helmut. *But I can feel it inside of me. We are one now. I won't tell him, yet, I am pregnant. This news should be for joy. Only for blessed joy. It should be for love. It should be because we want to be together, because we have created a blessed child. The news should not be to calm him. Not to force him. Not to threaten him. That's not the right way. We love each other. We need each other now. But what is it that he can't tell me?*

Chapter Twenty-Four

The little cubicle was quiet except for a furious scratching noise. The bright desk light was on, and the window shades were open. Inside Helen Hadley Hall, the rooms were warm, but Temple Street was an empty, snow-covered flatland. A hot pot full of black tea gurgled and steamed. Bharat Patel, consumed by his work, scribbled a torrent of numbers and formulas and explanations with astonishing speed. Yellow legal pad sheets were stacked in front of him, each covered with his hieroglyphics. The phone rang. He wrote down his last thought in a few seconds, and picked up the phone with a smile. In an instant, his face became uncharacteristically serious.

"Sarah! My goodness! I have been trying to reach you for days now. Merry Christmas!"

"Merry Christmas to you!" Sarah Goodman exclaimed happily. "Got all your messages. Did you get mine?"

"Sure I did." Bharat smiled again. "I have not erased a single one. I like to hear your voice. It makes me happy."

"I miss you so much. Still thinking about the night before I left. It was so special for me, Bharat."

"Sarah, you are the special one. I will never forget that night either. I want to see you as soon as you return. Sarah Goodman, you are my dream. I miss you too."

"Hey! I have great news! Got my Comp grades! I passed! With Honors! Can you believe that? I showed my mother as soon as I ripped open the envelope. She was so proud, Bharat. You should've seen her."

"Ah! That is great news! I knew you could do it! I am also very proud of you, my Sarah. You see what you can do if you believe in yourself? Now you know you belong here."

"Thank you. I could never have done it without your help. I'll never forget that, Bharat. My parents want to meet you."

"Of course. Maybe this summer. After the school year. Would that be possible?"

"That's perfect. Told them you were a brilliant, nice guy! The best!"

"Ah, but Sarah. They will be so disappointed when they see me! A poor mathematician, nothing more. You are the brilliant one. I also have some good news. I finished my prospectus and submitted it a few days ago. My adviser said it would be quickly approved. I am working on my first chapter."

"Hah! You see! You are brilliant! That's wonderful! Bharat, the steamroller! You're just amazing! Give yourself time to relax. I sent you those books about the history of Iowa, and a book of short stories too. You should get them any day now."

"Thank you very much. I will read them and think about you. For me, you are the beauty of Iowa."

"You are just so sweet."

"Sarah, I have another piece of news. Not good news, but I thought you should know as soon as possible."

"My God! What's wrong? What happened?"

"Sarah, Werner Hopfgartner was killed about a week ago."

"What? How? I, I can't believe that! Bharat!"

"It is true. A mugging. On Whitney Avenue. I read it in the newspaper first. I called your department and confirmed it. Werner Hopfgartner is dead. A tragedy. I don't think the students know about it yet, except those still in New Haven."

"Bharat! Professor Hopfgartner was killed?" she said, gasping and sobbing. "I don't understand! That's horrible! What? How, I, I, my God! He was my adviser, Bharat! My friend! How could this happen? Why?"

"I did not want to be the one to give you the terrible news. Sarah. Sarah, please. I wish I could be with you now. I will be with you when you come back. Tell your family what happened. They will help you. Sarah, please do not cry. Sarah."

"What am I going to do? Listen to me! I'm worried about my stupid dissertation and this poor man's dead! I'm absolutely disgusting!"

"Sarah, that's not true. Sarah, you knew this man and he helped you and you should grieve for him. But your first instinct is right! Sarah, are you listening to me?"

"Yes."

"After you grieve, after you do what is natural, you should think about what to do next. That's *exactly* why I wanted to tell you now, so you could come back with a plan to continue your progress. That's what your adviser would have wanted you to do. That's what you should do now and I'll help you."

"Bharat, I don't know anything anymore. Things were going so well for the first time. And now this. Feel like I've been struck by lightning! I can't win! Soon as I start winning, God crushes me!"

"Sarah, you know that is not true. It has nothing to do with God. You can survive this. You have made important progress. You have finished your Comps. The next step is to get a new adviser. But don't think about this now. In a few days. We will do it together."

"Bharat, this is awful," Sarah cried softly. "He was killed on Whitney Avenue?"

"That is right."

"Someone mugged him? They know who did it?"

"No. They have no suspects yet. I saved the newspaper articles, but I am sure your department will know more."

"Bharat, I don't know what to do anymore."

"Yes you do. Sarah, I am here for you. If I hear anything else, I will tell you. Remember: Tell your family about what happened. They will help you. And then, focus again on what must be done."

"Bharat, I wish I could be with you right now. Wish you could hold me. I feel so lost."

"Sarah, my dear Sarah. Please. I am with you. Call me tomorrow if you want. You know I will be happy only when I hold you again. Please, Sarah. Remember we can overcome anything together."

"This is a nightmare. I can't believe this is happening. When something good happens in my life, I should expect a catastrophe in return."

"Sarah!" he snapped, and then calmed down. "That is simply a destructive way to think. You won't do that with me! The key, I think, is to have no fear. No fear of success. No fear of failure. For that, you need self-respect."

"Self-respect?"

"Self-respect."

Chapter Twenty-Five

Jack Rosselli read the report he had submitted to his boss. It was most likely the official end of the three-week-old Hopfgartner case. The comprehensive report was well written. The logic was sound. Rosselli listed the facts of the case. Werner Hopfgartner had died on the night of December 16, most likely between 10:00 p.m. and midnight. The cause of death was massive internal bleeding from two large stab wounds to the upper chest and abdomen by a stainless-steel blade. The professor died on Whitney Avenue, slightly north of the Mill River dam. The body was discovered in the early morning hours by a jogger. There was a record in the logbook of a call from Mrs. Hopfgartner to the police shortly before 1:00 a.m. that night. At the murder scene, the police discovered only a bloody footprint, which was photographed and measured. A more expansive search of the neighborhood turned up the professor's wallet, minus any cash or credit cards, at East Rock Park. The DNA work on the body had been inconclusive.

The biggest break in the case was also the greatest disappointment. Two days after the murder, a pair of bloody shoes had been found on a vagrant about a mile away from the scene. Lab analysis proved the shoes were smeared with the professor's blood. Rosselli included his first and only interview with the vagrant, deleting his potentially explosive reference to "a goddamn Yalie." He decided it would serve "no official purpose." The old drunk died in his sleep from a massive heart attack only three days after his arrest on unrelated charges. Rosselli offered the opinion—an epitaph, as it were—that he did not think the vagrant was responsible for the murder. Others, he was sure, would think otherwise.

In his report, the detective also included the pertinent facts gathered from his interviews with members of the Yale faculty and staff, as well as family interviews. Detective Rosselli concluded the professor had probably been killed for his wallet, but that no suspects had yet been identified. He would follow any new leads that turned up, but that was about it. His boss told him he had covered all the bases. Rosselli sent a copy of his report to the Yale Police Department. Yale seemed satisfied too. The president's office offered a reward of ten thousand dollars for any information leading to an arrest and conviction in the murder of Werner Hopfgartner. But Yale was convinced the case had reached a dead end, too. This was the written and official word. The word accepted and authorized as the truth. But it wasn't the truth. At least Jack Rosselli didn't think so.

The truth might never be known, officially. He accepted that as often as he accepted a police officer apprehending a suspect in possession of an undeniable piece of evidence, and then that selfsame officer making a stupid mistake during the arrest to let the bad guy get away. You needed to know an endless list of rules and procedures. Forget any single one while you scrambled to avoid being shot in the head, and a lawyer would use your mistake to punch a hole for the rat to scurry through.

Sure, sometimes Rosselli just went through the motions. Sometimes he lost all hope. What was the point of all that extra effort? If society wasn't going to make it easier for him, why should he break his back to help society rid itself of crime? He would do his job, and nothing else. He would be officially clean, and take care of himself along the way. Society made it easier to have crime without punishment. It said, in no uncertain terms, through its newspapers and TV shows, that people did not bear any responsibility for their actions. The excuse of racism, of course, was the most pervasive. But it could be the poverty excuse. Or the I-was-abused-as-a-child excuse. Why didn't they label crime itself a historical form of discrimination, and criminals an injured class? Why didn't they do away with right and wrong altogether? People did whatever they could get away with, Rosselli thought. Only the police had responsibilities. The courts ignored common sense. The juries were often a mirror image of the worst in society. And the lawyers? Who expected anything but lies from them? *Do whatever you can get away with.* That should be the new motto under George Washington's chin on every American quarter.

So, if his report wasn't the truth, what did Jack Rosselli believe? He wouldn't discuss his theory even with his colleagues in the homicide division. This would be a truth only for his heart. Rosselli believed Jonathan Atwater had killed Werner Hopfgartner. Jonathan Atwater had been the malevolent force behind the murder.

The detective had shadowed Atwater. Rosselli watched the librarian leave his house on Chatham Street to go to work. Atwater seemed a clean-cut man in his forties who liked to wear bow ties. He always parked in the lot in front of the Whitney Gymnasium and marched straight into Sterling Library.

Rosselli measured Atwater's footprint from the snow and mud outside the librarian's front door. Atwater's shoe size was about one size smaller than the shoes on the old vagrant, but that was close enough. The thick layer of snow on that murderous night could've easily distorted the original imprint. Rosselli ran a background check on Atwater and got a copy of his driver's license.

That type of surveillance was always a judgment call. The alternative strategy would have been to confront the suspect immediately, a search warrant in hand, and hope to discover crucial evidence before its destruction or disappearance.

But that strategy depended on several factors that were missing in this case. Rosselli had Mrs. Hopfgartner's assertions that Atwater had been in love with Professor Hopfgartner. No judge in Connecticut would grant him a search warrant on only that. With that reasoning, Mrs. Hopfgartner herself could have been a suspect. The old bum had claimed someone from Yale had abandoned the shoes. Rosselli believed him, but who else would? The old man had been unable to provide any other details. Atwater also had no prior arrests or convictions. From a legal point of view, the librarian was as clean as a cardinal in a cassock. Rosselli had nothing to elicit official sympathy for the leap of faith he wanted to make. Moreover, he had followed Atwater several times during the week before New Year's Day. Atwater had done nothing the least bit out of the ordinary.

Twice Rosselli picked through Atwater's garbage. He found used emerald condoms. An empty carton of two percent low-fat milk. Empty low-fat plain containers. A slew of basmati rice bags. An occasional box of "Couscous Moroccan Pasta." An empty box of Kellogg's All-Bran. A cellophane wrapper of boneless chicken breasts. Also telephone bills—Atwater called a number in Boston most often, and one in Santa Monica—gas and electric bills, a statement from People's Bank, credit card bills, which showed Atwater often ate in cheap New Haven restaurants, probably alone. With his hands in surgical gloves, Rosselli also retrieved a gay porn magazine from Atwater's trash.

The first week in January Rosselli decided a radical change in tactics was necessary. It was time to push events forward instead of waiting for something to happen. He decided he would interview Atwater, unannounced, and question him about Hopfgartner. True, the tactic of questioning a possible suspect was always a gamble. The element of surprise would be lost. But the detective might make the suspect nervous enough that he would commit a careless act leading to an arrest. What choice did Rosselli have? In his gut, Rosselli was convinced Atwater was responsible for the murder. He just needed to prove it.

Atwater seemed intelligent and outwardly calm, but Rosselli could also smell the fear. The only way to crack Atwater was to confront him. Rosselli would get one shot at him. After that, Atwater would get a lawyer. The chief would ask why Rosselli was harassing a Yale librarian if he had no evidence.

A few minutes after 2:00 p.m., Rosselli yanked open the massive wooden doors of Sterling Memorial Library. It was practically empty early in the spring semester before the students returned. A librarian at the reference desk showed him past the guard to the stacks and pointed down a narrow corridor lined with thick metal bookracks. Atwater's office was closed, but Rosselli could see a glow of light through the opaque glass. He knocked sharply on the doorframe, and a hazy figure took shape through the glass. The door opened.

"Jonathan Atwater?"

"Yes, that's right."

"I'm Detective Jack Rosselli from the New Haven Police Department. I'm investigating the murder of Werner Hopfgartner. Can I ask you a few questions?"

"Why, yes. Of course. Please come in."

The change in Atwater's face was remarkable. The librarian had been grinning, as if he had just remembered a particularly delicious joke. But after he heard Rosselli's first words and calmly sat down again, Atwater's eyes shined with concentration. The smile vanished. His skin turned pasty white. Atwater offered the detective a cup of coffee. Rosselli declined. Atwater's body seemed suddenly tense and immobile.

As Rosselli talked, he searched Atwater's clear blue-gray eyes. This library gentleman looked frozen in terror. But Jonathan Atwater, Rosselli believed, also possessed fantastic composure. The librarian's mind seemed to be working at a frenetic pace behind that façade. This man did not yet display one movement out of character, not one jerk or lunge or flash of anger. Certainly Atwater appeared without any guilt or anguish.

"I'm just asking routine questions to all friends and acquaintances of Professor Hopfgartner," Rosselli said, smiling and pulling out a notepad. He felt energized. "As I'm sure you know, the professor was attacked and killed on Whitney Avenue. Near the Hamden line. We're basically gathering as many details as possible about the professor's life. To get an idea what happened. Certainly to get a picture of his last days."

Atwater gulped.

"Detective Rosselli," Atwater said, in a higher than normal voice, "I will certainly help you any way I can. It has been a great tragedy for all of us at Yale. But I thought this was a random act of violence. Another New Haven story. Wasn't it?"

"Well, sure. That's what we think it was. A mugging gone bad. But there's certain information—confidential, of course—that has led us to believe it could be otherwise. We need to get to the bottom of this mystery and we need your help. You knew the professor well, right?"

"Naturally. The professor was a regular in the library. Every faculty member is."

"What kind of person was he? I mean, did he make friends easily? Was he a loner? You know, I've changed my mind about that cup of coffee, if that's okay."

"Of course. Be right back," Atwater said. He brought the detective a cup of coffee and sat down again. "Professor Hopfgartner was just another academic. Kept to himself. Spent hours reading in his favorite corner chair in the German Reading Room. Expected his requests to be the first and only requests you fulfilled, just like everyone else at Yale. They can be quite demanding, these pedagogues." Atwater lifted his horn-rimmed glasses and rubbed his eyes. The facial skin underneath these orbs seemed translucent, even delicate.

"I can only imagine," Rosselli said. "Barely finished college myself. Would Hopfgartner make friends with anyone? I mean, would he befriend someone on the street, for example, someone who might kill him?"

"You think somebody picked him up and killed him? I don't understand. I don't think Werner Hopfgartner would have gotten into a stranger's car. Not willingly. He wasn't the type to hitch a ride. He loved walking home."

"It's just a possibility we're considering. Among other things." Rosselli put the cup to his lips and drank slowly. "Did the professor have any enemies? Someone who wanted to kill him?"

"Are you saying someone here killed him? That's ridiculous. Werner did not have any enemies and no one here would even think of such a thing. How on earth did you come up with that conclusion?"

"Well, how well did you know him?"

"I don't understand what you're saying. What exactly are you saying? That I had something to do with this awful crime? Are you actually serious?" Atwater's blue eyes blazed with surprise and outrage.

"I just asked you how well you knew him and I didn't get an answer," the detective repeated in a deadly drone.

"I don't know what kind of game you're playing, detective. I don't have anything to hide." The librarian seemed suddenly weary, even defeated.

"So answer the question."

"Werner Hopfgartner and I, at one point in time, we had been lovers. I'm sure you know that already. Now I want you to get the hell out of my office. I want you out now!" Atwater jumped up behind his desk, shaking.

"I was just asking you a few questions, Mr. Atwater. No need to become hysterical." Rosselli sat cozily immobile in the black chair. Atwater's eyes burned with rage. There was no doubt, Rosselli thought, this man could kill.

"Just get out of my office. Search until you're blue in the face. Search until you die, if that's what you want to do with your time. You can ask questions about me, ask anyone. You will find absolutely nothing. You're looking for a bogeyman, aren't you? Look until you're satisfied. I don't care. But if you bother me again, I'll charge you with harassment. You can count on that. I'll stop you. Being in love is not a crime." Still standing, Atwater trembled in his tracks.

"Fine. Thank you for your cooperation, Mr. Atwater. Oh, one more thing before I go. Where exactly were you Wednesday night, December 16?"

"At home. I was at home. Where I usually am after work." Atwater tried to hold his body still, but he was still quivering.

"Were you alone?" He almost had the bastard, Rosselli thought.

"Yes, I was."

"You didn't see Werner Hopfgartner that night? Tell me the truth, Mr. Atwater. That's all I want."

"No I didn't. Please leave now."

"A bit of advice. Don't go too far. I might be back with a few more questions. Thank you for your time. Appreciate it."

"Do whatever the hell you want."

"Thank you."

As soon as Rosselli stepped into the hallway, the door slammed shut behind him. Maybe Atwater would crack, he thought. Now that Atwater knew he was a suspect, he would be careful, maybe too careful. The librarian could figure out the police had nothing on him yet. But he would worry about it. Hiding the evidence would consume him. Getting the evidence away from him would become an obsession. Then Atwater might make a mistake. Stranger things had happened. Some perps almost wanted to be caught, as if they were desperate to grab on to the truth of their crime. Maybe Atwater was like these weak bastards. Maybe he would plunge headfirst into the redemptive bliss of his own criminal responsibility.

Chapter Twenty-Six

The memorial service for Werner Hopfgartner was on January 14. Jonathan Atwater, Rosselli thought, would surely emerge from his self-imposed seclusion. The emotions would be unshackled. The memories would fragment in the mind like a million bits of the sun. It was the night Yale buried the memory of Werner Hopfgartner. And Jack Rosselli would be there.

A solemn procession of congregants filed into Dwight Chapel. Rosselli had checked out the building as soon as he knew where the memorial service would be. He located the side entrances and where he could watch the ceremony secretly. The secretary at the German department's office had told him the memorial service would consist of a couple of speeches by colleagues and a formal eulogy by the family priest and possibly some brief remarks by a graduate student. Mrs. Hopfgartner would also be there.

Rosselli sat down in a dark corner near a side exit. Dwight Hall wasn't a real chapel, but a churchlike building with ornate spires. It was filled with rows of metal folding chairs. A huge oak table would be the altar. A wooden lectern had been placed upon the table, for the orators. Rosselli counted about forty mourners. About two minutes before the service began, Jonathan Atwater quietly slipped into a middle row.

Atwater took a seat next to Helmut Sanchez and Ariane Sassolini, who scooted over so the librarian was at the edge of the aisle. Five rows ahead, Frau Hopfgartner sat with Victor Otto and a few other senior faculty members. Everyone seemed attentive, ready for another lecture. Frau Hopfgartner turned her head to whisper a word to the chairman; Atwater slumped behind the heads in front of him and lowered his eyes. Ariane reached out and clasped Atwater's hand. He seemed startled at first and then smiled kindly at her. In the darkness, Rosselli kept an eye on all of them. He would keep an eye on Atwater, and follow him to the parking lot next to the gymnasium once the ceremony was over. Before leaving Chatham Street, Rosselli had seen the librarian load a shovel or a hoe, several planks of wood and possibly a coil of rope into the trunk of his car. Rosselli was convinced Atwater was planning something devious.

≈ ≈ ≈

Helmut glanced toward Ariane and Mr. Atwater, winked at her, and tried to smile, too. Did he look awkward or distracted? Helmut thought. Could anyone tell he was trying to think of nothing at all, and certainly not Werner Hopfgartner? Flashes of crimson exploded in front of his eyes like a bloody, palpitating sun. He was dizzy. Ariane touched his hand too, and everything came back into focus.

A priest began with a prayer and exhorted the crowd to remember the good life of the professor and not just its tragic end.

"We should all do this in time of pain and so overcome it, and overcome as well the danger of evil in this world, its pervasiveness and increase," the priest intoned. "Blessed be he who will lead us out of this night of despair. Blessed be he, Christ the Son of God. In the name of the Father, the Son and the Holy Spirit. Amen."

The priest took his seat next to Frau Hopfgartner and held her hand tightly. She seemed embarrassed by the show of compassion and bowed her head awkwardly. A retired professor from the German department stood up and talked about the first time he had met Werner Hopfgartner in Europe.

Helmut looked at the people in front of him. Almost all of them were male professors in their fifties or older. Many were from the German department, a few from other enclaves at Yale. A group of younger graduate students sat together. Helmut noticed a few administrators whom Hopfgartner had known for years, a representative from the president's office, who looked like an investment banker, family members and old friends. Not one of them seemed anguished.

Helmut wanted to leave the room and escape this nightmare. He turned toward Ariane, but instead focused on the two tears sliding down Mr. Atwater's face. The poor librarian cried silently and immovably like a grieving statue.

Another professor stood up. In a booming, theatrical voice, he recounted the academic successes of Werner Hopfgartner. The prizes he had won. The numerous honors and dedications. He then gave an overview of Werner Hopfgartner's ideas, the main topics behind his books, including their "singular rigor" and "monumental influence." He focused on Hopfgartner's "seminal work" on Nietzsche and Heidegger, which first brought "our dear colleague" to the attention of a wider international community of scholars.

This eulogy was just a preachy, self-important lecture, Helmut thought. A messianic gleam shined from the old professor's eyes. Like the others, this idiot was consumed by his self-importance. Helmut wanted to stand up and leave. Those fools didn't know Werner Hopfgartner. The man behind those "great" ideas. Helmut alone understood the truth behind this man. Didn't they understand what might happen when someone took these perversions to heart? Whose responsibility was it if someone acted against helpless individuals for the sake of a rancid good?

Helmut's head spun. This false rhetoric. The absolute lies. He had been right. Why didn't they open their eyes? He knew that the blood might haunt him for a while. Maybe the dread would always be there. He had killed a human being. But never would he doubt himself again. He had been right, Helmut believed. These idiots listening to the memorial service lived happily in a netherworld, preserving it with this ceremony of lies. He listened and squeezed Ariane's hand.

Mr. Atwater wiped his face with a wrinkled handkerchief. The priest was speaking again, but Helmut didn't listen. He kept his eyes on Mr. Atwater, who was shivering. The spasms that rifled up his shoulders slowly ceased. The librarian's chest heaved and was steady again. It was already fifteen minutes past nine. Everyone stood up.

The crowd spilled into the murky amber of the quadrangle. The graduate students scurried into the darkness to avoid facing their professors. Helmut tried to catch Ariane's hand, but she pulled it away, raised her eyebrows and tilted her head toward Jonathan Atwater. The librarian's eyes were bloodshot and hollow, his head bowed. He looked like a man for whom nothing mattered anymore. The three of them walked together toward High Street. Ariane asked Mr. Atwater how he was, and he said he was okay, but not another word. Ariane draped an arm around his shoulders and told him she could only imagine his pain. He said the memories were such a torment.

Helmut trailed them awkwardly. He was breathing easier now. He didn't have to listen to those lies anymore. He imagined flying toward the dark clouds, and escaping, and finally being free.

The three of them waited at the curb for the stream of headlights to stop. Just as they were about to cross Elm Street, a navy blue Datsun with tinted windows screeched to a halt in front of them. The car throbbed with the thunderous thump and grind of Dre XXX's "Fuckit." Laughing, four black teenagers poked their heads out the window. One yelled to Ariane, "Yo, bitch! Watcha doin' with 'em faggots! I be your daddy in here!"

Ariane quickly walked past the car. Helmut and Mr. Atwater pretended to be deaf. Then the car peeled away toward the New Haven green, veering sharply left at College Street.

Ariane and Helmut stopped in front of her Corolla parked on High Street next to the law school. She asked Mr. Atwater if he wanted to come over and have dinner or a few drinks. He was tired, he said, and just wanted to go home. Maybe next week they could do something together.

"Do you think he'll be okay by himself?" Ariane asked in the car. "You don't think he'll do something stupid, do you?"

Atwater looked so forlorn as he walked away from them, alone.

"I don't think he's like that. I'll call him tomorrow and see how he's doing," Helmut said, rubbing his hands together and trying to dispel this cold chill around them.

"I wish I knew what to do," Ariane said. "He's all by himself. Did you see him at the service?"

"Yeah. He must've really loved that old bastard. I don't see that at all." Helmut stared at her hands, willing her to start the engine. "Me neither. Werner Hopfgartner? God, I'm sorry he's dead. But what could anyone ever see in that old man? Maybe in private he was a different person." She started the engine and put the car into gear.

"I can't wait to get under the covers." Helmut squeezed her thigh.

≈ ≈ ≈

From the shadows of the law school, Rosselli watched Atwater split away from his two companions. Then the detective marched up Wall Street, took a right on York and a left on Grove to wait for the librarian. Rosselli figured the librarian would stay on Wall Street, and turn left on Grove, on his way to the parking lot in front of Whitney Gymnasium. Rosselli had parked there too. The detective would slip into his car and be ready to follow the librarian. What in the world did Atwater plan to do with a rope, a shovel and wooden planks? Maybe Atwater was ready to turn himself in, or kill himself.

Rosselli reached his car, jumped inside and waited patiently for Atwater to emerge from the shadows of Grove Street. Clouds concealed the half moon. What if Atwater did commit suicide? It would be justice in a way, and the end of this godforsaken affair.

Rosselli was freezing, and he wanted to turn up the heater. But what if Atwater noticed the idling vehicle? Rosselli buttoned up his coat and rubbed his knees together, and waited.

But Atwater was nowhere in sight.

≈ ≈ ≈

Jonathan Atwater crossed Wall Street and entered the heavy canyon of shadows between the law school library and Beinecke Library. He felt alone in the world, and so utterly empty. He had lost so many friends to the scourge of AIDS. That had been horrible. But that hadn't prepared him for the unmerciful blow of Hopf-gartner's death. Werner Hopfgartner's absence had left a hole in his heart.

Yes, Mr. Atwater knew Hopfgartner had not been a saint. The professor had even battered him. But just as he forgave himself for his own occasional failings, he had long ago forgiven Werner Hopfgartner. Instead, Mr. Atwater had treasured those moments when his lover had risen above the worst in his nature and bestowed upon him affection. He replayed scenes in his memory, important conversations. Even after they separated, Mr. Atwater would see the professor walking across the campus and know that he had sacrificed his own pleasure for the good of this man. There had been a reason for the pain. A purpose. Now all of that was gone forever. Worse, some imbecile cop blamed him, the only one person who had truly loved the professor. How could the world twist with such malevolence? There was absolutely no logic at all anymore, Mr. Atwater thought. In fact, there was evil reason, per-spectives devouring other perspectives, and senselessness at the end. He thought of turning himself in if only to reaffirm the wretchedness of his existence. In a momentary flash of self-indulgence, he had also imagined the relief of dying. He was still uncertain about that. But he was quite certain about one thing he had to do tonight.

Around the corner of the Book and Snake's ominous mini-Parthenon, Mr. Atwater thought he heard a rustling in the bushes, soft laughter. He walked quickly, and peered at the shadows trying to make out who it was. From behind, a hand grabbed his throat. Someone punched him in the stomach and kicked his face. He was gasping for breath, dazed. His feet swung into the air, hands all over his body. More laughter. The navy blue Datsun with the tint-ed windows was parked under the entrance to the Grove Street Cemetery, in front of the secret society at Yale. The car doors popped open and slammed shut. More gangly bodies sprinted toward the nascent revelry. High above on the portal, etched in red granite, were the words 'The Dead Shall Be Raised.'

They dragged him into the cemetery, behind the empty guard-house at the entrance, over a gravel walkway covered with bits of ice and frozen mud. The half moon shined against the vault sepulchers and tombstones from previous centuries. Stripped of leaves, the old elms swayed desolately. A massive stone wall surrounded the dead. In an alley of monuments, one boy repeatedly kicked the writhing figure on the ground, kicked him again in the throat, waited for just the right moment and smashed his heel into the groin. Others shouted encouragement and laughed. Another boy searched through the librarian's pant pockets—coins and keys spilled on the ground—and yanked his pants down to his ankles.

Atwater moaned in agony. Blood gushed from his mouth like black foam shining in the moonlight. He tried to stand up, pushed his torso up by grasping the white edge of a tomb. A knee crashed into his face. Someone else yanked him from behind, pulled at his jacket, ripped it off his body and threw him against a sharp corner, his back exploding in a flash of pain. A hand pulled at the leather strap of his watch, tugged it free and disappeared back into the shadows.

Mr. Atwater's body throbbed with deep bruises to his face, chest and abdomen. Two ribs were already broken. His skull was mildly fractured. His left eye socket had cracked. He thought he heard gleeful braggadocio in the distance. But the perpetrators were nearby, mindful of their anonymity and the sweep of further possibilities.

Mr. Atwater lay motionless on his back, breathing heavily. Blood bubbled out of his nose and mouth. He could see a blurry half moon. Then he was moving again. Someone was dragging him over a rough patch and yelling at the others. Mr. Atwater heard deep grunts and accusations, unintelligible mockery.

He was lifted onto a slab of cold marble. The clouds began to drift across the moon. Two boys were arguing about what to do next. One wanted to leave Mr. Atwater on the low, flat marble vault with a cross protruding from one end upon which 'Emerson' was etched. The other sounded angry, taunting the vacillator with stabs at his face and an occasional lunge of his muscled body. The others glanced at the wallet, the wristwatch and the jacket, thinking about which side to take, swiveling their heads to check the tombstones and the tall cemetery wall around them. But nobody else was there.

Mr. Atwater tried to lift his head but became dizzy, lost his balance and rolled off the tomb. He hit his face and moaned. Immediately he was hoisted back onto the vault. His movement stirred and coalesced their passions. Someone yanked his pants off. He lay there naked from the waist down, the civility of his shoes and socks incongruous with the blood splattered on his shirt and the wobbly red mass of a head. They pulled his arms so they were behind the tomb's marble cross, and tied his wrists together with one pant leg. Around his torso and the base of the cross, they pulled the other pant leg until it was tight against his chest, like a weird sash, and then also tied it behind his back.

Someone punched him in the groin again. A flash of light seemed to burst in front of his face. He tried to cross his legs, but wasn't sure if the movement he imagined was a command completed or just a purposeless quivering in a remote part of his body.

Jack Rosselli opened his car door and walked cautiously down Grove Street, peering at the shadows. Atwater's car was still in the parking lot. Rosselli crossed to the south side of the street, next to the back entrance of the law school, expecting Atwater to be on the opposite side of the street already, where he could more easily reach the parking lot. The detective stared at the tiny square with a park bench at the outside corner of the cemetery, at the thicket and the trees. No movement there either. He followed the cemetery stone wall to the corner of High Street, where the wall became a seven-foot high spear-like fence and the portal entrance. A streak of moonlight lay on the walkway, the uninterrupted shine along the wall, next to the fence and up to the portal. No one was walking up Grove Street. Where could Atwater be? Rosselli checked his side of the street, glanced behind him, but found nothing at all. A car rounded the corner of York Street and proceeded up Grove. As he reached the corner of High Street—the last place where he had seen Atwater—he heard low murmurs and laughter in the cemetery. He heard what sounded like a growl. Rosselli snapped open his gun holster. In front of the cemetery gate, he noticed that someone had left a car door ajar. The windows were rolled down.

He stepped inside the cemetery and around the empty guard-house, crouched and ready for anything. What the hell was going on? Rosselli thought.

He saw four figures lurch toward one corner of the cemetery. One of them was dragging a black mass on the ground, a man. His pants seemed to be at his ankles. But Rosselli wasn't sure. He had to get closer. Rosselli squatted behind a row of tombstones and ran quickly down a parallel pathway. The voices sounded gleeful. Was that Atwater on the ground with some of his little boys? Had Atwater been fucking them on those gravestones? Maybe they had wanted to give him a little more than he had asked for.

Rosselli breathed deeply to calm himself. He was about fifteen yards away. Rosselli recognized Atwater's coat in the hands of one of the boys. The four of them lifted Atwater's limp body onto a flat tomb that looked like an altar. He saw Atwater's lolling head. They had done a little dance on his face. The librarian wasn't moving much on the slab of marble. His hands were spasmodic around his waist. Atwater looked absolutely ridiculous with his pants pulled down on top of somebody's dead grandfather.

It served Atwater right, Rosselli thought. The son of a bitch was getting what he deserved. Why would this librarian flick out his pecker if he didn't know who the hell he was about to fuck?

Rosselli heard two boys arguing, but he couldn't understand the gist of it. The other two were watching the fun. Maybe they were deciding who was next. Maybe Atwater wanted it a little rough, and things got out of hand.

Atwater rolled off the tomb and fell to the ground. The boys lifted him up and tied him to the marble cross with his pants.

Rosselli winced. That must've hurt, he thought. Right between the legs. These shits were doing his job for him. Atwater deserved it. He had killed the professor in the middle of the night. Now it was his turn. Maybe God wanted it to happen here. In His out-house. Maybe there was justice after all. Rosselli decided to get the hell out of there. He had 'justice' and 'peace,' all in one neat fuck-ing package.

Rosselli snapped the holster shut and backed away from the scene. The four boys sprinted down the adjacent pathway, laugh-

ing and jostling each other and racing down to the guardhouse
and toward the gate. They went past him, a few feet away. He waited for them to leave the cemetery before he stood up. He heard the
Blue Datsun rev up and screech away.

Rosselli turned around and stared at the back of the tomb
where Atwater was tied. He could see a hand quiver. A dark cloth
was tied diagonally across the marble cross. That poor bastard was
going to freeze to death.

Rosselli walked toward the gate. As soon as he was outside
again, he marched toward the gymnasium and turned left as he
reached the parking lot. In a dark corner of the street, he took out
a white handkerchief and cleared his throat and stepped up to a
phone booth. He slipped his right sleeve over his hand and yanked
the receiver off the hook and punched in 9-1-1. He glanced
around, but the street was empty. The emergency operator
answered.

"Four kids in a navy blue Datsun just fucked up a guy at the
Grove Street Cemetery in New Haven. Got it?"

"Please identify yourself. What is your name and location?"

"Grove Street Cemetery in New Haven. Have a nice day."

Rosselli slammed the phone down and walked back to his car.
It felt good to be finally rid of this Hopfgartner mess. He pulled onto
Grove Street and turned left on Broadway to drive down Elm Street
toward I-91. He turned up the heater and clicked on the fan. His
nose was stuffed up; his face was numb. His legs felt stiff, like cold
rods of steel. The heat didn't kick in until he was on the interstate,
and it felt good to warm up. He remembered that he hadn't gotten
a good night's sleep in a long time. Tonight he might just sleep like
a baby. It was really good to put this case behind him. Rosselli
couldn't wait to climb in bed after drinking a nice hot cup of tea. He
would hold Rosie, soak up her warmth. She would tell him to get
himself another blanket and stop pestering her in the middle of the
night. He was so prone to cold chills, to the winter winds that
seemed to stiffen every joint in his body. Maybe they should retire
to Arizona. New England was simply too cold too long.

Chapter Twenty-Seven

The half moon seemed even more distant than before. Jonathan Atwater couldn't feel his legs. He drifted in and out of consciousness. He thought he was going to die. He felt as if he were underwater. When he inhaled, a dull ache in his chest metamorphosed into the sharp pain of needles piercing his insides. He tried to inhale more slowly, but that didn't help. He could taste the bitter blood in his mouth. His stomach churned, and he thought he was urinating. He wasn't sure. A burning sensation in his groin expanded to his hips and toward his legs. Atwater tried to pull his arms free, but the knot was too tight, a sharp pain in his back too forbidding. He thought his back was broken. How dramatic his death would seem, his body splayed atop a tombstone. He had style. At least he had that.

Mr. Atwater tried to straighten up, but the cloth pinned him in place. He was going to die like Christ, he thought, like a stupid martyr when he had never given a damn about religion or anything so high. He was in the *wrong* cemetery. Dead, instead of a maid for the dead. He had just wanted to be with him one last time. That had been his special plan. Why had he been punished for wanting to clean Hopfgartner's grave? Mr. Atwater asked himself in the darkness.

Suddenly Mr. Atwater heard voices behind him. He was afraid his friends had returned. Someone tugged on his bonds. He crossed his legs again, tensed his thigh muscles and readied himself for a final plunge into an abyss. Why couldn't they just leave him here? he thought.

God, oh God, why can't they just forsake me? Please don't torture me anymore.

Then his hands were free. Mr. Atwater heard a young voice. A blanket was laid across his bare legs. A dark blue jacket covered his chest. He looked into a woman's eyes. It was Mary Magdalene with a badge. More hands cradled him gently and carried him through the cemetery like a child sleepy and warm. He wondered if all of heaven's angels were dressed like cops. He fainted.

Deep inside the black mist of a forest, it rained. In his dreams, he was running. Rain fell over his face, caressed his skin and blessed him. Holy water from God's tears. Inside the forest, Jonathan Atwater was free. Free to live and help, free for the best of life. Free of the pain and the weakness of his body. Inside the forest, he was a man. Whole and complete, and with a place to be. And most of all, he was loved. Loved completely, loved and loved again. Emancipated from all hate. In the dark forest, Atwater could fly to the heavens. He flew up. High above the horizon of trees, to the clouds, beyond the clouds, toward the stars, high as high could be. He came to a light, which was even more helpful and welcoming than the forest. He jumped into its warmth and found what he was looking for and knew everything for the first time in a long time. For the first time ever. In that light, Atwater could be warm.

Then something shattered. Suddenly there was this shattering, like glass breaking. A merciless light blinded his eyes. Then he was falling. Falling into the world again. A breezy and stupendous fall. Falling back into terror and existence again. Falling and opening his eyes and feeling his pain again. So much cursed pain. Mr. Atwater closed his eyes tightly, but he could not escape. He still found himself there. In the hospital, in this body of pain.

The nurse tugged at the intravenous tube stuck in his arms, tugged it because she had inadvertently tangled her foot in it. Mr. Atwater opened his eyes. His head pulsed in dizzying waves. He saw a terrifically white light above his head. He turned his head slowly, and the nurse smiled at him and told him not to move too much. Most of his face was bandaged. His torso was tightly wrapped in stiff casing. His head was in an ugly contraption that looked like a cube-like halo from a high-tech band of angels. Mr. Atwater could feel his legs, but he could hardly move them. They were strapped loosely to the bed. His back had a spot that felt as if a branding iron had been left embedded in his flesh. The nurse told him he would eventually be all right, that he had suffered serious injuries but that they would heal. She told him his job would be to rest and let her know, by squeezing what felt like a rubber ball at his fingertips, when he felt uncomfortable, when he needed her. He squeezed his fingers around the rubber ball to practice.

"Perfect."

"I was attacked," he whispered hoarsely.

"Yes, we know. Just relax and get better. We still don't know your name."

"Jonathan Atwater. I work for Yale." Was that his raspy voice he heard? What had happened to his voice?

"We'll call your family. Don't worry."

"I don't have a family here," he said.

The next morning, as soon as Helmut heard the news, he called Ariane and they rushed to Yale-New Haven Hospital. The front desk at the hospital wouldn't give them much information on Mr. Atwater except to say that he was in stable condition. He could not have visitors. Helmut glanced at the nurse's information sheet. Mr. Atwater's room was on the sixth floor. He told Ariane they'd wait in the cafeteria. They had to pass a security guard and the elevators to reach the dining room. When they were past the guard, they darted into an elevator and rode it to the sixth floor. They told the floor nurse that they were the only family Jonathan Atwater had, that they were old friends from Yale who had talked to him minutes before the attack. The nurse looked them over, asked to see their Yale ID cards and requested their names and phone numbers in case Mr. Atwater needed help getting something from home. She said his injuries included a mildly fractured skull, a bruised liver and kidneys, and a fracture in one eye sock-et. The patient also had back and groin injuries, and they were sta-bilizing his neck as a precaution.

"But he'll recover in due time," the nurse said.

Ariane began to cry. The nurse handed her a tissue.

"He's heavily sedated," the nurse said. "But you can see him for a moment."

Helmut and Ariane walked into Mr. Atwater's room.

Helmut's head swam in a murk so overwhelming that he almost stumbled into the mobile tray with a pitcher of water and paper cups. Mr. Atwater's face was barely recognizable. He lay motionless under clean white sheets. His left cheek was unbeliev-ably swollen, as if someone had implanted an orange underneath the skin. Under the bandages around his head, you could see his eyes, puffy and teary and nearly shut. Tubes ran from his nose and mouth; smaller tubes dangled from his arms. Boxlike machines hummed and pulsed around Mr. Atwater. Ariane did not make a sound, but tears streamed down her face. She said she was going downstairs to buy flowers for the room.

As soon as she left, Helmut sat down in the chair and stared at his friend. His mind was empty. All that mattered was Jonathan Atwater. His friend in a world of peace and recovery, blood slow-ly coagulating, bandages wrapped neatly and carefully, warm lights hovering overhead.

Who in the world would do this to Jonathan? Helmut thought. The poor man had never hurt anyone in his life. Helmut was the one who deserved such a thrashing. He was the one who should have been mercilessly pummeled. He was the guilty one. Helmut had chosen to be a demon, not poor Mr. Atwater. There really was no justice in this world anymore, Helmut thought. There was simply awful pain and a life of lies.

Ariane returned and arranged the flowers on the tray next to the bed and wrote a note saying they'd be back for another visit tomorrow.

Helmut had to drive the Corolla back to Harkness Hall because Ariane was immersed in an unrelenting river of tears.

"Who would do that to Jonathan?" she asked, sobbing. "I hate this place! I hate this horrible city! Who could be so cruel? I don't understand anymore. I don't understand anything at all. Helmut, what's happening? First the professor, then Jonathan! My God! How can we help him? You think he'll be all right? I just don't understand what's going on anymore. They almost killed him! Animals! Oh, my God! This is madness!"

Helmut drove slowly through the traffic, trying not to focus on anything in particular. He wanted to stop moving. He wanted to be safe, but he wasn't safe. He wanted to know what was right and what was wrong in the world. But he was the guilty one, Helmut thought. There was no pretending anymore. He was the guilty one, and his heart was engulfed by the darkness that had already consumed his mind. Helmut stopped the car in the parking lot, gave Ariane the keys and stepped into the sun. The innocent were suffering for his sins, Helmut imagined. The half-truths and lies had not been obliterated. Instead, he had inherited and reinvigorated their power.

Chapter Twenty-Eight

On Saturday night, Helmut and Ariane returned to the hospital. They brought a fresh change of clothes and books for Jonathan to read. Mr. Atwater was still heavily sedated and had not opened his eyes. The nurses again reassured them that Mr. Atwater's injuries, although severe, would eventually heal. Helmut did not say much. They watched their friend for an hour, and then returned home.

Later in the day, Ariane slept in her bed while Helmut lay motionless beside her. He had noticed that, before brushing her teeth, she had checked the windows and doors, glancing at the street before she closed the micro-blinds. A baseball bat lay next to her bed. She was afraid a stranger would break into her apartment, attack them. She said after a while it would probably go away, this fear.

Helmut went into the dark living room, closing the bedroom door behind him. His mind erupted with bloody images again. His mind seemed to have a life of its own. Suddenly Helmut imagined how Mr. Atwater might have been attacked. What kind of depravity was this? Helmut thought, disgusted with himself. He recalled his fateful night with Werner Hopfgartner. Helmut stared at his hand and thought he was holding the knife. He saw the knife and he saw himself plunge it into Hopfgartner. A gurgle of vomit surged up his throat and receded into his stomach, leaving an acid sting in his mouth. Helmut was woozy, so he sat down and tried to shake off these infernal images. The innocent were suffering for his sins, he imagined. There was no doubt. His blood had become guilty blood. Forever guilty blood. A sea of guilty blood to drown in.

In his mind, he knew he was an animal, too. A spiteful animal. He transformed good into evil, and then evil into this new morality. But when had there ever been a 'good' unadorned with blood? When? Where was that pristine beginning? The awful truth was that it was a complete sham. And that was the only truth that mattered. The road was littered with corpses and they called it "civilization." What judgment? Helmut thought. What rightness? There was only hate. He had simply gotten away with it! He had made a horrific assertion. It had been simply a matter of taking the knife and using it when no one else would. It had been a matter of skill and temerity and some luck.

Damn the gods! he thought. Damn every single last one of them! They were simply the best with the knife! They took it and cut cleanly with it, and again! They simply had no doubt about it. No doubt and no guilt. None of this wretched guilt. From that birthright of terror, everybody, too, could cut flesh and be free.

Helmut imagined a madman bursting into the dark room. A madman with an ax. He shuddered with an eerie delight. A crimson light drenched him. This titillating anticipation. The purity of action. He asked himself: Who was virtuous here? Why was morality ever a question?

Immersed in a black cloud, he imagined a shrill cry escaped his contorted face. The ax came down and chopped off his arm. The bones cracked and split. The muscles shredded. Blood poured and flowed like an eternal stream that carried him away. The madman vanished. He was alone again, in bits and pieces.

The reason for morality? To be safe, Helmut muttered to no one in the darkness. What happened when that goal was relinquished? Other images invaded his mind. A rat came up to his bloody shoulder and stuck its greedy snout into the wound. Its razor teeth chewed on a sinewy strand of flesh, tugging at it until it snapped free. He was food for rats. Werner Hopfgartner had been his food. Only this food was left. This food, and this insatiable hunger.

Helmut refocused his eyes on the room in Ariane's apartment. A small knife was in his hand. Only the innocent and the guilty existed, he thought. Only a knife separated them. Only a knife could bring them together. Another pristine beginning from a wound of hate. A task for only a chosen few. A desire for absolute justice and the thrust of a blade. A desire for absolute glee. The guilty were food for the innocent. The guilty were eaten alive, he imagined. The innocent remembered the acts of the guilty, revered them. But they were not enamored with the details of these immortal acts. The guilty—oh, those ignoble idiots!—acted and were set free, absolutely free. The monstrous freedom of demons and archangels. And so the guilty were banished from the world.

The blade in his hand glimmered in the moonlight. He sliced into the fatty tissue of his right forearm. He felt exquisite pain. Blood, hot blood, gushed from his arm. Helmut clenched his fist, and the red stream became fuller, warmer, quicker. He knew he was condemned to this band of the guilty. He could not go forward, and he could not step back. He opened his shirt and dragged the blade across his right ribs, sinking it deeper on a wave of exquisitely hot pain. Helmut yelped against his will. The knife fell free.

"Oh, dear Lord, what have you created?" he called to the darkness. "What ugly beings? What lies? What impossible freedom and disappointment?"

The blood soaked his shirt. The cut in his arm dripped blood onto the shiny wooden floor. He was breathing in spasms now.

In his mind, he was again in a sunlit field awash in crimson. But this time the color seemed welcoming. He imagined a flash of metallic ruby in the stale air. It was electrifying. Rain fell all around him. Helmut was losing consciousness. From a field of red tulips in the rain, tulips swaying gently in a breeze, he reached out and clenched the knife tightly in his hand again. He could not yet be safe.

~ ~ ~

Ariane thought she heard a noise in the other room. Was someone crying? She reached out in her half sleep for Helmut, but he wasn't there.

She pushed the covers to the floor and stepped on the baseball bat by the bed. Maybe it would help. She carried it like a walking cane. She didn't want to smash it on Helmut's head by mistake. Ariane patted her way through the darkness. The chair. Her dresser. A suitcase. The bedroom door. Before she opened the door, she heard it again. A high-pitched moan and sobbing.

What was going on? she thought. Was that Helmut on the chair? The room was pitch black except for the weak moonlight from the window. She couldn't see his face clearly, but yes, it was Helmut. She knelt in front of him.

"What's wrong?" she asked. "Why are you crying? Please, Helmut! What happened?"

She felt something moist on her hands. She found a light switch and flicked it on. Blood was on her hands! A twitch disfigured her face. Her heart raced wildly, but when she glanced around the room no one else was here. They were alone together. The chain was still on the door.

"My God! You're bleeding! Helmut!" she cried.

He dropped the knife on the floor. She stared at it incredulously, as if she had half-expected it to leap and plunge itself into her own ribs like an object possessed. She grabbed the knife and threw it in the kitchen sink and yanked the dishtowel from the magnet on the refrigerator door. The bat was still in her hands; she dropped it with a clang. Everything suddenly seemed in slow motion.

"Helmut! Speak to me! Are you out of your *mind*?"

His head lolled against the back of the chair in a red ecstasy. Tears poured from his eyes. Blood soaked his shirt. Blood was splattered on his pants, on the floor. Rivulets trickled from his chest. She wrapped the dishtowel tightly around his forearm. Ariane glanced at the living room again, almost expecting an assassin to rush up behind her, yank her neck back and slash her throat open. But no one else was here, she assured herself, breathing hard and trying not to panic. She stared at Helmut. He was lost inside a storm of anguish. His chest heaved with deep sobs, and blood still dripped down his chest.

She ran to the bathroom, more possessed of her senses. She grabbed a towel. Ariane almost fainted. Back in the living room, she knocked over the coffee table, sending newspapers and the candy bowl full of little chocolates and mints, and three Italian ceramic tiles crashing onto the floor. Helmut was still conscious. Had he wounded himself deeply? The dishtowel on his arm was soaked with blood. She pressed the bath towel against his chest and managed to wrap it around him and secure it tightly with a thick knot. Her head was exploding with thoughts. Should she call an ambulance? What would they say about Helmut? Why had he done this?

Suddenly she grabbed his hair and pulled his head up and yelled, "What's wrong with you? What's wrong?" She was angry and confused.

He opened his eyes and stared at her, half-astonished too. She ran to the telephone, crushing chocolates underfoot.

"Greg, it's me. Ariane Sassolini. Listen to me. I need your help badly. My friend's hurt himself. He's bleeding. Please come over and help him. Yes, I'm still at the same address. Oh, God! I don't know why. So many things have happened. He was depressed. He's right here, on the sofa chair. He's conscious. I don't think it's terrible. No, he doesn't have to go to a hospital! I think the bleeding's stopped. Yes. No, on the forearm and across the chest. With a knife. I did that. Yes. Just see him. See if he's all right. Yes. All right. Okay. If you say so, he'll go. But I want you to see him first. It would be worse if that happened. Okay. Hurry!"

She slammed the phone down. Helmut was looking at her, his eyes still teary. His head hadn't moved. At least his eyes were open, she thought, and he seemed calmer now. She knelt next to him and checked the makeshift bandages and pulled the knots tighter.

"Helmut, listen to me. Greg's coming. Why did you to do this? Please talk to me. I love you. Why did you do this to yourself? Please stop crying. Everything will be all right. I'm not leaving you for one second. We'll get through this together. Please talk to me."

She brushed back his hair and wiped the tears from his cheeks and his eyes. She planted kisses on his lips and kissed his eyes, and this seemed to revive him. His face became recognizable again, yet it was still ashen.

"Ariane, it's my fault! I'm the evil one! Why did they attack Jonathan? Why? It's all my fault! The innocent are tortured and killed! The guilty are set free! Ariane! I did it to all of them! It was even *easy*! *Ach!*"

New rivulets of tears covered his face.

"What are you talking about? You had nothing to do with these things. It shouldn't affect you this way. Jonathan's not dead. He'll be all right. Don't worry, please."

"Oh, Ariane! You don't know the madman you're with! Do you still love me?"

"Of course I do. I'll always love you."

"It's all my fault! You have to *know*! It's me! No one else! I don't know what to do!"

"Please, what are you saying? We'll be all right. Let's get out of New Haven. That's what we should do. No one's safe here. Don't blame yourself. It's not your fault. Please, Helmut, stop crying. I *do* know you. You always do your best. You try so hard. You are nothing but a *good* person. You *are* good. The world isn't perfect. Don't worry about anything anymore. Please."

"I hate myself! If you only knew! You *must* know! You are looking at a demon!"

"Please, here. Clean yourself up. Stop saying that. You'll be all right. Greg should be here soon and he can look at you. He's already a doctor. Don't worry about anything anymore. You'll be Okay. Just rest your head."

"Ariane, I have to tell you what's in my heart. I love you. I will always love you. These next words, I don't know. But I have to tell you! You'll hate me and I won't blame you. I won't deserve your love if you don't know. I won't!"

"Helmut, just don't say anything. I love you too. That's all that matters. I don't understand what you're talking about. You're scaring me."

"Ariane, I killed Werner Hopfgartner!"

"What? What are you talking about?" Suddenly she stood up and backed away from him.

"I killed him! I stabbed him! It's my fault, Ariane! I am the one! Please don't be frightened of me! Please!"

"Oh, my God! Helmut!" She collapsed onto the floor a few feet in front of him, her face stricken. She began to sob and gasp. "That's not *true!*"

"Ariane, this, my God! This is my worst torture!"

"Helmut!" The air seemed to lack oxygen. She stood up, as if in a dream, and clasped his hand tightly and stared at him, still searching for any other truth but *this* one. There was none.

Helmut sobbed too. He felt even more desperate than before.

"Helmut, why?" she continued. "Why? What did he do to you? I don't understand!" She kissed his hand as her tears fell on his fingers. A knot seemed to grow in her stomach. She thought about the secret she had not yet revealed to him; she imagined their baby thrashing inside of her.

"Oh, Ariane! I love you, Ariane! Why don't you just leave me to my misery? Why? You're blinded somehow! I don't deserve you! I deserve to die too!"

"Helmut! That's horrible! That's worse than what you did! *This* is why you suffer! Helmut, I love you too!" she said.

"Don't leave me, Ariane. Please don't leave me."

"I won't! I don't care what happens! I love you, Helmut. I love you with all my heart! But *why?* Helmut, are you out of your mind? How could you do this? You *killed* Professor Hopfgartner? You? What happened?" She reached up and stroked his hair. Suddenly the blood on her hands and thighs seemed more precious than ever. She was frantic. "*Why?*"

"You won't understand my explanations. No one will. It doesn't matter anymore. I'm a murderer! That's the simple truth! That's what you should know, Ariane! I killed him! I killed him! I wish I had died too. I wish the old man had choked me. I wish I had never ruined our love. That's the one thing that matters to me now. But I've destroyed it. Maybe I shouldn't have told you. I don't know what to do. I'm going out of my mind! These nightmares! I told you so I could save myself. See how selfish I am? I'm a disgusting animal! You should run away from me, run as far as you can."

"Helmut, please! Stop this! Just tell me why! I'm not going anywhere! I'm staying here with you! Does anyone else know?"

"No," he said. "You are the only one. Maybe the police will find out. I don't know what they know. Maybe I'll go to prison for the rest of my life. Ariane, that would be better than this nightmare! I would gladly kill myself for my sins!"

"Helmut, please stop talking like that," she said quietly, more in control of her emotions. "I don't know what we're going to do. Did you steal his wallet? Is that why? I can't believe that! You know I would give you every penny I have! Why did you do it? *Why?*"

"Oh, Ariane! You will laugh at me! The whole world will laugh at me! I killed him because I *hated* him! I killed him because I could kill him! For once *I* had power over this evil man! For once! For once he paid in blood and it wasn't enough! I had the knife in my hands. He was there. Alone in the dark. No one would know. I didn't want to, then I wanted to stop, but he tried to choke me. I plunged the knife right into his gut! I did it! I hear his screams in my ears every day."

"Helmut, please. What are you talking about? You *hated* him? You simply hated him? I don't understand at all. I want you to tell me *why*. Exactly why. What did he do to you?"

"I don't know, nothing. I killed him because he was there. I killed him because I hated him. Who cares anyway? It's done. I am what I am. What's the point of explaining it? I killed him for my own reasons. I killed him for myself. How do you 'explain' this act? I had the knife in my hands. I could have turned away. I could've simply forgotten everything. I could have let the world forget. Nothing 'explains' it. I simply did it. At that moment, I did it and it's a part of me."

"Helmut, I will understand. You have to trust me. Don't know what we're going to do. I don't know what we should do. How could you kill him? How could you hate someone that much? I just don't understand what you're saying. What could you have forgotten? What? I love you, Helmut. Please tell me."

He opened his teary eyes and stared at her face. Her cheeks were streaked with tears. Her brown eyes were wide open, waiting for his answer. She held his hand tightly and huddled next to him on the floor, as if she had been afraid he would fly away if she let go. Her shoulders shivered, and she was fragile. Gone was her self-confidence. Ariane had already given herself to him. She would not abandon him. She still had faith in him. He saw that in her eyes. But if he did not believe in himself anymore, then maybe there was nothing left for her. Then maybe she had indeed made the worst mistake of her life. Her eyes. Her love. This brought him forward, and he winced as he straightened up in the chair.

"I killed him because he raped and murdered a young girl years ago. I killed him because he deserved it!"

"What? Professor Hopfgartner? How? I don't understand, Helmut. How do you know this?"

"I found things he had written in Europe. Remember I told you about it last summer? I didn't know everything then. Later I found out he was accused of war crimes. Who cares about this anyway? It's irrelevant now! I'm a murderer, Ariane! That's the only thing that matters!"

"Please, Helmut. I want to know everything."

"I broke into his office and found a note about files he had hidden in Melk."

"Melk! Is that why we went?"

"Yes. I have these files, Ariane. Take them and burn them if you want! Take them away from me! It's all there! He raped her. Anja Litvak. He raped her when he was a soldier. He raped her and then he slaughtered her. And he got away with it! He lived an incredible life, full of rewards and ceremonies! But I knew who he was! I knew! How could I let him escape again? How?"

"Helmut, please stop crying. I believe you. I'll always believe you. Who was this Anja Litvak?"

"She was a beautiful young girl from Lithuania. She and her mother were on a prison train, but her mother died. I don't even remember the story very well. She ended up in Mühldorf, near Munich. That's where Hopfgartner killed her. He admitted he killed her when I confronted him that night. He still didn't care. He wanted to kill me."

"Helmut, you know something? I thought she was an old girl-friend or a childhood sweetheart."

"What are you talking about?"

"You said her name in your sleep. A month ago. You said once, 'Anja! Let's hide in the trees!' I thought you were playing with her. Two children playing . . . I think I hear Greg's car. Don't worry about anything anymore. We'll be okay. Just rest your head. We'll talk about this later. I'm not going to leave you. I love you with all my heart. I want you to promise me one thing. Just one thing."

"What?"

"If you ever want to do this again, just remember, you're doing it to *my* flesh."

"Oh, I would never hurt you!"

"I know that. I know. But remember: when you hurt yourself, you're hurting *me* now. Remember that."

"I would never hurt you!"

"I know. That's why I want you to remember, so you won't ever do this again."

"I would never hurt you."

"Okay. So remember what we've talked about. Everything will be all right. The worst of it is over."

When Gregory Winters walked into the living room, he was carrying a large plastic bag. He didn't say more than a hello to Ariane and immediately started to work on Helmut. Suddenly embarrassed, Helmut said nothing. Greg cleaned the wounds and said, to no one in particular, that these wounds were deep enough to require stitches. He stared at Helmut for a second, almost disdainfully, and asked Ariane to hand him a few things from the bag: sterile towels, a disinfectant solution that looked like blood, a syringe and a tiny medicine bottle.

Greg gave Helmut a local anesthetic and sewed closed the two wounds. He covered them with fresh bandages. He didn't bother to look at Helmut's face again as he told him what Helmut needed to do to keep the wounds free of infection.

"I'll be back to check you later today," Greg said.

Ariane followed Greg out onto the porch of the apartment complex. In a few moments, a car pulled away. Ariane returned from the freezing cold.

"Greg's not worried about you," she said, "Know why?"

"No. I'm sorry. I'm sorry for all of this."

"He said you were ashamed. That was a good sign."

"I love you, Ariane."

"*Are* you ashamed?"

"I'm ashamed he saw me like this."

"You are not ashamed before the eyes of God? It is against God's law to kill another human being. Helmut, please tell me you believe in God. Maybe the devil took control of you for a few seconds that night, but I can't believe you're completely possessed by evil! I know who you are! Helmut, please answer me."

"I don't know how to answer you! I know there's good in the world. God, whatever it is, is responsible for it. We're a part of God. What I did was a part of God. That doesn't mean God's evil. It's just how he works! I *thought* about what I was going to do. I didn't want to do it at the end, but then I did it anyway. He *deserved* to die, Ariane! That was God's will! Maybe I needed the hate to do it that night. But it wasn't just hate. I can't explain it with my feeble words. It sounds so stupid to me when I explain it. You're right about what you said. I did love Anja Litvak. I didn't know her. But I loved her as a human being, simply *because* she was a human being. I didn't need to know her. She was like me. As much as I hated Werner Hopfgartner, I loved Anja Litvak. I can't separate them in my mind anymore."

"But why *you*?" Ariane asked. "You're not God! You can't decide when someone should live and someone should die! Who are you to decide that? Why did you take this into your own hands? Why? I don't know what you call this. A certain lack of humility. It's dangerous. What if everyone started doing the same thing? I don't understand this. Maybe Hopfgartner had it coming to him. But why you?"

"You think I'm an arrogant murderer possessed by evil? Maybe you're right. I don't know. Maybe I should've stabbed myself deeper. I'm a coward! Look at me! Look at the lurid spectacle I've created! I should've simply snuffed myself out quietly! But Ariane, I didn't want to be great! I didn't want to be anything. I just felt miserable and angry. I didn't want to know about Anja's murder. I didn't ask for it. I have no explanations anymore! This is who I am! Maybe your

God will tear me apart! That would be a blessed redemption for me. To know that God cares enough about my stupid world to obliterate it. *That* would be better than knowing God just doesn't give a damn."

"What are we going to do?" Helmut looked capable of anything tonight. She felt exhausted. What was *she* going to do? She imagined their child inside of her. The knot in her stomach had disappeared, and had left behind only a dull ache. What kind of family and world would he or she inherit?

"Maybe I should turn myself in! Maybe I should spend the rest of my life in jail! I deserve it. You said so yourself."

"That's ridiculous, Helmut. First you want to kill yourself. Then you want to ruin the rest of your life, and mine. These extremes! What's wrong with you?" she shouted at him, exasperated, standing up. Even Helmut was startled.

"Let's think of a solution. Together," she continued. "A practical solution to get out of this mess. You should know, first of all, that I would *never* do what you did. Never. Maybe you're right. But think about what it's done to you! And to me! What about your family? You certainly didn't think of anyone else except yourself when you charged into this *quest*! You abandoned yourself and everyone else, and here we are, with this catastrophe! You should think about that! I don't condemn you completely. Please understand that. If I did, if I had a doubt Hopfgartner was guilty of what you said he did, I'd leave you in a second, I would leave you forever. But I would never do what you did. We're completely different that way. But let's survive this. That's all I want. In a way, you're *better* than me. You did it from the goodness of your heart. I see that. But that same goodness is so close to what's evil. Stay away from it. Don't go near it. Suddenly you might not know which side you're on."

"Please help me."

"We need a solution. We need to get the hell out of New Haven. The police don't know anything yet and probably will never find out. Let's go to your mother's place in New Mexico. I thought it was a good idea before, and I think it's a *great* idea now. This will be our secret, Helmut. We'll keep it to ourselves. When you want to talk about it, we'll talk. That's not a problem. But the best thing to do is to get out of here. That's what I think we should do. That's the first step. After that, a new beginning. After that, we'll just see what else we need to fix. This will make your mother the happiest woman in the world. That, in itself, is a good enough reason for New Mexico."

Chapter Twenty-Nine

Sarah Goodman rubbed her calves and forearms. They were warm and sore. It was the second week of March, and she was in a wonderful mood. She didn't even mind the cramped cubicle assigned to her in the attic of Harkness Hall. Her body was so tired, yet she felt strangely refreshed and invigorated. Bharat had put her through his "little workout" of morning calisthenics. She already loved his body for its perfect proportion and supple muscularity. He had told her about his morning regimen. But until she joined him, she hadn't understood the discipline, the focus. It had been like exercising with an Indian-version of Rudolf Nureyev. Bharat had only encouraged her at every turn and promised her that, soon, she would roar with incredible energy. Well, she wasn't a jaguar yet, but every muscle in her body did throb with joyful warmth.

Sarah reread Professor Steiner's comments and smiled. Her prospectus was ready for official approval as soon as one more professor signed up to complete her dissertation committee of three.

Sarah had nailed down her topic as soon as she returned from her Christmas vacation in Iowa. She had convinced Professor Steiner to be her new thesis adviser. She wanted to explore the role of female writers in postwar Germany and Austria. What distinctive roles had women played in writing literature during this age of denial and confession, defeat and resurrection? What were their philosophies and dramas about? Did their characters show any particular tendencies or concerns?

Sarah believed that women had been more practical in their interests, more focused on daily life rather than the abstract life of the mind. Did female writers primarily focus on the importance of making common sense? Or did they also concern themselves with the absolute? Strident distinctions of right and wrong, Sarah believed, would be an anathema to most female writers of this period.

Professor Steiner told her that her early theoretical work would have to distinguish clearly between what was "abstract" and what was "practical." It could be she would end up proving the picture was muddier than what she had thought initially. In any case, her topic was certainly "intriguing," the professor had said. Now, after weeks of work, her prospectus was a detailed plan of where she wanted to go, what she wanted to do.

Sarah had thought about Professor Hopfgartner often since the awful news about his murder. She remembered how warm he had been and how he had also pushed her to excel in the months before his death. In many ways, his influence was all around her. She would never again be satisfied with anything less than an all-out effort. Whenever she thought she had understood something clearly, she'd disassemble it one more time and force herself beyond the obvious. She was a much more critical reader now. She questioned and probed what she thought others took for granted. Professor Steiner himself had told her that her completed prospectus was one more step toward the writing of an important work.

Even the other graduate students had started to treat her differently. Word had spread that Sarah Goodman had been one of the few who had achieved an Honors for her Comps. A circle of "friends" formed around her when she flipped through her mail in the main offices of the German department. She ignored the distractions and focused on her work. Bharat had also helped to make that state of mind the norm for them and their relationship. It was good to be with someone who was exceptionally intelligent, genial and supportive. He told her that, for the first time, he was also happy. *She* had made him happy. That in itself seemed incredible to her.

Sometimes Sarah would also think of her greatest fear, that she was inferior, that she wasn't good enough, that no matter how hard she tried she would never belong at Yale. She knew she wasn't a natural genius, yet she could still be competent and interesting and even innovative. That was all she wanted. Her affair with Hopfgartner seemed like a bad dream. Now Sarah would not have plunged into such a stupid episode. She was beginning to experience what she thought was real love. Maybe she and Bharat would end up in different places, at different jobs. But at least now they cared for each other, and that's all that mattered to her.

Sarah heard voices outside her door. Other graduate students? No one ever came up here. It was so desolate and out of the way. The back stairwell led only to a small hallway of three doors, and she didn't recognize the names on the other two offices. She heard footsteps in the hall outside her door. There was a moment of silence. Then someone knocked on her door.

"Hi," Sarah said, momentarily thunderstruck. "Please come in."

It was Regina Neumann.

"Thank you," Professor Neumann said, and sat down in a dingy, brown loveseat the previous occupant of the cubicle had left behind.

Her black coal eyes stared uncannily at Sarah, yet Neumann did not appear hostile. The professor was wearing the slightest hint of make-up and a touch of lipstick. It was a dramatic change. Regina Neumann was actually beautiful. Her face radiated a classic serenity. "Thank you for seeing me. How have you been, Sarah?"

"All right. It's been a hectic six months, but I'm in good shape, I think."

"I certainly won't keep you from your work. First, I want to tell you I know you have done well. You deserve my congratulations for that."

"Thank you, Professor Neumann. I'm doing the best I can," Sarah said, thinking about closing her eyes, about the bliss of being alone to work, about bursting into tears. She *did* belong here. She knew that now.

"Second," Regina Neumann said more slowly, and even softly, "I wanted to apologize for what I said to you the last time we met.

You didn't deserve it. You *are* a good student. You are *becoming* a good scholar. That is exactly what you should do at Yale. I was angry and I allowed my worst instincts to control me. You simply did not deserve the harsh words I said."

"But Professor Neumann! I'm the one who lied! I'm the one who should be apologizing to you! I'm sorry I lied about Professor Hopfgartner. I'm sorry it ever happened. I was stupid and I didn't know what to do."

Sarah had the sudden urge to hug Regina Neumann, but those black coal eyes, even in apology, were still intimidating. "I'm not proud of what I did," Sarah continued. "I'll regret it for the rest of my life."

"Well, Sarah. We have both done things we are not proud of. Maybe one of these days I will tell you about the *dozens* of things I would have done differently in my own life. I would very much like to get beyond what happened last year. You simply do not have to explain yourself and I hope you don't ask me to explain what I did. It is enough to know we are of one mind on the matter now. I am not about to hold a grudge against you and I hope you do not hate me too. It happened, and now we have a chance to create a much better history between us. What do you think?"

"I think I would like that very much," Sarah said quietly. She would not cry now. She certainly would not cry.

"Sarah, Professor Steiner showed me your prospectus this morning. I like it very much."

"What? He did? I can't believe that!"

"I would like to be a part of your dissertation committee, but I thought we should have this talk first. I believe your ideas show real promise. Of course, I have some questions too. I will be as critical as ever. I promise that. But I hope we can work together on your dissertation. I would like to help you. In fact, I am just a bit jealous of Steiner, that he will be your major influence."

"I don't know what to say, Professor Neumann," Sarah said, almost in a whisper. The words just wouldn't come out easily. "I would be pleased if you were on my committee."

"Then it's settled. I will tell Steiner this afternoon. Before I go, may I ask you a question about Professor Hopfgartner? If you

don't think you want to talk about him, I will certainly understand. I honestly don't mean to put you on the spot. I'm just curious in a way."

"That's okay," Sarah said quietly. She didn't think it was a trap.
"Please ask me whatever you want."

"Well, let me just put it as clearly as I can. This isn't easy for
me either," Professor Neumann said. "I hated Werner Hopfgartner.
I am sure that was always quite clear. Sometimes my hate was
wildly excessive. Now, after his death, this hate has dissipated. In
fact, I often think about his faults in a fond way, as if they were
just the faults of an otherwise ordinary man. I find myself thinking that maybe I overlooked his positive qualities when he was
alive. But then I 'correct' myself and condemn him again. Yet I do
so without any real conviction anymore. Why did you like him?
What did you see in him?"

"I can't really say I *liked* him," Sarah said. "I was desperate and
weak when I did what I did. I simply allowed it to happen. Maybe
he could see that, that I simply wouldn't resist whatever he wanted from me. He was nice to me when I felt alone. He made me feel
safe. He was like a father to me. I never knew my father very well.
My parents were divorced when I was real young. Professor Hopfgartner wanted to help me, maybe for his own selfish reasons, I
admit that. But I needed someone. I needed help. I needed someone to be on my side no matter what. I think that's what a real
father should be. A real mother, too. I didn't have those here at
Yale. Maybe I should've been an adult from the start. But I wasn't.
My relationship with Professor Hopfgartner was a way to survive
a place like this. A bad way. But I didn't have anything else. Now
I know what I need to do and how to do it."

"I am sure you do, Sarah."

"You always hated Professor Hopfgartner?"

"Well, yes. He was *too* much like my abusive father. That is a
secret I can talk about now. My father convinced me that what he
did to me was something I wanted. But *he* was the one who was
wrong. I also admired Professor Hopfgartner too, just like my
father. So even I feel a sense of loss now that he's gone."

"Me too."

Chapter Thirty

Helmut stopped by the German department's main office to pick up Ariane, who was finishing writing a letter on her computer. While he waited, Helmut glanced nervously. For several weeks now, he had felt like he was being watched. The feeling had started after Hopfgartner's murder, and intensified once he confessed to Ariane. His self-inflicted knife wounds had healed and were now faint, pink scars.

He and Ariane talked endlessly about the murder, his reasons, his reactions. Sometimes it seemed like that was the only thing they talked about. He told her how he felt at the time, what he had believed then. She told him why he had been wrong, *absolutely* wrong. She had not convinced him, but he had stopped arguing with her. The arguments didn't matter to him anymore. Hopfgartner was dead. The deed was done.

Ariane needed to rid herself of her own doubts, about *him*, and so he stopped arguing with her. The only thing that bothered him was a lingering restlessness. The fear of being watched. He knew this paranoia was only in his head. No one else would ever find out. Yet once in a while, Helmut still imagined a hot breath behind him. Sometimes he imagined footsteps scurrying around the corner. Maybe a hand waited inside a patch of darkness, about to grab him and pull him down. But nothing ever happened. Rationally, he knew it would probably be that way forever. Yet his nightmarish deed was also a fading memory. Even for Ariane, it seemed less important after a while. She really did love him. Now he only needed to shed this fear that sometimes would not let him sleep at night. Much of his self-torment had vanished as soon as he confessed to her, as soon as he knew in his heart she wouldn't leave him. He wanted to probe her feelings, to find out why she didn't just leave. But he didn't press her for an explanation, and decided simply to believe what she said. Maybe Ariane herself did not know exactly why she still thought of him as a man and not a monster. Helmut did know one thing. Ariane had saved him. Whenever she kissed him, it felt like a miracle. Whenever she asked him if he was all right and stroked his cheek, he felt shocked by her warmth. She healed him. Nothing would ever matter more than that.

Two weeks after he told her, Helmut gave Ariane the files from Melk. He found the old files on a bookshelf. He left them on her desk, and the next day they were gone. Periodically, he would see an article or document being read on her desk. It took her forever before she asked him a few questions about what she was reading. And even then her questions were perfunctory. She had always believed him. This now seemed clearer than ever. She believed what he said about Hopfgartner was the truth. Helmut felt liberated. He could share his entire life with her. She did not agree with what he had done. She never would. But in the space between her shock at finding out the truth about Hopfgartner and his anguish over what he had felt compelled to do, there—in that space—they could live together.

When Ariane revealed to him she was pregnant, it was her turn to shock him. Inexplicably tears welled up in his eyes, and for the first time he had felt deeply ashamed of himself. Of course she wanted to keep the baby, she told him. Of course they would start a family together. They loved each other, wasn't that what mattered? When Helmut heard these words, he knew she meant them, and perhaps these words were easier to say once she had convinced herself of Hopfgartner's guilt. But Helmut could only think of what he had wrought in the world. Yes, Ariane had saved him, and given him another chance and a promise for the future.

They left the German department and walked to the car.

"Somebody's coming over to look at the dresser at six," Ariane said, walking in front of him to open the car door.

"What time are we supposed to be at Jonathan's?" he asked, sliding into the passenger's seat.

"Around eight. I finally talked to Otto today. I'm so relieved. I can't believe we'll be in New Mexico one week from tomorrow!"

"What did he say?"

"Nothing new really. He said they'd give me my vacation days. They also said they're down to two candidates for my job. They already have somebody for yours. An ex-graduate student, I think. He wants me to send pictures of the baby. Wasn't much of a conversation, really. Think he's been to Santa Fe once, bought something called 'tablos'."

"You mean *retablos*. Religious offerings. Some people collect them as art. In Germany, my mother hung one above her bureau. From my grandfather. She used to pray to it in Spanish every night. Gave me the creeps."

"We haven't gotten our tickets in the mail, have we?"

"No. I called them yesterday. They said they should be here tomorrow or Monday."

"I can't wait to get down there. You think your mother really won't mind if we stay with her for a while, until we get our own place?" Ariane turned up Whitney Avenue.

"Well, *you* heard her. What do you think? My ear still hurts. I never thought anyone would go so wild about being a grandmother. My God."

"It was very cute. She sounds more excited than we are! Can't wait to finally meet her in person! You think your relatives will like me?"

"They'll like you more than they like me. I really don't know them either. Hey! Boxes! Over there, behind that strip mall." He squinted his eyes for a better look.

"Give me a second. I'll make a U right here."

≈ ≈ ≈

Helmut stuffed his philosophy books in a thick-sided, waxy box used to ship bananas. The doorbell rang. It was an assistant professor who had come to look at the dresser in their bedroom. He heard Ariane in their bedroom, talking up the other items they were trying to sell.

As soon as the professor left, Ariane jumped in the shower to get ready for Mr. Atwater's "farewell dinner." The librarian was leaving to visit his mother in Boston. Ariane hummed in the hot shower while Helmut marched around the apartment, the twilight surrounding him like a cage. He peeked through the Venetian blinds. No one was out there. The street was empty. Still his heart yearned to escape his chest.

Anja Litvak flashed in his mind. A younger, blonder version of Ariane Sassolini. In his daydream, Anja sprinted through a field of marigolds. The sun shined in her eyes. She ran toward a gnarled tree trunk by a stream, away from him. She was free. Helmut shook his head clear and stood up. Suddenly Ariane dashed into the living room. She pressed her warm and wet body against his, almost knocking him back, and kissed his neck and his face. He almost fainted.

Mr. Atwater had outdone himself, even by his own extraordinary standards. On his dinner table was a lavish centerpiece of white and purple lilies, orchids, two chrysanthemums and an orange bird of paradise. His fine bone china had been carefully arranged next to wine goblets and water glasses and his best silver.

"I rarely get a chance to use it, so I might as well do it right when I have it out. Why not approach the end of the millennium with style?" he said.

Helmut was glad he had worn his best dress shirt and shoes, but he was worried about which fork to use with the salad. They sat in the living room and started with hors d'oeuvres of marinated shrimp and mushrooms stuffed with crabmeat. Flamenco guitar music wafted around them. Helmut sipped a glass of white wine. Ariane took a glass of seltzer from Mr. Atwater, who was bedecked in a bow tie, a light dinner jacket and gray wool slacks.

She asked him about the music, and he said it was Paco de Lucia's *Castro Marin.*

They talked about New Mexico. Helmut said he kept thinking he was finally on his way "home," but he knew next to nothing about the place. He had in fact never visited the Southwest. Except for his mother, he didn't really know anyone there.

"It has to be better than New Haven," Mr. Atwater said, spearing a shrimp with his toothpick. "You know how I fell in love with the New Mexico? Georgia O'Keeffe's landscapes. *There* was a woman with a provocative eye! I went to Phoenix for a few days last year, for a conference of university librarians. The big sky! The absolute beauty of the desert! I simply could not believe how beautiful it was. But it was hot."

"Have you ever cooked New Mexican food?" Ariane asked, reclining against the back of the sofa. Her black slacks did not mute her shapely figure. Did all women get sexier when they were pregnant? Anything she wore, Helmut thought, would look fabulous on her. It wasn't just her body, but the way she moved and relaxed, with an easy and elegant rhythm.

"Oh, most certainly," Jonathan said. "I use a powdered *chile* from the El Paso Chile Company whenever I serve *chile con carne.* I have a friend who lives there. But that's not too ambitious. I'd like to try my hand at something more challenging. Green *enchiladas.* Or *buñuelos* topped with a touch of honey. What absolute delights!"

"Helmut's mom makes great *tamales.* Even sweet *tamales* with raisins, nuts and chocolate. I can give you her recipe before we go."

"That would be tremendous!" Mr. Atwater exclaimed. "We have to change with the times. I'm bored with pasta with pesto sauce and beef bourguignon. And yet, *tamales* were an Aztec dish originally. How the pre-Columbian is suddenly à la mode!"

They moved to the dinner table and savored carrot soup tinged with ginger. Afloat exactly in the center was a sprig of mint. Helmut and Ariane never ate like that at their place. They usually had one of Ariane's elaborate salads or homemade soups, quick and hearty. But never this carefully staged extravaganza. Mr. Atwater passed them fresh sourdough bread from the oven.

Eventually the conversation shifted to Mr. Atwater's recovery from the attack he had suffered, in another epoch, it seemed. He said he was in good shape now, with only a slight loss of vision in his left eye and an occasional dizziness the doctors said might eventually go away. Ariane caught Helmut's eye and winked at him. Mr. Atwater mentioned vague painful spasms. The attackers, Helmut surmised, had probably ruptured one of Mr. Atwater's testicles with their blows. Once in a while, the librarian was unable to sit or stand or even crouch. Sometimes the waves of torturous pain caused him to gasp for breath. Whenever those traumas consumed him at Sterling Library, he hobbled to one of the private employee bathrooms. But mercifully, he had had no pain for several days.

Ariane and Helmut noticed that Mr. Atwater's left eye looked less pink. When Mr. Atwater wasn't smiling, the skin under his left eye sagged. Ariane stood up and quickly collected the plates and the soupspoons.

"Did the police have any luck catching who did this to you?" Helmut asked.

Mr. Atwater said that a few hours after his assault the police had stopped four teenagers in a navy blue Datsun, on an anonymous tip to 9-1-1. But Mr. Atwater had not been able to identify these teens as his assailants. He had never seen who attacked him. Of course, they denied ever seeing him too. Even if the boys had been responsible for his beating, they were minors who would have gone free in a matter of months.

"It really doesn't matter," Mr. Atwater said, passing them two plates with baked red snapper, asparagus and mushrooms. "I'm just glad to be alive."

Suddenly Helmut forgot the presentation of the food. He was angry. He felt stupid for being angry. "That's horrible," he retorted. "I think it should matter. Don't you think they'd want to confess if they did it?"

Mr. Atwater coughed, his mouth full of mushrooms, and then cleared his throat and chuckled. Finally he caught his breath.

"Oh, my dear boy. I, too, wish we lived in a nineteenth-century novel! All of us would be better off. But today's criminals don't possess half the grace of a Raskolnikov. It's just an awful world and we have to accept it as it is."

"Why do you think it's so different today, Jonathan?" Ariane asked, glancing at Helmut, who was lost in his own private world again.

"Well, that's a central question, my dear. I have a theory. Probably nonsense. But here it is. Table talk to save the world! Two important things have gone by the wayside, in my opinion, and I believe they've affected each other in a miserable manner. Family and truth. Now, of course, you have to understand what I mean by 'family' and 'truth.' Oh, this is simply too boring! You really don't want this harangue!"

"Please, Jonathan. Please go on. It's certainly *not* boring," Ariane said.

"Well, by 'family' I mean that we belong together. That we are a 'we,' so to speak. Our notion of family certainly begins with blood relations, but it doesn't end there. We can consider 'people like us' to be friends, neighbors, fellow workers, fellow worshippers and so on. When we lived mostly in villages, say three hundred years ago, our place was local. We met people usually of the same religion, of the same race, within a relatively confined geographical space. We were 'people of the desert' or 'people from the mountain' who spoke this or that common language, and so on. No jet or TV could whisk us to another exotic land at the blink of an eye! We also weren't an overcrowded world. We were more like dozens of isolated worlds, in the remote corners of Africa, Europe, Asia, Latin America.

"But the point is that when we had this 'family' or 'community' in its local version, it was much easier to know what was right and wrong. Truth was primarily something understood, rather than something codified into law. Without empathy for the other members of your community, the law became something to manipulate for your selfish benefit. It's certainly not about truth or justice anymore.

"Anyway, to finish this verbiage, let me just say this. It's not just the fault of the 'family' expanding and becoming meaningless. Idiotic philosophers also started to think of 'truth' as only something abstract, universal, exact. Quite different from 'community truth.' Maybe they simply didn't have a choice. The world was changing. Really, we have no more villages anymore. Sparta and Athens are simply quaint memories. So you have rational abstractions, certainly after the Renaissance, passing for what used to be meaty, virile truths. And you have groups of individuals, whole nations, and then the entire planet as cauldrons of religions and races and languages. Boom!

"I am sorry. Didn't mean to be histrionic. You see, now, what genie you've uncorked! I'm practically in a lather! Let me just take a sip of wine. Much better. It is certainly hot in here, isn't it?"

"But Jonathan," Ariane said, "I don't understand what that has to do with modern criminals not confessing anymore."

She glanced at Helmut again, who was paying polite attention to Mr. Atwater. She knew Helmut was dealing with what he had done. They had long ago stopped avoiding certain subjects. He would be okay. He had made a terrible mistake. But it was in the past now. Every soul could be redeemed. That was God's Word, or at least that is what Ariane had told him. The future was what mattered.

"Well, Ariane, you are quite right," Mr. Atwater said. "I've given you the foundation and left the home I promised you to your own imagination! This is what I mean. Rational discourse, this flight toward abstraction, always depended on non-rational things, like a village or community in which people would tell each other the truth. If your father asks you a question, you will probably tell him the truth, because you love him and feel a connection to him, which would be jeopardized by continual lying. If you don't tell him the truth he'll find out anyway since he knows you so well. He knows how you grin nervously when you're lying. He remembers that certain look in your eye from your younger days. The point is that in a real community (please set aside the dysfunctional exceptions for a moment) the truth will often come out. Either you will feel compelled by your guilt to blurt it out and unburden yourself, or the truth will become 'evident.'

"Now, zip to the end of the twentieth century! There is no community left, really. Maybe some living museums exist here and there, but modernity will eventually infect them and destroy them with TV! You have only an abstract, legalistic connection to your fellow man. He is most certainly not a 'relative' or a 'neighbor.' You avoid him. You do only the minimally required to have a cold, civil relationship with him, which means nothing. 'Don't bother me, and I won't bother you.' If you can steal from his fruit trees without him noticing it, you do it. Why not? He'd do it to you if he could. You have no personal connection to him anymore. He's Jewish and you're Muslim. Or he's Algerian and you're French. Or he speaks with a thick foreign accent and, well, you're at least the second generation in this bleak town. Anyway, the only way he can force you to face the truth is to film you with his Sony Handycam!

"You have to understand this abstract nature of modern relationships is ubiquitous. One lover sees another as a good piece of taut flesh or as a gold mine. Why? Because we're a community of transients! Aunt Helen isn't about to scold me for breaking poor little Ricardo's heart, because she's in Florida fending off the instant messages from MrMagestic. Or the abstraction can be something like: She doesn't understand me because she's white. Or she's one of those who believes money is everything. Or she actually thought X was a great president. Or she's an infidel. The point—my God, the point, the point, the point!—is that at the end of this millennium we have a notion of truth as abstraction without any kind of community to make sense of it. It's a righteous sword run amok! It's your abstraction against my abstraction. Your terrorists against my freedom fighters. One community against another community. It's your word against mine. Everything is politics! It's a war of all against all, and make sure you've got a jury specialist on your defense team! Why confess? You'll have to catch me red-handed, and even then you better have clear color video! The criminal of today has no guilt because he can convince himself he's really not guilty! And who's to tell him otherwise? Who's to say this truth is better than that one? And there you have it! The nonsense of truth!"

"I think I understand more or less," Ariane said. "Society is falling apart. We really don't help each other out. We really don't belong together anymore. So you won't ever have these old Hollywood confessions at the end of the trial or when the criminal is confronted with the 'truth.' You can lie and that's as good as the truth, because 'having truth' always depended on people believing in each other. Communities clash against other communities, and there's no one referee everybody trusts. But why can't we have a bigger 'community,' with everyone included? I mean, do we really have to be the same race or religion, speak the same language, be from the same place, to be a community? I know sometimes Jews marry Catholics, and Germans fall in love with Spaniards. It happens. Maybe not enough, but it happens. There's the potential to understand each other intimately, even if we're really different."

"I agree, Ariane," Mr. Atwater said. "There is that sliver of hope. But look around you. There is too much of this group against that group. People are getting away with murder! Tell me the last time strangers welcomed your comments on how to raise their children? Maybe what we are seeing now is the hundred years of growing pains of the 'community of earth'! I guess I'll die thinking that. But I really don't know. How can a gigantic planet be anything like a local community? Just wait until idiotic politicians or religious zealots try to tell us what to do. Then we'll really see some bloodshed."

"Well, the end isn't quite here yet," Helmut said quietly into the silence left by Mr. Atwater's last words. "I want to confess something to you, Jonathan. It's hard for me to say it, but it shouldn't be."

Helmut's eyes were teary, yet his face looked resolute. Ariane stared at him in disbelief and stood up, as if to say something, to stop him. But her mouth did not move. Her entire body was frozen. Helmut stood up too and wiped away a tear on his cheek. "I'm really going to miss you, Jonathan Atwater."

"Oh, my dear boy, so will I!"

They gave each other an *abrazo* and toasted the future with another glass of wine. With tears in her eyes, Ariane rejoiced too. Maybe they would make it together.

Chapter Thirty-One

The pastel colors in geometric designs and the turquoise bolo ties and black cowboy hats were the first things Ariane and Helmut noticed as they strolled through the Albuquerque International Airport.

Eva Sanchez had not been waiting for them at the arrival gate, and Helmut was getting angry. Ariane dashed into a store and tried a black cowboy hat, which the clerk said was too small for her. They found a better one, and the clerk explained how to take care of it, how to get it blocked when it lost its shape, and where she could find a Tony Lama store for a good pair of boots. She bought the hat.

Helmut sat down on one of the benches of the cavernous concourse, fuming now. Ariane walked up behind him, wheeled around in front of his face, and tipped her hat with a flick of her hand and dropped her hands on her hips. She looked sweet and sexy. It was the first time Helmut smiled in New Mexico.

He started to relax. They waited for their luggage. Helmut glanced at the strange faces in the crowd, looking for his mother. Several men stared unabashedly at Ariane. He turned to Ariane—she did look fantastic as a pregnant cowgirl—and kissed her. She wrapped her arms around his neck and wouldn't let him go.

"Oh, you lovebirds! Just can't keep your arms off each other, huh?" Helmut heard his mother behind him an instant before another pair of arms wrapped themselves around them. Eva Sanchez covered their faces with kisses and hugged them with such whoops of delight that others just stood back and enjoyed the display. They were finally home.

It was a long, hot drive to Cloudcroft. It was a godsend that Eva Sanchez's new Ford pickup had air conditioning and even a cab with two rows of seats. Helmut could feel the heat by touching the dashboard. The dusty horizon danced with heat. It was the first day of spring. Not taking her eyes off the interstate, his mother reached over and planted a kiss on Ariane's forehead and squeezed her shoulders. Eva—she had immediately insisted Ariane call her that—asked them about their trip and switched the radio dial from a country station to a deep-throated narration of mysterious stories.

"Listen to this, kids. It's that Ricardo Montalbán—remember him on *Fantasy Island* with that poor little midget?—he's from around here, I think. It's about the Jornada del Muerto, this flatland we're driving through now. He's telling you about its history, the reason it has that awful name. Some conquistadors died on this part of the Camino Real. They died of thirst or they froze to death at night, I think. Isn't that something? Makes you feel like you're driving through a storybook. Keep your eyes open. Maybe you'll see one of those old *gachupinos* on horseback, with a pointy metal hat. A lost Don Quixote looking for the Río Grande."

Ariane grinned and searched the horizon of the Sacramento Mountains. The shadows and bright surfaces sketched the peaks and valleys. It was more magnificent than she had ever imagined. They turned west on 380 and advanced toward the mountains.

"M'ija, I know a store in Alamogordo where we can find you a good pair of boots. Antelope or shark skin, if you like," Eva said, pushing on the cruise control.

When they reached Alamogordo, about two hours later, Eva pulled into a gas station and filled both tanks of the pickup. They still had to climb the mountains. Gas was cheaper down here than on Route 82 near her house. Helmut noticed how different his mother looked. Her skin was deeply tanned and almost leathery, with a hint of crimson on her cheeks. She wore a white embroidered cotton blouse, jeans and a leather belt with a big, silver buckle. She looked younger than he remembered her, younger and bolder and even attractive. Even with her salt-and-pepper hair in a bun, his mother seemed vivacious. She had also lost weight, he thought. She seemed to move in bursts. Ariane fell in and out of sleep on his shoulder. Helmut watched his mother as she gunned the engine and put the truck in gear. He felt *older* than her. Eva turned toward him and blew him a kiss, and he blushed.

"I'm allowed to do that, you know. I'm your mother. I'm so happy you're here, I could kiss you all day!" she said cheerfully, glancing at both of them. "She's so beautiful, *m'ijo*. And so *cariñosa*. When are you two getting married?"

As they started their assent, Helmut quickly noticed the change in temperature, the vegetation becoming greener, more abundant, the pine trees growing taller. Even the air had a cleaner, fruitier scent. Helmut told his mother he thought he smelled apples, and she immediately turned off the air conditioning and opened the windows.

"Take a whiff," she said. "That's real mountain air."

They passed an old, boarded-up stand selling apple and cherry cider and fresh peanuts. In a couple of months, she said, dozens of stands would spring up around Cloudcroft. Tomorrow they could see what fruits and vegetables were available now. Ariane was sound asleep. His mother told him that Cloudcroft was pretty much a tourist town, with skiers in the winter and campers in the summer. Only two or three thousand residents actually lived in town year-round.

When she had returned from Germany after Helmut's father had died in a military accident, she had a choice of living in Alamogordo or anywhere else nearby. She had grown up in Alamogordo, and most of her family still lived there. But she didn't want to go back to the same place where she had been born. That small town was too inbred; too many things reminded her of old high school anxieties. She also wanted to have the sense of changing and improving, not of regressing to something in the past. "And anyway," she said, "it's too hot and dusty down there."

She had first gotten the notion, when Helmut had been in school in Freiburg, to live in El Paso. It was a big city with more shopping and movie theaters and concerts, and it was right across the Río Grande from Juárez, where she knew some old girlfriends. Money was no problem, not with the military pension and her savings.

"And now," she said with a smirk, passing a Nissan Sentra with a back seat loaded with camping gear, "I've actually made a nice bundle investing in the stock market and I get monthly checks from my bond funds. You know, your mother's no dummy. I can send away for anything I want by dialing eight-hundred numbers."

El Paso, however, had never felt right. Eva said it felt lonely. If you didn't belong to a family there, you were left out. There were too many people. Too many cars. Too much noise. Too much pollution.

She moved back to Alamogordo, went on a camping trip with some cousins to Cloudcroft, and fell in love with it. Her family told her she was crazy to live up here. Hungry bears and other strange animals ran wild in the mountains. Mountain lions and rattlesnakes. Who would help her if she got sick? What would she do in the snow?

Eva hadn't listened to those naysayers before, and she wasn't about to start now. So she shopped around and finally bought a two-story house on a five-acre parcel next to a stream. The house reminded her, in a way, of the houses she had seen in the Black Forest with her husband, Johannes. Yet, in New Mexico, she could actually understand what people said to her. No one gave her that look of pity reserved for foreigners and stupid animals. In fact, she *loved* the people of Cloudcroft. They were simple and straightforward and real friendly. She had dozens of friends here. She belonged to the volunteer fire department. She also tutored three kids in math and Spanish. For four years, she had been one of the main organizers of the summer arts and crafts festival. She had even started to paint landscapes after enrolling in classes with the artists who lived in nearby Ruidoso. This was better than a small town. It was a *pueblo*.

Eva turned off Route 82, onto a smaller, paved road that meandered toward a lush valley. A dark mountain rose behind a cluster of evergreens and a wide field. Helmut saw a few barn-like houses at the other side of the valley, but nothing else. There was only Route 82, which they were leaving behind, and the handful of cars driving into the center of town. His mother said it was about a ten-minute drive into town. She zigzagged down the side road, through the trees, until she came to another, smaller valley hidden from Route 82.

This valley was greener than the first, but flatter. It was a wide, sloping field between two mountainsides, like a secluded landing pad of grass for a spaceship. Two black horses galloped through the field. A few more houses circled the rim of this valley, scattered about half a mile from each other, some tucked away from the valley road behind conifers, others at the end of long gravel driveways. Each one, Helmut noticed, had a white satellite dish pointed toward the heavens. Helmut spotted an old tire hanging from a thick cable wrapped around a branch of an old pine. "You know, a doctor and his nice family live in that house. His practice is in Alamogordo. He's a cardiologist, but he's already given me recommendations for Ariane and the baby. Stan is crazy about fly fishing."

The pickup pulled into one of the gravel driveways. Eva Sanchez's house was tucked behind a line of pine trees. The front yard was cornered by two neat gardens of wild flowers. A carpet of old pine needles covered the ground. Thick pines surrounded the white clapboard house. Streaks of sun and the clear blue sky poked through the ceiling of pine branches. Ariane finally woke up when the pickup's engines went silent. She glanced around, smiled and then stared at the house and the pine trees and the bright sun, astonished.

"My God," she said to Eva. "This is like a dream!"

Helmut's mother smiled too, kissed Ariane's cheek, wrapped her arms around her as they walked up the steps together. "This is yours, honey, as long as you and Helmut want to stay here," she said. "We can finally be a family after all these years. Let me show you around."

Eva took them through the living room, which was sunken around a massive stone fireplace. She showed them her favorite spot under the sun, on a plush sofa, where she loved to read and knit and call her friends. She showed them the eat-in kitchen, with sliding glass doors that overlooked a backyard with more flowers and pine trees as far as the eye could see. At least a cord of wood was underneath an open shed. "The river's down there," she said, pointing beyond the shed.

She took them to a supply room, stocked with seven-foot high shelves of canned food, flour and sugar and rice and beans in giant glass jars, and a massive meat freezer abutting the far wall. They walked upstairs. She pointed out the bathroom and her bedroom and then, in the far corner of the hallway, opened the door to another big bedroom overlooking the backyard. A brand-new queen-size bed was in the middle of the room. A pine chest of drawers and a full-length mirror were in one corner. A red quilt was draped over half the bed, and big blue pillows rested against the headboard. An ornate brass reading lamp sat next to a rocker, both of which she had purchased at an auction a few years ago.

"This is where you two are staying," Helmut's mother said. "Why don't you relax and unpack and I'll start making sandwiches for lunch. Tonight we're staying home. That way you can rest. But tomorrow night we're driving into town for a nice dinner at a place a friend of mine just opened last year. I want you to meet *mis compadres y mis comadres*."

Helmut and Ariane took it all in with a touch of amazement. They could not help but think, simultaneously, how lucky they were to be there.

After lunch, Helmut lay in bed, falling in and out of sleep, catching snippets of conversation. His bones felt weary, and his head ached. There was simply too much heat in his head.

Ariane and Eva started to search for pastry recipes and finally decided to try one on the fly, following Ariane's vague recollection of a delicious dessert she had once cooked with her mother years ago. Ariane told Eva about Italy and her family and why she had left for America. She said she had just wanted to find out who she was.

"Don't think you ever know the answer to that question," Eva said, turning on the kitchen radio to a classical station. "I think you only wind up having things you did that might tell you what kind of person you were in different situations. When Helmut's father died, I thought my world had ended. I loved Johannes so much. With all my life. I even cursed myself for going to Germany in the first place, for uprooting my life that way. But I know I did it. I know I loved him. I know I lived there without ever forgetting my New Mexico. And I know I came back. But I don't know what it all means. I don't know what it says about me. I just know that coming back here, to Cloudcroft, makes me feel right. I know I'm home. With *mi familia*. My beautiful Helmut is a part of me. My blood. And so are you, my dear. You're welcomed here with open arms. You're welcomed here for being *you*. That's all. There's no need to know who you are, to have all the answers . . . ."

In the darkness, Helmut opened his eyes and looked around. He heard voices laughing downstairs, dishes clattering. His headache was gone, but his head was still warm and fuzzy and deep within the absolute darkness of the room. He pushed himself off the bed and stared out the window. Was anyone out there? Was someone watching and waiting for him? Would anyone else find out what Helmut had done? How would he be as a father? Would his son or daughter ever find out the truth about him?

No, he told himself. No one was out there. What he had done, what he had done . . . well, it was over. Helmut stared out the window and found the dark shadows of the pine trees swaying in the night's breeze. He touched the window glass, and it was cold. The whole room felt much colder than before.

After dinner, he would suggest taking a stroll in the darkness outside. He wanted to see the darkness up close, to face this fear that something was out to get him. Animals might lurk in the dark forest. All manner of creatures might attack them if they pranced around at night. But most animals—he had heard—would be afraid of humans. Perhaps they should be. Besides his mother did love to walk. Maybe she'd jump at the chance. Ariane was fearless too. She'd probably lead the charge out the door. He thought he would take a stick just in case something popped out of the bushes. Maybe they'd laugh at him. They'd laugh, but maybe they'd secretly be glad he had a stick to protect them. It would make him feel better. It would be a little something to help him overcome his fears. That's all he needed. Only a little something, and he'd be on his way.